I0655111

Pawns:

Kings in Check

PAWNS:

KINGS IN CHECK

BY

DON KESTERSON

Pawns: Kings in Check. Copyright Don Kesterson, 2018. All rights reserved. No portion of this book may be reproduced in any form whatsoever, except for brief quotations in reviews, without the prior written permission of the author.

ISBN-13: 978-0998470733 (Amber Publishers Company)

Library of Congress Control Number: 2018903923

http://www.donkesterson.com

Cover design - Eric Fritzius

While historical timelines, persons, and events are depicted, the main characters of this work are fictitious. They interact with historical figures as a way to show a view of the depicted historical events.

OTHER BOOKS BY

DON KESTERSON

The President's Gold

Gold of the Spirits

Pawns: Magic Bullet

Chapter One

December 29, 1963
Long Tieng, Laos

Major Steven Hebert was startled awake as the C-47 lurched forward and bucked as it dropped out of the sky toward the small runway. The two other men looked over at him as they talked in low voices. *Wonder if they are talking about me. They must know something about me. Who are they?*

Within a few minutes, they landed roughly and lurched to a stop at the edge of the runway. Hmong soldiers with guns drawn emerged from the trees and surrounded the plane. Steven looked over at the two men as he unbuckled himself. One thing was for sure, he'd let the two men exit the plane first. He was uncomfortable having them behind him, plus, the Hmong soldiers may get a little too excited. He started to fidget with his duffle bag so they would walk past him.

Both pilots ducked through the cabin into the main deck then sauntered over as Steven got up. The Captain looked at his watch and exclaimed, "If you're going back with us, we'll be wheels up at 16:45. Be belted in, ready. Otherwise, won't be back for a week."

Steven got up and swung his duffle bag on his shoulder. "Understood."

Steven ducked through the door, and the humidity the heat, the smell of the jungle surged over him. His home near the swamps of Louisiana was hot and humid, but the jungle of Indochina was different, oppressive. Something a man could never forget.

The two other passengers moved rapidly into the jungle toward Vang Pao's headquarters. Clearly, they had been here before. As Steven approached the headquarters, Nguyen Tao came out dressed just like a Chindit. *Must have just returned from a mission.* Tao walked up to Steven, grabbed his hand and shook it fiercely. Steven was pleased. Tao looked good, and it was a welcome relief to see someone who actually wanted to see him—other than his mother and brother. Steven was not even sure about his brother, as he had acted really strange.

Tao pointed him away from the headquarters. "Come on, let's walk and catch up. Too many ears right here."

Steven fell into step. "Fine by me."

Tao slipped along the jungle floor toward the six cheap lawn chairs on the edge of the clearing. He nodded at a Hmong guard, who slipped into the jungle. It was if he literally disappeared. Steven smiled, remembering how easy it was to become invisible in this part of Indochina. *Wouldn't it be great to do that in life?* He dropped his duffle bag and flopped down in a chair.

Tao pulled out a cigarette, lit it, blew out smoke. "Why are you hanging out with those two?"

Steven frowned as he twisted his back, tight from the plane ride over from the States, his back had never been right from his years as a sniper. "Who? The men from the plane? Never seen them before."

Tao made eye contact. "Good. Let me tell you who your travel companions were. The guy in the fatigues is Pop Buell, CIA. Helping the Vang Pao's men grow their crops, if you know what I mean."

Steven raised his eyebrows. "Poppies *and* a few other crops?"

Tao looked around. "The guy in the fancy shoes is Julian Romano. He represents the French Corsican Brotherhood. Julian is here to arrange for the movement of drugs out of here. He is responsible for keeping everyone honest. A real bad character."

Steven could not believe his ears. *French Corsican Brotherhood? Did he know who I am? Was he watching me, too? Restoring my trust with*

General Lansdale and Ambassador Lodge was complicated enough, now Lucien Sarti has someone watching me. Steven attempted to be nonchalant,

"I wasn't aware Vang Pao was involved with the French Corsican Brotherhood."

Tao took another drag and nodded petulantly. "Me neither. I just learned since I've been here this time. Things have changed a lot since we were here, but you'll remember Conein was with the Corsicans."

Steven was focused on the fact he had been on the plane and now was stuck in this camp with a high official from the French Corsican Brotherhood. He had tried to find out all he could about the Corsicans while he was still in the States but was unable to learn very much. Steven drew a deep breath, refocused his mind.

"Do you suppose Lansdale knows?"

Tao shook his head but looked away. "I don't know. I can't help but believe he does. You know, he seems to know everything."

Steven nodded. "Well, Lansdale wanted me to tell you that the talk in Washington is General Harkins is going to be replaced. Soon."

Tao raised his eyebrows. "*What?* How come?"

Steven looked around then leaned forward. "According to Lansdale, one of Harkins's top officers advised him that Harkins has been altering reports. Making things look more favorable, particularly territory in the South controlled by the VC."

Tao rubbed his jaw with his right hand. "I can't believe it. I was under the impression that the general was a good leader."

Steven nodded. "Me, too. I had some limited dealings with him. I don't get it."

Tao glared. "Did he say where he got his information?"

Steven shook his head. "No, you know Lansdale, he wouldn't elaborate."

Both men sat quiet for a minute. Steven looked around then leaned forward.

"Okay, tell me about Diem."

Tao pounded the cheap lawn chair until Steven thought it was going to come apart. "I had Diem rescued! I had a chopper… Then he wanted to go to church. I will never ever forget that as long as I live."

Steven rubbed his chin. "I knew Diem was a devout Catholic, but that doesn't make sense. It is almost like he wanted to get caught?"

Tao took another hard drag off his cigarette. "I've almost quit smoking, but when I sit down and think of trying to relax, the desire comes back. Anyway, my two men were killed. I went out to get my car and ran into Conein. I fought him, but he was too much for me. He stuffed me in the trunk of my Peugeot. I thought I was going to die there."

Steven shrugged and held his hands out, palms up. "Conein told me he sent you here, and you went willingly and could come and go as you pleased."

Tao laughed so hard he started coughing. "Come here willingly? *No!* But since I've been here I feel safer here than in Saigon, considering all that has happened. I believed the South Vietnamese generals or some of our guys would kill me. No one would believe my story, if I even got a chance to tell it…" He rubbed his chin with the back of his hand. "Since I've been back here, I have gone back to the Trail. I've seen tremendous activity."

Steven shook his head as he sat back in the lawn chair. He had already decided he would rather be on combat duty than Embassy duty.

Tao took another long draw off his cigarette. "What happened to you?"

Steven looked away from Tao for a minute. Could he tell Tao the truth? He decided to wing it, let Tao's reaction be his guide. "Ambassador Lodge recommended President Kennedy honor me for protecting the Embassy Staff during the Diem Coup. On November 22, I was to meet the President in Dallas after his speech at the Trade Mart. Lansdale picked me up on a military transport the day before. He was recruiting a team to operate, you know, the way we used to. Then, well, you know the rest of the story. The President ends up dead."

Tao gave him a puzzled look. "I'm afraid Kennedy's death changes everything."

Steven felt likeTao might know more but that now was not the time to elaborate. "Lansdale told me two days ago, it's too early to tell. He is proceeding like he and MacArthur can still convince Johnson and the decision makers."

Tao took a final puff off his cigarette, snuffed it out. "I'm being recruited by several different CIA groups to lead teams here. What about you?"

Steven lowered his head. "Before, Lansdale wanted me to join him. Now, he wants me back at the Embassy. He said it was important since Johnson is now president. So that's where I'm headed. Who knows? I don't have a good feeling about any of this. I really want back on combat duty. Lansdale wanted me to meet up with you to show me a good spot to set up snipers and sabotage the Ho Chi Minh Trail."

Tao nodded. "Tomorrow, I want to take you for a little tour along the border. I have a couple of places you should see. Do you need to see Vang Pao?"

Staring off at the surrounding jungle, Steven rubbed his forehead before he stood. As they walked toward Vang Pao's headquarters, the general stepped through the door. Vang Pao stopped Tao and Steven and vigorously shook Steven's hand.

"Major Hebert, you will bunk down in the barracks with my men. Tao will show you the way. We'll catch up tomorrow."

As Steven followed Tao toward the barracks, he looked back and saw the two men he had flown over with watching out the window of the general's headquarters.

December 30, 1963

Several hours before daylight, Steven Hebert, dressed in marine fatigues with two M1911s on each hip and carrying an M14NM, exited the barracks toward the landing strip. As he walked he heard the thump, thump, thump of an approaching Huey helicopter. Just before he got to the runway, lights came up, illuminating the landing area. He could see Tao at the controls of the chopper.

Tao landed but did not turn off the bird. He gestured for Steven to join him. Steven held down his Boonie Camo bush hat as he ducked under the churning blades. Steven crawled in the chopper, and before he could close the door, Tao was throttling up to lift off. As they moved over the jungle below, Steven peered over the thick foliage. His mind drifted to a place he had not been in years. It was exhilarating to again be flying over the jungle. His brain was firing all synapses, just like it did seven years ago.

Tao punched him in the leg and pointed at a landmark on the horizon, snapping Steven back into this reality. As they approached the Ho Chi Minh Trail, Tao flew just out of range of automatic weapons.

"The activity of the North Vietnamese Army has been considerable over the past two months." Tao said loudly over the rotors. "If the US is to have a chance at winning this, we *have to* shut it down."

Steven nodded slowly, fixated over on the jungle below.

Tao continued. "Lansdale wanted you and I to come out here together to see if we could come up with any ideas."

Steven looked around, stretching over to peer on both sides of the chopper. He pointed to a spot. "Can you set down there?"

Before Steven could complete the sentence, Tao had the Huey nosing down toward the spot Steven had picked out. Just off the edge of the Ho Chi Minh Trail, it did not look any bigger than a postage stamp. As soon as they were on the ground, Steven motioned to check it out as he slipped his rifle on his shoulder and pulled his M1911 pistol. He started moving east stealthily away from the chopper from tree to tree toward the trail, glancing up and down each time before he moved. Bringing up the rear, Tao followed one tree behind, checking behind him as he moved. Once they were about fifty yards away from the chopper, Steven's instincts put him on full alert. He waved for Tao to move up to where he was. Off in the distance they heard the rumble of some type of vehicle. He holstered his handgun, crouched and swung his M14NM around. He focused on a spot due west of their position along the crown of the road.

Tao moved up, drew his M1911, and whispered, "How many, do you think?"

Steven shook his head slowly. "At least two vehicles coming toward us. I don't think we have to identify them."

Tao nodded. "Must have heard our chopper?"

Steven nodded as he scanned the area directly ahead of them.

"I'm guessing they're after us. Better get out of here." They started moving back toward the helicopter as fast as they could while keeping an eye on the road for the vehicles. Three small vehicles carrying several Viet Cong in each chugged into view. Steven looked at Tao then through his M14NM scope at the head of one of the men in the first vehicle. He zeroed in on the spot and without looking up. "Tao, when I pull the trigger, all hell is going to break loose. We need to keep moving toward the chopper. You keep moving. We have to get that bird in the air, ASAP."

Tao lightly touched his shoulder. "On your shot, I'm moving."

Steven didn't remove his eye from his scope, remained ridged and focused. As soon as the vehicle slowed down, he moved his finger from the side of his rifle to the trigger and pulled. A man dropped dead, Tao moved to the next tree as VC bullets rained. Steven identified at least five shooters as he focused his next shot and fired at another point. Another man down.

Now the bullets clustered on him. Tao moved to the next tree. Steven fired another round; another man down. Steven quickly shouldered his rifle, crouched as low as he could and moved with amazing speed to a large tree. He turned and swung his rifle into ready position and fired another round. A miss. More VC bullets rained as the Huey blades thumped. Again, Steven crouched and moved like a cat, zigging and zagging to the last tree on the edge of the clearing. Tao was waving for Steven to come on as he throttled up the chopper. Steven ignored him and crouched back down. *Sixteen shots left, got to make them count.* He made one more study of the area. *Come on, someone show yourself.*

Just on cue, two men stepped into his line of sight, charging toward Steven and the chopper. Steven fired at both. The enemy on the left went down; the other kept charging. Steven pulled his handgun and fired three shots, wounding the charging man, just as two others stepped out to his left and charged. Again, he fired his handgun—got one but missed the other.

Steven took a deep breath, swung his M14NM. *One man to beat.* He nodded at Tao and started his sprint across the small clearing to the chopper. Tao pulled his handgun and fired continuously at the enemy charging Steven from behind. Then Tao dropped the gun in his lap and lifted the helicopter just barely off the ground and spun it so that Steven could enter straight into the chopper. As Steven ran, the shooter came out firing. Two bullets missed Steven but hit the helicopter. Steven jumped in, spun in his seat, and fired his M14NM rifle. He missed.

Tao throttled up, pushing the helicopter up as Steven continued to fire until empty. He dropped the magazine, jammed in another, and continued.

Within seconds, they were away well in the air. All the enemy soldiers were dead. Steven and Tao drew deep breaths, attempting to gather their wits. Steven looked down at Tao. "You've been hit."

Tao glanced at the blood soaking through his lower pant leg. "Wow, must not be much. I didn't feel it."

Steven patted Tao on the shoulder. "I was just about to say that was a good spot to place some snipers and blow up the trail to slow movement on the trail."

Tao frowned as he nodded. "Pretty good exhibition, wouldn't you say?"

Steven just nodded.

On the flight back to the base camp, Steven nudged Tao. "Can you tell me any more about those men I came here with?"

Tao shook his head and pointed down at the Ho Chi Minh trail. "There... that might be another good place to destroy the road."

Steven concurred. "You're right. How's that leg?"

Tao shook his head several times without a word.

Steven and Tao flew quietly as they looked over the terrain below. After a time, Steven inquired, "Are you okay being back to trail-watching duty?"

Tao sighed deeply. "I was hoping to get away from it, but honestly it has been a personal mission for me since my wife, my daughter, and my home were burned up by the VC."

Steven sat back and raised his right eyebrow.

"You see, over six months before the VC attack my village, a number of northerners moved into our village. At the time, none of us thought anything of it. I knew the CIA was encouraging northerners to come down. But I should have investigated them more than I did."

Steven shook his head. "You think they were all VC?"

Tao frowned as he continued to steer the helicopter. "I don't know, but I've always believed some were. I've searched for them, any of them. Not a trace. They all just disappeared."

Steven shifted in his seat as he wiped his brow. "It doesn't make sense. All of them disappeared?"

Tao looked down for a second, ignoring the question. "When Luc and I got back to the village, everybody was gone, but only my home was burnt up."

Steven jutted his jaw. "You believe the VC knew you were working for the CIA and was sending you a message?"

Tao sullenly nodded. "Yes. I don't know what happened to the other residents. I don't know whether they are in prison or were killed, too. I have never found any of them. Not a one… You would think… If only I had been there. I had taken Luc to CCD class at the Catholic Church in Da Nang. Our home was near Hoa Ninh, about a thirty-minute drive into Giao Xu An Thuong."

Steven shook his head. "You and your son might have died that day. I'm sure you've thought about that."

Tao looked away from Steven. "It's weird, when I was at the church with President Diem for the Feast of the Souls and went to the front to participate in the sacraments, I was happy to say a prayer for my wife and my daughter." Tao paused for a minute, then continued. "It did give my soul some peace."

Steven felt Tao's emotions, yet he felt helpless at the same time.

Tao said, "I still carry the list of the names of those who moved in from the north. I have kept a file since that time. Even have a few pictures of some. When I find them, they shall experience a painful death."

Steven eyes widened. "I never knew any of this."

Tao continued. "My family meant and means everything to me. I still to this day remember walking through the charred remains of my home, finding the charred remains of my wife shielding my daughter… They took my engraved golden chalice, which was given to me by my friend, a priest

14

in the Philippines. While it is very valuable, *I couldn't put a value on it...* My family Bible burned to a crisp. More than three hundred years of family genealogy prepared by my grandmothers and aunts. No, I will never forget."

Steven sensed Tao's rage. *This man is trail watching so that he can inflect revenge. It must burden his soul.* Steven remembered the old movie *Kind Hearts and Coronets*, and the quote, "Revenge is a dish which people of taste prefer to eat cold." It had always stuck with him. He had contemplated it himself since his father's death in the line of duty serving on the New Orleans police force.

As the helicopter moved over the small landing pad, he thought about the men he had flown with into Vang Pao's camp—one was CIA and the other was a Corsican. The words of Lucien Sarti popped back in Steven's head: *So, should word get out that instead of an assassination, Kennedy's death is a coup—which is what it truly is—your country will be implicated in two coups within a month. That would relegate it to some third world country. Your people would rather believe a lone, crazed gunman pulled this off.*

These were words that he had to live with, similar to Tao's burden. The only difference was he could not talk about it. He could not get it off his chest or he would be implicated or his mother or brother killed. The Corsicans were cold-blooded killers, without conscience. Steven would do whatever it took to protect his mother and brother.

15

Tao started his descent to Vang Pao's landing strip. He wiped his face. "It's still difficult to talk about. I just wish I had been there. I might have been able to make a difference. So, to answer your question, I don't mind being on the trail again. When I was in the Philippines, I watched the enemy, the Japanese. When I came back here with Lansdale, I was watching the enemy, the North Vietnamese. When I was in Saigon, I was watching our Allies, the South Vietnamese generals, and they killed my president. It's mentally easier to fight the enemy you know than to worry about being betrayed by your allies."

On their descent to the landing strip Steven sat very quiet, just thinking. He had learned a lot about the Ho Chi Minh Trail but also a vital part of his friend's life story. Still, try as he might to focus on his world here, he could not shake his thoughts about his brother, Jeremiah. Over Christmas, while Steven was home on leave, Steven sensed something had been bothering him. *What is wrong with Jeremiah?*

The bird landed, and Steven picked up his gear and started toward his assigned barracks. As he walked, he was considering Jeremiah's situation. His brother's grades were okay. His track coach had sent home a positive, encouraging letter with his training schedule. Jeremiah had spent most of his time by himself or away from Steven and their mother. That could be expected, a boy his age; however, Steven didn't think Jeremiah was meeting up with his old friends. That was different. Steven had confronted Jeremiah about his attitude, but his brother got real defensive. He never used to do that, and it nagged at Steven. Jeremiah claimed he was stressed over rushing a Negro fraternity and feared he would not get accepted. While that might have been true, Steven knew his brother and could tell he was in trouble. Whatever it was was much more than some fraternity. But what?

The next morning Steven turned the door handle to General Vang Pao's small headquarters, and Tao walked in first. Vang Pao was glad to see his old friends and introduced Steven to William Young, CIA operative and translator. Vang Pao pointed to two old chairs for them to sit. Steven asked for Vang Pao's assessment of the Indochina conflict.

The general leaned back and folded his arms over his chest. "Major Hebert, my men are the only troops confronting the Pathot Lao, the North Vietnamese Army, *and* the Viet Cong. We are holding our own, with some help from Central Intelligence, and I can only hope we can make some progress."

Tao added, "Just since I've been here, I've reported the VC and supplies pouring over the borders into South Vietnam. The South Vietnamese Army has done nothing to stop it."

Steven frowned. "I am going to report this to Lansdale as soon as I get back to the Embassy."

Vang Pao snarled, "My men and I will continue our effort to the bitter end. I am fighting for my country, too. The North Vietnamese and the Chinese are heavily supporting the Pathot Lao to try to keep me occupied. So far I have been able to fight them off."

Steven nodded as he twisted his back around one way then the other, stretching. "Lansdale is hoping to get back in here and start working like we did several years ago…"

Vang Pao held his hand up. "This is too big now for that type of counter-insurgency to be effective alone. I can tell you the enemy we are fighting now is much better trained and better armed than when you all were in here. *The lost time* has been devastating."

Tao leaned forward. "Do you think General Minh can get the Army engaged?"

Vang Pao shook his head. "I don't know. We can only hope. But he must engage now. Two years, nothing."

Steven stood. "Thank you for meeting with me. I desperately needed this information. I have learned much between this meeting and the things Tao and I saw earlier in the week. I have learned a lot in my stay at Camp."

JANUARY 1, 1964

As Tao waited for the incoming Air America flight, he heard singing

"Stars shining bright above you,

Night breezes seem to whisper,

I love you,

Birds singin' in the sycamore trees,

Dream a little dream of me"

He knew Major Steven Hebert was approaching the landing strip. Tao nodded as Steven set down his duffle bag and his weapons.

"Going somewhere?" Steven asked.

Tao pointed Steven. "Yeah, with you. I am going to Saigon. I have to get some answers."

Steven tilted his head to the right. "Pretty risky, don't you think?"

"Maybe, maybe not." Tao sat down on his suitcase. He reached into his pants pocket and pulled out his passport. "Haven't used this one in years, since my days in the Philippines. Kept it active just for such purposes."

Steven drew a deep breath as he raised an eyebrow. "Where are you going for these answers?"

"I'm going to visit Pham Xuan An."

Steven pursed his lips. "The man who seems to know everything?"

"Where better to get answers?"

Steven looked up, shaded his eyes with his hand, as he heard a plane coming. "Do you expect him to know?"

Tao rubbed his hand over his mouth and chin. "I believe I can get the answers I seek. Might have to do a little interpretation of the answers."

Steven chuckled as an Air America C-47 tried to stop on the short runway, its engines roaring. He shouted over the roar. "Hell, you might as well go talk to Conein."

Tao raised his eyebrows and spoke sharply. "Who knows, I might? I've got to find out if the South Vietnamese generals are out to kill me. Time has passed, and nobody has come after me. I'm tired of hiding. From what I hear they are so busy fighting among themselves they don't have time to worry about me or anybody else. Tao sighed. "I am beginning to fear the enemy within more than any other."

After the C-47 came to a stop, Tao reached down for his suitcase. Before he could pick it up, Vang Pao and the two men Steven had flown to camp with drove past and onto the landing strip, followed by a large US army truck with a tarp thrown over its cargo. With incredible speed ten Hmong gunmen stepped out of the jungle from all directions surrounding the stopped C-47. Tao knew it was poppies. Vang Pao, Edgar "Pop" Buell, and Julian Romano walked to the plane as the captain lowered the airstairs. Vang Pao and Romano boarded the plane. After a short time, Vang Pao skipped back down the steps and signaled the truck to pull up alongside the C-47. As Tao and Steven started toward the plane, two of the gunmen stepped in front of them to prevent them from boarding.

After the plane was loaded with the poppies, those same men unloaded large bags of raw rice and some medical supplies and placed them into the Army truck. As soon as they were finished, the Hmong gunmen disappeared into the jungle. Tao and Steven were now free to board the plane. Before either man was seated, the co-pilot pulled the airstairs up as the C-47 started to taxi down the runway. The co-pilot walked toward the front of the plane, looking at his watch, and shouted to the Capitan. "Best time yet. On the ground just under twenty-five minutes."

Just as the plane lurched into the air, Tao looked at Steven while he fastened his belt. "Here we go."

Chapter Two

January 2, 1964

US Embassy

Saigon

Major Steve Hebert had dreaded the last leg of his trip, returning to the Embassy. Now, he had to walk into Ambassador Henry Cabot Lodge's office and act as though nothing had gone wrong on 22 November. One thing was for sure: No one could know what had happened the night before the assassination because his mother's and brother's lives depended on it. Steven had to hope that whatever endorsement Lansdale or MacArthur provided would be sufficient to get him back into Embassy Security with full responsibility for the Ambassador. He looked out the window of the plane as it descended into the Tan Son Nhut airbase. While Saigon had not changed physically in the short time he had been gone, Steven felt very different about his return. Life had changed in both his country and the country he where he would serve out his military mission.

Steven went straight to his quarters, unpacked his duffle bag, and put on his dress blues. He headed to Ambassador Lodge's office to report back to duty. *Might as well get this done.*

Steven walked into the ambassador's office and was greeted by a great big smile from the new girl, the woman who had taken Cindy Scott's place. An attractive brunette. She quickly turned over something she was writing and jumped up from her desk. She shook Steven's hand vigorously. "Why, you must be Major Steven Hebert. It's a pleasure to finally meet you."

Steven blinked, wide eyed. *Quite different from Cindy Scott.* "Yes, ma'am. Who do I have the honor of meeting?"

The young lady finally let go of his large hand. "My name is Meredith Brown. The Ambassador wanted to see you as soon as you arrived."

Again, she flashed a big smile and pushed the intercom button. She spoke cheerfully. "Major Hebert is here, Ambassador."

Ambassador spoke, "Pick up the phone please, Miss Brown."

Meredith picked up the phone, nodded several times. When she hung up, she looked at the Major. "Please have a seat. The Ambassador said he would be with you shortly."

Steven sat down stiffly in the plush leather chair and held his dress cap squarely on his lap. *Figures. He's going to let me sweat.*

Shortly, the intercom buzzed. Miss Brown picked up and pointed Steven toward the door. "The Ambassador will see you now."

Steven stood. He pulled his dress coat down and placed his hat on his head, adjusted it. As he walked toward the door he straightened his shoulders. Just as he reached for the door knob, the Ambassador opened the door.

"Major Hebert, please step in. Miss Brown, hold all calls unless from the MAC-V or the President."

Steven sat there staring at the Ambassador as he read over a letter. Several times the Ambassador looked at Steven over his glasses. *Surely he read this when it arrived, and it didn't just arrive.* Finally, the Ambassador laid down the letter and looked directly at Steven. "This is the letter General Edward Lansdale sent me regarding what happened to you on November 21 and November 22. Do you care to explain yourself?"

Steven was unsure what to say. He believed he knew basically what General Lansdale had put in the letter. Anything he said would only leave an opening for the Ambassador to pounce on. Steven looked straight into the Ambassador's eyes. "I was only following orders, Sir."

The Ambassador leaned back and put his finger on top of the letter. "You are aware that many of my supervisors at State don't hold the general in very high regard."

Steven sat straight in his chair. "No, Sir."

The Ambassador fixed his gaze on Steven for a minute.

Steven knew the technique: Stare at someone, try to make them nervous so they will start talking, but Steve was not going to bite on the old trick.

Finally, the Ambassador leaned up. "Son, you better tread lightly from now on around here. I am not buying all this nonsense. There are things which I feel I have not been told, and I don't like it. Do you understand me, Major?"

Steven stiffened. "Yes, Sir."

Again, the Ambassador stared at him.

Steven didn't budge, blink, or move. He remained fixed in the chair, eyes forward. The Ambassador was not going to intimidate him. Tougher men had tried.

Finally, the Ambassador said, "You're dismissed, Major."

Steven stood up, saluted, and left the office. Quickly, he walked through Miss Brown's office, returning her smile as he exited. That experience of sitting across from the Ambassador only confirmed his notion that he would rather be on combat duty than Embassy duty. The politics were complicated, and he remembered the need to parse every word he said or heard.

As he continued through the building, he encountered yet another change around the Embassy. On the door of CIA Chief of Station was the name Peer de Silva. Steven's eyebrows raised; he was impressed. The man had been a real climber in the CIA, but Steven knew him more for his role as an army officer. Steven let out a breath he had not realized he'd been holding. De Silva might be a man worthy of working with in Saigon.

Meredith Brown heard the Ambassador pick up his phone on the call she had placed for him to Secretary of State Dean Rusk. She had a few minutes to try to finish writing her letter to her best friend, Rita Sullivan. It had been her intention to write since arriving in Saigon two weeks ago, but she'd been too busy learning the ropes of the Embassy. The last time she had spoken with Rita, she had just completed her interview at the Department of State. She did not feel she had interviewed well, but Rita assured her that family connections would make the difference. After all, her final interview had been conducted by long-time family friend, Averell Harriman. Rita tried to reassure her that the only reason she felt she didn't perform well in the interview was that her expectations of herself were too high. Meredith thought Rita was just trying to make her feel better, but Rita's family and the Harrimans had been friendly for more than thirty years.

Meredith picked up the pen and continued to write about how excited she was to be in Foreign Service. It had been a life-long dream, and she was now in the middle of one of the hotbeds of the world, South Vietnam, working for another family friend and former vice presidential candidate, Henry Cabot Lodge. She truly felt honored and lucky. Just as she was about to ask how Rita's job-hunting was proceeding, Ambassador Lodge called her into his office. Meredith quickly placed the unfinished letter in the drawer and grabbed her steno pad.

SAIGON
THAT EVENING

In the darkness, Tao slipped up the street toward the Continental Palace Hotel. He went to the side of the hotel to enter through the side door. He stood silently at first to make sure no one entered the elevator. At the last second, he slipped in and pushed the button for Pham Xuan An's floor. Once the elevator doors opened on fourth floor, again, he looked down the hallway to make sure it was empty. Quickly, he slinked down the hallway to An's room. He tapped on the door.

A muffled voice on the other side: "Who is it?"

Tao whispered, "It's Nguyen Tao. Let me in."

"Just a minute."

Tao glanced around the hallway. Just as An's door opened, he heard the door on the opposite side of the hallway started to open. Tao pushed his way past his friend before the person in the opposite room could get a look at him.

Tao invited himself to the kitchenette table seat. "I am sorry to barge in on you at this late an hour."

An went over to the refrigerator, pulled out two beers, and sat one down in front of each of them. He offered Tao a cigarette. Both men lit up and Tao began. "I really need some information."

An looked at him, sucked hard on his cigarette. He exhaled and took a long drink of beer. "What can I do for you, my friend? I notice you are no longer selling mopeds."

Tao didn't anticipate An's question. "Ah, yes, I am selling the business. I— I thought I could live in the city, but as it turns out, it's really too big for me. I like living in the smaller villages."

An nodded but kept up his hard stare. "What information do you need?"

Tao took a long swig of beer and a puff off his cigarette. "Lansdale needs to know your opinion on the Buddhist situation. Do you think it has quieted down since they removed Diem?"

An scowled. "Yes, quite a bit, but since Thich Tri Quang was not added to Minh's cabinet, he has tried to keep things stirred up. I believe the Buddhists and students are waiting to see how Minh treats them."

Tao exhaled his cigarette smoke. "I don't think Minh wanted him in his cabinet."

An smiled. "Not true. It was Ambassador Lodge that told them not to include him. But I still haven't figured out exactly why."

Tao shook his head. "Funny, they talk about wanting peace. But I don't think they would be able to practice their religion if the communists take over." Tao paused and drew a breath. "Do you believe Diem's Strategic Hamlet Program will be maintained by Minh?"

An took a big swig of beer and laughed. "The Strategic Hamlet Program has been an utter failure. The Vietnamese people didn't want to be herded around like a bunch of animals."

Tao knew of some of the failures of the program, but to hear it called a total failure was surprising. "Do you think Minh is going to make it?"

"I hear the younger generals are already plotting against him."

Tao realized that explained why there had not been much South Vietnamese military engagement with the Viet Cong and the North Vietnamese Army. And why they were pouring over the border along the Ho Chi Minh trail. Tao knew before he left Saigon he would have to get this information to Lansdale and Hebert. Another coup could be happening at any time. *I predicted the instability that would occur with Diem's removal.*

An leaned forward. "Tao, that is not why you came to see me. I saw desperation in your eyes."

An's statement snapped him back to reality. Tao thought he had hid his emotions better, but An had always been good at quick reads of people and good snap judgments. It was why he had such a good relationship with Lansdale. Tao said, "I want to know if the South Vietnamese generals or the police are looking for me. I've been told I was implicated in the assassination of Diem?"

An stared at Tao silently, taking a long drag off his cigarette. "I have not heard anything like that. Where did you get your information?"

Tao thought about ignoring the question but instead slugged down his last drink of beer and snuffed out his cigarette. "Let's just say old friends told me. They didn't want me in Saigon." Tao got up and headed for the door.

As Tao got to the door, An smiled. "Please get this information to Lansdale."

Tao looked back. "Will do."

January 7, 1964

Nick's Pool Hall near University of Southern Miss, Hattiesburg, MS

Jeremiah Hebert just racked the balls at the pool table then pushed the que ball at Bobby to break. Since he had walked into the pool hall, Nick had been standing at the back corner near the last table, talking to two men. Jeremiah wanted to stay as far away from Nick as possible. After Bobby broke on his shot, he sank the two ball, so he was solids. He missed his next shot but buried the que ball where Jeremiah had no shot whatsoever. Just as Jeremiah was about to line up a really bad shot, Nick started talking louder to the two men. Jeremiah could not hear everything but it was something to do with markers and payments. Following his shot, in which he left Bobby an equally bad placement, he slipped around to Bobby's side of the table and asked if he had any marijuana to sell. He added that they better finish this game fast and get out of there.

Bobby, a fellow Southern Miss student, shrugged. "What's the rush?"

Jeremiah looked down at the table then back at the two men talking to Nick in low voices. Nick wasn't saying a thing. Jeremiah looked back at Bobby. "That's just making me uncomfortable." He didn't want to tell Bobby, he might be part of the cause of Nick's conversation.

Bobby leaned over the table again to line up his shot. He bounced the que off the rail and perfectly hit the seven ball into the side pocket. The que was left for a really good shot on the five ball. Bobby answered, "Yeah, I can get you something tomorrow night. You want the usual?"

Jeremiah just raised his eyebrows for his answer.

The conversation between the two men and Nick got loud again, with Nick doing most of the talking. The only thing Jeremiah could understand was Nick saying he would handle it, the markers. Jeremiah noticed the two men had gotten up real close to Nick. When Nick was done talking, the two men crossed their arms and stood there in front of Nick not saying a word. He looked real nervous, yet Nick was bigger than both men. Finally, one the men spoke in a tone Jeremiah heard: "I want those markers and your book."

Jeremiah knew he had to get out of there. Fast. He looked over at Bobby again. "Come on, I'll just say you win. I got to get back to the dorm and study."

Bobby raised both hands one with the que stick in it. "No, I'm going to win in two more shots. What's your rush? It's the first of the semester, when do you become the big student?"

Jeremiah looked back over at the three men talking in low voices. He couldn't hear a thing. As Bobby sunk the five ball and left the que in position to make the six ball. Jeremiah saw Nick point directly at him as the two men turned and looked at him. Jeremiah didn't even see Bobby make the six ball and leave himself without a shot on the table.

Bobby shouted at Jeremiah to get his head in the game, and Jeremiah realized it was his shot. As he lined up the shot, he glanced over to see the three men now walking toward the back, where Nick's office was. Jeremiah knew this was his chance to get out of there. Jeremiah lined up a shot on the fourteen ball that was perfect—if he hit it just right it would bounce off it and sink the eight ball in the side pocket. Jeremiah really concentrated on this shot as he pulled back the que stick. As the que ball hit the fourteen, it went into the left corner pocket, Jeremiah faked excitement for the shot as he watch the que ball hit the rail hard enough to ricochet back hard toward the eight ball and tip it in. Jeremiah slammed the que stick down.

"Damn it. I thought I could actually get on a run and give you a game." He reached in his pocket, produced a dollar bill, and laid it on the table for Bobby. "I'll see you here tomorrow night same time?"

Bobby walked around picked up the dollar bill and nodded.

Jeremiah looked back towards Nick's office, the two other men had disappeared. Jeremiah glanced around as he walked out of the pool hall into damp, chilly night air. Before he got five paces away from the doorway, two men stepped around the side of the pool hall. Jeremiah crossed to the other side of the street to avoid them. They crossed to remain in front of him. Both men had on fedoras and long, dark rain coats. One of the men blocked his path, while the other slipped around to his side. It was the two men from the pool hall that had been talking to Nick.

The man blocking Jeremiah looked up, his fedora still shading his eyes. "We need to talk to you."

Jeremiah frowned. "Excuse me, sir, what is this all about. I don't know either of you."

The man reached in his jacket coat and pulled out a piece of paper. "You're right. You don't know us, but that's okay. Look, Mr. Marcello's *friend* Nick made a bad mistake, *a real bad* mistake, and he needs your help. You know we just had a talk with him a few minutes ago. He said you could probably help us and him at the same time 'cause you owe him a lot of money." The man pushed the piece of paper into Jeremiah's face. "Your number, right, *Mr. 38?*"

Jeremiah just nodded, sucking on his lower lip.

The man held the paper in front of Jeremiah's face. "Since we can't see real well in the dark, can you read *what that number is* on this sheet, Mr. 38?"

Jeremiah did not need to even look at the paper. He mumbled, "Twelve hundred dollars."

The two men nodded and exchanged glances. The man in front continued. "What are you going to do to help *our mutual friend,* Nick, who made a bad mistake in letting you get these kinda numbers."

Jeremiah shifted his weight again as he looked down. "I'll get you some money. I promise, sir."

The man standing to his side spoke for the first time. "Mr. Marcello is a very patient man, but I am scared he is running out of patience. Those markers go back to November. So when are you going to help Nick out?" Just then he punched Jeremiah hard in the stomach.

Jeremiah doubled over and tried to catch his breath. Saliva dripped off his lips. When he straightened up he glanced at both men. "Give me a couple of weeks, I promise I'll get you at least $250.00 to start."

The first man raised his hand. "You are on the track team here, right. *Big track star*. We might have some alternate ways to collect. We really want to protect your legs and knee caps from any harm, right." He pointed to the other man. "We want to take care of you and keep you healthy." He stood there nodding. "We're just a couple of friendly guys. We'll give you two weeks from tonight but no more. Meet us right here, same time, in two weeks. Get us some money, then we'll talk further."

A car was coming down the street. The man punched him again in the stomach. Jeremiah doubled over again and coughed a couple of times. The man pushed him onto the ground.

The two men looked at Jeremiah, nodding their heads for a few more seconds, then turned and walked back into Nick's Pool Hall. Jeremiah lay there in pain for a few seconds in the cold night. He believed if the car had not come down the street they would have beaten him much worse. He looked around to see if anybody else was around then got up, took off staggering then jogging toward his dorm room.

NEXT NIGHT

HATTIESBURG, MS

UNIVERSITY OF SOUTHERN MISSISSIPPI

Jeremiah Hebert stood outside in the cold damp air, his hands stuffed down in his pants pockets, fuming mad. His bad day had just gotten worse. First, he got an "F" on a pop quiz in English 102, then his track coach had given him a hard time in practice for not training hard. The icing on the cake was that he had just been thrown out of Nick's Pool Hall because of his outstanding gambling debt. Nick had been pissed and told him in no uncertain terms not to come back until he brought some money. As mad as Nick was, Jeremiah could see the fear in his eyes from those two thugs working for Carlos Marcello's thugs. Nick had told Jeremiah when he could not pay in full, they threatened him. Jeremiah knew this was going to happen sooner or later. The pool hall was where Jeremiah was supposed to meet Bobby to buy the marijuana. Now, he had to stand outside in the cold hoping to catch Bobby.

After a half-hour, Jeremiah saw Bobby walking toward him. Bobby waved. "Why are you standing outside?"

Jeremiah decided it was best not to directly answer the question. "I just wanted to get some stuff, then get back to the dorm and study."

Bobby pointed toward the alley. "So, you are still trying to feed me that student story. Come on, let's get around back so no one sees us. How much do you want?"

Jeremiah shivered, pulled his hands out of his pocket and rubbed them together. "I only have five dollars. Can a get enough to roll five joints?"

Bobby put his hands on his hips. "Shit, I came all the way down here just for that?"

Once they were behind Nick's, under a dim light near some trash cans, Bobby opened his winter coat, pulled out a couple of small paper bags. He looked at a couple before handing Jeremiah one of them.

Jeremiah pulled out a wad of dollar bills, counted out five, and stuck the remaining single back into his pocket.

Bobby half smiled, as he stuffed the money in his hip pocket. "Hey, Jeremiah if you want, I can hook you up. You can sell some reefer and keep some for yourself. I know a couple of guys. I can definitely hook you up."

Jeremiah looked around, nodded but didn't say anything. He pulled out a Bugler rolling paper and sprinkled reefer in. He licked the paper and rolled it up in his fingers. He stuffed the bag in his pocket.

The two young men started back toward the front. At the front door, Bobby went in and Jeremiah kept walking. Once he was away from the business lights, he pulled out a matchbook and lit the joint. *Maybe I should take Bobby up on his offer.*

CHAPTER THREE

JANUARY 24, 1964

WASHINGTON DC

WASHINGTON STAR NEWS OFFICE

Rita Sullivan ripped the last page out her Smith Corona then headed toward the editor's office. The word count was right for her normal Sunday column and the close was right, too. Finally. She pushed her horn-rimmed glasses on top of her head—time to get it to the editor. Ed Boland had been hired at about the same time she had, and Rita had good relationship with him. He had really helped her tighten up her writing, but he also encouraged her by complimenting her talent.

Boland's door was closed when she got there. She rapped on the door then flung it open, as usual. Ed peered over his glasses.

"You're late, Blondie. Take a seat and wait your turn."

Rita plopped down on the hard wooden chair, as far away as she could get from the pipe that constantly burned in his ashtray. Rita stared randomly at the same pictures she had seen every week for the last year. She nervously patted the tight bun of her hair. Finally, it was her turn to get the dreaded red pen. Two minutes later, Boland looked up from her column and nodded. He picked up his pipe, tamped the tobacco, and re-lit it. "Blondie, this is your best work yet. Only two mistakes. Get 'em fixed and get 'em over to the Chief, immediately."

Rita smiled. "You really liked it?"

Boland stuck his chin out. "Excellent personal interest story. Should attract a lot of our readers. Do you have good pictures to go with it? It's a side of the war that has been forgotten."

"Of course, great pictures. What did you expect?"

Boland leaned back in the chair and stoked his pipe a couple of times. After he got his pipe going, he asked, "How did you come up with the idea?"

Rita Sullivan smile got even bigger as she rocked her wooden chair back on two legs. "I saw a picture of Rosy the Riveter and thought of some stories my mother told me. I sought out women who worked in factories here in the US, then I thought I would expand it to cover women who served."

Ed bit the pipe in his mouth as he placed his palms on his desk. "Still, how did find these ladies?"

Rita rocked back forward. "A little bit of luck. I was introduced to one lady who, as it turned out, played in a bridge club and three of her friends were the other women interviewed."

"Sometimes, luck has the answer in it. Sometimes you stumble into it." Ed grabbed his pipe with his left hand.

Rita nodded. "I'll call this one luck. I tried and tried to figure out how to end this column. Then it hit me, the one WAC had been a clerk handling coded messages for the command staff at the airbase. She was on duty when the Japanese attacked Hickam Field. She told stories about spending the rest of the day helping the nurse's staff with the wounded and the dying. Despite having a weak stomach when it came to the sight of blood, she had been able to assist all day. However, when the WAC finally got to sit down that night, she got deathly ill. She puked her guts out and cried uncontrollably for more than an hour. She had never told that story to anyone, as she didn't want to talk about it."

Ed replied, "Good, Blondie. Now hustle. This needs to get down to Copy, ASAP.

Rita felt very positive about her column, but how would Petit respond to it? Jonathon Petit was the executive editor, but everyone called him Chief.

41

Before the story went to Copy, it had to go to him. Rita thought for sure the Chief would love it. After all, he had done something in "the Big War," as he always used to call it. Not so much lately.

She also couldn't wait to hear what John and Miriam had to say about it. Rita had looked up to them since she'd arrived at the newspaper. John Sherwood had been one of the premier reporters during World War II. He had so much experience, and his stories were captivating. Miriam Ottenberg was different. Rita couldn't put her finger on it precisely, but she was, well, *different*. Rita liked her for basically two reasons: She was the only woman, plus her desk was pushed up against Rita's in the news room. Rita believed her column showed her readers that women had stories just like the men who had served in the war. They too tried to suppress them, were reluctant to talk about them.

Rita drew a deep breath and knocked on Chief's closed door. From the other side, she heard a muffled, "Come in!" The Chief looked up as Rita entered and held out her column. He grabbed it and grunted something that Rita thought meant, "Pull up a chair," so she did, calmly. *Anticipating a good word.* The Chief spent two minutes reading and finally looked up from the pages of typing.

"I don't like it," he said. "The women that served in the War had very minor roles. The women who were at home had no choice but to work. You have certainly over glamorized their roles in the war effort. As to those in the service, well…" He looked up at the clock above his desk then dropped his fist down on the paper. "Take it to Copy, get it in the paper. It's too late to go back to the drawing board on this. In the future, get your columns in sooner."

Then the Chief looked away from her and waved his hand for her to leave. Rita knew better than to argue with her boss; she quietly reached over the desk, picked up the column, and walked out of the room without so much as a word.

As fast as she could in her high heels, she marched toward the Copy Office. Rita tried to cool off, but temper was getting the best of her. The Chief did not like her column because it was about *women*, whom he felt did not have a role in World War II. He was a tough man to please. Rita's father had died when she was very young, one of the casualties on Iwo Jima. She wondered if her father had been like the Chief.

As she walked, it dawned on her that her column would appear in the Sunday *Washington Star News*. All was right with the world, at least for the next week.

January 26, 1964
Washington DC
White House

President Lyndon Johnson was sitting in the Oval Office going over several reports on the domestic issues he had not paid much attention to. He was looking forward to meeting with Secretary of Defense Robert McNamara regarding new operations in Vietnam. President Johnson was on the phone when his personal secretary, Geraldine "Gerri" Whittington, announced McNamara's arrival. As soon the President was finished, he buzzed the secretary to send him in.

President Johnson moved over to one of the two couches in the Oval Office. McNamara entered the large room carrying a briefcase and sat down on the opposite couch. "Good afternoon, Mr. President."

"I'm anxious to hear your report."

McNamara opened his briefcase and handed him a file. "I have two bits of good news. The changes we made in our Navy Seals program have improved operations. Placing them in Da Nang with Marine Intelligence has made them much more efficient with their ambushes, and they have been able to grab supplies and capture North Vietnamese Officers. I still haven't been able to ascertain the reason for the slow intel from the CIA."

President Johnson tossed the report on the coffee table between the two men. "You said you had two bits of good news. What else, Bob?"

McNamara reached in his briefcase and produced another file, which he handed to the President. "On your orders, Mr. President, the Joint Chiefs have implemented the first phase of OPLAN 34A. The MACV-SOG personnel will provide the sea and river routes for operations. This should greatly enhance their psychological warfare against designated targets in North Vietnam, ASAP."

President Johnson leaned back on the couch and smiled. "These two operations should really add to the success we are experiencing over there, Bob. Keep me fully briefed on both."

McNamara closed his briefcase and scratched his chin. "Mr. President, how is Geraldine working out for you? That was a bold move appointing a Negro secretary."

"Yeah, when word gets out, it should get me some votes come November."

Hattiesburg, MS
University of Southern Mississippi

Jeremiah walked out of the tiny dank weight room toward Scott Hall, his dorm. A damp chill filled the night air. After half a block he noticed two men standing in the shadows up ahead. Although he couldn't tell for sure, he thought they were the two men looking for his gambling money. Jeremiah hadn't shown up three nights before, as he had agreed. It must be those two men, fedoras and long, dark rain coats. Jeremiah turned and walked in the opposite direction, away from his dorm.

He glanced over his shoulder. *Uh oh, they saw me. Should I try to run? Am I in for another ass-whipping?* He ran. *No place to duck away from the street.* Within a minute a Lincoln pulled up beside him, the passanger pointed a gun at him. He stopped running. The two men got out; one blocked his path, while the other slipped around to his side.

The man who blocked Jeremiah's path looked up, his fedora still shading his eyes. "Jeremiah, you didn't meet us like you promised. Mr. Marcello *insisted* we stop by and talk to you, tonight."

Jeremiah bit his lower lip. "I forgot, I swear."

The man in front looked over at his friend. "Looked to me like Jeremiah here saw us and was going in the opposite direction. What do you think?"

Jeremiah looked over at other man who only stared coldly and pursed his lips. One hand was in his rain coat, something tenting the coat out. *Is he still pointing his gun at me?*

The man in front poked Jeremiah in the chest hard with his index finger. "Do you have Mr. Marcello's money yet? He has become a little nervous about your empty promises. We certainly don't want Mr. Marcello to snap his cap."

Jeremiah looked down at the ground and shifted his weight. "No, sir."

The man stepped closer to Jeremiah. "Look, Mr. Marcello's *friend* Nick is in a little bit of a bind. Have you been down to see him? Oh, that's right, he ain't around." He folded his hands on his chest. "*Mr. 38,* what exactly are we supposed to tell Mr. Marcello?"

Jeremiah nodded, sucking on his lower lip. He shifted his weight and looked down. "I'll get you some money real soon. I promise, sir."

The man standing to his side spoke for the first time. "Mr. Marcello has run out of patience with you. Those markers are too old. Now, you can still help Nick out, *so to speak.* But this is your last chance. When are you going to get us Nick's money? Or should I say, Mr. Marcello's money?"

Jeremiah glanced at both men. "I haven't had a chance to go home. I have to go home *to get it*. I promise I'll get you at least $250.00 to start."

The first man raised his hand. "You have exactly two weeks, not a day more. *Mister track star.* We might have some alternate ways to collect." He pointed to the other man. "We want to take care of you and keep you healthy. *And* you don't want to let your mother and brother down. We really don't want to have to talk with them." He stood there nodding his head. "We're just a couple of friendly guys. Meet us right here, same time in two weeks. *No more time.*"

The second thug pulled back to throw a punch. But the first thug stopped him. He poked Jeremiah in the chest again with his index finger. "We are civilized businessmen here. The boy just said he was going to bring us some money. This time I think he means it."

The two men stared at Jeremiah for a few more seconds, then got back in their Lincoln. After watching the car pull away, Jeremiah stood there in the cold night, watching the car drive off. He took off jogging toward his dorm.

Chapter Four

January 27, 1964

Marseilles, France

Atonine Guerini was seated at the large table in the private room in the back of the restaurant with Julian Romano and Lucien Sarti and a bottle of good French wine. They had just enjoyed a large meal of seafood-stuffed lasagna, French bread, and fresh salads sprinkled with ricotta cheese and olive oil. Atonine motioned the two waiters and his personal guards out of the private room.

"We have had an excellent situation handed to us in Indochina." Guerini lit a cigar, blew out the smoke.

Lucien Sarti smirked. "Yeah, those generals will be too busy reorganizing their government. They will not pay any attention to us."

Guerini waved his arm around with the cigar. "No, there is more. Another big development."

Sarti took the napkin off his lap. "What's that?"

Guerini leaned forward. "The CIA has consolidated their power around Vang Pao. They want him to be more aggressive, taking on the Pathot Lao, the North Vietnamese Army, *and* the Viet Cong. Conein tells me this could be a huge break. He said with the CIA backing the general, they will put more assets at his disposal."

Romano finished a long drink of his wine. "Vang Pao said he could ramp up their crops for our O and H production, if we needed. The CIA has sent in an agent to help them improve their growing techniques." He looked at his glass of Merlot. "Can you believe it?"

Sarti swirled the wine then drank it down. "What do you want me to do, Atonine?"

Guerini sat back. "I want you to go to Colombia and Argentina to re-establish our network. Make sure our old contacts are still with us. You must convince them. *Tu comprends?*"

Sarti nodded. "I think I'll go in through the Bahamas. Me and my boys better stay out of the good ole U. S. of A." Lucien cracked half a smile as he took a drink of his wine.

Guerini refilled Sarti's glass, then held up his. They all toasted and slugged down the remainder of the contents. The general sat back, took a draw off his cigar. "Julian, I want you to go back to Vietnam soon. First, meet with Conein, then go see Vang Pao. I want to keep Conein in the loop on this. He knows everything going on in Indochina. If you don't believe it, just ask him." Guerini let out a big laugh.

Sarti sat his glass down and placed both hands on the table. "So you still want to use Miami for our route into South America?"

Guerini pursed his lips. "At the moment, yes. Miami has served us well since we lost Cuba. We still need Trafficante. Trafficante and I have worked well together, but we don't trust him. Understand. Let's not tip anybody off." Atonine looked over at Romano and pointed directly at him. "This includes you. Don't say anything to Conein or Vang Pao. We keep this conversation in this room, *tu comprends*."

WASHINGTON DC
WHITE HOUSE

President Johnson walked into the room for an off-the-books, last-minute meeting with Secretary of Defense Robert McNamara and Head of the Joint Chiefs, General Maxwell D. Taylor. He continued to stand, towering over the table. and threw the top secret memo on to the table top. Then he took his seat at the head of the table. Johnson stared at both men intently.

"How sure are you both of this information?"

General Taylor spoke first. "It's been confirmed by Peer de Silva."

McNamara chimed in. "I received confirmation from both Ambassador Lodge and the Deputy Secretary."

General Taylor looked away for a minute then returned his eyes to the President. "I have confirmed this through another source, Mr. President. Lieutenant Colonel John Paul Vann has been imbedded with General Cao, trying to teach the South Vietnamese how to fight, and has been at odds with General Harkins for a year. Lieutenant Colonel Vann told me that he has seen Harkins alter battle reports."

President Johnson took a deep breath and exchanged glances with both men. "Maxwell, your old friend has really let us down. I can't believe that General Harkins would alter reports from the field. I mean both the CIA reports and Military Intelligence. How much territory do we now believe the Viet Cong control?"

General Taylor shook his head. "That is unclear, Mr. President."

President Johnson drummed his fingers on top of the memo as he sucked in his lower lip. He shook his head, trying to control his temper. "General Taylor, it sounds like we have total chaos in South Vietnam. For

God's sakes, I thought just the government was a mess, and now I am hearing that our military operation and intel is a bigger mess."

McNamara drew a deep breath. "Mr. President, I think we need to get on top of this immediately. I will start to come with some proposals. That is, if we are going to have any success with this conflict."

General Taylor looked down at the memo under the President's hands. "Well, I think we need to replace General Harkins. I will make a recommendation for a replacement, ASAP. If I can, Mr. President, I'd like to recommend we verify all our information and just get Harkins to retire. I would prefer not to embarrass my old friend."

President Johnson held his chin in the palm of his hand. "That may not be an option, dammit. I do want a verification of all of this, but I want it *fast*. And I will take those recommendations for a replacement within forty-eight hours. It's critical to learn how much territory is actually controlled by the Viet Cong. I am not going to be the President to lose this war."

Chapter Five

January 28, 1964
Washington DC
White House

President Johnson was sitting at his desk in the Oval Office when Gerri Whittington buzzed him that General Edward Lansdale had arrived. The President asked that he be shown in immediately. The door opened the Secret Service Agent stepped aside for Lansdale. The two men shook hands, and the President pointed toward a chair. Lansdale took a seat.

The President sat behind his desk and leaned back in his chair. "Ed, I called you into this meeting to discuss your plan for Vietnam, the one you were working on for President Kennedy."

Lansdale sat up straight in his chair. "Yes, Sir, Mr. President. I never finished it?"

Johnson leaned forward. "I was in that meeting last November when you briefed the Cabinet. I want you to finish it." He poked his finger on the desk repeatedly. "Look, I am aware that President Kennedy kept saying he was going to send you to Vietnam. Within the next few months I do intend to send you, but I want to see that plan first."

Lansdale nodded. "Mr. President, every time I get close to completing it, something dramatic happens and the situation changes."

Johnson folded his hands. "Ed, I'm very aware of that and things are changing fast on my end, too. I need to get up to speed and stay ahead of this situation." Johnson stared at Lansdale, then leaned back and ran his large hand through his balding hair. "You can't fool an ole' country boy like me. I know you still have contacts over there, and I'm willing to bet you're still talking to them."

Lansdale half smiled. "I'll deny nothing, Sir."

Johnson chuckled. "Look while you are putting the finishing touches on it, I want you to keep me abreast of any development. Will you do that for me?"

Lansdale took on a pensive expression. "Yes, Mr. President. May I ask if your plan for my return to Vietnam will include my team?"

Johnson cupped his chin in his palm. "I'm hopeful things will work out that way. I'm sure you're aware, a situation has come to my attention that has caused me great concern."

Lansdale fidgeted in the chair. "Yes, I'm aware of some discrepancies in some of the reports. My sources tell me the VC have penetrated much deeper into South Vietnam than has been reported."

Johnson raised his hand up to his chin; his test had proved valuable, Lansdale's contacts were still very good. Johnson continued, "Yes, that's true, but I'm about to get that handled. I know I don't have to tell you that Station Chief de Silva is overseeing certain clandestine operations now. Plus there are others at Langley implementing operations in North Vietnam, including one of President Kennedy's pet projects, the Navy Seals. All these operations incorporate facets of your old operation."

Lansdale rubbed his hands. "Mr. President, I will try to get this wrapped up within the next couple of weeks."

Johnson stood and shook his hand across the desk. "Thanks for stopping by on short notice. Now, don't forget to keep me in the loop on any information you get from over there, too."

President Johnson met Secretary McNamara outside the side entrance to the White House, and both men slipped into the presidential limousine for their trip over to the Pentagon. Johnson looked over at McNamara. "Just met with Lansdale. Got him to agree to finish his proposal for Vietnam."

McNamara stroked his chin. "You know Lansdale doesn't have many friends left in either the CIA or the State Department."

Johnson nodded. "I know you know that. I bet he knows that, too, but he has contacts in Vietnam that can be valuable to us and having him finishing his proposal will make him receptive to telling me things I need to know."

"You really going to send him back over there?" as McNamara made eye contact.

Johnson looked out the window as the limousine exited the grounds. "I don't know. I'll be sending him back the way he wants. But if he thinks we really want to keep US troops out of Vietnam… We do for a while, until I get this election behind me. He'll give me information. Maybe information no one else has. Let's find out."

McNamara raised his eyebrows. "Your call, Mr. President."

Silence hung in the limousine as President Johnson looked out the window. After a few moments, he turned back to McNamara. "Bob, I have to get this Vietnam situation under control, so I can work the domestic… I'm thinking about calling it the Great Society."

McNamara took off his glasses and closed his eyes. "Has a nice ring to it."

They arrived at the presidential entrance to the Pentagon. As soon as they came to a stop, the President and McNamara were greeted by two military police officers. The two men began their trek to the Pentagon's

Situation Room to meet with Chairman of the Joint Chiefs, General Maxwell Taylor. Within the last forty-eight hours, President Johnson's situation had gone from cruise control to damage control. His expectation was to walk out of this meeting with an update on the Viet Cong status and a recommendation for a new MACV for U.S. and South Vietnamese troops. Johnson stretched his long legs and McNamara almost had to run to keep up. Johnson was trying to keep his temper in check, but the last two days had been difficult. His political future lay in keeping the chaos in Vietnam behind a curtain to conceal it from the voting public.

Johnson and McNamara were shown into the room just as the meeting of the Joint Chiefs was finishing up. Each officer saluted then quickly exited the room. General Taylor remained standing until the President sat. President Johnson started the conversation.

"Less than a week ago, General Taylor, you and the other Joint Chiefs sent a memo to Bob, claiming that if Vietnam falls to communism, Cambodia, Laos, Thailand, Malaysia, Japan, Taiwan, South Korea, and the Philippines will also fall. Let me make my position very clear. I must get this general election behind me. I want the country to see Goldwater as the war candidate, assuming he's the nominee. The table is set for that. I want the public to see me as the more reasonable, peaceful candidate. If we escalate now, I have no position to distinguish myself from Goldwater. I will not be able to talk about some of *my* initiatives. Now, once the election is over, Maxwell, I let you and the Joint Chiefs have your war *and we will win* in Vietnam," President Johnson said, stabbing the table with his forefinger for emphasis. He took a deep breath and sat back before speaking more quickly.

"But right now, we have bigger, more pressing problems. What do you propose to resolve the situation with General Harkins? It must be done very quietly. I don't need any scandal with the military after Diem. I want to know the status on the Viet Cong and the North Vietnamese Army, and I want a name for Harkins's replacement."

General Taylor looked at McNamara, jutted his jaw then turned back to the President. "Mr. President, we, the Joint Chiefs, have discussed a plan among ourselves. I, we, propose you send General William Westmoreland over to serve as deputy commander of the Military Assistance Command, Vietnam, directly under General Harkins. We need to tell Harkins he must retire, very soon. Westmoreland is the best we have, and we can ease Harkins out without it getting too messy, if you will. Naturally, Harkins has to accept this proposal."

President Johnson nodded. "I am sure his general's pension will cause him to stay in line. Don't you think?"

General Taylor exchanged looks with both men. "Mr. President, we can only hope that will be the case. Harkins's term is over in six months. Westmoreland will begin to shine in his role. I believe Harkins could just quietly retire. Naturally, I will advise him we've been made aware of some revisions in reports. We will investigate further *if* we need to."

"Arm-twisting is a good thing. Sometimes it shows the wisdom of one's own decisions. Besides, Mr. President, we are clearly relying on Ambassador Lodge for as much information as we can get." McNamara jutted his jaw, as he leaned on one elbow.

President Johnson stood up and leaned over the table. "We want everything to be very calm in South Vietnam and in our own military. That way my re-election will almost be ensured."

Evening January 29, 1964

Saigon

US Embassy

Major Steven Hebert was making his rounds about the US Embassy to check on his security staff. The outside grounds were in good order. He decided to go inside, stop by communications and visit with Sergeant Tim Mitchell. Steven rapped on the door to the communications room. From the other side of the door, Tim said to come in. Steven opened the door.

"Tim, what do you have going on this evening?"

Tim looked around the room. "Major, you are looking at it. I am headed to my quarters to just groove on some music. There are a couple of new albums out, Beach Boys and Rick Nelson. I'm pretty excited."

Steven smiled. "Sounds like a good idea. You know, Tim, you are one of the few soldiers here who doesn't go out in Saigon. I'm glad. I don't have to worry about you drinking, chasing prostitutes, or getting arrested."

Tim started to straighten up his desk area. "Major, all I want to do is serve my time and get an honorable discharge."

Steven folded his arms on his chest. "What are you going to do when you go home? Jobs are tough to come by."

Tim pursed his lips. "When I go back to the States, I want to settle somewhere on the West Coast. Maybe just hitchhike the Pacific Coast for a couple of months. Maybe find a Beach Boys concert along the way."

Steven started to ask another question when the phone rang. Tim reached for it. "Communications, Sergeant Mitchell." Tim nodded a few times then said, "Yes, as a matter of fact, he is standing right here." Tim extended the receiver. "Miss Brown wants to talk to you."

Steven took the receiver. "Yes, Ma'am?"

"Major Hebert, there is someone here to see you. A Sergeant Graham. Shall I send him down to communications?"

"No need. I'll be right there." He hung up the phone.

Steven started out the door when Tim hustled over and grabbed it. "Care if I tag along?"

Steven and Tim started out the door, walking quickly up the hallway. "You must really be bored, if you want to walk up and meet a friend of mine."

Tim got a sheepish smile. "Naw, *while I do* want to meet your friend, I don't want to miss an opportunity to stick my head in the door and look at Meredith."

Steven stopped in his tracks and looked at Tim, then busted out as big a laugh as he could remember. "Well, I should have known." He stomped his foot. "Damn, I sure missed that one."

Tim turned two shades of red. Steven finally got under control and wiped the tears from his eyes on his white gloves as he started back up the hall. At Meredith's office, he opened the door and let Tim walk ahead of him. No sooner was Steven in the room than Ethan Graham jumped up from a chair and extended his hand for a firm handshake. "Thought you went home, got out of this place."

Ethan rubbed his face with his right hand. "Hey, you didn't have to put on your Blues just to see me. And yes, I tried to go home, but I didn't like being out of the service."

Tim raised both palms. "You got to be kidding me."

Meredith laughed and feigned a serious look. "Sergeant Mitchell, that's not fair."

Steven pointed toward the door. "E, why don't you come down to our dining area. We can talk there." Steven turned his hand and pointed at Tim and Meredith. "You all are welcome to come along, too."

Meredith spoke first. "Steven, that is really nice of you. If you don't care I might tag along for a minute."

Ethan nodded. "Great. I can't stay long. I am shipping out at midnight."

Tim continued to stare at Meredith and just nodded.

As they walked down the hallway, Ethan turned to Meredith. "Does Steven still sing that song? *Stars shining bright above you.*" Ethan was *way* off key.

As Meredith shook her head, Tim piped up. "Yes, that how we know he is coming. We hear that baritone voice."

Steven fained a punch into Ethan's arm.

When they entered the dining hall, a few other soldiers and civilians were sitting randomly around the large room. Steven and his entourage walked over to the coffee pot. The coffee had that burnt smell it got from being kept heated for hours. They all grabbed cups, then proceeded to a table in the corner. Steven and Ethan sat down before Tim and Meredith. Steven leaned over and whispered, "E, where are they assigning you?"

Ethan looked around to see who was within ear shot. "Da Nang. Top Secret Mission, part of a team to provide security for the Navy Seals and OPLAN 34A personnel. Didn't want to say anything in front of the others because of security clearance."

Steven wanted to ask him more, but Tim and Meredith joined them, so Steven changed the subject. "E, you couldn't make it as a civilian so you re-upped."

Ethan leaned back in his chair and looked at all of them. "Hebert, I tried civilian life. I got a job working at a grocery store, you know, just to get started. But it wasn't any good. Don't get me wrong, the people were great, but I quickly discovered I missed fighting."

Steven shook his head. "You are certainly true to your heritage." He looked around at Meredith and Tim. "If you couldn't guess from his red hair and accent, Ethan is one hundred percent Irish." Everybody at the table laughed. Steven, the first one to sip his coffee, made a sour face. "Wow, is that coffee old. Everybody better put your hands over the cup. It's strong enough to get away."

Ethan said, "There is that dry sense of humor I missed."

Meredith spoke up first. "*Sense of humor*? What do you mean? Since I have been here, we've never seen it."

Ethan laughed and put his hand on Steven's broad shoulder. "This is a real funny guy. Cajun humor, some people wouldn't get. But I know what you're talking about. When we were being tested for the Force Recon, he was so buttoned up you'd never know he even heard of funny."

Steven started to speak, but Ethan put his finger to his lips and whispered. "You know why. He was the only Negro in the group, so he was afraid to cut up any and—" He nodded. "For good reason. But after he made it and I didn't, we went out on the town one evening and he had me cracking up. We've been close friends ever since, even though we don't get to see each other very often."

Steven grabbed Ethan's shoulder this time. "Okay, E, that's enough. Don't you have to go?"

Ethan waved his arms. "Well, since your friends are here, I want to tell a story about Steven. We were both trying to become Force Recon at the same time, and as I said, he made it, I didn't. Now I grew up in the country and could always shoot, but let me tell you, Steven was the best sniper you have ever seen. I think the trainers still tell new recruits about his scores."

Meredith winked at Ethan and smiled. "Tell us a story about young Major Steven Hebert."

Ethan scratched his head. "Well, then, one day we were doing a timed run in army boots. Anyway…"

Steven interrupted. "Oh, come on! Please don't tell this story again."

Tim and Meredith both chimed in, "Oh, please, Ethan, tell us," Tim said. "The Major never tells us anything about his background."

Ethan laughed. "Okay, we had to run a mile under six minutes in army boots carrying, I don't know maybe a one-hundred-pound backpack."

Steven put his head down for a minute, knocking his cap off, exposing his short cropped hair.

Ethan continued. "Well, there were ten of us. Through the first three laps we're all together running. As soon as we all hit the last lap, I decided to take off. Running is the only thing I could do and compete with these guys. About a quarter of a lap I was pulling away from everybody. Then, with just a half a lap to go, here comes Steven, pulling up beside me and passing me. Now, he had never outrun me before, so I just figured I would go with him. As we are coming down the final straight stretch, my feet were killing me. I put on a charge and we were side by side. All you could hear is the clop, clop of those damn boots hittin' the track, but I wasn't going to let him beat me. Well, apparently, he felt the same way. So down the stretch we went. What it was, was he outleaned me at the finish line. We both were timed at just over five minutes. I don't remember the exact time. Then both of us got to see our breakfast again."

Meredith made a face.

Tim chimed in. "That's our Major... but it is disgusting to think of you guys laying there getting sick. What did..."

Just then Captain Jefferson came bolting into the dining room. "Major Hebert, we have a situation."

Steven jumped up from the table and went out the door like a shot, with Jefferson close behind him. Jefferson said, "Damn it, you were right, Major. General Nguyen Khanh is trying to overthrow General Minh."

Steven snarled. "Come on, let's move." The men ran down toward the Marine quarters.

As they moved through the Embassy, Steven exclaimed. "Have you doubled the perimeter guards?"

"Yes, Major"

Steven drew a deep breath. "Did you determine if all of our communications are still up? You remember when they took out Diem, they cut our communications."

"Haven't had time to check, Major. I came to notify you as soon as I shored up security."

"Good. Okay, Captain, you take care of communications. I'll check on the Ambassador. Let's meet at the front entrance. ASAP." Steven ran off in a different direction.

Steven ran toward the Ambassador's quarters, and when he arrived, he caught his breath before knocking. He came to attention as he heard stirring on the other side of the door. The Ambassador opened it. "Major?"

Steven saluted. "Our intel from inside the city has advised us that General Khanh has started his attempted coup of General Minh."

The Ambassador frowned. "Has the Embassy been properly secured?"

Steven nodded. "Yes, Ambassador. Captain Jefferson came and notified me after doubling the parameter guards. He went to communications while I came to your quarters."

The Ambassador looked around. "Major, I believe I will not notify the President until we have more information." He half-turned and mumbled, "Who knows what the outcome of this damn situation will be? Keep me posted. Every development! I'll go to my office as soon as I get dressed."

Steven saluted then rapidly moved toward the front of the Embassy to meet the captain. *This is why the South Vietnamese have not engaged the Viet Cong. They could have had the upper hand if they had only taken some action. And General Harkins has altered the reports…* As Steven rounded the corner, he met Captain Jefferson at the front door. Jefferson saluted.

"Major, I have rechecked all the perimeters. All is secure."

Steven returned the salute. "The Ambassador is on his way to his office. I believe he was aware of the situation before I got there. Captain, excellent job getting everything buttoned up."

9:00 AM, JANUARY 30, 1964
SAIGON
US EMBASSY

Major Steven Hebert sat across from the desk of Ambassador Lodge, who was speaking on the phone with President Johnson. Steven was unable to hear what the President was saying, but at one point, the Ambassador raised his eyebrows. "President Johnson, this coup is not a surprise. I saw the report of Lieutenant Colonel Lucien Conein. It *was* sent to the State Department."

Steven bristled at Conein's name but forced himself to sit expressionless in his chair.

The Ambassador nodded occasionally as he listened yet seemed disinterested. "Yes, Mr. President, I just wanted to report that the coup is complete. Totally bloodless, at least at highest levels of their government. We should have the full report sometime this morning. General Nguyen Khanh is the new leader. I actually think he will be an improvement over General Minh. I am going to try to meet the Khanh later today or tomorrow."

Ambassador Lodge sat for a moment, listening, then, "Yes, Mr. President, I intend to make the meeting as low key as possible. I am aware you do not want to attract the press." He peered at Steven over his glasses

69

for a moment before saying, "Yes, Mr. President. Thank you, Mr. President."

He hung up, and as soon as he did, he looked straight at Steven. "I want a security detail on standby, ready to move out. We will be going to Mr. Dunn's private residence. This motorcade will be low key."

Steven stood up and saluted. "Yes, Ambassador." Steven left his office. He wondered why they were conducting this meeting at Lieutenant Colonel John M. Dunn's residence. *Why are they sneaking around?*

On his way out, Steven passed through Meredith's office. He stopped when he saw that she looked concerned.

"Major," she said, "*what* is going on?"

Steven winked and whispered, "Nothing to worry about, Meredith. Everything's going to be fine. You are in the most secure place in Saigon." Steven continued out the door.

Once back in his office, Steven put together a security team for standby. Choosing the duty officers was a little tricky: fewer cars, fewer soldiers. He needed the best of the best. As Steven went over the list of names, he sat back in his chair. *Another coup within 90 days. Conein had known it was coming; the Ambassador knew it. The only way I knew anything was because Tao talked to An.* Steven went out to the hall and posted his security team.

JANUARY 30, 1964

WHITE HOUSE

President Johnson had called for several members of his cabinet and advisors to come in to the White House to review their information on the coup in South Vietnam. National Security Advisor Walt W. Rostow, Assistant Secretary of State for Far Eastern Affairs Averell Harriman, Director of Central Intelligence John McCone, Secretary of State Dean Rusk, and Secretary McNamara and Chairman Maxwell Taylor all waited for him in the White House conference room. The President walked in and took his seat at the head of the conference table.

"Gentlemen, I called this meeting to give you the latest information regarding the coup in South Vietnam." Johnson glanced around the room to get each man's reaction to see if he could detect who might already be aware of the details. He figured if anybody knew something it would be Harriman. Harriman and Lodge were part of what Johnson had told Bobby Baker was the New England Cabal. No one flashed any signs that Johnson could read, yet he believed at least one person had known what was going on before him and he did not like it.

Johnson picked up the phone and buzzed Gerri to bring in copies of the cable from Ambassador Lodge. He looked at them as he passed them out. "Please read this and give me your opinions. I need to stay out in front of it if I want to get elected in ten months."

Johnson watched carefully as they read.

The first man to speak was Dean Rusk. "We had no inside information on this coup."

"That is because you ignored a report in December from that CIA Officer Conein!" Johnson roared.

McCone jumped into the conversation. "Mr. President, I wish you wouldn't refer to Conein as CIA. We all know he *was* CIA but has... retired. Besides, he works closer with Ambassador Lodge and Lansdale."

Johnson pounded his fist. "I want answers not damn semantics!" He paused and looked at each man. "First off, I want your opinion on General Khanh as a leader. He has promised to engage the enemy and work closely with the US military and government. What do you all think? Our official statement has to be just right, and I want to make sure when I release my statement. I don't leave my behind exposed. Surprises in an election year are never good. Number one, we have to get it out that we were unaware of the coup and had *absolutely* no knowledge of it until this morning."

Robert McNamara placed both hand on the conference table. "I think we respond slowly to the new government."

Johnson shook his head. "Khanh brought an entourage of reporters with him to the meeting at Colonel Dunn's residence. This story will be in every newspaper in the world within twenty-four hours. Lodge says he tried to make it low key but it didn't work. Khanh wanted it high profile and succeeded."

General Taylor made eye contact with everyone. "General Khanh may be the finest officer in the South Vietnamese Army. If Khanh says he is willing to work with us then let's put him to the test."

Johnson pouted. "That is long-term view. Right now, I need to get a statement prepared."

Rusk said, "Let's say, 'General Khanh has removed General Minh as the leader of South Vietnam and is currently forming his government. We believe there is a real chance that the—'"

"Pardon me, Dean," Walt Rostow interrupted, "but, Mr. President, why do we have to say anything? While everyone knows we are in Vietnam, saying nothing might give the best impression."

Johnson leaned back in his chair and closed his eyes. "*Perhaps* that is the best course to take. Say nothing, don't hold a press conference or even release a statement."

Silence fell over the conference room. Finally, McNamara spoke up. "Reacting to Khanh's next moves may be a better choice. It will give us time to work behind the scenes to see how this plays out. That certainly could quell any reaction to statements made from the White House."

Johnson sat back up. "Okay, that's the plan. But all of us, including Lodge and de Silva, damn well better start communicating about what the hell is going on! No more damn surprises. Everybody understand?"

Chapter Six

February 8, 1964

Saigon

Street Cafe

Major Steve Hebert was off duty, sitting in a little café in downtown Saigon. *Wonder how many Viet Cong are around me right now?* He was sipping on a cup of tea waiting for his order of lemongrass with sticky rice. He looked down at his watch: Maxton was five minutes late. About that time, the waiter brought his rice, and Colonel Andrew Maxton walked up to Steven's table and sat down. Steven looked him in the eye. "What is so important that we have to meet in civvies off base?"

Colonel Maxton looked all around him and whispered. "I need information. From the Embassy."

Steven shook his head a couple of times. "Not sure I'm your guy. Ambassador Lodge doesn't tell me anything." *Particularly since I came back.* "Most of what I ever learned was from observing."

Maxton leaned even closer. "I picked up word that General William Westmoreland is being assigned over here. Coming in as a second, but I can see the writing on the wall. You have not heard anything at the Embassy?"

Steven knew a great deal but he could not talk, even if Maxton was one of his few friends and a good source of information. "If there is any scuttlebutt at the Embassy, it hasn't trickled down to me."

Maxton bit his lower lip. "Supposedly, there is an investigation into General Harkins and his staff, including me. But I can't find out anything."

Steven kept his best poker face. *Word is getting around fast.* "I don't know anything. If I hear anything, I'll let you know." Steven changed the subject. "What is going on with the South Vietnamese Army? Understand Khanh is one of their best generals."

Maxton leaned back wiped his mouth with his hand. "Well, I suppose you know about the latest screw-up"

"No." Steven shook his head. "Tell me."

"Just a couple of days ago, one of our choppers spotted a large contingent of Viet Cong at Long Binh. It's—"

"Near our big army base." Steven finished Maxton sentence.

Maxton nodded, waved him off and continued. "Anyway, Khanh ordered the South Vietnamese out and they surrounded the Viet Cong with superior forces. After eight hours of more or less pretend fighting, they let the VC get away."

"You have got to be kidding me! How is that possible?"

Maxton placed both hands on the table. "They had superior numbers. The VC were surrounded, but they still wouldn't engage. They relied on artillery and bombing the VC from the air."

Steven shook his head. "What do you think is going to happen? We have to engage the VC or we are going to get overrun. I'm beginning to think some of the commanders are scared of the VC."

Maxton bit his lip. "General Harkins told me just this morning that Khanh is removing five division commanders. But this is the culture of the South Vietnamese Army—they just aren't very good fighters. Don't get me wrong, they have some vicious fighters, just not enough of them." Maxton pushed away from the table.

"Aren't you going to get anything to eat?"

Maxton shook his head. "No, I've got no appetite. Really, I should go."

Steven looked around as he finished his tea, looked down at his rice. "I have lost my appetite." Steven stood and reached across the table to shake hands with Maxton. "I've got to go, too. I'll let you know if I hear anything."

Steven figured it was the last time he'd see Maxton. He surmised that Westmoreland was going to replace Harkins soon and Harkins's staff would be recalled to the US.

Steven reached into his hip pocket for his wallet to pay for his meal. He felt a hand on his shoulder. Thinking Maxton had returned, he looked up: Julian Romano, Corsican Brotherhood, dark sunglasses and all. Steven aggressively removed the man's hand. Romano slid into the chair just vacated by Maxton.

"Stevie Boy, how ya doin'?"

Steven sharpened his stare. "I was just leaving."

Romano waved his arms to make a scene but spoke softly. "Stevie Boy, don't leave on my account. I came by with a compliment. Lucien Sarti wanted me to tell you you're doing a great job at the Embassy, keeping your end of the bargain."

Steve pursed his lips and continued to stare at the Corsican.

"Sit," Romano said softly before continuing in a louder voice. "By the way, looks like your little brother might have a pretty good future as a track star at Southern Miss." He leaned back in the chair and whispered, "But it seems he has discovered marijuana." Romano laughed real hard as he sat up straight.

Steven leaned across the table as he reached over and grabbed Romano's shoulder. "Quit your lying to me. You and your kind stay away from my mother and brother. You hear me. I'll keep my end of the bargain."

Romano threw his arms up in the air again. "Wooh, Stevie Boy, calm down. Thought you'd just want some good news about your family. Don't get so excited."

Several of the other patrons in the café stared at the two men. Steven knew he should walk away. His next step had to be to defuse this situation and his temper. With great restraint, he aggressively pushed his chair back, pulled out his wallet and tossed twenty piasters on the table and walked away. It was a very difficult thing to do, as he could hear Romano laughing as he walked away.

As Steven walked, he wondered if what Romano had told him was the source of his brother's problems. Steven knew he had to confront Jeremiah about this; smoking marijuana was totally unacceptable for a Hebert. For Godsake, their father had been a police officer! *Where the hell is he getting the money to buy it?*

MARCH 11, 1964

WASHINGTON DC

WASHINGTON STAR NEWS OFFICE

Rita Sullivan had heard the name Cassius Clay but knew little about the man. However, over the past couple of weeks of research she had learned what a charismatic individual he was. But who and what he was had exploded in the last two days since his announcement he had changed his birth name from Cassius Marcellus Clay, Jr., to Muhammad Ali. Clay was named after his father, who had been named after a 19th century Republican, a staunch abolitionist. Clay had been raised a Methodist by his mother and father but had joined the Nation of Islam. This caused a considerable stir throughout the United States. His brash attitude had already brought him considerable notoriety, but this latest pronouncement quickly converted him to a more polarizing figure. Since the newspaper had a predominately Negro audience, Rita believed the article she was working on would be well received by all, except maybe the Chief. But maybe, because of the controversy surrounding Ali, from the Chief's prospective he would let this article slide.

When Rita first sat down to write she realized she could only write two sentences about the man: Ali had defeated Sonny Liston for the world heavyweight title, and he had changed his name. She was off to the archives to research the period from his youth until March 6 of this year, when he announced he had changed his name at the behest of Elijah Muhammad, the leader of the Nation of Islam. Rita quoted Ali's reason for the name change: He believed Clay was his "slave name." Much of her column focused on his personal background, including problems with growing up in segregated Louisville, Kentucky. Her research included Clay's friendship with the controversial Malcom X. Clay first started boxing at the age of twelve, which culminated with a gold medal in the Rome Olympics. Sonny Liston was now the champion, but Clay was the number one contender, with a 19-0 record, even though his record had come with some controversial decisions in his early fights, including his being knocked down in two fights.

When Clay stepped into the ring to fight Sonny Liston for the title fight, he was a heavy underdog. Yet throughout the lead-up to the fight, Clay had promised to win by a knock out. That's when he first started using a phrase that had become famous: "float like a butterfly, sting like a bee." Liston had a questionable past, including being an ex-con and having ties to the Mob. Rita contemplated including some reference to Liston being bought off, but with the theme of her column, she was afraid she'd go over her 500-word limit. She thought if the Chief liked the column—or at least tolerated it—she might follow up in a couple of Sundays covering that aspect of the fight. Right now, she wanted her column to focus on his youth and his philosophy of life. The sportswriters may end up covering the gambling side anyway.

She waltzed in to Ed Boland's office, handed him the column and sat down, waiting for his reaction. His eyes got big several times during the reading, but she noticed he only picked up the punishing red pen twice in the 497-word column. When he was finished, he puffed on his pipe several times, then leaned back in his tattered swivel chair. Boland told her that her column was well thought-out and well written. He even told her he had learned a few things about Ali's past that he didn't know. This brought a smile to Rita's face. Boland was a boxing fan. She thought he might be a gambler but was afraid to ask. He warned her that the Chief might blast her because he wouldn't like the column, but he'd probably let it slide into the paper because of their subscription base. Rita appreciated his advice. She was still learning how to handle the Chief's gruff nature.

After making the corrections, Rita headed for the Chief's office with her column in hand. She sat down across from him and watched him read. When he finished, he leaned back in his chair.

"Miss Sullivan, this is an excellent article. We will definitely use it this Sunday. You know, I had high hopes for Clay, after he won the gold and all. But he's a self-serving glory hound. This—the way he's behaving—is more than I can take. Liston had a terrible reputation. I didn't think they should allow him to hold the title. I hated it when he beat Floyd Patterson." The Chief almost flashed a smile. "I really liked Patterson, another Olympic Champion. Go ahead and take this down to Copy."

Rita was in shock—no fighting to get this in the paper. The Chief does know his audience. She did not understand why everyone was so upset with Ali.

CHAPTER SEVEN

MARCH 12, 1964
SAIGON

Major Steven Hebert was sitting in his quarters writing a letter to his mother. He especially wanted to inquire about Jeremiah. Steven had a sense his brother was in some kind of trouble, but he didn't wish to discuss that with their mother just yet. If Romano was right and Jeremiah was smoking marijuana, it could explain some of his behavior. Was there more? Steven and his mother had always exchanged letters monthly. He elected to stick with that pattern. He had contemplated calling her but was afraid that would scare her. He was walking a fine line between his own concerns and overreacting, all while tip-toeing around his mother. Just then his phone rang. Tim wanted him in the communications area.

Steven walked into the communication area and saw Meredith Brown. *Strange.* Tim had called him down to the area. *Must have called Meredith, too.* Tim motioned for him to close the door. Steven looked bewildered. "What gives, Tim?"

Meredith nodded. "Yes, you made me wait here until the Major got here—what is going on?"

Tim was barely audible. "Ha-Ha-Has the Am-Ambassador said anything to either of you?"

Steven shook his head.

Meredith chimed in. "No, about what? I think we need more information. He was pretty happy this morning... Actually, come to think about it, he's been pretty cheerful the last two days. Why?"

Tim pulled out news he had received from the United States and laid it on the table in front of them. Steven's eyes widened, Meredith looked at Steven, then Tim. Finally, Tim looked at Steven. "What do you make of all of this?"

Steven read the headline out loud. "Henry Cabot Lodge, a write-in candidate, won the first Republican Primary of the season in New Hampshire." Steven moved his finger down and continued the opening sentence. "The results came as a surprise to everyone. Senator Barry Goldwater finished second, and the favorite, Nelson D. Rockefeller, the former governor of New York, finished a distant third. Lodge, the current US Ambassador to South Vietnam, didn't campaign for a single minute in the state—"

Meredith interrupted. "So, Major, what does that mean?"

Steven laughed. "Well, it means he has been happy for the last couple of days. How the… *heck*, do I know what that means? We all knew he had presidential aspirations, but this beats all."

Tim chimed in. "No official cables in the last thirty-six hours."

The room got quiet. Finally, Steven rubbed his chin. "Bet he goes back to the States to run for President."

Tim said, "If you are right, who will replace him?"

Steven shook his head. "I'm a soldier not a politician. I'm clueless."

They both looked at Meredith; Tim raised one eyebrow. "You work for the State Department. What do you know?"

Meredith sheepishly looked at Tim. "He has had several personal calls from friends and politicians over the last few days, but I thought it was either private conversations or State Department business. He has not dictated anything to me, and his door has been closed the entire time."

Steven said, "Okay, here's one thing I can tell you. We can't say a word to him. He has to bring it up to us, agreed?"

Tim and Meredith both nodded.

Steven said, "It's a deal."

MARCH 12, 1964

WASHINGTON DC

WASHINGTON STAR NEWS

Rita Sullivan hustled into the very small conference room and settled into a seat next to Miriam Ottenberg. Chief Petit continued to stare at her until she got out her note pad. Petit walked over to the blackboard, grabbed a piece of chalk, then wrote April 12 on the board and underlined it three times. He spun around but continued to tap the blackboard with the piece of chalk while looking at John Sherwood. "This is the date. All of your columns in for this Sunday paper. John, you are up first."

John nodded. His plan was to interview random people as he walked about the various Cherry Blossom Festival events. He named seven different events, complete with the dates and times. His goal was to come with between four and six good interviews for commonman-on-the-street stories from DC area. The Chief turned back to the blackboard to make notes of the events and the number of interviews that John would attempt. The Chief stepped back and looked at the board, nodded.

Petit pointed his chalk at Miriam Ottenberg. "Your turn."

Miriam tipped her pencil over several times, tapping on her steno pad. She wanted to write about the business impact of the Festival Events, focusing on the hotel business and how many of them raise the rates for the three-week period of this tourist season. As she talked, Petit stood there, legs spread, nodding. He made some notes on the blackboard, put his hand on his chin. "Ottenberg, I want you to focus on the lower rated hotels, no five stars."

Rita looked back down at her steno pad and appeared to write some notes. The Chief pointed at her and nodded.

Rita opened her notepad. "Last night, I went to the Quorum Club and met with a number of socialites from the DC area who were organizing art and music events. The chairman could not meet with me, so he sent some lady named Mary Pinchot Meyer. She is a local artist."

The Chief folded his arms on his chest and laughed. "Do you know who Miss Meyer is?"

Rita shrugged her shoulders. "A local artist?"

"Well, Miss Sullivan," the Chief said, "I can tell you haven't been in this town very long. The Quorum Club is one of the elite clubs in this city, and Miss Meyer is one of the elite's elite. Her brother-in-law is Ben Bradlee, and before you say anything, yes, the editor at Newsweek. Plus, he was once with the CIA."

Rita got lost in the Chief's statement. *There was a man sitting in a dark corner of the club just staring at us.* After the Chief cleared his throat the second time, she looked back down at her notes.

"Okay, Miss Meyer handed me this copy of all of the more "high brow" art and music events." Rita flipped over a couple pages, then grabbed a piece of folded mimeograph paper. "Chief, I would like to cover some of these music events. Some of the more modern jazz music. I hope to find some groups that I know a little bit about so I can write some previews."

The Chief turned back to the blackboard, made his notes, and put his hands on his hips and stared for a minute. He turned back around. "This should be a good overview of the Cherry Blossom Festival period. Here is the challenge for each of you: Every column must incorporate the blossoms into it. Everyone get to your typewriters and get started." The Chief waved his right hand toward the door.

Last out of the room, Rita dipped her head as she moved past the Chief.

Rita was sitting at her desk and staring off into space. While she was not assigned to the political section, she knew her friend Meredith Brown worked at the US Embassy in Saigon for Ambassador Lodge. If she was going to get out of her special interest weekly column, she'd have to make a bold move and perhaps her friend Meredith could…

Miriam Ottenberg's voice cut through her thoughts. "Rita! You better get to work on your column or Petit will be upset with you for being late."

Rita shook her head, half-smiled and looked back down at her Smith Corona. She had not even prepared the opening paragraph for her column. She started typing, her story focusing first on the cherry blossoms getting ready to bloom in Washington over the next couple of weeks. She knew once she had that part written, adding in the jazz music would be easy. She glanced up at the clock—almost lunch time. Perhaps that was what she needed, a walk and some fresh air to get her focus.

Rita slowly descended the steps to the ground floor and went out into the cold afternoon. She took a couple of steps and stopped to feel the sting of the cold air on her face. She stopped and leaned against the building. Growing up, she had always said you can't force creativity—she was wrong. She forced it often in her columns.

John Sherwood and Miriam Ottenberg walked by her. John snapped his fingers twice in her face, asked if she'd be interested in joining them for a quick bite. Rita nodded and fell in step. Perhaps life had just handed her the opening she needed.

The three of them sat at the lunch counter and ordered coffee with a variety of set ups from black to cream to sugar. The short order cooks banged and clattered as they worked, and Rita tried to block it out. Miriam started to speak, but in her rush to speak before her thought was drowned out, Rita interrupted.

"I have this dilemma. One of my best friends works for Ambassador Lodge. I sent her a letter about the coup, but this New Hampshire election result has made me want to contact her. See if she can get me an inside story?" Rita nervously patted her hair pulled into a bun.

She paused, suddenly embarrassed by her lack of respect for her elders.

John took a sip of his steaming coffee. "An inside story on what exactly? You can't break either story. So where are you going?"

Upset with the answer, Rita started to reply, but Miriam jumped in. "As John says, you can't break the story, so do you have to have an angle or believe there are some inside facts? But for that you must have an open mind. Are you looking at the story with the facts in mind?"

Rita rethought her objective while not knowing what to say. About that time the waitress behind the counter walked over to get everyone's orders. Rita nodded at the other two, to get their orders first, as she finally opened the menu. After John ordered a hamburger with a pickle and tomatoes and

Miriam ordered a garden salad, it was Rita's turn. She frowned. "Get me a roast beef sandwich with a side of potato chips. Please."

John restarted the conversation. "Rita, do you see what Miriam is saying? Okay, you have a source, so you have an angle to build your story. The coup—what is your play? Now, the election angle is interesting to the American people. Everyone thinks it's Goldwater's nomination to lose. However, Rockefeller was supposed to win the more liberal New Hampshire. Do you think your friend is going to have a story?"

The waitress returned and refilled their coffees. Rita took a sip. She didn't like the answers she was getting, but it was great insight. She knew why these two were such excellent reporters. Rita looked at them. "What should I do?"

Miriam glanced at John, who motioned her to go ahead. "I'll take the war, you take the background side."

John nodded.

Miriam pulled out her notepad and scribbled down some ideas. Miriam was the President of the Washington Press Club and a Pulitzer Prize winner. She knew how to tease out a story. Miriam tore out the sheet and pushed it to Rita, who immediately looked at it: Lodge's background and what might his next moves be.

Just then the waitress brought their lunch.

Rita picked up a couple of potato chips and stuck them in her mouth. She cleaned the grease off her fingers with her napkin.

Miriam finished chewing, then continued. "What do you see different about the coups in South Vietnam? Can you determine how they affect Vietnam? Get into the background of Lodge, build a story from those answers. That will add depth to your story. Never forget the background of the individual, it can provide powerful insight."

John asked, "In your letter to your friend, what did you ask about the two coups in South Vietnam?"

Rita replied, "Why all the information from the Kennedy Administration and virtually no information from the Johnson Administration on the coups on their watch?"

John nodded. "That could be a great angle. The Vietnam conflict—is it a civil war or is this an extension of the Cold War? This may end up leading you to the political side, but remember, always be open to the facts. Try to get inside the politician's heads."

Rita took the first bite of her roast beef. She thought she had some good ideas for approaching Meredith. Plus, she could apply these things that Miriam and John had pointed out to finish her column. Rita looked at both. "So, this Mary Pinchot Meyer is a big deal in this town?"

Miriam nodded. "Her former husband is or was a very high level CIA agent. They were personal friends with the Kennedys at one point in time."

Rita looked at John then back to Miriam as she bit her lip. "There was a man sitting in a dark corner of the Quorum Club the whole time I was interviewing her. He didn't move. I really got an eerie feeling about it. Even when I looked at him, which I tried not to do, he just sat there."

John frowned as he exchanged glances with Miriam. "It's a club. It's supposed to be dark. He may have just been checking out two pretty women. Who knows, Bradlee may have problems with someone from another publication talking to his sister-in-law." John started laughing then Miriam and Rita joined in.

Rita felt slightly relieved. Still, the man was creepy.

As they were walking back to the newspaper, Miriam said, "Your friend at the Embassy, write her and find out if she will be an unidentified source. Maybe she could even get you an interview with Lodge? But most of all, tread lightly. Your friend is your friend, don't use her to abuse her."

John held the building's door open. As Rita entered she realized that she had been given a lesson in journalism. Now apply it in the proper fashion to continue to climb the ladder.

CHAPTER EIGHT

MARCH 14, 1964

WASHINGTON DC

It took Lansdale about thirty minutes to drive from CIA headquarters in Langley, Virginia, to the White House. *Time to think.* While Lansdale never envisioned General Minh leading South Vietnam, he had hoped his Buddhist background could help unify the broken country. Obviously, Lansdale had misjudged Minh. Thich Tri Quang had known things about Minh's staff or had simply planted stories implying they were conducting negotiations with the French and the North Vietnamese.

Cannot imagine Minh wanting an independent state, which would allow the French back into the country. General Khanh had jumped in to take advantage of the continued unrest throughout South Vietnam. What concerned Lansdale more were the Buddhist and the student protests.

95

Something was not adding up. Lansdale had hoped Khanh would let General Minh be president, while Khanh would assume the role of prime minister. That could improve the situation, including Khanh re-establishing military intelligence for the South Vietnamese Army. However, in the first month of the relationship nothing had changed. *If Johnson does not officially send me over there, I'm going to send myself. Before long the odds will become insurmountable. My relationship with Johnson is not as good as it was with Kennedy. So far, the results have been the same: all talk no action.*

When Lansdale arrived at the White House, he was shown into the empty conference room. After a few minutes, President Johnson entered the room carrying a piece of paper. Lansdale stood up to shake hands.

"Ed," President Johnson said, "thank you much for stopping in on such short notice. I wanted to talk with you about the developments in Vietnam, bring you up to speed on some things that are going on behind the scenes."

"Yes, Mr. President."

The President leaned back in his chair and ran his hand over this thinning hair. "I want to show you my level of commitment to Vietnam, but at the same time be cognizant of their government. I have jotted down some notes from which I am going to prepare a cable to Ambassador Lodge." The President reached in his pocket for his glasses, leaned over the table. "Forgive me, I'm reading from my notes, 'We want South Vietnam to be independent and noncommunist. I want their leaders to understand, but also we want to be firm in our position. South Vietnam must be free. But I want to be clear we do not wish to put any demands that they establish a Western-style government."

Lansdale nodded. "If I may be so bold... I know the Khanh has said he wants to work with us, but, Mr. President, their Army must engage the Viet Cong. We need to imbed more of our officers in their troops, like we have done with Lieutenant Colonel John Paul Vann. Also, we need to start directing our attention to the Ho Chi Minh Trail."

Johnson jerked his glasses off and tossed them on the table. "You know, Ed, McNamara recommended we start bombing North Vietnam. So, I hear what you are thinking. I know we are not doing enough. This is why I want your opinions. You know things. I assume that is going to be part and parcel of the plan you are preparing, and I desperately need it, ASAP."

"Yes, Mr. President."

The President folded his hands over his hand-written notes. "There are some developments. I assume you are aware the Navy Seals are now active."

Lansdale raised his eyebrows and nodded.

The President continued, "OPLAN 34A has started, but it is off to a rocky start. They were getting their intelligence from the CIA, but they are slow to identify and hit targets. De Silva has some operatives trying to mimic your activities from the 1950s. I want to get you over there. Put your team on notice. Sometime this summer I am sending you over there in some capacity. Do you know anything that I should know?"

No wonder the CIA was getting slow intel they ran Richardson out of the Country and took months to replace him. Lansdale ran his hand over his mouth and down to his chin. *I'm sure as hell not telling you all I know.* "No, Sir, Mr. President. I'm ready to get over there. I'll get it finished."

President Johnson stood. "Okay, get back to work. Let's get this done. Time is of the essence."

Lansdale got up and exited the conference room ahead of the President. *I hope Johnson really means this. I will be headed back over there. I need to get this information to General MacArthur. I hope he is feeling better. Perhaps this news will perk him up.*

President Johnson looked at his watch. He pushed the intercom button on his phone. "Gerri, send McNamara in as soon as he gets here." Johnson leaned back in the chair. *I wish I could still call on Bobby Baker, if anybody could*

dig up anything that I could use on Lodge, Goldwater, or Lansdale, it would be him. I got too many people around me I cannot control.

The President leaned back over to reread his daily briefings. After he finished he reached for another file and pulled out the memo from Senate Majority Leader Mike Mansfield and reread it. It was third time he'd read it. Mansfield was predicting that the coup of General Minh would not improve the situation in Vietnam. Mansfield even predicted that there could be more coups, because he believed whoever was in charge would be pushing to control the money coming in from the US.

Several minutes later, there was a knock on the door. President Johnson said, "Enter!" and a Secret Service Agent escorted Robert McNamara into the Oval Office. The Secret Service man exited, and President Johnson pointed toward one of the two couches in the oval office. The President got up from his desk and moved to the opposite couch. The President pulled out his note, again, and handed it to McNamara to read. McNamara glanced over the paper and laid it down on the coffee table.

"I met with Lansdale earlier today to ask him his opinion." President Johnson relaxed on the couch.

McNamara nodded. "What did you say?" McNamara took off his glasses and cleaned them with his tie as he continued. "What are you going to do with him?"

"Naturally, Lansdale liked it. I told him about some of our operations and some of our difficulties. He didn't flinch. So, his insiders had already told him everything I told him."

McNamara raised an eyebrow. "What are you going to do with him?"

Johnson shook his head. "Don't know yet. The man has many enemies, but he also has his contacts. Right now, *I need* those contacts."

"Well, just keep him out of the room with Taylor and Krulak." McNamara laughed as he spoke.

Johnson rubbed his forehead. "Boy, to tell you the truth, I'm not comfortable with having Lodge in Vietnam either, but right now he's the front runner for the GOP presidential candidate. I need to keep him in Vietnam as long as possible."

McNamara looked around. "Thought you were worried about Goldwater?"

Johnson leaned over. "*I don't want* to worry about any of them boys. This election is mine to win if there aren't any surprises."

McNamara nodded. "I still have grave reservations about the potential of the domino effect in Indochina. We must get those South Vietnamese generals involved in the fight. Seems like the only thing they want to do is fight over their personal power."

Johnson tapped repeatedly on the coffee table. "Bob, I've been thinking we may need to take a more active role if things don't start going our way soon. I'm going to send you to back over to Vietnam."

McNamara leaned back. "Whatever you want, Mr. President."

Johnson scowled. "Damn it, Mike Mansfield called this. He said the overthrow of Minh would not make much difference. The Vietnamese have sat on their damn hands while the Viet Cong get stronger and stronger. And our people haven't told us the truth. But if we do anything more that will be what I am forced to talk about, maybe even campaign on. I just have to hold off until after the election. I really want to get to work our domestic agenda. I want to be able to campaign on the great society."

MARCH 18, 1964

WASHINGTON DC

WHITE HOUSE

President Johnson finished dictating a letter to Gerri just as he was informed by the Secret Service Agent that General Taylor and Robert McNamara arrived for an off-the-books meeting to discuss the findings from his trip to South Vietnam. Johnson could barely contain himself as the situation was much worse than he had expected. Johnson wanted to get feedback from the Chairman of the Joint Chiefs before making his policy.

As soon as both men were seated, Johnson pounced. "Maxwell, what is your reaction to Robert's report?"

General Taylor jutted his chin and tugged his jacket in place. "I cannot believe that twenty-two of the forty-three provinces are controlled by the VC. They have achieved more in the last few months than anyone could believe possible."

Johnson spoke up. "Yes. Several provinces around Saigon. This is part of what I can't believe. How could they let this happen?"

McNamara shook his head. "Large portions of their population are apathetic about the entire situation. That's worse. Moreover, they seem to be turning against the U.S. contingency in their country. The Viet Cong continue to terrorize the villagers in the countryside."

General Taylor interrupted as he opened his arms. "We need to get our forces in there as soon as possible if we are going to save this country from the communists. If we don't get in there soon, all of Indochina will fall very quickly."

McNamara continued with his point. "The Diem coup caused changes in the political leadership of many of the provinces. These changes have not benefited the countryside."

Johnson opened his palms. "I thought the Catholic leadership was bad."

McNamara nodded in agreement. "My trip was too short to determine whether it has to do with the Catholics or the Buddhists. All I can tell you is the leadership change at the local level may be part of the problem."

General Taylor nodded. "The thing that concerns me, according to my sources, they have surrendered their weapons in many of those in the strategic hamlets to the Viet Cong. Plus, I just don't believe in the South Vietnamese army. Khanh doesn't have his government or his military under control. I believe this is why we need to get in there and take over the entire military operation."

Johnson waved his hand as he interrupted. "Now, Maxwell, I told you and the Joint Chiefs we need to get this election behind us. Then you can have your war. I can't start the fighting now or Goldwater or Rockefeller could get the upper hand."

Taylor sat back on the couch and pursed his lips.

McNamara decided he better speak up. "Look, I believe our only advantage is Khanh will likely do what we tell him to do. He is very pro-US."

Johnson ran his hand through his thinning hair. "I think we have to stress to him that there can't be any more coups."

McNamara nodded affirmatively. "As you have seen, that is part of my report. We need stability and confidence in the Khanh government."

Taylor jumped back in. "But their army is still on the sidelines. Him being pro-US is great, but it isn't winning any battles."

Johnson looked at Taylor. "What do you think about paramilitary action?"

Taylor shook his head. "If their regular army can't find it in them to fight, how are they going to organize a paramilitary force?"

McNamara looked at Johnson. "I think we have to try, don't you?"

Johnson continued. "You mentioned de Gaulle in your report. What is your opinion? Can he stir up the South Vietnamese and turn them against us?"

McNamara shook his head, obstinately. "de Gaulle is still pissed off. He thinks the US forced the French out of South Vietnam, but what he refuses to believe is most of the Vietnamese still dislike them. He has to paint us to be like them. At the moment, I don't see him affecting the situation. The rest of Europe, who knows?"

Johnson nodded. "De Gaulle has become so anti-American lately, but I think he can only play to that element in Europe." Johnson picked the report up and flipped the page. "I will try to work the diplomatic channels to try to get Prince Sihanouk to allow us some access to his country to fight the VC. The only place we seem to be winning is in Laos, and damn it, we can't even talk about it."

The room fell quiet. Finally, Johnson spoke. "What are your all's final thoughts or suggestions?"

Taylor said, "Get our military in there as soon as possible."

McNamara looked at Taylor then to Johnson. "Well, I do think we need to add some troops to fortify Saigon. There's just too much VC activity around the city. It could fall before we even got into the war."

Johnson sat there fuming. This Vietnam situation was not working out the way he wanted. He looked at McNamara's report.

"Gentlemen, thanks for coming by. I want to think about this some more at this point."

CHAPTER NINE

MARCH 18, 1964

NEAR PLAINES DES JARRES (PLAIN OF JARS), LAOS

HO CHI MINH TRAIL

Nguyen Tao was back in his blind observing movements on the Ho Chi Minh Trail. This had become his favorite place since he and Major Hebert had picked this spot several months earlier. Over the past several days, Tao had made notes up and down about twenty miles of trail. He tried to get as much detail as possible, the bombing runs could be effective. General Lansdale had sent word to Tao to start mapping. Tao had a CIA map that had been taken on a flyover reconnaissance.

Tao was about to head back to camp when he felt a rumbling under his feet. Tao sat patiently. First, he checked his backpack for extra magazines, then checked his M1911 and Colt M16, which Tao had started carrying in

106

his last two scouting missions. If there was some small convoy on the trail, he could ambush them by himself. Within a couple of minutes, two small old vehicles slowly drove by his position, each pulling carts with supplies for the Viet Cong. Tao noted three men in each car, none of the whom appeared to be carrying any high-powered weapons. This might be his chance to pull off an ambush. As soon as the two vehicles had passed, Tao slipped out of his blind and moved surreptitiously onto the Trail. He pulled up his M16 and fired off six rounds at the trail vehicle. He slipped behind a large Koda tree just as the trail vehicle crashed. The lead car stopped all three men bailed out and ducked behind nearby trees for protection.

Tao observed only one man crawling out of the wreckage of the trail vehicle. As the man moved to the safety of another tree, Tao stepped out and fired four rounds. The VC dropped where he stood. Bullets zinged around Tao, so he quickly moved deeper into the jungle. He secured himself behind Bael tree. Again, bullets rained around him. Not so deep as to take his line of sight off the remaining VC. Tao peeked around the tree. More bullets were fired at his position. Tao realized he'd lost his advantage; he had to change the odds. He chose to keep his bullets rather than to fire randomly, wasting them. He moved closer to the three VCs. This time they did not fire at him. The VC had moved. Obviously, attempting to surround him.

Tao could not let them triangulate on his position, so he slung his M16 on his shoulder, pulled his M1911, and retreated the way he had come. As he moved he heard a sound on his immediate right and saw one of the VC, rifle raised. Tao evaded the shots then fired five rounds from his handgun as he continued to run. One less VC to worry about. He continued to move to another secure position.

Tao believed the other two were still behind him as he retreated, and if they were to advancing on his position, one would be on his immediate left, while the other was directly behind him. He moved slowly and deliberately in that direction. When he found a secure large Koda tree to position himself, he holstered his M1911, swung down his M16 and sat. His strategy was to listen for the movement. *Think. Think. What is their strategy? They might make a run for their vehicle and escape.* Tao could not let that happen.

Tao was also concerned both men would attack his position simultaneously. Hopefully, they were not trained soldiers. He sat quietly and continued to listen. No movement anywhere around him. They were using the same strategy as him. Tao decided to make a bold move: He was going to their vehicle. Again, Tao shouldered his M16, pulled his handgun, and moved out in a circular direction, hoping to encounter one of the two remaining VC. As Tao moved, no one shot at him. *Very strange. Did they tuck and run? Are they doing the same thing, moving to their vehicle?*

Tao zigzagged from tree to tree, each time checking the area all around him, listening for any sound. Within a couple of minutes, he reached the wrecked vehicle. The driver was not dead but dying; his passenger was dead. Tao couldn't take the chance of shooting the dying man to give up his position, so he moved on. *I wish I had a knife; on his next trip, I will.* Tao reached inside the vehicle, pulled all the guns out, and threw them far away from the vehicle. Tao looked at the other vehicle. He could not afford to stay in one place too long, so he moved toward the lead vehicle. Tao positioned himself just off to the side of the trail near the vehicle and waited.

After a short time, he heard rustling off to his left and his right—both men must be coming. Tao laid a magazine beside him and pulled up his M16. He peered around the tree. No one in sight. *Where were they?* Finally, he saw movement to his immediate right and focused in that direction. This movement was on the same side of the vehicle that he was. Tao was ready, and the sounds got closer. Tao dared not close his eyes. Finally, Tao saw one of the VC, moving from tree to tree but with his gun pointed down at the ground. He watched for the ideal time to strike.

Tao timed his move perfectly. As the VC stepped from behind a tree, just thirty yards away, Tao dropped with a quick burst from his M16. Man down. Tao dropped low back behind the tree. Finally, the odds were even.

Tao guessed after the gun burst, the remaining VC would assume a defensive position. He was across the Ho Chi Minh Trail, so neither man could cross out into the open as either would lose their advantage. Tao reached down and dropped his magazine and put in a fresh one. He thought of going on the offensive but changed his mind and stayed near the vehicle. Tao looked around both sides of the tree for a clue to the last VC's position. He kept the M16 on his shoulder and moved forward to the vehicle, which brought a rain of bullets from a stationary position fifty yards ahead. Tao unloaded the magazine at the spot. No more bullets came from there. Tao quickly dropped the empty magazine and inserted another without taking his eyes off the spot. Tao cautiously moved forward toward it. In a few seconds, he was standing over the dead VC.

Tao's work was almost done. He hustled back to his blind and quickly gathered up his maps. He had to make sure this spot was accurately mapped. He slipped over, uncovered his vehicle, and sped off toward Vang Pao's camp. The first bombing run needed to attack this site to eliminate his ambush. Tao pushed down hard on the accelerator to go as fast as possible back to camp.

When Tao arrived at General Vang Pao's headquarters, he slammed on the brakes. He leaped out of the jeep and went in to the general. The Air America pilot was already there, impatiently waiting on him. Tao pushed up to the desk where Vang Pao had his map out. Tao pulled his map out and laid it down. Everybody immediately leaned over Tao's map as he pointed at each point that he had seen activity over the last week. He felt these were the key bombing points on the Ho Chi Minh Trail. Tao straightened, folded his arms on his chest, and proceeded to tell about his experience at the last site. When he was finished, the Air America pilot pulled out his map and marked the spots Tao had picked out. The Air American pilot folded his map and left. On his way out the door he said, bombing should start within twenty-four hours.

After the pilot exited the headquarters, it hit Tao some of Lansdale's plans were finally getting implemented. CIA operatives were flying old US air planes, marked as Laotian Air Force, to attack the Ho Chi Minh Trail. Not exactly the ideal battle strategy, but at least something was being done to try to stop the flow of supplies into South Vietnam. Hopefully, it was not too little too late.

CHAPTER TEN

APRIL 1, 1964

SAIGON

When Major Steven Hebert walked into Meredith Brown's office, dressed in civilian clothes, he was greeted with her usual happy smile. "How are you doing, Major?" Before he could answer, she continued, "I'm so excited... Richard Nixon is coming."

Steven was assigned to his security detail by the Ambassador, which was why he was here in civilian clothes. Steven had spoken with General Edward Lansdale a week earlier and was aware that Nixon was coming. He would be assigned to Nixon's detail. Lansdale told him that Nixon would discuss a matter with him and he needed someone Lansdale trusted. Steven knew that meant no further communication via the telephone.

"You are more excited for him than for McNamara, eh?"

Meredith's smile widened then turned puzzled. "I don't know, he was the vice president. My dad says he's a really big deal, lots of connections. Connections most diplomats don't have."

Steven was about to reply when Ambassador Lodge stepped out of his office. He looked at Meredith, half grinning, then at Steven. "So, you are excited to see Richard?"

Meredith looked up at the Ambassador. "Sir, I have all of your reports typed up and read for your meeting. Is there anything else you need?"

Lodge stepped forward to reach for the papers. "Step into my office, please," he nodded toward Steven.

Steven sat down opposite the Ambassador and waited for him to speak. Steven believed he was about to receive his itinerary for Nixon. Finally, Lodge looked at him across the desk. "You and one soldier you will proceed to Tan Son Nhut and pick up Nixon. Nixon will be meeting South Vietnamese Foreign Minister Phan Huy Quat and bringing them directly back here. You get Nixon back here as discreetly as possible. Do you understand, Major?"

Steven looked puzzled. "This is a worldwide tour, announced weeks ago. There are certain members of the press traveling with him. Sir, how do you propose to keep this low-key?"

Lodge looked at him for a second. "Don't be surprised if Nixon holds a brief press conference or, at least, makes a statement. This is to be expected. I want you to blend into the woodwork when you leave the Base."

Steven drew a deep breath. "Are you expecting trouble? Do you know something that I need to be briefed on?"

The Ambassador stuck his chin out. "No, Major, just the opposite. I expect nothing from the VC. Actually, I want to avoid the South Vietnamese public."

Steven tilted his head. It was the strangest answer he had ever received from the Ambassador. He tried to process the situation. "Are there any other instructions?"

The Ambassador folded both hands on his desk. "That will be all, Major. Follow these orders. We have placed considerable trust in you. Don't let us down."

As Steven walked down the hallway toward his assignment, all he thought about what the Ambassador had said—*Don't let us down*—and added, *this time,* in his own head. Outside, Steven dismissed the team he had previously assembled, got in his jeep, and drove off toward the base.

As he drove, about to embark on one of his most important mission, all he could think about was the disturbing letter he had received from his mother. The coffee can where she had hidden her stash of money was empty, the two hundred and fifty dollars gone. She did not know what had happened to it. Steven had a pretty good idea that his brother had taken it. But why? What was going on that Jeremiah had to steal from his mother?

Steven arrived at Tan Son Nhut and showed his credentials to the security. The sentry saluted but signaled that he should hold right there. The sentry turned toward the nearby small building and pointed at Steven's vehicle. Puzzled, Steven looked at his watch. This had never happened before. He was supposed to meet Nixon and Quat in less than thirty minutes, and it was his responsibility to make sure the military police had the press corps line fully established and secured.

Within a minute, a plainclothes man walked up to the driver's side and flashed his ID: Sergeant Hollis Kimmons. This was the man Lansdale had told him was assigned to work with him on his detail. Kimmons moved quickly around the front of the vehicle and got in without a word.

On the drive over to the tarmac, Steven began to tell Kimmons of his steps to secure the press area. When he was finished, Kimmons described the steps the military police had taken to secure the perimeter pending Nixon's arrival. He also detailed the time of the arrival of the Foreign Minister. As Steven pulled his vehicle to a stop, he believed the situation was well in control. Lastly, Steven looked at his watch—right on schedule. A soldier from ground crew chief ran over to him and moved toward their vehicle and signaled *five minutes to touch down.*

Within a couple of minutes, the military plane was taxiing toward their location on the tarmac. The ground crew chief signaled the military police, and Steven knew it was time to look sharp. He stood at one end of the press corps line, while Kimmons took the opposite position.

The ground crew rolled the airstairs up to the plane's door and within seconds Richard M. Nixon was descending to the tarmac. He moved to a makeshift lectern to issue his brief criticism of previous policy but went on to praise Defense Secretary Robert McNamara's recent comments against the communist insurgents. Steven noticed that Quat started walking toward the vehicle and got nervous about him going toward the car without either of them. What if he planted something? After a few brief questions of little consequence, Nixon ended the Q-and-A with his signature wave and a smile to the small assembly of press as he walked toward Sergeant Kimmons and the awaiting vehicle. Steven brought up the rear to verify security. When Steven was in the car, he looked around, and saw that Quat and Nixon were both ready to roll. With a nod to both men, he shifted into drive and drove out of the airbase toward the Embassy. Steven traveled a different direction than he had come through Saigon to be inconspicuous as possible. The drive was completely quiet from Tan Son Nhut to the Embassy.

After arriving at the Embassy, Steven and Kimmons exited the vehicle first to make sure everything was secure. Once certain, they signaled that it was safe for Nixon and Quat. They escorted the two diplomats to the Ambassador's office. They were greeted by Meredith with her usual smile.

Before Meredith could strike up a conversation, Ambassador Lodge stepped out to meet both Nixon and Quat, then lead them into a closed-door meeting.

Lodge had told Steven and Kimmons to wait in the outer office. After a little more than thirty minutes, the three diplomats emerged from the Lodge's office. The two soldiers stood to attention.

Nixon said to Steven, "I have a dinner meeting with Minister Quat. When it is over I want you to drive me back to Tan Son Nhut. All of us will be spending the night in the 145th Aviation Battalion tonight so we can get an early start in the morning. Major, pack your gear, including your weapons for a mission to last for several days. I have made arrangements for your fatigues."

Steven and Kimmons saluted. Steven went to his quarters to pack the clothing he would need. He picked his two M1911 handguns with several magazines and his favorite M14NM sniper rifle and several magazines, then returned to Mcredith Brown's office to wait. She still had that giddy grin as she conversed with Richard Nixon. Steven was happy for her. She had been so excited to meet the former vice president. After another minute or so, Nixon turned to Steven, "Son, are you ready to go?"

Steven saluted and opened the door for them to exit. As he walked out, he turned and flashed a smile at Meredith, who was beaming.

Outside, Kimmons was leaning against the car, staring up into the night sky.

"Looking for divine intervention?" Steven asked.

Kimmons and Nixon laughed. Steven walked around to the driver's side while Kimmons let Nixon into the jeep. The three men were quiet on ride over to Tan Son Nhut.

Once at the quarters for 145th Aviation Battalion, Nixon waved his arm for both men to follow him. Steven and fell in behind Nixon and Kimmons and followed them into the building. Nixon gave them their room assignments.

"Be at the jeep ready to roll at 4:30 AM," Nixon said. "Wear the fatigues that are in your quarters. Get a good night's rest."

Steven looked at his watch, 2330. Morning was coming fast, mission unknown. Like the old days with Lansdale.

CHAPTER ELEVEN

04:30

APRIL 2, 1964

SAIGON

The next morning, Steven walked out of his room with two side arms on his hip. He was carrying his rifle and was surprised to see Richard Nixon already in the hallway dressed in the same fatigues as Steven and the sergeant and carrying three army boonie hats. Nixon looked at both men.

"Here, put these on," Nixon said as he handed out the hats. "Both of you have been selected to protect me on an above top secret mission due to your various knowledge and skills. If you have any identification with you, lose it now. Let's go."

119

They moved swiftly to the jeep. Once in, Nixon leaned up between the two men in the front. "Major, turn right on the tarmac and go to the farthest end of the runway. There will be a Chinook, engines ready. Pull up to it."

Steven replied without looking in the rearview mirror. "Yes, Sir, Mr. Vice President."

Nixon tapped Steven on the shoulder. "Let that be the last time you use that title until we are back here. It is Dick. Is that understood? Both of you?"

Steven thought this might be the strangest build-up to a mission he had ever been on. Both Steven and Kimmons nodded.

Just as Nixon said, there sat the Chinook, but oddly, it had no markings. No *USA*, no *Army*, no *Air Force*, nothing. *What is going on?* He pulled alongside the Chinook and stepped out to make sure it was okay for Nixon, who got out of the jeep at Steven's signal. Nixon walked to the opposite side of the Chinook and gave the slit-throat signal to the two pilots then motioned for them to come down. *What is this all about?*

Steven watched the two pilots double-time over to Nixon. None of those pilots had name tags or rankings. When all four men assumed at ease shoulder to shoulder, Nixon placed his hands on his hips and addressed the men.

"The mission you are about to embark on is above top secret. As of this moment you all have volunteered or been volunteered without any knowledge. I hope none of you want out because you have been hand-selected due to your various skills, but if you want out I will understand." Nixon looked at each of the soldiers. "We will proceed to Phuoc Binh where I am scheduled to meet a man by the name of Nguyen Loc Hoa." He turned toward Steven. "You know this gentleman."

Steven nodded. "If you are speaking of the Catholic priest. Yes, I have had dealings with him in the past."

Nixon nodded as he folded his arms over his chest. "Yes, son, that is one of the reasons you were chosen for this mission." Nixon looked at each man. "I must have a private conversation with Father Nguyen Loc Hoa. After that we will go on to our next destination, which is to be determined by my conversation with the priest. I should add that with each successive move this mission gets considerably more dangerous. So gentlemen, if you want out, now is the time to decide."

Steven did not make eye contact with anyone but Nixon and assumed each of the other three did the same thing. No one moved.

Nixon looked up at the sky, where dawn was breaking. "Okay, gentlemen, let's go. I want to be in the air before daylight."

They rapidly boarded the Chinook. Steven placed his rifle on the seat beside him. As soon as the helicopter was in the air, Steven's mind began to recall facts to get his mission face on. He had not seen Father Nguyen Loc Hoa in years. Hoa had provided information to Lansdale when he was in Vietnam. He had fought the Japanese in World War II, then Mao's communists in China. When Mao's forces defeated the side he fought on, he fled to Cambodia. That was the last location he had known of the priest. *I wonder if this is the right man.* At least now, Steven knew why he was on this mission. Lansdale had sent him along to identify Hoa. *Maybe Lansdale is starting to trust me again.*

It was a short helicopter ride to the small village of Phuoc Binh, an area known for heavy VC activity. The pilots flew high enough to avoid automatic gunfire then swooped down at the last minute to an open field near an old church. The pilots were instructed by Nixon to stay in their seats and keep the chopper running and ready to get out fast, just in case anything went wrong. Steven nodded at Kimmons, and the two men got up to lower the steps. Steven started to pick up his M14NM, but Nixon looked at him.

"Leave it. You can keep your side arms. That's all."

Steve felt very uncomfortable with that decision, but he did as ordered. Kimmons looked over at Steven, eyebrows raised. Both men walked off the helicopter ahead of Nixon. Once they were on the ground and clear of the turning blades, a small Vietnamese man dress in a black cassock stepped into the clearing. He was by himself. He appeared to study the men and the Chinook. Nixon ducked his head a little and continued walking with Steven and Kimmons falling in stride beside him. He spoke in a low voice. "Is that the priest you remember?"

Steven narrowed his eyes as he studied the little old man in the black cassock. "Yes, Sir."

Nixon let out his breath, but never changed his stride or expression. Steven had heard stories about Nixon's background; it was about to be tested. The three men closed to within fifteen yards of the priest when Nixon looked to both men and held his hands away from his waist. "Wait here."

Steven did not like that idea. One of his jobs was to protect Nixon at all costs, but both he and Kimmons did as ordered; they stopped then stood at ease.

The priest looked past the approaching Nixon. "Is that you, Captain Hebert?"

Steven did not know what to do or how to respond. Nixon turned around, looked at him and nodded. Steven knew it was safe to talk, "Yes, Father Nguyen. It's Major Hebert now. It has been a long time." Steven remained in his stance.

The priest replied, "Yes, my son. You look well." Then the priest looked at Nixon. Nixon spoke to Father Nguyen under his breath, too softly for Steven or Kimmons to hear. The two men proceeded into the small chapel. Steven looked over at Kimmons, who pursed his lips. Steven believed Kimmons was as puzzled as he was and neither knew whether to move toward the chapel or stay put. Then Kimmons began surveying the area. "I think it would be prudent to police the perimeter of this field."

Steven chuckled nervously. "Agreed, the priest is okay, but this is VC territory. Surely someone heard or saw that Chinook coming, and I assume we will have to take off at some point. That could be when a trap is executed."

A half-hour after going into the church, Nixon and the priest walked out. They were chatting as Steven and Hollis Kimmons walked up to the two men. Nixon did not stop them from approaching this time. He looked at Steven. "You two do have a little history, I understand."

Steven nodded and without a word, reached out and shook the old priest's hand. The priest grabbed the hand and pulled Steven into a hug.

Nixon then turned to Kimmons. "Please say hello to the priest."

Without a word, he also extended his hand and greeted the priest, who accepted the gesture with a smile. Before they left, the priest said a Catholic blessing over the three men then made the sign of the cross. "Peace be with you." The priest raised his head. "Please hurry away."

The three men double-timed it back to the waiting Chinook. The pilots saw the men coming and revved up the motors. The blades began turning ever faster. As soon as Nixon was aboard, both Steven and Kimmons looked around the perimeter of the field one last time then climbed aboard themselves and tugged up the walkway. Once in, Kimmons moved far enough forward to signal the pilots to lift off. The Chinook lurched forward into the air within seconds.

When the helicopter was in the air, Nixon shrugged and rubbed his hands together. "Well, off to dinner with the Ambassador."

Steven looked at Nixon, over at Kimmons, then leaned back in the jump seat. *Wonder what's our next action?*

As soon as they were back on the ground at Tan Son Nhut, Nixon gathered everyone from the Chinook helicopter. "We start again in the morning, same time. All of you will spend the night here, except for you, Hebert. You will escort me back to the Embassy for my dinner with Ambassador. After dinner you will bring me back here." Nixon nodded. "Major, we both need to change into civilian clothes before going to the Embassy."

On the drive over to the Embassy, Nixon did not say a word. Most of the time he leaned back, his eyes closed. When they arrived, Nixon was escorted by Hebert into the large building. They walked down the hallway toward the Ambassador's office.

In the office waiting room, they were greeted by Meredith's smiling face. She picked up the phone to notify the Ambassador of Nixon's return. Nixon sat down and started a very friendly conversation with her. In a few moments, Ambassador Lodge came out of his office and ushered Nixon in. As the door closed, Steven heard Lodge ask if Nixon was ready to come to his quarters for dinner. The last thing Steven heard was Nixon saying they had much to discuss and asking if de Silva got the product yet. *What will they be discussing today's activities or Lodge's politics, likely both.*

Once the door was closed, Meredith smiled and looked at Steven. "What is it like running around with the vice president all day?"

Steven shook his head. "I wish I understood what we were doing."

Chapter Twelve

April 3, 1964

Saigon

Tan Son Nhut Air Base

At 05:00, all five men assembled next to the Chinook helicopter awaiting their orders. Nixon pursed his lips. "We are headed to An Loc. As I mentioned yesterday, this mission will be considerably more dangerous. What you are about to witness today, well… you will not divulge to anyone." Nixon pulled out four papers and handed one of the papers to each man. "Should any of you violate this agreement, you will be locked up so deep they will have to pump in sunlight."

After each man signed, everyone boarded the helicopter. Steven sat down and closed his eyes. *Why sign those letters? What are we getting into?* They were going to An Loc, which was another hotbed for VC activity.

Within seconds the Chinook was in the air, flying to An Loc. Nixon leaned backwards to look out the small window. He watched for several minutes, then Nixon release his seatbelt and walked carefully up to the cockpit. Steven watched him speak to the pilot and the co-pilot, but he couldn't hear what was said. Nixon returned to his seat and re-fastened his seatbelt. He looked at Kimmons and Steven. "Get ready. We're almost there."

As Steven checked his rifle and side-arms, he glanced over at Kimmons, who nodded. The helicopter was starting its descent. Shortly, they were on the ground, but as it had the day before, the Chinook remained idling. Steven got up to lower the walkway, but Nixon stopped him. He stood up and signaled the pilots to join him. Everyone gathered around Nixon, who stuck out his chin.

"Gentlemen, I have put a lot on you while giving you little information. Now I will tell you what you have been volunteered for. Sometime ago, five members of our OPLAN 34A were captured by the Viet Cong while on a mission in Cambodia. None of these men are soldiers, but they are critical operatives. Their mission was tipped off to the Viet Cong, so they walked into a trap. Some of the men I know personally, so I have taken it on myself, with the blessing of the President and two high level CIA operatives, to get these men back. Yesterday's meeting with the priest was to set the table for today's meeting."

Nixon pointed at Hebert and Kimmons. "When you open this door, I'm going to exit the chopper first. Both of you will follow me out as rapidly as possible and deploy on either side of me. We will proceed west to the end of this clearing. Be prepared as a Viet Cong lieutenant will step into the clearing as we walk in that direction. You will do nothing to him. When he steps out, you will stop walking and I will continue forward. And yes, you can carry your rifles and side arms. It will be expected, in case this is a trap. I intend to negotiate the terms of exchange, in that field in your plain view, to get those five men back. If all goes well, we will board the Chinook and leave. If it is a trap, it is your mission to get me safely out of here. Do you all understand?"

All the soldiers nodded without a word.

Nixon looked at the four men. "Let's get started."

Kimmons walked over to the door and lowered the walkway, with Steven positioning to survey one side and Kimmons to survey the other. They both nodded to Nixon, who started down the steps. As Nixon started walking, Steven and Hollis Kimmons quickly came down the walkway and came alongside Nixon, Steven on the left and Kimmons on the right. Both men had their rifles over their shoulders. Steven did not like this situation because the sun was behind the position where the VC would emerge. *We are getting a long ways from that Chinook, if this is a trap.*

After they'd walked about fifty yards, a small Vietnamese man emerged from the overgrowth of vegetation. He wore a baba and was armed with a US-made AK-47, a nine millimeter handgun on his side. When Steven and Kimmons stopped walking, the VC carefully knelt to lay down his automatic weapon. With two fingers he grabbed his sidearm and laid it down. Steven looked for military markings, as Nixon had mentioned the man was a lieutenant. The Vietnamese man slowly stood and started walking again toward Nixon, who was now about thirty-five feet from Steven. Their ability to rescue Nixon was getting more complicated. Once the two men stood about ten feet apart both stopped almost as though choreographed. The two men started speaking to one another, but Steven could not hear what was being said.

Nixon continued his conversation with the Vietnamese man, while Steven and Kimmons continued to scan the open field and what they could make out in the jungle. At one point, Nixon raised his voice. "What evidence do I have?"

The Vietnamese man showed his hand to Steven and Kimmons and slowly opened his baba then reached inside. Steven's senses intensified as he watched. The Vietnamese pulled out a small piece of paper. Steven relaxed a little, assuming it was a picture. The conversation continued awhile longer, then Nixon turned to Steven. "Is your Vietnamese good?"

"Yes, Sir."

Nixon replied. "What is a hôp?"

"It's a box."

Nixon turned back around. Steven still could not hear what was being said, but noticed the conversation again grew more intense. In moments, though, the tone settled down. In a few minutes, Nixon turned around and walked back to Steven and Kimmons. Nixon almost walked into both men as he walked past. Steven and Kimmons walked backwards, watching as the VC lieutenant recovered his weapons and disappeared into the foliage. As quickly as possible, the three men boarded the Chinook. Nixon gave the pilots a thumbs-up, and he throttled up the motors. The big helicopter lifted up off the open field. Nixon sat quietly the entire flight back to Tan Son Nhut.

As soon as the Chinook was on the ground at the airbase, Steven opened the walkway, everyone exited. On the tarmac, they huddled around Nixon, even the pilots, and stood at ease.

"Gentlemen, this is now your mission to complete. I have negotiated an exchange with the Viet Cong to return our five operatives in exchange for three boxes of gold." He pointed to the two pilots. "As soon as we load the boxes, you will precede immediately to Phumi Kriek, Cambodia. There, the gold will be exchanged for the five men. If the VC keep their end of the bargain, you will bring those five men back with you. If this is a trap, you will bring back the gold, at all costs. Is that understood?"

Steven and the other three men nodded.

"Hebert," Nixon continued, "since you speak Vietnamese you will meet the same lieutenant. He is supposed to show the five men first. Then you will bring out the gold. That's the agreement."

Nixon told them to follow him and walked toward what appeared to be an old abandoned hanger on the far end of the airbase. When they opened the side door to the hanger, they were met by Nguyen Tao, who turned on one bank of lights in the dilapidated hanger. Tao and Hebert exchanged discreet glances. Tao led them over to the back corner of the building. He pointed to five boxes. Nixon looked at the CIA operative.

"We will only need three of these boxes. Thank Santa Romana." Tao nodded silently. Nixon did not wait for the response and turned to the four men. "Can any of you drive a fork lift?"

None of the men acknowledged their ability or their willingness to try. Nixon looked at Tao. "Will you load three boxes on that Chinook?" Nixon pointed toward the tarmac.

Tao did not say a word, just walked over to the small fork lift on the opposite side of the hanger.

Nixon motioned toward the hanger door then at Hebert and Kimmons. "You two soldiers get that door open." Then he pointed to the two pilots. "You two get over to that bird and get ready to load those boxes." Within ten minutes, all the boxes of gold were loaded, and Tao disappeared back into abandoned hanger and closed the door.

Everyone assembled next to the Chinook. Nixon placed his hands on his hips. "You have a mission to accomplish. When you have completed it, give your uniforms to Kimmons. Kimmons, you are to burn these uniforms. Is that understood, Sergeant?" Kimmons and the other three men saluted then boarded the helicopter.

Nixon stuck out his chin. "Look sharp." Then turned and walked off.

The Chinook was airborne, flying toward Cambodia within a minute. As they flew, Steven looked at Kimmons. "How do you see this playing out?"

Kimmons patted his hand on his knee several times. "It could be a problem, I'm not going to lie to you. It is going to take three of us to carry each box. It means three trips back and forth to the helicopter."

Steven frowned. "Since I am to talk to the lieutenant, I'll keep him and his men occupied, while you and the pilots unload the gold. Then we'll load the five prisoners. You have those pilots get this bird ready to fly, and I'll back myself aboard to try to keep them from any shenanigans. You cover me from the doorway."

Kimmons cracked a half smile. "Well, you figured out a way for us to do all the heavy lifting." He laughed heartily.

Steven rubbed his chin and nodded. "You don't have to worry about me. I'll just be keeping the VC busy." He leaned back and closed his eyes. This mission was more dangerous than anything he had anticipated, standing face to face with the enemy, trusting them while the exchange was made. Very risky.

After about forty-five minutes, the co-pilot shouted back and gestured with his hand when they were about to the target site. Steven and Kimmons came up to the cockpit, bent to look out the windows. Looking around, they saw a man in a baba waving a torch. Kimmmons slyly stated, "This must be the place."

Steven and Kimmons went back to their jump seats, buckled up, and immediately started checking their weapons. As the helicopter started its descent to the open field, Steven closed his eyes to focus on his mission. Once on the ground, Steven unbuckled his belt, picked up his M14NM as he moved to the door. Just before he lowered the walkway, he looked at Kimmons. "You got my six."

Kimmons picked up his rifle and moved behind Steven to the door. "Before you're on the ground, buddy."

The pilot shouted back—the Vietnamese man had disappeared! Steven looked at Kimmons, turned his head slightly to the right. "I don't like the sound of that, look sharp. You know we could end up in a fire fight, out-manned and out-gunned as soon as we get on the ground."

Kimmons laughed nervously. "Yeah, and all Nixon would be upset about is losing the gold."

Steven grabbed the door release and lowered the walkway. He surveyed the area then descended into the open field carrying his rifle in a ready position. When he stepped off the walkway, the VC lieutenant stepped back into the clearing on the opposite side of the field carrying his AK47. He and Steven both froze, studying each other. He took several slow steps into the open field. When he stopped, he pulled his automatic weapon to the ready position. As Steven walked through the open field, the heat and humidity seemed to intensify, but he continued his steady walk, displaying as much confidence as possible. Within fifty feet of the lieutenant, Steven stopped and spoke, asking to see the five soldiers. "Cho tôi xem năm lính." Steven realized even at this distance he towered over the VC lieutenant.

The lieutenant cautiously swung his AK47 onto his shoulder and waved to the far right side of the field. Steven knew his next move would put him in extreme danger. He swung his M14NM on his shoulder and, taking his eyes off the lieutenant, Steven turned his vision toward where the lieutenant pointed. Five captives were aggressively pushed from the jungle foliage, followed immediately by three VC with automatic weapons pointed at the five men. Steven assumed there were many more soldiers in the jungle ready to respond or, possibly, be aggressive.

Steven looked back at the VC lieutenant and nodded. The lieutenant wanted to see the gold. "Bây giờ, chỉ cho tôi vàng."

Steven turned around and waved at Kimmons. The helicopter was shut off. Within about a half minute, the three Americans began to carry the first box of gold into the field in the direction of Steven and the lieutenant. They awkwardly carried the first box until the lieutenant held his hand up. The men lowered the box to the ground and hustled back toward the helicopter.

Steven continued to shift his eyes between the five captives and the VC lieutenant, attempting to make sure everyone was protected. Once again, they slowly came down the steps and moved as quickly as possible to the same spot to set the box down beside the first box. It was a struggle for the three exhausted men to carry the last box. The box may have been heavier, or it may just have *seemed* heavier after carrying the first two. The humidity had the three men sweating profusely by the time they set the last box on the ground.

The men returned to the Chinook. Steven nodded to the VC lieutenant and back-peddled toward the boxes of gold. Steven maneuvered behind the boxes, positioning himself between the boxes and the helicopter, slightly closer to the five captives. He heard the helicopter motors starting, and the blades begin to turn slowly. The VC lieutenant lost his focus on Steven; he was fixated on the boxes. When he reached the boxes, he opened each box and meticulously maneuvered several of the bricks to make sure he had received exactly what he had bargained for. Steven spoke to him sharply, ordering the men's release. "Giải phóng năm người đàn ông," Steven commanded.

The VC lieutenant straightened up and looked hard at Steven for several seconds, then he waved to his soldiers to move the five men forward. Steven looked over to the five men and watched VC soldiers aggressively shove the men so hard they stumbled forward. The men staggered toward the Chinook. When they were within thirty feet of the helicopter, Steven glanced at Kimmons, who nodded. Steven started to carefully walk backwards toward the Chinook.

Steven stopped about twenty feet away from the walkway and watched the five operatives board the helicopter. Another very dangerous situation, this was the second-to-the-last best chance for an ambush. Once the five were on the helicopter, Steven continued to move backwards. The Viet Cong were now beginning to move toward the boxes of gold. *Hope they get occupied with that gold and how to move it. That will allow us to get out of here without incident.*

Steven moved up the steps slowly while giving a thumbs-up to the pilots. He continued in the ready position. He felt the lurch of the helicopter and, at the absolute last second, pulled up the walkway and secured it. He lost his balance as the helicopter accelerated up and away from the VC, back toward Saigon and Tan Son Nhut.

As soon as he sat down, the five men started shaking his hand and Kimmons's. Then they asked the tough question: How had their safety been secured? Steven looked at Kimmons, then back to the men. "We are under strict orders not to speak about this."

Within forty minutes, they returned to Tan Son Nhut Airbase. When they landed, two military ambulances sat waiting. The pilot and co-pilot joined Kimmons and Steven, all four of them watching as the men solemnly walked toward the abandoned hanger. Steven wondered who was on the other side of the door to greet those operatives. One thing was for sure, he would never know.

This had been a very intense but successful mission. Kimmons motioned for all of the men to follow him to their quarters to change out of these uniforms. Steven turned and lethargically walked in that direction. Right then, he was longing even more to return to the battlefield. The exhilaration he'd felt that morning could not be touched by anything he was doing at the Embassy. *Will those five operatives ever learn Vice President Nixon negotiated their release? Where did that gold come from? Obviously, someone Tao knew. How will bargaining for their release affect the conflict effort?*

CHAPTER THIRTEEN

APRIL 4, 1964

SAIGON

Steven knew he had to push his relationship with Lieutenant Colonel Andrew Maxton, since Steven knew he would likely be reassigned to General Harkins soon. Steven did not know how deeply Maxton was involved in adjusting figures on the Viet Cong strengths and altering the maps of their strongholds, but he was too close to Harkins to be left in the theater. They were about to meet in a local bar off the beaten path. Steven seldom drank, especially after the previous November, but he thought alcohol might loosen Maxton's tongue. Steven hated taking advantage of his acquaintance, but he was still trying to get information to get in Lansdale's good graces. He hoped to gather some information on the South Vietnamese government, from the military's perspective.

Maxton walked into the bar with his head down and his St. Louis Cardinals ball cap pulled low over his face. He walked over to the dark corner where Steven sat. Maxton sat down and repeatedly glanced around the room. *He looks nervous.* Hebert was concerned about his actions drawing attention, just what he was trying to prevent. Steven signaled the waiter, who came right over to take their orders.

Neither man spoke, and the waiter returned quickly, with a cup of tea for Steven and a vodka and tonic for Maxton. After Maxton had taken his first drink and settled a bit, he reached inside his hip pocket and pulled out a piece of paper. He discreetly passed it under the table for Steven. The bar was too dark to read, so Steven placed it in his back pocket.

"What do you have for me?" Maxton asked Steven

Steven took a sip of his tea. "When McNamara was here on his fact-finding mission, he was satisfied with General Khanh. He believes the South Vietnamese government is going to be okay."

Maxton frowned. "We—or should I say *General Harkins*—thought Khanh would engage the enemy almost immediately. But that hasn't happened. Everyone believed Khanh is the best fighter among the generals. But so far, nothing."

Steven nodded. "Obviously, the CIA decided not to wait any longer. They've started bombing the Ho Chi Minh Trail."

Maxton looked around and held up his glass trying to make eye contact with the waiter. He leaned toward Steven. "The CIA is ill prepared to do this. We have more planes here plus we can place carriers offshore. They should be doing the bombing."

The waiter brought over another vodka tonic and set it in front of Maxton.

Steven raised his eyebrows and placed both hands on the table. "Andrew, we see the problem the same way. The VC already have camps around Saigon. You know our embedded military advisors have been frustrated with their lack of action."

Maxton downed the rest of his second drink. "You know Westmoreland is due here any day. Have you heard any more about his role?"

Steven nodded. "No. Not a word at the embassy."

Maxton pursed his lips as he shook his head. "That's no help at all. I don't like it. Our command was doing just fine. Now we have some hotshot general coming in. It's just not right." Maxton slammed down his glass, drawing more attention.

Steven knew not to take the bait, but he had to calm down Maxton. "I thought he was coming in as a second in command to help with the guerilla warfare side. Maybe oversee the Seals?"

Maxton looked out the dirty window for a long time, not saying a word. "It just doesn't feel right. We are being punished because of the South

Vietnamese. I'm guessing we will be bringing in more American troops very soon."

Steven downed the last of his tea, wiped his mouth with the back of his hand. "I've got to get back to the Embassy."

Both men stood and walked out of the bar together. Steven watched Maxton walk away. As soon as he was in his jeep, he reached in his pocket and pulled out the piece of paper Maxton had passed to him.

> South Vietnamese Government is ending Strategic Hamlet Program, despite 5000 strategic hamlets completed, 2000 more under construction. May not finish. Program deemed a total disaster. Many of our weapons given to defend them have fallen into the hands of the Viet Cong.

Steven shook his head. He knew the South Vietnamese could not properly build them despite funding from the US Department of State AID. The plan had some merit, but the people never bought in. They were uprooted from their homes and moved into newly constructed villages. However, the reality of the program was to monitor who was going into the villages. In other words, to keep them safe from the Viet Cong. There was no way they could keep up the pace. Now, they were ending it. *Worse yet, our troops are being shot at by our own weapons,* thought Steven. *This could turn into a total disaster; we are inadvertently arming the VC.*

Sunday Morning April 5, 1964
Washington DC

General Edward Lansdale was sitting in his kitchen with his morning coffee. He was about to read over his Washington DC newspapers. It was not uncommon for him to pick up two or three national newspapers besides the local press. He wanted to stay on top of developments as told to the public, not only in the nation's capital but also around the world.

After finishing his second cup of coffee, he reached over his head and grabbed the telephone from the wall to call Walter Reed Medical Center. He dialed information on the fourth floor nurse's station. He had talked one of the nurses into giving him their private number. On the fourth ring, a young voice answered: "Fourth Floor Nurse's Station."

"This is General Lansdale. Can you give me the latest on General MacArthur?"

There was silence for a moment, then the nurse spoke in a broken voice: "The general passed away early this morning."

Lansdale despondently hung up the phone. The last six weeks had been very tough on MacArthur, but Lansdale never doubted for a minute he would pull through. He stared at the kitchen wall. A distant church bell snapped him back to reality. The man he had served and respected for as long as he could remember was gone. Lansdale suddenly felt very alone. *Why hadn't anyone called me? Surely someone at the CIA or in the White House knew how close we were.*

Lansdale looked at his watch. He'd have to notify Tao and Hebert and, of course, his old friend, Santa Romana. He went into the living room. *I knew things weren't good when MacArthhur went into a coma... Three major operations in six weeks, who could survive that? Damn, just gone in for gallstones. I can't believe this. The complications with the last surgery...*

For a moment, Lansdale felt totally lost.

Rita Sullivan walked into the office and headed for her desk. Before she can reach it, she heard Jonathan Petit, the Chief, shout for her to come to his office immediately. She walked to her desk to put her purse down, but the

Chief bellowed again—he wanted her in there *now*. Rita slung the purse strap over her shoulder and scooted in her high heels in his direction. No sooner was she in the doorway than he pointed at the chair next to John Sherwood and Miriam Ottenberg. Rita plopped down, set the purse on her lap, and gave the Chief her full attention.

"I want the three of you working up stories on General MacArthur. Sherwood, I want you on the World War II angle. Find me some personnel background stories. Ottenberg, I want you working up a story about his time in Japan. And Sullivan, I want you on Korea." The Chief stared at her, rubbed his chin. "No, I want you to address his time in the Philippines before World War II. It's more of a personal story, more up your alley."

Sherwood and Ottenberg asked if there were any additional instructions. The Chief shook his head as he pointed toward the door. "I want those stories ready to run tomorrow."

Rita got up to go when the Chief asked her to wait. She let Sherwood and Ottenberg slip between her seat and his desk, then sat back down.

Once they were out of the room, the Chief walked around the desk and leaned back on it. He pursed his lips. "I have special instructions for you. I made a last-second decision to take you off Korea. It would have been a tough assignment. MacArthur and President Truman didn't have a good relationship. I didn't want you to have to figure out a way to write your article without painting either of them with bad paint, *got it*? The Philippines is a much easier assignment, without potential problems."

Rita furrowed her brow. *He does not like my writing, I'm too controversial for him.* "Let me do Korea."

The Chief leaned forward and pounded the desk with his right hand. "Did you not hear what I just told you? *No*, I just told you I don't want to see that column. General MacArthur was a great man. President Truman was a great president. I don't want them tainted, that's all I'm saying. Now, get to work. I want that for tomorrow's paper. This is *big*. Everybody loved MacArthur. He was our greatest general."

Rita stood up and headed out the door. Before she sat down at her desk, she decided the best thing to do was head to the archives to review some of the old stories about MacArthur.

Rita finished typing the final paragraph of her column, which was due to the copy room this afternoon. She looked up at the clock: 2:50 PM. Rita rolled the cylinder backward so that if there were any typos she could easily fix them. She reached over to the other pages that she had already proofread. As she scanned over the article, she was pleased. Rita looked over her notes.

MacArthur had a history in the Philippines beginning in 1935. President Roosevelt picked him to go as a military advisor to what was a US territory at the time. He was tasked with building a defense force. The Chief's timeline helped her avoid writing about his time as Chief of Staff of the Army and his decision to remove the World War I veterans from the temporary camp in Washington DC. That had been a nightmare to send the Army to remove veterans. She tried to brush over the debacle of the fall of the Philippines to the Japanese and his famous quote, "I shall return."

What few Americans knew was that Roosevelt had ordered MacArthur to abandon his troops in the Philippines—it was essential that he escape. Upon his return to the Philippines on October 20, 1944, he began his campaign to rid the Archipelago of the occupying Japanese. On February 5, 1945, MacArthur finished liberating the city of Manila with a loss of only 1,000 men. Many Filipinos believed that because of his slow actions and his unwillingness to destroy the historical buildings of Intramuros, the walled city and the original capital of the Philippines, 100,000 civilians had been slaughtered by the Japanese. The Rape of Intramuras had been similar in many ways to what happened in NanJing.

Rita looked at the last page, still rolled in her Smith Corona. MacArthur discovered that Yamashita had escaped Manila and gone into the Cordillera Mountains to carry out guerilla warfare tactics against the superior forces of MacArthur. While MacArthur's brilliant plan, called island hopping, allowed the United States to retake the Pacific Ocean and each territory in the Pacific, it did not come without its faults. Some even believed that

Yamashita's War Crimes Trial was a sham due to his humiliation of MacArthur in the last days in the Philippines.

Rita rolled the last page into her hand then grabbed the other two pages. She stacked them sharply against the desktop and walked to Boland's office. The door was open, so Rita walked in and pushed her column in Boland's face. He did not look up at whose work it was, only grabbed it at the same time he drew the dreaded red pen. He zipped through, occasionally looking up at Rita over his glasses. Finally, when he got to the last page, the summary paragraph, he dropped the page on his desk and leaned back in his chair. He frowned at Rita for a short time and drew a deep breath

"Rita, you have a few grammatical errors, but I'll tell you, the Chief will come unglued when he sees this last paragraph, which I won't even edit because it is a waste of my time."

Rita dropped her hands in her lap. "All I wrote was the truth from both perspectives. MacArthur was a great general, but he wasn't a flawless man."

"Blondie, you must learn that in writing a column sometimes you have a theme. The Chief gave you a theme. Here it was to honor the man. You are trying to do reporting." Boland ran his hand over his hair, picked up his pipe and stoked it. He added, "Something that you're very good at, but it needs to be brushed aside in this kind of assignment."

Rita was not happy. She reached over, picked up the paper, and went back to her desk. As she walked she realized Boland was right. It spared her from being shouted down by the Chief. This just boosted her determination to get out of the column side of the newspaper business and into the reporting side.

Rita went back to her desk and re-wrote the last paragraph. Then she went through and corrected the errors pointed out by Boland. After getting approval from him, she was off to see the Chief. Rita took a deep breath as she entered his office and stretched out her hand with the column.

"Chief, bringing this in for your approval."

The Chief grabbed the three pages from her hand and read. After three minutes, he looked up.

"I like this. Get it down to Copy. You're late. I want you to go watch the funeral procession, the caisson carrying MacArthur's body, and follow it out to the internment in Norfork. I want you to see the appreciation this country had for MacArthur, from a military prospective and the public's."

Rita was speechless, first, because the Chief liked her column, and second, because he was sending her through entire process. Just to watch, to understand, not to report.

Chapter Fourteen

April 14, 1964
Washington DC
Quorum Club

Rita Sullivan pulled into the parking lot outside the Quorum Club. She was scheduled to meet Mary Pinchot Meyer outside the membership club. Rita let her blonde hair down and ran her fingers through it several times then checked her lipstick in her rearview mirror. Rita glanced up just in time to see Mary walking toward the front door. Rita quickly stepped out of her car, waved at Mary, and headed in her direction. As Rita walked, she noticed a black Cadillac pulling into the parking lot. The man leaned out of view as Rita tried to look back at him.

As Rita reached the front door, Mary opened it for them both, and they walked right past the man checking memberships and their guests. Rita thanked Mary for the nice thank-you card she had sent after Rita's column on the Cherry Blossom Festival that had featured the events Mary had pointed out in their first meeting. When they sat down, a waiter immediately appeared at their table. Mary ordered an expensive bottle of Louis Roederer; since Rita was still working she ordered tea. Mary folded her hands on the table.

"Miss Sullivan, I really love your writing style. You have such flare! I think you have a real future in writing Society articles. I'd like to start working with you, providing advance notice of cultural events. Next year, when the Cherry Blossom Festival comes around, I want to take you to some pre-planning meetings and to the invitation-only events. What do you think about that?"

Rita had a big smile on her face by the time Mary finished. Still, she had to think about what Mary was offering. Clearly, it was an opportunity to work with one of Washington DC's elites. She could really advance her career. However, was that the advancement she wanted? Rita wasn't going to turn down an opportunity, but she thought she would mention her goals. Subtlety, of course. *Who knows who I might meet that could advance my career. Got to take this opportunity.*

"I really appreciate your offer," Rita replied. "I'll talk with Mr. Petit, my executive editor, about this. See if he will approve me reporting on that area.

I know they were very impressed that I was able to interview you for our newspaper."

The waiter brought the chilled bottle to the table and a pot of hot tea. After Mary had approved the wine, she drank about half a glass.

"Rita. May I call you Rita?"

Rita nodded with a smile.

Mary continued, "So you are stuck in the weekly light Society and Regional columns?"

Rita finished swirling around her teabag, squeezed it into the pot with her spoon. "I have tried to write some hard news stories, but they were shot down by Mr. Petit."

Mary frowned and finished off her glass of wine. "I'm going to guess you have tried to write some anti-war stories? I've noticed your paper always runs pro-Johnson or pro-Vietnam articles."

Rita looked down at her tea. "I haven't written anything about Vietnam, but I had a hard time getting my women in World War II article in the paper, and then I tried to write a factual article on MacArthur, which got shot down real fast."

Mary looked around the room, then back at Rita and spoke in a different tone. "Perhaps someday we can meet in a more private place and talk."

Rita glanced where Mary had seemed to focus: a man in the dark corner. *Was it the same man I saw the last time I was here? Was he following Mary, or me?*

Mary waved at the waiter. When he came up, she asked him to put the bottle of Louis Roederer for her to take. Mary leaned forward with a stern look. "I need to go. Give me your phone number."

Rita pulled her steno pad from her purse and wrote the phone numbers at work and at home. She pushed it toward Mary. "If you don't find me at my desk working, I am likely at home. I would really enjoy talking again."

As soon as the waiter brought her bottle of wine, Mary got up and rushed out the door. Rita sat for a moment trying to discreetly look at the man in the dark corner. Rita decided she would get a better look close up. But as soon as she started in his direction, the man got up, lowered his face, and headed deeper into the club. Rita tried to catch up, but someone bumped her hard, slowing her down. She watched the man slip through a door behind the bar and disappear. Rita turned for the front door, hoping to catch him in the parking lot. By the time she was out the front door, the black Cadillac was gone.

Chapter Fifteen

May 6, 1964

Saigon

Major Steven Hebert led the motorcade around to the front of the Embassy and waited for Ambassador Lodge. Steven made sure all posts were secure then ushered the Ambassador to his car, the middle car of the motorcade. The Ambassador seemed to be regaining some confidence in him. Steven wasn't sure why the Ambassador was meeting with General Khanh. The last couple of meetings had been contentious and unproductive, and it was obvious that Khanh had not earned the Ambassador's respect. Clearly, he believed that Khanh was no better than Diem. Unlike the last couple of meetings, the Ambassador requested Steven accompany him into their meeting today.

Steven followed the Ambassador into the President's office. After the Ambassador took his seat on the opposite side of the General Khanh's desk, Steven stood guard a few feet behind him. Khanh started the meeting.

"Out of respect for our two country's relationship, I wanted to give you notice we intend to execute Ngo Dinh Can tomorrow."

From where he was standing, Steven could not see the Ambassador's face, but he imagined the Ambassador's standard scowl as he snapped, "The United States government has asked that I formally request you commune his sentence to a short prison term. The President and the State Department requested that you exercise restraint, to try to offer all sides a peaceful solution. We have grave reservations that the Can execution will turn the American Catholics and maybe the balance of the Catholic Church against your government."

General Khanh calmly folded his hands on the table. "As you know, Ambassador Lodge, he was found guilty in his trial. You yourself have witnessed the Buddhist and student protests. The Buddhists—via their designated voice, Thich Tri Quang—have been very persuasive. They still resent Can, his rule in Central Vietnam, and more particularly, his ordering the attack on Buddhists in May 1963. As for Major Dang Sy, we have only sentenced him to life in prison. There is your leniency. He was the man who carried out the orders."

Lodge jumped back in to try to win Can a reprieve. "General, Mr. President, I implore you to reconsider. Your leniency with respect to the

Major makes my point. Put Can in prison, spare his life. This family has had enough death."

Khanh pursed his lips. "Ambassador Lodge, you are a very popular figure in the city, in the country. The people of my country would be very disappointed to learn that you are opposed to our verdict, considering the man received a very fair trial."

Steven felt the verbal jab at Lodge. The Ambassador was very much tuned into his personal popularity, particularly since he was running for the Republican presidential nomination.

"Mr. President," Ambassador Lodge countered, "I hope *you* reconsider. Talk to Tri Quang, again, see if he will be more compassionate. We both know his role is crucial in resolving this. Win him over and you win the day. Here you must exercise your role as a politician not as a general."

General Khanh got up from the table and walked around to the Ambassador. Steven squinted and rose slightly on the balls of his feet. Khanh stretched his hand forward. "Ambassador Lodge, the decision has been made. It was made in the best interest of our people. Thank you for coming."

Steven looked at Ambassador Lodge as he got up from his chair and the man's face told the whole story. Steven did not take his eyes off the general as the Ambassador moved toward the door. Steven reached for the door knob, turned it, and escorted Lodge into the hallway. The two men walked quietly all the way to the motorcade.

As they traveled through the city traffic, Ambassador Lodge spoke to Steven for the first time. "Major, you were with me when I met with Thich Tri Quang. He has this administration and the Buddhist monks under his spell."

Steven was not interested in entering this debate. "Yes, Ambassador."

Steven looked in the rearview mirror at the Ambassador, who was looking out the window at the crowded streets as the car slowly moved between the mopeds, bicycles, small cars, and rickshaws throughout the crowded city.

"Tri Quang is very difficult to figure out," Ambassador Lodge said. "I protected him from Diem, and this is how I am repaid. He is playing his country right into the hands of the North Vietnamese."

Steven decided to speak out. "What do you think will be the outcome of Can's execution?"

Lodge looked at Steven in the rearview. "I don't believe for a minute that it will benefit the Buddhists or the effort to unify the country." The traffic was starting to pick up. The Ambassador continued, "Major, I said it before and I'll say it again, a monk advocating the execution of anyone makes me ponder…"

Steven had had several conversations with Lansdale and Tao. Steven believed that Tri Quang was sympathetic to the communists and had been certainly instrumental in undermining the war effort. This was the first time since returning to the Embassy Steven felt he might be getting back into the

Ambassador's good graces. Steven was determined to do everything he could to restore his credibility.

MAY 12, 1964
SAIGON

Steven Hebert, dressed in civilian clothes, was escorting Ambassador Lodge to a secret meeting with Thich Tri Quang at the designated Buddhist Temple. Ambassador Lodge told Steven that the purpose of this meeting was to attempt to sway the radical monk's stance with respect to some of his views of the Khanh government. Lodge hoped that if Tri Quang took a softer position, the Khanh government would be more lenient toward the Catholic population. It would cause the world to hold a higher opinion of South Vietnam and, tangentially, the United States.

Steven steered the limousine silently as the Ambassador spoke of the up coming meeting, as they drove across the city. Perhaps the United States government was more concerned about how it is perceived throughout the

World than defeating the Viet Cong and the North Vietnamese. He wondered why this was the thought process.

As they walked into the Temple, Ambassador Lodge spoke softly to Steven. "I want you here as a witness. I don't think we have to worry about my safety, so pay attention to everything he says. He will interpret your presence as protection not as a witness. Plus, Tri Quang got used to seeing you at the Embassy, so he may be very comfortable. The fact that I protected him from Diem will allow me to get a returned favor. Pay close attention."

Steven maintained his pace alongside Lodge. "Yes, Sir. Ambassador."

Steven and the Ambassador were met in the Bell Tower by two monks clad in Orange robes. They motioned for the two Americans to follow them. They quickly walked through the Drum Tower then the Hall of the Heavenly Kings to the main hall where Thich Tri Quang was waiting. Tri Quang, dressed in a white robe, waved the two other monks away. Tri Quang greeted the Ambassador then glanced around at Steven but did not acknowledge him.

"You wished to speak with me, my friend?"

Ambassador Lodge sat down while Steven remained standing behind him. "Yes, I wanted to see if we could come to some sort of an agreement to soften your stance on the Catholic population in South Vietnam."

Tri Quang maintained his eye contact with Lodge. "I have no issues with the Catholics. My issues are with a few of the *leaders*, who happen to be Catholic."

Lodge shook his head, but Tri Quang continued.

"Nhu Dinh Can and Major Dang Sy carried out vicious attacks in my home town. We were conducting a peaceful protest when Can decided to shut it down, which the Major did with extreme violence. This was not the first time, Can had always been tough on those he ruled over in Central Vietnam."

Lodge reached out, both palms up. "We, the United States, want to have the support of the Free World, which of course is predominately Christian, and we fear this execution of Can will have an impact on their view of our role in your country."

Tri Quang was quick to counter this. "If the United States government wishes to have the support of the Buddhist population in this country in their fight against communism, Can's execution was essential. The people must know that the old Diem crowd is no longer in control." Tri Quang opened his arms and continued. "Mr. Ambassador, you are very popular in South Vietnam. Should the Vietnamese people find out you are attempting to usurp our legal system, it would hurt their opinion of you."

Steven heard Tri Quang speak nearly the same words Khanh had said to Lodge on that point. Lodge responded, "Are you for or against the Khanh government?"

Tri Quang continued to maintain direct eye contact. "Naturally, we support Khanh. He is our President. We, as a country, must give him time, but we are cautiously watching his actions more than his statements."

Lodge remained steadfast in his questioning. "Will you continue to support our government and our efforts in South Vietnam?"

Tri Quang nodded slowly. "Of course, we Buddhists know we will no longer be able to practice our religion under communist rule. It appears that the United States government is our only hope, as our government is doing little unless involved with the United States. Ambassador Lodge, I would like for you to speak at the Dinner of the Unified Buddhist Association at the end of the month."

Ambassador Lodge nodded. "Thank you for the invitation. I accept."

Tri Quang put both hands together, is if preparing to pray. "We would be honored. I want to reiterate our position, so it is clear. What is the difference between being repressed by the Can Lao or the communists? Should Khanh not continue to remove all of the remanence of the Diem government, you may find that the Buddhists will no longer support the fight against the communists and leave it to the Americans and the Catholics, alone."

With this comment, Ambassador Lodge got up, thanked Tri Quang for the meeting, and headed out with Steven fallen in pace.

On the drive back to the Embassy, Steven observed Ambassador's sour look. It was obvious he didn't get any concessions. Once at their destination, Lodge reminded Steven to keep this was a meeting a secret. Steven felt he may be regaining some of the Ambassador's trust, even if it was forced by circumstance.

CHAPTER SIXTEEN

MAY 14, 1964

PLAINES DES JARRES, LAOS

Nguyen Tao moved like a cat along the perimeter of the Pathot Lao army, which was advancing on Plaines des Jarres. Tao was having considerable trouble estimating the size of the communist army, but it was the largest assembly he had witnessed since scouting the Japanese army in the Philippines. Various skirmishes, using guerilla hit-and-run tactics, allowed Vang Pao's army to keep the communists at bay all the while inflicting considerable damage on them. Vang Pao had challenged the Pathot Lao and the North Vietnamese Army. Up until the last month the battles between the Pathot Lao and Vang Pao had more or less been stand-offs. Since then, the tide had turned against Vang Pao.

But now, with the assistance of the North Vietnamese and the Chinese, they were bringing a formative force that was well-armed and equipped. The only factor on Tao's side was that the size of the communist army kept them from moving too fast as they engaged some of Vang Pao's troops. Earlier in the day, Tao had witnessed other forces in the area, and if they and their extra equipment joined up, it would be a daunting force. Tao quickly estimated this army would soon to be more than 10,000 strong, once the other divisions caught up. This time the communist army would be too large for Vang Pao to confront directly. Tao believed they were headed to the Plaine de Jarres camp; Tao had to get there ahead of them, so he could warn them and they could evacuate.

Tao continued to traverse the terrain, staying out of their sights until he made it back to his jeep. Tao looped around the Pathot Lao's advancing position, hoping not to run into any other forces traveling to Vang Pao's high plains camp. Upon his arrival, Tao ran into Vang Pao's headquarters, shouting. "The Pathot Lao are advancing on our position with a combined army of Laotians and North Vietnamese!"

Vang Pao jumped up. "How large? Do we have time to get our bombers in here?"

Tao shook his head. "*No!* You must bug out immediately."

Vang Pao ordered one of his lieutenants to assemble his commanders. As they came into the headquarters, he pointed at two of his officers.

"You two, take your divisions and go with Tao to fight off the communists. The rest of us will destroy the camp. We will meet at the main camp at Long Tieng. Vang Pao stepped around the table and grabbed his youngest commander by the shirt collar. "Get me as much time as you can. Do you understand me?"

The general let go of the scared commander. Tao thought that commander was just a boy, not more than eighteen years old.

Tao nodded. "I know just the place. Let them follow me."

Vang Pao kicked a chair. The general got nose to nose, again, with his youngest commander and snarled. "Go, go, go."

Tao sprinted out of Vang Pao's headquarters, waving his left arm. "Come on, the Pathot Lao are coming. We must get at least halfway down the mountain and get dug in to establish a position for our fighters to retreat to. We fight there as long as we can."

Vang Pao stood in the doorway waving his arms. "*Give us enough time* to destroy everything here."

Tao waited impatiently in his jeep as the two commanders assembled their men. The transports came up behind his position loaded with well-armed Hmong fighters. Tao floored the jeep, heading off with all the transports in pursuit. After driving about twenty minutes, he stopped, picked up his 1911 as he jumped out and waved for the two commanders to join him.

Tao pointed out why he believed this was a good place to dig in. After quickly assessing the position, the two commanders passed the word for their troops to position themselves along this shallow ridge, a strong, strategic position that would also would provide them with their best pathway to escape, if something went wrong. Tao watched nervously as the Hmong soldiers fanned out. Tao moved quickly to a secure spot behind a bank of trees. He looked around and watched all the Hmong troops get into place.

The two Hmong commanders came over and squatted down by Tao. Their ambush was in place against the superior force of the communists. *Time to sit and wait.*

Within thirty minutes, the retreating Hmong soldiers moved back to fortify this position with the entrenched soldiers. Their commanders gestured silently for them to hunker down and hold their position. Tao watched the commanders signal along their lines for them to be on the lookout for the advancing Pathot Lao.

Within ten minutes, the lead trucks and transports advanced into sight. They were a combination of North Vietnamese and Chinese vehicles. Tao stood up far enough to place both hands on his knees as he watched the two commanders signal the closest men. The signal passed up through the line. Those same commanders looked to the forward positions. The signal came back up line: The communists troops were in range.

The commander nodded as he waved his hand over his head in a circular motion. All hell broke loose. The entire jungle came alive with gunfire.

Tao held his position, firing toward the road leading toward the Plaines des Jarres camp site. He was able to get the drop on several Pathot Lao soldiers as they stepped from their transport. Tao slipped in behind to his original position just as several explosions could be heard from on the mountaintop. He ducked back into the position with the two commanders.

Less than thirty seconds later, both commanders signaled to open fire on the advancing Pathot Lao just as they were preparing to renew their attack. The battle was fierce for several minutes as the Hmong inflicted huge casualties on the Pathot Lao. However, it seemed to have virtually no effect. They barely slowed. As the casualties mounted, finally, the Pathot Lao was forced to stop and take some defensive positions.

The Hmong soldiers continued to pepper the Pathot Lao position. Unfortunately for the Hmong, soon the Pathot Lao started lobbing mortars into the Hmong positions.

Tao leaned toward the commanders. "We need to get out of here while you still have an army."

The two commanders ignored Tao's comments. They continued to signal to their men to stay in the fight. Tao could see the communist soldiers advance, then drop down in position. Tao fired his 1911 in the communist direction. Then another round of mortars, dialed in tighter, hit the Hmong position. Following the bombardment from the communists, the Pathot Lao started moving forward again. This time they moved much faster. More emerged from the back as men up front were killed. The commander looked down the hill to see how his Hmong soldiers were faring. They were holding their position and firing while taking heavy fire from the advancing communists.

Tao snarled at the two commanders. "You're about to get overrun if you don't get out, now."

After hearing several more explosions Tao assumed came from Vang Pao's outpost, the two commanders finally signaled their soldiers to move out to the west from their current position. As the Hmong soldiers moved, bullets came raining down on them from all positions, inflicting heavy losses on the escaping soldiers.

The surviving Hmong soldiers got out of the line of fire. The fighting came to a halt, and the jungle fell silent. The Pathot Lao army moved past their position, they paid absolutely no attention to the Hmong soldiers, who sat down around their vehicles. Finally, Tao could hear the vehicles moving back out. Their mission was a success. They had provided enough time for Vang Pao's forces to blow the remainder of the camp and escape. Tao followed up to his jeep. His was the last vehicle out, following the gallant soldiers of Vang Pao toward their camp. *Thirty-minute fight at most. They had taken some casualties but certainly not as many as Pathot Lao.* Tao hated the game. If their army inflicted more casualties than they took, the US considered the battle a victory. It made no sense. Vang Pao lost a key outpost, which doubled as a landing strip for the CIA's Air America planes. Tao knew this would be a huge set-back. The CIA had been using Vang Pao's army to keep the North Vietnamese Army and the Pathot Lao in check. The loss of this strategic position would likely cause a change in the conflict.

CHAPTER SEVENTEEN

MAY 15, 1964

SAIGON

Major Steven Hebert sat across from the Ambassador, waiting to find out why he had been called to his office. The Ambassador sat behind his desk and continued to write. He flipped over the second page of his legal pad and was still writing without so much as acknowledging Steven's presence. Steven sat erect in the chair, impatient on the inside, patient on the outside. Finally, after the Ambassador had written about halfway down the legal pad, he laid down his pen, took off his glasses, and folded his hands on his desk. It appeared he was about to speak, but he took a deep breath, closed in eyes, and leaned back in his high back leather chair,

"Major Hebert, I called you down here for an unusual reason. I want you to review a plan I have drawn up. You have much more experience in this area than I ever will. But first I have another question."

Steven wondered what was going on. "Yes, Ambassador."

The Ambassador picked up a piece of paper and waved it. "This is a memo from George Allen. He states that through his research, and with consultation of the higher ups in the CIA, they believe Tri Quang wants American forces out of South Vietnam. It also says the monk is in favor of some sort of neutralism, but not like the position of the French President de Gaulle. They even believe he may be a communist sympathizer. Did you get that impression from our meeting?"

"Not at all, Sir." While Steven had heard these same comments from Tao, he wasn't about to volunteer any more information.

The Ambassador nodded. "I concur. I think I know him better than anyone in the US. I think he is just a man who is enjoying his power by keeping the Buddhist protests going strong."

Steven only nodded this time. He could not decide for himself what side Tri Quang was on, other than his own side and whatever suited it best.

Lodge stroked his chin with his right hand. "The other reason I need to speak with you. I just prepared a draft of a cable for President Johnson. And I want your thoughts based on your background before you took this assignment."

Steven frowned, "What do you mean, Sir?"

171

Lodge leaned back and opened a drawer. From it, he lifted a file that he laid on his desk. He leaned forward and tapped the top of the file. "Listen, Major Hebert, I know you were assigned to General Edward Lansdale's psy-ops team, as a sniper, operating in and out of North Vietnam. Since receiving the letter about you from General Lansdale, I researched his service record and role. Well, what's in the file anyway. I know you served with Lieutenant Colonel Lucien Conein, who I have discussed this with. But I wanted another perspective… yours." Lodge looked hard at Steven, but Steven knew not to react or talk. Lodge continued, "You also have knowledge that I need because in my cable to the President I'm recommending terrorist attacks on North Vietnam. To send them a message."

Steven believed the Ambassador had done his homework. "Yes, I'll try to help in any way I can."

Lodge squinted. "Here is what I am proposing be done in the next couple of weeks. Plus, I need to know who to recommend for this operation." Lodge handed him the draft of the cable, then leaned back in his chair. "I call it my Thirty-Day Scenario."

Steven read it over. The Ambassador was proposing several teams of men go in and out of North Vietnam sabotaging industries, killing key political and military figures. Quick strike missions. It mirrored what Steven had done with Lansdale's team. Steven was aware of several similar operations in Vietnam at this time. Steven wondered what the Ambassador wanted that was different. *I don't believe I'm being told the whole story. Why would you propose something that is already being done and act like it is new? Was it setting up something? Thirty-day scenario?*

Then it hit him. the Ambassador's plan could possibly help keep ground troops out of Vietnam. He smiled slightly and nodded.

Lodge anxiously sat up. "Well, what do you think?"

Steven was surprised that he had been entrusted to this proposal. He handed the Ambassador the two pages of legal paper. "I would use CIA operatives, maybe some of de Silva's men. They are better trained for that kind of mission."

Lodge rubbed his chin. "I knew you were aware of the problems with General Harkins. His days are numbered. Still, the Defense Department has taken over one of the CIA clandestine programs and assigned it to Harkins." Lodge shook his head. "Poor decision. But I think you are right about CIA operatives, so I concur with your opinion. This operation must not have the signature of any military operation. The CIA picked the wrong people to scout missions, so they were slow to execute. They used antiquated planes and all that. Not a program worth giving up to the military. You modify it, improve it."

Lodge seemed pleased with himself. He leaned back in the chair.

"One more thing, Major. Look, I'm going to resign very soon, go back to the United States to run for President. I want to make an impact on the conflict here before I leave."

Steven was speechless, which was probably a good thing. He had finally regained the trust of the Ambassador only to find he was planning on going back to the States.

Lodge cautioned the Major. "You are the first person in the Embassy I have told. That will be all, Major."

Steven stood up, saluted, then walked out of the office.

Washington DC
Next Day

President Johnson was sitting by himself in the Oval Office, having just completed his morning intelligence briefing. He was laughing. *General LeMay just wants to bomb everything in sight.* Gerri Whittington interrupted his thoughts with the buzzer to tell him Secretary Rusk and Secretary McNamara had arrived. The Secret Service Agent let them into the Oval Office. President Johnson stepped away from his desk, then leaned over the back of the couch where the two men sat, towering over them before taking a seat on the opposite couch.

President Johnson asked both men if they had read the Cable from Ambassador Lodge. Secretary Rusk acknowledged that he had read it and there was little to react to.

McNamara jumped in. "He damn near just proposed everything that we think Lansdale will propose?"

Johnson sat down, folded his arms on his chest, drawing a deep breath. "Lodge really believes that focused surgical strikes inside North Vietnam in the thirty days leading up to the talks will help Seaborn in his negotiations."

Johnson leaned forward and rapped his knuckles on the coffee table. "I cannot afford to have a plan connected with *Ambassador Henry Cabot Lodge* change the course in Vietnam. For God's sakes, I may have to run against him in the Fall."

McNamara pursed his lips as he looked over at Dean Rusk. "Have you had any more conversations with Blair Seaborn?"

Rusk nodded. "Seaborn says he wants more information regarding our future plans."

Johnson shook his head. "How the hell do we know what comes next?"

McNamara raised both palms. "What more does he want? I thought we were pretty clear with our future plans."

Johnson pounded his hand lightly on the couch arm. "If you think this Canadian diplomat is our best choice, we probably better give him close to what he wants. I've been thinking about this. First off, we must make sure

Seaborn looks innocent in his mission. I don't want it to look like anything more than a normal meeting with Ho Chi Minh, so the Press won't pay any attention. I really believe Seaborn's role at the International Control Commission will allow him to go in and out of North Vietnam unnoticed. However, this first meeting is critical as far as I'm concerned… It sets the tone because there may not be another one until after the election, so this one must be the one to accomplish things."

Rusk raised his eyebrows. "Seaborn has said repeatedly he plans to be in Hanoi more than his predecessors. We might get another chance, Mr. President."

Johnson stared at Rusk. "We can't afford to take any chances."

McNamara opened his briefcase, pulled out a document and laid it on the table. "I have Lodge's cable right here. I want to compare it to our purposed memo to Seaborn." McNamara fumbled for his pen and scribbled to see if it would write. "I want to make some notes about Lodge's reply. See if there is any merit before we finalize our notes to send to Seaborn."

President Johnson got up and started pacing behind the couch. "Our objective was to get into Ho Chi Minh's head, to learn what he is thinking. Does he believe the Chinese are going to have his back? I don't for a minute think he believes that he can take on the USA by himself. Particularly, if we bring down the full force of our military. What will the Soviets do? Will they get more assistance from the Chinese? How much assistance can North Vietnam provide?"

Rusk leaned back on the couch. "He is pretty confident. He has been in and out of the Soviet Union and China since the 1930s. They—"

Johnson interrupted as he sat down on the couch. "I don't care that he has been a good communist. As long as we promise we won't invade North Vietnam and go all the way to Hanoi, I want to plant an element of doubt in his head. Will the Soviets or the Chinese help him if we go in full force? I believe Khrushchev is about as involved as he cares to be at this point. North Vietnam is all in helping. China, China is the wild card."

McNamara asked, "What do we give to Seaborn?"

Johnson leaned back. "You boys better look again at what Lodge says."

Rusk picked up Lodge's memo and read over it. "Well, Lodge thinks we should try to get Ho to become completely independent of the Chinese. I'm not sure exactly how we could facilitate that."

"Right now, no one has pushed back," McNamara said. "The South Vietnamese have done virtually nothing over the last four or five years. When I was over there, Khanh blamed the Buddhists, which has been his focus. Meanwhile the Viet Cong have had free rein. As a result, territory has been lost. Ho has every reason to be confident."

Johnson got up and started pacing again as he worked his right arm around in circles to stretch his shoulder. He frowned at Rusk. "Let's focus on what we can do, not what the South Vietnamese haven't done. I think we have Seaborn tell Ho that we are determined to keep the South free. We are prepared to bring the full power of the military down on them. Let's tell Seaborn to give Ho examples of our real power."

Rusk nodded. "Basically, Lodge wants to give him the option, given enlarging the war effort verses withdrawing. The US will increase our presence and retaliate for every effort the VC or North Vietnamese make."

McNamara chimed in. "Let's see if Seaborn can question Hanoi's intentions. Have him remind Ho we are not the French. We have no intention of establishing any bases in Vietnam or Laos."

Johnson leaned over the back of the couch, his arms spread wide, both palms on the edge of it. "Damn it, Bob, we can't bring up Laos. That is like admitting we are in there."

Rusk rubbed his mouth with his right hand. "Here I think Lodge makes a good point. It is in North Vietnam's interest to have as few Americans in the South Vietnam as possible. I think that's what we all want."

Johnson sat down on the couch and closed his eyes.

Rusk looked at McNamara and pursed his lips. Before he could continue, Johnson spoke up. "We want to tell the North Vietnamese there are many examples of Free countries existing next to communist's countries. Why, we can even promise trade with them, of course, with the right cooperation on their part. But by God, they must agree to stop their aggression against the South."

McNamara crossed his arms on his chest. "What are we going to do before the conference?"

Johnson leaned forward. "The Joint Chiefs said the Japanese terror raids didn't work during World War II. Why would they work now? General LeMay and the Joint Chiefs believe that they can bomb strategic sites in North Vietnam prior to Seaborn's meeting. Just give them a little taste."

Rusk reached his hand toward McNamara. "Give me those notes. I'll get them drafted up and find someone at the State Department to send for a meeting with Seaborn, we don't want any attention."

Johnson jacked his jaw forward. "I think Seaborn has a real chance here. It would be great to stop this war right here. It would ensure my election."

CHAPTER EIGHTEEN

MAY 17, 1964

SAIGON

Nguyen Tao arrived in Saigon in the early afternoon. He had been sent to pick up a CIA operative in a bar and escort him back to Vang Pao's camp at Long Tieng. The only description that Tao had was the man had blonde hair and horn-rimmed glasses. Tao was to meet him at the bar in the Duc Hotel. Tao thought while he was in the city he would meet with Major Steven Hebert to discuss the latest developments in Laos. If he had time, he would also catch up with his friend, Pham Xuan An.

Tao had arranged for Steven to meet him at the back door of his scooter shop. As he walked the streets of Saigon, toward his shop, he thought it was funny how his and Steven's roles had reversed since Tao had been assigned to the Laotian Army. Now, it was Steven who was communicating with Lansdale.

Tao opened the front of the store, turned over the open sign, and hustled to open the back door. He peeked out to see if Steven was there. No Hebert. He relocked the door.

Tao sat down at the small desk in his shop office. After a few minutes, there was a knock at the back door. He let Steven in, who entered and immediately turned a chair backwards as he plopped down. Steven drew a deep breath.

"Tao, things are not good, are they?"

Tao laid out all the events that had just unfolded in Laos. Steven acknowledged the loss of the Plaines des Jarres would affect the Laotian effort to disrupt movement on the Ho Chi Minh Trail. Steven told him about the disruptions being caused by the monk Thich Tri Quang, without mentioning the secret trip he'd made with the Ambassador.

Tao sighed. "I am in the city to pick up a CIA operative to take back to Long Tieng."

Steven nodded. "The CIA is *sure* cozying up to Vang Pao. Speaking of being in the city, Lansdale said to order you to get your ass back in Saigon keep an eye on the developments. He said to remind you that you work for him, not Conein or Vang Pao. He said to remind you he didn't set you up in that front business for nothing."

Tao's level of frustration was climbing. He got up and paced around the shop, adjusting mopeds and aggressively brushing dust off with his hand.

Steven followed him. "Tao, the VC control many of the districts of South Vietnam. They have camps right outside Saigon."

Tao turned around with rage in his squinting eyes. "*General Khanh* is doing the exact same thing as all of the other leaders. Keeping the best fighting forces in around the city to protect himself, as did Diem, as did Minh. I'm beginning to fear the odds are really stacking against ever fighting off the North Vietnamese or the VC. Lansdale's plan worked in the 1950s. It might work now. *I don't know*. Major, the South Vietnamese don't get it, the US doesn't get it. Ho Chi Minh and North Vietnamese Army have been fighting for thirty years. Remember, Ho Chi Minh led the fight against the Japanese. They know how to fight in this terrain."

Steven stopped pacing to ponder what Tao had said. It had never occurred to him how long these people had been fighting. Fighting had become a way of life. Steven ran his hand over his short-cropped hair. "I haven't had a chance to tell you that the US has put a team of Navy Seals in Da Nang. They put some Marines in to guard the post. A friend of mine is part of the guards. I don't like the idea. I fear they will be sitting ducks in these camps."

Tao looked at the ground. "Not good news." Tao started pacing again, then pointed directly at Steven. "Mark my words, the US will be portrayed as occupiers, just like the French."

Steven drew another deep breath. "I really want to get back into the fighting. My role at the Embassy isn't working like it did. Lodge has had some private meetings with Khanh, but he only allowed me into a few meetings lately. I'm more or less out of the loop. Plus, no big meetings at the Embassy. I don't know if he is on to me. Despite all of this, Lansdale wants me to stay. I'm being wasted."

Tao looked at his watch. "I need to get moving to keep my schedule."

Steven smiled. "Before you go, I have to ask about your meeting with Nixon. You ever met him before?"

Tao started locking up the building. "No, never have. What exactly was going on?"

Steven shrugged. "I'm under strict orders not to speak about that mission. What about that gold?"

As both men exited through the back door, Tao looked up. "My friend in the Philippines. That's all I can say."

Steven exaggerated a pout. "I need to get back to the Embassy." He got in his vehicle. "Let me know when to meet again. Don't forget what Lansdale said."

Tao locked the back door and headed out to see if he could meet up with Pham Xuan An over at the Continental Palace Hotel. But when he got there, An was nowhere to be found. Tao did run into his assistant, Ba, who he spoke with for a minute, long enough to learn that An was out of the city. She said An would be returning soon.

At the scheduled time, Tao entered a dingy bar on a back street to meet the CIA operative. All he knew about the man was the description he had been given. Tao walked in, looked around the dark bar. In the far corner was his contact, a New York Yankee baseball cap pulled down low.

Tao ordered a drink, then went over to the man's booth. The man did not look up. Tao slipped into booth. "I am from Vang Pao."

The man still did not look up. Tao set his drink down on the table and started to introduce himself. The man stopped him by raising his fingers to his mouth. "I know who you are. Take a seat, I'm waiting on an old friend before I brief anyone."

Tao sat quietly sipping his drink with his back to the door. Shortly, he heard a commotion as the door swung open. He turned to see a man in an Aussie bush hat. Tao saw a smile come over the blonde man's face, but he still did not raise his head. Within in a few seconds, Lieutenant Colonel Lucien Conein sat down at the table on Tao's side and pushed him hard against the wall opposite the blonde man. Conein looked at Tao and smirked. He leaned across the table toward the blonde man.

"Shackley, how the hell are you?"

Shackley started to speak, but before he could, Conein interrupted him. "Men—that includes you, Tao—down your drinks. We only discuss business in a secure location. My jeep is outside."

They quickly downed their drinks, and Tao followed both men out of the bar. Conein and Shackley talked as though Tao was not even there.

The two jumped into the front seat of the jeep, and Tao slid into the back. Shackley looked back at Tao then over to Conein, as he pulled out into traffic. Shackley pointed his thumb toward the backseat. "Is it all right to talk in front of him?"

Conein looked over to Shackley. "Ted, he's CIA, but he works with Lansdale. So what brings the Blonde Ghost to Saigon?"

Shackley cracked a half-smile, as he glanced toward the backseat. "Langley has demanded we change how we execute this conflict here in Indochina. Some of us are going to start our own operations. If we don't, this country is in big trouble and these people don't even know it. De Silva is overseeing some clandestine operations in North Vietnam, a la Lansdale. I'm here to gather information." Shackley turned, looked in the back seat, then continued. "The OPLAN 34A missions were not real successful. They were getting bad intel, blaming it on us."

Conein stopped at a traffic light. "So, what do you need from me?"

Shackley looked out the window up and down the street then leaned over and barely whispered, "I'm going to meet with General Vang Pao, try to see what he needs to increase his fighting capabilities. Langley believes the only way to save South Vietnam is to keep the fighting going on in Laos. But Langley wants to keep this mission off the record. What we want from you is… to help us get in better standing with Vang Pao. We need him and we need you to help us."

As the light turned green, Conein accelerated away. "My friend here in the back seat has been sent to escort you to his camp. Now I see. What are you going to do with the operatives already in the camp? Young, ah… ah… Poe and… ah… Buell?"

"You have been fighting with Vang Pao for several months. What do you think?"

Looking at the backs of their heads, Tao said, "Without the South Vietnamese Army fighting the Viet Cong and the North Vietnamese Army, this whole thing has been going backwards. I've witnessed many VC and weapons pouring over the Ho Chi Minh Trial. I'll let Vang Pao speak for what his needs are, but the US needs to focus on cutting off that trail. The South Vietnamese have completely ignored it."

Conein laughed. "Shackley, you just heard Lansdale's solution. Are you going to meet with de Silva while you're here?"

Shackley looked at Tao again. "No, all my moves are strictly off the record, Lodge and de Silva don't know I'm here."

Tao sat back in his seat. He got the code. There were still two distinct divisions within the CIA. Shackley was sent to meet with Vang Pao and there was obviously more to it than just concern about fighting supplies. Shackley was here to increase black-bag financing.

SAIGON
04:00

Tao drove his Peugeot up onto the abandoned air strip outside Saigon. He flashed his headlights. Immediately the landing lights of the C-47 came on, and he could hear the two engines start up. Tao pulled his car under the camouflaged canopy. He looked over at his passenger, Theodore Shackley. "Ready."

Shackley did not say a word as he exited the car. He walked back to the trunk and pulled out his suitcase. He brushed his blonde hair back with his hand, then checked his handgun in his shoulder holster. The two men did not speak as they walked toward the plane. The CIA did not like to fly in and out of this old air strip, but sometimes it was necessary, particularly when they did not want to have people see key personnel moving around inside Vietnam. The flight to Long Tieng, Laos, was very quiet as both men tried to catch some sleep.

Once on the ground at Vang Pao's encampment, Tao lead Theodore Shackley into General Vang Pao's headquarters. Tao knew this meeting with Shackley was critical for the general and believed the CIA could bring him the help he desperately needed. The loss of the Plaines des Jarres had been devastating.

Both men gathered around the desk of the general. The general began with a description of what his Hmong soldiers had accomplished over the last two years; holding off the Pathot Lao while also engaging North Vietnamese and Viet Cong. Vang Pao made the point that his army was fighting and dying while the South Vietnamese Army was still more or less coalescing around Saigon. Then the general stated that the South Vietnamese were losing territory to the Viet Cong. Tao observed Shackley's expressions during the general's presentation: He was really disturbed by these facts. Had he not been told or had he ignored all the CIA memos regarding these developments? Tao had also periodically glanced at other man, who seemed totally disinterested in what was being discussed.

Shackley pushed his glasses back up his nose and slicked back his hair. "The CIA sent me to find out what kind of help you needed. I am to report back to them. We know there is a real need to regain the Plaines des Jarres so we can get our planes in and out of there to attack the Ho Chi Minh Trail."

General Vang Pao leaned back and folded his arms. "We need to get more food, particularly rice, and medical supplies for our men and families. We also need more, no make that *better* air support. When we call in, we are getting old US planes and flying them with Laotian markings at your government's request."

Tao knew that with Shackley receiving Conein's blessing, there would be a new player in the drug operation. After all these years, Conein was still a power broker in Indochina, whether with the military, the CIA, the Underworld, or the South Vietnamese. Tao was beginning to believe Conein may be more powerful than Lansdale in this part of the world.

Shackley looked at the general. "General, the CIA is willing to assist you with your banking, establish accounts for you around the world. You know, help you invest your money, help you take your production to a different level."

Silence fell over the small operation's room for several minutes. Tao looked at the three men. *Is the CIA more interested in the poppy production or in defeating the North Vietnamese and Viet Cong?*

189

General Vang Pao finally spoke. "For me, it is really important to find a way to retake the Plaines des Jarres from the Pathot Lao, Shackley. What can you do to help me accomplish this?"

Tao was pleased to hear this question. At the moment, the Hmong soldiers may be the only hope of keeping South Vietnam independent and the American troops out of the theater.

CHAPTER NINETEEN

JUNE 25, 1964

MARSEILLES, FRANCE

Atonine Guerini paced several steps behind his desk before sitting down and looking over at Lucien Sarti, who was standing on the other side. "Are you ready?"

Sarti walked over to a chair in the corner of the large office and nodded. "I'm ready."

Guerini nodded at the bodyguard at the door to his office. He opened it, and Julian Romano was escorted into the dimly lit office. Atonine looked at his bodyguards on either side of his desk but did not make eye contact with his visitor as he pointed to a large leather chair in front of his desk. Guerini continued to read the letter that he had received from an anonymous source. Guerini surmised that the letter must have come from one of the top lieutenants in one of the US mafia families. *Somebody must be looking for some favors or an offer to move up with backing.* The letter detailed conversations between the Trafficante and Sam Giancana. The letter was explicit about Trafficante's desire to work with certain individuals in the CIA to develop a direct network with Vang Pao's Hmong poppy growers.

Sarti spoke up. "General, do you want me to pay a visit to Trafficante?"

Guerini calmly looked up from the letter, then folded it back up, but left it on his desk. "Let's get some facts first."

Guerini cleared his throat, drawing Romano's full attention. Romano was nervously looking around the office, while frequently glancing at the two bodyguards. Guerini licked his lips a couple of times, as he squinted.

"Do you know anything about this? How has Vang Pao acted toward you lately?"

Romano shrugged. "Same, distracted but who wouldn't be in his position. Our figures have matched, but I don't think he trusts many of us."

Guerini held up a tri-folded paper. "I just reread this letter I received from someone in the United States who believes the US families are going to try to cut us in Laos."

Romano started to speak, but Guerini put his finger to his lips then pointed to the corner.

"Lucien said he didn't know anything about this."

Romano turned and looked over his shoulder at Sarti then back to Guerini. General Guerini continued to speak. "*However*, Lucien Conein said he didn't know anything, but there was something in his voice. He wasn't his usual cocky self."

Romano raised an eyebrow and attempted to speak, but again, Guerini put his finger to his lips.

"I *did* expect this to eventually happen. I expected them to show some respect since we took care of two presidents for them, cut them in on our operations, allowed them to network our products. *This* is how we are repaid?" Guerini slammed his fist down on his desk, sending the pictures leaping off his desk. He stood up abruptly. *"Well, is it?"*

Guerini drew a deep breath. "We are respectable businessmen here. *We're borgatta.* The increased chaos in Indochina has offered opportunity. No, make that *allowed the Hmong farmer to increase their production* and our profits. *Everybody* profited, *everybody* made money *but it sounds like somebody* is about to get greedy."

Romano leaned over and picked up some of Guerini's pictures, including some of the broken glass from one of the picture frames, nicking his finger. "What do you want me to do? I am at your service, General."

Guerini sat back down hard in his chair and leaned back, closing his eyes. The mantle clock ticked in the background. When the clock struck, Guerini leaned up and placed both palms on the desk. "We've been paying Indochinese officials for years. We aren't getting our money's worth. Go back to Saigon, talk to Conein. I want to know what he knows."

Sarti snarled as he spoke. "While you are in Saigon, go pay a visit to Hebert. He needs to be reminded we are watching him."

Guerini stared at Sarti then leaned over toward Romano. "You go and get the truth out of Conein. Whatever he knows about Vang Pao's operation." Guerini reached over and grabbed Romano's collar. "And whatever he knows about the CIA. I want the truth."

Guerini's anger had left some spittle on Romano's chin, and Romano had the fear of God in his eyes. "You know meeting Conein on his turf will put me at a disadvantage."

Guerini released Romano. "His confidence will allow him to be looser with his tongue. He is one of us. *Or he was* one of us. Conein knows everything going on in Indochina, has for years. He's been my eyes and ears there for more than a decade. I want him to know *I'm* asking the questions. I cannot believe he would betray me. *Tu comprends.*"

Romano nervously nodded. Sarti cleared his throat in the background.

Guerini wiped his mouth with his hand. "After you talk to Conein, go talk to Vang Pao. Since Vang Pao lost the Plaines des Jarres to the Pathot Lao, we lost our ability to fly our planes in and out of there. But we made alternative plans. We worked hard to get other ways to get our O and H. Everybody still made money." Guerini stood up. "Get me a deal. Don't come back without one. *Tu comprends.*"

Guerini looked up at both of his bodyguards. "Show him out." As the bodyguards moved Romano toward the door. Guerini shouted, *"Julian, I want answers."*

SAIGON

Major Steven Hebert walked out of his private meeting with CIA Intelligence analysist George W. Allen after a very candid conversation. Steven knew little about Allen, but Allen knew a lot about Steven. When Steven had gone into the meeting, he was not sure which faction of the CIA Allen represented, but by the time the meeting was complete, he had a good idea. Steven was totally impressed with Allen's in-depth knowledge of the situation in Vietnam, very realistic views. Allen believed the situation was not nearly as rosy a picture as the brass had painted. Allen's reasoning was solid, and he had prepared the original 1962 report in detailing Viet Cong strengths and activities. A certain colonel who was assigned as the intelligence officer for the MACV had failed to keep it updated. Allen went so far as to call the officer an incompetent alcoholic. *I wonder why Allen isn't giving me the name of the colonel. Is it someone I know?*

As Steven walked down the hall, he thought about Richardson and how Ambassador Lodge used Lucien Conein rather than his own staff. Richardson was a well-qualified CIA operative, and it looked like Allen was cut from the same cloth. *Someone to respect.*

Since it was slow around the Embassy now that the Ambassador had resigned, Steven decided he'd drop in on Meredith Brown. As he walked down the hallway, he started singing "Stars shining bright above you, Night breezes", Steven walked toward Meredith's open door. Of course, he had to be sure to leave it open. A negro man in the office with a white woman would be viewed with suspicion otherwise.

Steven sat down opposite Meredith, and they began to discuss who might replace the departed Ambassador. Meredith seemed sad that Lodge had resigned. Steven was reluctant to say too much, choosing silence as the best way out. *Just when Steven was restoring his credibility, the man resigns.* Meredith leaned over and whispered as though there was a crowd of people sitting around her desk.

"I have heard from my father that Johnson has a list of six men: Robert McNamara, Robert Kennedy, Sargent Shriver, Roswell Gilpatric, William Gaud, and McGeorge Bundy."

Steven shrugged. He knew not to express an opinion, but he knew Johnson would not select two of his closest advisors, Bundy and McNamara.

"It is beyond me. I can tell you we need somebody who can get along with the South Vietnamese, inspire them."

Meredith shook her head back and forth in an exaggerated fashion, which caused her brunette hair to flip around. "Major, you don't get it, my father said it will be a political appointment. It is *always* a political appointment. You know, whatever will get Johnson the most points for his reelection."

Steven knew Meredith was right, but before he could reply, there was a sharp rap on the open door. They both looked up and saw Tim Mitchell. Steven shook his head in mock sadness.

"Why did you knock instead of just walking in?"

Tim stuttered for a moment, tried to speak. Steven knew the real reason: Tim was bashful. Finally, Tim composed himself. "I just got off duty, was looking for someone to talk to. Need to get some new albums. With the Ambassador gone, I'm bored out of my mind."

Steven let out a hearty laugh. Tim turned red as he realized why. From her befuddled expression, Meredith did not. Steven decided he would get in a little dig.

"So Tim, did you come here because you heard my dulcet tones?"

Once again, Tim appeared to get Steven's zing and changed the subject. "Major, the situation here is constantly changing. I really never believed there would be such chaos in an Embassy assignment."

Meredith looked at Tim, Steven, back to Tim. "Are you afraid?"

Tim shook his head. "No, but when I joined the service and worked my way through signal school, it just never occurred to me that some of these assignments would be so volatile."

Meredith frowned. "Aren't we safe, Major? Since I'm new here, I've always assumed it was a very safe assignment. Just a career stop. Exciting but a career stop. Perhaps even a stepping stone." Then she got a big smile. "We should make a pact, Major, are you in?"

Steven raised an eyebrow. "In... on... what? What's so volatile? The Ambassador resigned to go back and run for President."

Meredith put her hand out, palm up. "We are all in this together, and we leave here together. And Major, it is your task to make sure that is so."

Tim quickly put his hand on top of Meredith's. "Count me in... Major?"

Steven thought for a minute what they were asking him to commit to. At that moment, he saw the both for what they were, Tim was still a freckle faced boy and Meredith was a naïve young lady. After thinking for a couple of seconds about wanting to return to the battlefield, he placed his big brown hand on top of the other two. "Sure, it's a pact. We all leave here together."

Meredith added, "Safe and sound."

Tim parroted her words. "Safe and sound."

Steven refused to say those words. He recognized both of his friends needed to hear them, but he simply looked at them and nodded silently.

LATE NIGHT
JUNE 24, 1964
HATTIESBURG MS
SOUTHERN MISS CAMPUS

Jeremiah walked quickly down the dark alley up the black Lincoln and crawled in the back seat. He pulled a wad of ten and twenty dollar bills out then counted out two hundred and fifty dollars as he handed it to the thug in the passenger seat, who immediately recounted it. Then handed Jeremiah a paper bag. "There another pound of marijuana. Oh, if any of your friends request it, I can get you some hashish and opium, if anybody asks."

Jeremiah opened the bag and looked in then rolled it up tight. "I should be well past halfway paying you all off now."

The thug rubbed the right side of his face with the back of his left hand. "Boy, you have paid down to seven hundred dollars with this payment. You have forgotten to figure in interest on how long Mr. Marcello carried you without a payment. Mr. Marcello is a respected business man and is going to charge you interest just like he does anybody he gives a real estate loan."

Jeremiah squirmed in the back seat. "That's not fair. I have sold over five hundred dollars. My interest has been like two hundred dollars."

The thug turned around fast and barked. "You're damn lucky you're getting to work this off. You'll do as we damn well say, or else we be paying a visit to your mother and even your brother in Vietnam. Now, get your ass out of our car before I lose my temper. We'll be back here in two weeks. You best have all of this sold by then."

Jeremiah took the rolled-up bag of marijuana and stuffed it under the side of his shirt, got out without saying a word, and took off running down the alley. All he could think of was no one had seen or heard from Nick in almost six months. Whatever happened to Nick he didn't want it to happen to him.

CHAPTER TWENTY

LATE NIGHT

JUNE 26, 1964

SAIGON

This had been "one of those days", everyone wanted a piece of Lucien Conein. First, the meeting with Julian Romano. After that he felt it necessary to discuss with General Atoninc Guerini the movement of poppies out of Laos. Last but far from least, some of his old South Vietnamese general friends had called to complain about getting cut out of General Khanh's future plans for the country. Conein had decided the best solution to his day was to go hang out at some of his favorite watering holes. He had spent the evening drinking and carousing with old friends. Tonight, it felt like old times again. Finally, time to go home.

201

Lucien Conein glided to his jeep and started toward home. He felt vibrant until he looked at himself in the rearview mirror. As he looked into his eyes, he began to fret that once again he was getting himself in a problem similar to the Diem Coup. This time, he found himself in a balancing act between the Brotherhood, which he had been a part of since World War II, and the CIA, who seemed to be working with the American mafia. They had been on the same side in the Diem matter. *I was paid handsomely, too.*

His relationship with the Corsicans was very important in his life. *I love how they set up that big Negro in the Embassy. That was some fast thinking to involve him in the conspiracy to earn his silence.* Conein started laughing. *Still, I like Hebert. He saved my life when he was working with Lansdale.* But it was just so much fun to get under his skin, too easy of a target.

Conein got serious again. As much as it felt like the times before the Diem coup, this situation had some differences. He could smell a drug war coming. And this situation would not be finished by the simple removal of a political leader. This was going to be intense. There was a lot of drug money on the line. Clearly, there were going to be winners and losers in this war. *I'm not sure I can come out a winner. I've been able to maintain my control over the movement of drugs for years, but the last thing I want is in the middle of this war. Too much money involved.* There would be blood on a lot of people's hands.

Conein tried to focus solely on the situation in Vietnam. He believed if he had Lansdale over here now, between the two of them they might be able to turn the momentum against the Viet Cong. However, his relationship with Lansdale had been gravely damaged by his role in the Diem coup. Besides, Lansdale would want to run everything. Anyway, by now he had probably forgotten I gave him all of his contacts in this damn country. *I am still the powerbroker over here.* It was dawning on him that this was clearly part of his own dilemma.

As Conein continued to drive across town, he started laughing about his old friend Lansdale and some of the times they'd had. Their raids into North Vietnam had been fun. *God, I love the danger, the riskier the better.* He looked at himself in the rearview. "Alas poor Yorick, I knew him, Horatio."

Conein thought about how much he enjoyed living in Saigon. Maybe his decision was as simple as that. If South Vietnam fell, he sure as hell didn't want to be here. It was clear, the conflict within Vietnam could not be solved without the United States. He thought about the friends he'd made within the CIA. Over the last few years, in a strange way he'd developed a closer relationship with them than the Corsicans. They had fought shoulder to shoulder against Soviet and Chinese agents. Howard Hunt, Theodore Shackley, and many others were truly friends, if he had any. Perhaps a visit to Vang Pao would be enlightening. He hadn't been there in a while. *Yeah, that's what I think I'll do.*

He pulled up in front of his house. He got out and leaned against his jeep. He sniffed the air, Monsoon season would start any day now. *Boy, I sure hope there is some American beer in the refrigerator. I think I'll drink a couple then go upstairs and wake up my wife to have some fun.*

SAME DAY

WASHINGTON DC

The warm sun beat down on General Lansdale as he drove up to the side entrance of the White House. He picked up his briefcase and opened the car door before remembering to take his handgun out of his ankle holster and place it in the glove box.

As Lansdale walked up to the door, he was more confident than ever he could make an impact in Vietnam. The Secret Service agent ushered Lansdale into the conference room near the Oval Office. Lansdale sat down in one of the side chairs to wait for the President. He opened his briefcase and pulled out his report, "Concept for Victory in Vietnam." Seemed like he had been working on the report forever, he had been preparing the 22-page report for almost a year.

Lansdale thought about how things had changed both in the United States and Vietnam during that year: President Kennedy and General MacArthur had died, Vietnam had been through three different presidents, and the Viet Cong was making incursions into South Vietnam every day. The new perspectives the changes brought had always resulted in revisions. Lansdale's work was cut out for him. He had proposed his old team from the Philippines: "The Force" included his top lieutenants, Major Napoleon Valeriano and Bo Bohannan, but this time he was missing Lucien Conein. Truth be told, Conein had been critical to his operation in Vietnam in the '50s. Conein knew everybody and was going to be hard to replace. The three French Corsican men he had met back in November had at first decided they would come on board, but too much time had passed. They took another assignment. Lansdale had really hoped that Lucien Sarti would joined him; he had the reputation as the best shot among the three men. He was a little bit crazy, something Lansdale needed. Plus, he was also a good organizer. *Should I go back and talk to Conein? Try to mend fences?*

President Johnson entered the room with Secretary of Defense Robert McNamara close behind. Both men took their seats on either side of Lansdale with the President sitting at the head of the table. After an apology from the President for running behind on his appointment, Johnson said,

"Edward, I can't wait to see this report. I know how successful you were in the Philippines and Vietnam. We desperately need a game changer."

Lansdale pushed forward his original of "Concept…" then reached in his briefcase a produced another for McNamara. He sat quietly while the two men read. His eyes darted back and forth, but he tried to be discreet.

After about ten minutes, President Johnson took off his glasses and leaned back against the high leather executive chair.

"Ed, I want to read this all the way through again, but I have a couple of questions. Or I should say I need some clarifications." Johnson folded his hands on the conference table. "You really believe we need to change our strategy to night fighting?"

Lansdale glanced at McNamara then made direct eye contact with the President. "Mr. President, when do the Viet Cong inflect the most damage? At night. Our troops don't know during the day who the Viet Cong are as they move among the South Vietnamese population. Who is friend and who is foe?" Lansdale held up open palms. "Reveille at night, all duties accomplished at night. I mean our men walk among the population all day not really knowing who is friend or foe, *but at night*, at night, they know."

Johnson looked at both men. "Well, there is a lot of truth to that. But I don't know how the military will respond."

Lansdale leaned forward with both hands on the table. "That's part of the point. We don't want that many troops in the theater. Fewer camps, fewer sitting ducks. My plan calls for the Vietnamese people to free themselves, but with our help. Vietnam is no place for ground troops. We already know the VC try to call the US occupiers like the French. My team, which will quickly expand to more teams of men mimicking my First Team, they will conduct raids in and out of North Vietnam and on some of the Viet Cong strongholds."

McNamara spoke up for the first time. "So far, we have not seen that the South Vietnamese generals have the will to fight at all. What makes you think that will change?"

Lansdale raised his palms. "We can change the momentum with our success. We need to put the North Vietnamese on defense, something that has not happened since I was last in the country. We do things with them then give them the credit. This will uplift and inspire them." Lansdale paused. "Look, I have Valeriano and Bohannan, my top lieutenants, ready to get in there and start immediately. I cover this in my section of that report under 'Command Action.'"

Johnson shook his head. "I still don't see how the South Vietnamese Army will change. You know the saying: the leopard never changes his spots. Our generals tell us the Vietnamese expect us to do the fighting. That or they are unprepared to fight. It seems to be one or the other."

Lansdale nodded. "Yes, I've heard the same thing. I've read some of Colonel Vann's reports about this very subject. But we must embed more of our soldiers, teach them to fight. More importantly, we must get the South Vietnamese army and government to do a better job protecting their population. This is where the VC are really winning by intimidating and creating fear. I believe my proposal addresses this. Mr. President, I can tell you no matter what the Vietnamese brass say or want, their people will not trust our troops in there. Lastly, we must swing the perception of the VC."

Johnson stood up and grabbed the proposal. "Ed, let me read through this again. I will have more questions. I want to think about it. I want to look at what the Seals and OPLAN 34A groups are doing to see how they compare."

Lansdale stood up closed his briefcase. He shook both men's hands and went out the door. Lansdale looked at the floor as he moved down the hallway. *If Johnson wants to win this battle and his election, he better get me in there sooner rather than later.*

NEXT EVENING

SAIGON

Steven pulled out of the Embassy on his way to a dinner with his friend Ethan Graham, who was still on leave. Monsoon season had definitely arrived; one could not pour water out of a bucket harder it was coming down. As Steven drove across the city, he noted that a car had pulled out behind him at Embassy and was still tailing him. Even when he turned down side streets, the tail stayed with him. He was followed right up until he pulled into the restaurant parking lot.

I know I wasn't imagining that tail, he thought. Despite the rain, Steven hustled back to the street, looked up and down—no sign of that car. He turned and ran toward the restaurant to meet Ethan. They had argued over the eating establishment that met both of their desires; Steven wanted a restaurant where he could eat a dinner in comfort and relax, while Ethan wanted one close to the less reputable bars so he could unwind in a completely different way. He wanted to find some wild place to drink and maybe find a woman for the evening.

Ethan was already at their table with a large glass of Irish whiskey. "Major Hebert, it is good you decided to show up." Ethan let out a great big laugh.

Steven plopped down in the chair and grinned ear to ear.

Ethan swirled what was left of his glass. "I need some action. I have been so bored at Da Nang. I need to get into some fights somewhere."

The two men talked over their poorly prepared steak dinners. At least that's what the menu called them. Steven wasn't so sure, but he enjoyed an hour visiting about absolutely nothing but old times. *I'm getting spoiled by the Embassy food*, he thought as they took turns asking about acquaintances they had not seen in a while.

"E, you mentioned that you were bored. Nothing going on at Da Nang?"

Ethan waved at the waitress as he held up his empty glass, looked around the room and whispered. "I'm very bored. I have done nothing but watch a couple of our Navy Seals train the Vietnamese guerilla teams. They've been very active."

Steven spoke in a low tone. "Really."

Ethan continued. "They are not supposed to communicate with anybody in the camp but since those Seals know I flunked out of the Force Recon program, they come in and talk to me. Everybody else in our squadron is a bunch of green Marines."

Steven swirled the last bit of his water. "So, the South Vietnamese have been active?"

The waiter set down his fresh Irish whiskey. Once the waiter was away from the table. Ethan took a big swig, wiped his mouth with the back of his hand. "Ummm. Yes, there are three men from Navy Seal Team One here. They have got these Vietnamese doing all sorts of night raids into North Vietnam. Sabotaging facilities and killing high ranking officers. These guys are really getting good at guerilla warfare. Heck, they even named these guys the Brown Water Navy. The Vietnamese love it."

Steven smiled. "This is really good news. I was getting concerned about the lack of activity."

Ethan stuck his finger in his drink, stirred it around and sucked the liquor off. "I'll tell you these Vietnamese are being trained right for jungle fighting. You know, using guerilla tactics, they can be very effective. They are really creating havoc in North Vietnam. They just need more men trained this way."

Steven realized these guys were implementing things that they did in the 1950s in Lansdale's Force. It is working now—it just needs to be expanded. Steven said, "Conventional war tactics will never work in Indochina." Then he asked, "Where are they getting their intelligence for their targets?"

"The US navy has ships in the Gulf of Tonkin, picking up transmissions."

Steven saw Ethan look down at his watch. *I can take a hint.* Ethan wanted to go get wild somewhere. Steven excused himself, telling his old friend to be safe and that he would catch up with him before he returned to Da Nang.

Steven walked outside. While it had stopped raining, the night air was still hot and muggy. It was so thick, Steven felt as if he could wring out the moisture with his hands. As he approached his military vehicle, he saw a man leaning against it.

"Hey, what the hell do you think you are doing?"

The man did not reply. Steven picked up his pace toward the vehicle. Then he recognized the man: Julian Romano, the Corsican.

"Stevie Boy, how are you doin'? Lucien Sarti wanted me to stop by and say hello to you."

Steven got nose to nose with the man. "Well, you said your hello. Get out of my way before I knock the hell out of you."

Romano put both hands in the air. "Stevie Boy, you're not being very friendly. I didn't do nutin' to cause such a response. Just wanted to say Sarti wanted to make sure you knew you were cared for."

Steven looked him in the eyes. "I'll not say it again. Get off my vehicle and out of my way." Steven grabbed his shoulder. Just then Steven felt cold hard steel press against his back and a familiar voice. "*Back down, Tizzun.* Now, step back."

Steven released his grip on Romano and slowly backed off. He turned to see Lucien Conein. Steven put his hands on his hips.

Conein holstered his .357 nickel plated magnum. "Julian thought you might get a little excited to see him, so he asked me to join him. Interrupted my evening on the town."

Steven snarled. "*You* are part of this blackmail plot."

Conein and Romano both laughed.

"Major Hebert," Conein said. "That's harsh. What blackmail plot are you talking about? You know me. I'm just a Boy Scout. I came along to make sure everyone played nice." Conein shrugged at Romano.

Romano shrugged back. "No one here said this sniper was involved in the assassination." Romano pointed at Steven.

Steven looked at Romano then back to Conein. "I should have assumed you were part of this."

Conein shook his head. "Whatever I told you, how could you believe it? You know I'm an excellent liar. Besides, you know we are on the same team."

Steven briefly stared at Conein, then stepped toward his vehicle. "I'm leaving."

Romano stepped in front of him again, stopping Steven in his tracks. Romano folded his arm across his chest. "Hey, your mother has been working really hard lately, but the heat is wearing her down. And your brother, Jeremiah, oh tsk, tsk. He has been such a bad boy. He discovered pot last winter. One of his track teammates introduced him to it. And he seems to really like it. Now, I hear he is dealing drugs around his college."

Steven burned with rage, but he didn't move because Conein just might shoot him. "I'm leaving. I'm not going to say it again."

Romano stepped aside.

Steven got in the car and sped off. Now it was clear why his brother had decided to stay in Hattiesburg. It had nothing to do with the Negro fraternity or practicing with the track team like he had told mother. It was becoming clear that his brother was screwing his life up and could easily end up in some serious trouble.

CHAPTER TWENTY-ONE

JUNE 28, 1964

WASHINGTON DC

President Johnson looked at his watch then took off his glasses. He rubbed his eyes with his left index finger and thumb. General Maxwell Taylor was due at any moment to discuss the future of Vietnam and his new assignment as the Ambassador to South Vietnam. Johnson had many objectives to accomplish: he'd gone against conventional wisdom when he selected a military man to serve in this diplomatic role. Johnson was convinced that he needed a military man; it was his intention to ramp up fighting effort in Vietnam as soon as he was re-elected President.

His mind went back to his review of Lansdale's "Concept for Victory in Vietnam." It had many unique qualities, but the military was already implementing many of his plans with limited success. The lack of activity by the South Vietnamese Army still caused the most problems. Perhaps a military man as Ambassador could inspire this change. Johnson got up from the desk in the Oval Office and slowly walked toward the conference room for his meeting.

No sooner had President Johnson entered the conference room than he was notified General Taylor, Secretary of Defense Robert McNamara, and Secretary of State Dean Rusk had arrived. Once the men were seated around the conference table, Johnson wanted to define General Taylor's objectives in his new assignment. Johnson folded his hands on the table and leaned forward.

"Maxwell; Bob, Dean, and I have prepared some objectives we would like for you to accomplish as fast as possible. Most importantly, I want you to get these South Vietnamese ready to fight the damn enemy, the Viet Cong, and stop fighting amongst themselves. Right now it looks like they trying to see who can amass the most power."

Taylor nodded. "I'm ready to make things happen over there. I've been there enough to have some real solid ideas for achieving our objectives."

This comment brought a smile to Johnson's face. He glanced at McNamara and Rusk with nodding approval. "Having Westmoreland as the MAC-V, your relationship should only enhance that situation."

Taylor sat straighter in his chair. "Mr. President, Westmoreland and I have had a few candid conversations about the situation, our advisory role at this point, and about General Harkins. I told Westmoreland we need to fight like we did in France during World War II. I think that is how we need to engage the enemy."

Johnson rubbed his chin with his left hand. "Well, all I know is we have to do more. By the way, what did you think of Lansdale's plan?"

Johnson could tell he hit a nerve. Taylor jutted his chin. "With all due respect, Mr. President, Lansdale's schemes are hair-brained. I'm tired of CIA types telling us in the military how to fight. They need to go back and do the things that they're supposed to do and let the military do the things we're supposed to do. Lansdale and his 'Force' are a bunch of ruthless butchers."

Johnson was surprised by the sharp, direct response. "I was thinking of sending him over there to implement his plan with his team."

Taylor drew a deep breath. "Mr. President, I have accepted this mission, this new assignment, but I implore you not to have Lansdale anywhere near me. His ego is a too much. He always thinks he is in charge."

Johnson was stunned by Taylor's bluntness. Johnson had his objectives, and he had his men almost in place. To get Taylor, he knew he had to accept his requests. Johnson believed it was going to take a US military response to win the South Vietnamese independence. He looked at McNamara then at Rusk. "You boys got any questions or comments for *Ambassador* Taylor?"

Both men shook their heads.

President Johnson got up from the conference table and reached across to shake the general's hand. "Good luck."

Maxwell Taylor nodded at McNamara and Rusk, then looked at the President. "I'll be reporting to you as soon as I am in place and organized."

Once General Taylor had left, Johnson sat back down and looked at both men. Johnson took his glasses off; the room fell silent. "Looks like Taylor is just what the doctor ordered."

Rusk drew a deep breath. "I hope so, Mr. President."

Johnson leaned forward. "As soon as this election is over, we are going to do everything in our power to win freedom for South Vietnam. I need a military man in that Embassy."

Rusk rubbed his chin. "I hope the press doesn't identify your move. It could change the course of the election. There is a poll out that says Americans are against putting troops in South Vietnam."

Johnson looked concerned and McNamara chimed in. "Remember, I promised Westmoreland I'd give him the troops he needs to execute his role as the MAC-V."

Before Johnson could address that comment, Rusk spoke up. "What are you going to do about Lansdale? You told him to prepare to return to Vietnam with his team."

Johnson frowned as he put his glasses back on. "I'll handle Lansdale. Everything is on hold until after the election. One thing is for sure, I don't think Vietnam is big enough for both Lansdale and Taylor. I've got to have Taylor in there right now."

JULY 2, 1964

US EMBASSY

SAIGON

Major Steven Hebert was standing outside on the Embassy Grounds, speaking with one of the guards, when he saw Sergeant Tim Mitchell running toward him. He was waving a couple sheets of paper, and Meredith Brown was right behind him. Steven frowned at the two of them as they approached. Tim was running faster than Meredith, who tottered a bit in her high heels. Tim stopped several steps away from Steven trying to control his excitement as an out-of-breath Meredith caught up.

Steven laughed. "Sergeant, what is the big deal? Did the Beach Boy's just announce a new album?"

Tim glanced back at Meredith, then back to the large Negro man. "Major, we…" Tim pointed back and forth at Meredith with the papers. "Think you have to see this." Tim held out the papers.

Steven reached for the papers, read them, and a broad smile broke across his face. "Tim, Meredith. Thank you very much. This is really important to me... The Reverend Dr. Martin Luther King is one of my heroes."

Tim and Meredith were nodding in unison as Meredith said, "Major, read the article. President Johnson got President Kennedy's Civil Right Bill passed through Congress."

Steven looked back at the papers. Silently, he focused with great intensity on the article. When he'd finished reading, he looked up. "You can't imagine how much I appreciate this, Tim, Meredith. President Johnson really did what he said he would do—complete President Kennedy's work. Kennedy should have acted sooner, but that's okay. Johnson finished it. It's important to keep you word. *I* may not benefit from this, but many who come after me will." Steven let out half a smile.

Meredith reached over and gave Steven a one-armed hug. "Major, we better get back inside. We just wanted you to be the second to know, naturally, after General Taylor. He gave us permission to mimeograph you a copy of this."

CHAPTER TWENTY-TWO

JULY 24, 1964

WASHINGTON DC

Edward Lansdale walked over to his bar and pulled out a bottle of favorite old Scotch. He poured three fingers in his glass. Lifting his glass, he sat down to read over the speech Frank Church gave on the Senate Floor the day before. *Where did Church get his information? How could he really believe 25,000 Viet Cong carried backpacks through the jungle to supply their effort in the South?* Church was a very powerful senator. He had to know that the North Vietnamese Army, not to mention the Russians and the communist Chinese, would help them move supplies on the Ho Chi Minh trail. The intelligence community knew all about that. Church has been involved in military intelligence since he served in the CBI theater in World War II. Lansdale took a sip of his scotch. *Does Church know and just not want to put this information on the official record? Maybe he is making a power play.*

The speech was troubling, but it might also be helpful for Lansdale's position. Church did read the actions of the navy as indicating the US effort was being expanded. It certainly didn't look like they were trying to come up with a way to reduce their role. *Maybe I have just discovered a powerful ally in the senator. Maybe he could help me with President Johnson. Several weeks ago, Johnson had promised I'd be returning to Vietnam, but I've heard nothing since then. The appointment of Maxwell Taylor was a not a positive sign.*

The senator opposed bombing North Vietnam because it would accomplish little or nothing. Despite some industrial growth in North Vietnam, there were still few targets there. One thing was for sure: Church nailed it when he said we were pouring money into South Vietnam and producing absolutely nothing. Lansdale knew he could accomplish more with much less but he was sidelined, just like he had been by President Kennedy.

Lansdale looked at his watch. He needed to get in touch with both Hebert and Tao.

By the time Lansdale finished speaking with both men, they had relayed information about developments in Lao, Vietnam, and Washington DC. Both expressed a desire to come back onto his team. He was willing to bring

Tao over. Tao had been trusted for two decades. But Hebert was right where he wanted him. Perhaps he could find out what Taylor was up to. That was vital. Time was getting tight and developments were coming fast.

Lansdale walked over to the corner table and poured another two-finger shot of scotch. *Johnson is playing me. He sent Taylor. He's not sending me.*

SAIGON

Major Steven Hebert sat across from Ambassador Maxwell Taylor, who continued to look up at him then back down at the file he was reading. After a few minutes, Taylor said, "I've reviewed your file and Ambassador Lodge's. Neither one mentions anything about you working with Thich Tri Quang, that Buddhist monk. At least not during the time Lodge protected him here at the Embassy. Did you have any direct contact with the monk?"

Steven pursed his lips. "No, Sir, Mr. Ambassador. I was around him but not in an official meeting." Steven was determined to honor his agreement with Lodge.

Ambassador Taylor breathed deeply. "Would he recognize you?"

Steven nodded. "I believe he would, Sir. As you know, he was here for several months."

Taylor rubbed his chin with his right hand. "Let's put it to a test. Immediately."

Steven sat erect, expectant. Taylor got up from his desk. Steven stood up immediately, acknowledging the Ambassador's military rank.

"At ease," Taylor told him and went on to explain what he had in mind. Steven could not believe it. Ambassador Taylor wanted Steven to contact Tri Quang, see if he would be willing to open a dialogue with the Department of State. Steven did not like the idea, as he believed that Tri Quang was part of the reason the South Vietnamese people wouldn't buy into the effort to stop the North Vietnamese and the Viet Cong. The monk was very likely either a communist sympathizer or maybe even a communist. More personal to Steven, he believed that Tri Quang hated all Catholics.

Taylor ordered him to go in civilian clothes. While the Ambassador specifically advised Steven it was not an undercover operation, he did not want Steven going in officially representing either the military or the Department of State.

"When do you want me to search for Tri Quang?"

Taylor looked away for a minute. "As soon as you can get Captain Jefferson to relieve you. And Major, this mission is top secret. Not a word to anyone. Report back to me only. Understood, Major?"

Steven stood up and saluted. "I will grab the Captain as quickly as possible."

Steven had a good idea which temple to begin his search at—the one he had escorted Ambassador Lodge to. When Steven entered the Temple three monks materialized before he could walk into the Drum Tower. They wanted to know what he was doing there. *They certainly wouldn't believe me if said I was a Buddhist coming to worship.* He looked at the three small Vietnamese men.

"I would like to speak to Thich Tri Quang."

One of the orange-clad monks stepped close enough to Steven to make him nervous. "What do want to talk with him about and why do you think he will want to talk with you?"

Steven kept his cool. "What I want to discuss with him is private. Why don't you ask him if he is willing to speak with Steven Hebert?"

Two of the monks stood by Hebert while the other walked through the Hall of the Heavenly Kings and disappeared behind the middle alter. Steven gazed around the ornately decorated worship area. It was filled with sculptures of the Heavenly Kings and the Maitreya, the laughing Buddha. It seemed like there was gold everywhere. The minutes passed slowly. He had not had a chance to study the architecture the last time. At last, the monk reappeared.

"Follow me, Steven Hebert."

Flanked by the other two monks, Steven followed the monk through the middle alter, into the main hall, through the lecture hall, then into the refectory. They turned down a long hallway with doors along each side. The monk leading the procession stopped at the last door on the left, which was cracked open. The monk pushed the door open. Thich Tri Quang was seated in the lotus position on a mat in a room without any other decorations. He rose from the mat with one fluid motion and stepped forward. He placed his palms together and bowed. Tri Quang pointed to the mat.

"Please, sit." Tri Quang waved the other men away. "I will be fine." He sat in the lotus position.

"Thank you for seeing me." Steven sat down on the floor, leaned his back against the wall, and placed his arms over his knees.

Tri Quang tilted his head. "So, Major Hebert, what brings you to see me?"

"Ambassador Taylor sent me to talk to you about opening dialogue again with you and a representative from the State Department."

Tri Quang nodded. "Of course, I would be glad to talk with Ambassador Lodge."

"Well, I don't believe that will be an option. He is in the United States."

Tri Quang looked down at his crossed legs for a long time. "I really don't see that we have anything further to discuss here. I will talk to Ambassador Lodge, and I will talk to you. But I am not…" He trailed off, looking down.

Steven started to speak but paused because he didn't want to interrupt the monk if he was deep in thought. Tri Quang nodded for him to speak.

"Tri Quang, do you have a message I can take back to Ambassador Taylor?"

Tri Quang got up from his lotus position and moved toward the door. "Major Hebert, yes. I'm pro-American yet I am not wishing for my view to be made public. It might compromise my religious role. There are those in the US government that already know that. You are aware I was against Diem because of how he treated the Buddhists. While I am for Khanh, I fear he is too weak and inexperienced to lead South Vietnam." Tri Quang bowed his head and opened the door for Steven.

227

Steven walked back into the hallway. He paused long enough to stretch his back and his neck. The three monks met him and silently walked him to the front door.

Perhaps I was wrong about Tri Quang, Steven thought. *Unless I'm being fed a lie. Is he just giving me a line?* He had learned much and Taylor was not going to be pleased with his message.

Chapter Twenty-Three

August 5, 1964
Saigon

Nguyen Tao slipped in the back door of his Vespa Scooter business. There was dust everywhere. Tao didn't turn on any lights so as not draw attention to the store front. He couldn't keep up much of a front business because he was never there. And now it was time to follow Lansdale's orders. *I just can't leave Vang Pao without quality personnel to watch the Trail.*

Tao sat in the dark and contemplated developments over the last couple of days. Vang Pao's forces had encountered more of the North Vietnamese Army, which continued to work in concert with the communist Pathot Lao. Vang Pao's army was holding its position, but any attempt to retake their camp at Plaines des Jarres was out of the question.

Just then there was a light rap on the back door. Tao opened the door to let in Steven Hebert. He offered Steven a stool and got right in his face.

"I need to get you up to speed. Things in the Gulf of Tonkin have not been officially reported. Has General Taylor said anything?"

Steven ran his hand over his short-cropped hair. "No, I have not had much contact with him. You know, no one-on-one's since he arrived. Taylor has been very engaged with the South Vietnamese leadership, but his secretary said the White House is going to go before Congress and request authorization to start bombing the North. *Officially*, of course."

Tao looked up at the ceiling. "Hope it works, but what are they going to bomb?"

Steven raised his shoulders and both palms. "No clue. You know General LeMay."

Tao nodded. "Let me finish telling you about the Maddox. They were providing intelligence to the Laotian Air Force and the OPLAN 34A missions. *They were in* North Vietnamese waters. They had been feeding it to those conducting raids into North Vietnam for the past several days. I know the official report is they were ten miles out, but that wasn't the case. They easily repelled the attack with a few shots from their guns and a couple of planes from the carrier Ticonderoga."

Steven rubbed his chin with his big hand. "It's about time we start attacking. Isn't that what we should be doing?"

"Bet the North got tipped off by the Russians or the Chinese. I don't think the North Vietnamese have the technology to make that determination, do they?"

Tao shrugged. "No, we haven't seen any evidence."

The room was quiet for a minute.

Then Tao asked, "Have you had a chance to talk with either Peer de Silva or George Allen about any of this?"

Steven looked away. "No, both of those men are very low key, really buttoned up. Allen is always preparing reports with his door closed. I did have a briefing with him, and he thinks the way we do. And de Silva has been out of his office a lot this summer. My attempts have failed to gain the information we need."

Tao yawned and rubbed his eyes with his right hand. "Sorry, I'm really tired. Been up for two days straight. Anyway, it gets worse. The next night there was *no* attack. The captain of the Maddox reported there was an attack, but showing his experience, he questioned the data and issued a revised report as soon as they had completed their analysis."

Steven's eyes widened. "Are you sure about this? Every official report that has come through the Embassy said there was an attack on the second night on both the Maddox and the Turner Joy. We even decided to increase our security at the compound."

Tao shook his head. "I'm in the middle of CIA communications. We got both reports. Second report came in fairly quick. Something about the weather creating false readings. I didn't pay much attention since the first report was countermanded."

Steven nodded. "That is starting to make sense. Mitchell, the boy in charge of communications, showed me a report that said the North Vietnamese filed a formal complaint to the International Control Commission. Regarding our activity in the North. Huh, you know rules with our fighting effort."

Tao shook his head. "Yeah, we have to play by the rules and the North and the VC don't."

"Plus, the damn VC knew the rules we are playing by."

Tao continued. "Anyway, they dispatched a team from India to Da Nang to investigate. But the navy got a head's-up and moved all their swift boats to Cam Ranh Bay. They will be there until the ICC completes their investigation."

Steven got off the stool and started pacing. "I think I agree with Lansdale. The government and the military are getting ready to up the stakes. I never had a chance to tell you, but before Lodge left, he had corresponded with the President about attacking the North prior to something, some event. I was never able to ascertain what the event was, but something was definitely up."

Tao looked down at the floor. "Is there any way Taylor knows?"

"Without him calling me into his office to give me orders, I don't know. It may be part of our increased security."

Tao maintained an intense fixed gaze at Steven. "This task we've been assigned, it's getting away from Lansdale because of the politics not the mission."

Steven nodded adamantly. "I'm going to make an effort to get information from Allen and de Silva so we have some better intel. It will make it easier to get information to Lansdale with you back in the city." Steven got up and left.

Tao sat there in silence. *Getting back into Saigon might be best for the mission.*

WASHINGTON DC

Edward Lansdale sat at the bar finishing his dinner by himself. A number of individuals were scattered about on either side of him. Several patrons ate and drank in booths around the restaurant. Lansdale had never been here before, but William Colby had said they prepared very good meals that one could eat in peace. Colby was right: The food was good, no one to bother him, and while there were people around, Lansdale could barely hear anything. Great acoustics.

Lansdale had received word from a couple of his CIA friends that President Johnson was going to give a speech that night to the American people. Lansdale was prepared for worst. The events over the last few days had been made dramatic by the press and the politicians, while in Lansdale's mind, they were not really out of the ordinary in a theater of conflict. Lansdale scooped up a bite of mashed potatoes and was about to finish off a dinner roll when the network programing switched to the lectern behind which the President would speak momentarily. Lansdale put down his roll, took a sip of water, and asked the bartender to turn up the sound.

President Johnson began to speak.

"My fellow Americans:

"As President and Commander in Chief, it is my duty to the American people to report that renewed hostile actions against United States ships on the high seas in the Gulf of Tonkin have today required me to order the military forces of the United States to take action in reply…"

The bartender asked, "Is that was loud enough?"

"The initial attack on the destroyer Maddox, on August 2, was repeated today by a number of hostile vessels attacking two U.S. destroyers with torpedoes. The destroyers and supporting aircraft acted at once on the orders

I gave after the initial act of aggression. We believe at least two of the attacking boats were sunk. There were no U.S. losses…"

Some of the patrons in the bar cheered. Lansdale strained to hear what Johnson was saying.

"… performance of commanders and crews in this engagement is in the highest tradition of the United States navy. But repeated acts of violence against the armed forces of the United States must be met not only with alert defense, but with positive reply. That reply is being given as I speak to you tonight. Air action is now in execution against gunboats and certain supporting facilities in North Viet-Nam, which have been used in these hostile operations…"

Lansdale looked down at his plate. His meal was no longer so appealing. It was not the food. Lansdale believed Johnson was getting ready to do the one thing Lansdale had been trying to keep from happening. There might be no turning back.

Lansdale refocused on the President.

"I have been given encouraging assurance by these leaders of both parties that such a resolution will be promptly introduced, freely and expeditiously debated, and passed with overwhelming support. And just a few minutes ago I was able to reach Senator Goldwater and I'm glad to say that he has expressed his support of the statement that I'm making to you tonight.

"It is a solemn responsibility to have to order even limited military action by forces whose overall strength is as vast and as awesome as those of the United States of America, but it is my considered conviction, shared throughout your government, that firmness in the right is indispensable today for peace; that firmness will always be measured. Its mission is peace."

Lansdale disgustedly threw a ten-dollar bill on the bar, pushed away from the stool and walked out. The words *Its mission is peace* played over and over in his head. *The President is perpetrating a lie to the American people about the second night.* Clearly, he has been planning this for some time. He just needed to find a way to pull the wool over the eyes of the American people. That's why he sent Taylor over there and put Westmoreland in charge of the troops. *We can defeat the communists but the South Vietnamese people must be involved with* our *help.*

CHAPTER TWENTY-FOUR

AUGUST 7, 1964

WASHINGTON DC

Rita Sullivan briskly walked out of the *Washington Star* news office. It was a very warm evening, and to get to her bus stop she'd have to hustle. As she walked, she freed the long blonde hair of her top bun and shook it out. She ran her fingers through her hair, loosening it more. *Rather than catch the bus at this stop, I think I'll walk up the street a ways.*

It was another day that the Chief had blasted her, yet again, for a column she had written. The confrontations were becoming more frequent, but she knew her place. Still, she didn't like it. It had just been a bad day in general. Mary Pinchot Meyer had called her to see if she could meet to go over planning for the scheduled arts and music events that Fall in the DC area. Rita had to put her off due to scheduling conflicts.

The evening air reminded her of her days in college at the University of South Carolina. Warm night walks about the night life of Columbia, South Carolina, with her friend, Meredith Brown. At the moment, she longed for the simplicity of those nights. Thinking about old times calmed her. She wondered about her friend. Meredith had never responded to her request for an interview, nor had she commented on Rita's suggestion that she might be a source for future stories. Perhaps Rita had pushed too hard.

She noticed a black Cadillac limousine driving slowly past. *Was that the second time?* Rita stopped, pulled out her memo pad, and wrote down the license plate number. She was not certain it was the same because so many big shots traveled that way on the streets of DC.

She continued to walk but now paid closer attention to the traffic. Her bus stop was in sight on the well-lit street. She felt safe but the limousine kept her curiosity. She sat down in the sheltered bus stop and fanned herself as she looked up the street. A little more than a block away, her bus wheezed toward her.

As the bus approached, the same limo pulled up and parked on the opposite side of the street. Two well-dressed men got out and hustled across the street, beating the bus to her location. One of the men spoke to her, while the other man looked around pensively. They were aides to Senator Wayne Morse of Oregon. He was in the car and wished to speak with her in private. He pointed toward the limousine.

Rita frowned as she ran her fingers through her blonde hair. "The senator can come down to my office at the newspaper or invite me to his office. We can talk all he wants."

The aide shook his head. "No, he needs to speak with you *this evening*, in a quiet, discreet place."

Rita tilted her head to the left. "This is… highly unusual. What is this all about?"

The aide shrugged. "I'm just an aide, but the senator believes it is important he talk to you immediately."

Rita nodded as she her bus pulled up. The driver opened the door. Rita waved the bus on.

"There is a secluded restaurant just around the corner. We can talk there."

One aide started back across the street to the limo, while the other said, "We are authorized to offer you a ride."

Before Rita could reply, the senator rolled down the window and signaled for her to come over to the large car. Rita recognized him and was mildly surprised it really *was* him. The two aides scurried across the street though the sparse traffic.

Senator Morse looked up at Rita. "Miss Sullivan, I need to talk to you, but only my trusted staff can know about our meeting. Would you be willing to get into the limousine so we can talk?"

Rita's put her fist up to her mouth then she looked at the two aides, who were nodding their heads in unison. "Okay."

An aide opened the door, and Rita slid into a seat opposite the senator. The limosine started and pulled away from the curb.

Senator Morse sucked his lower lip and frowned. "I have heard about some of the columns you have written, the ones which *have not* appeared in your newspaper."

"Who told you about those columns?"

The senator continued, "It's not important. Let me continue. I believe you wish to be a reporter beyond the assignments you are getting from the *Star News*. Would I be correct in that assumption?"

Rita frowned. "Senator Morse, what is this all about?"

The senator pouted. "I need you to answer my question before I continue, Miss Sullivan. Are you wishing to expand your role to that of a serious reporter?"

Rita nodded. "Of course, Senator. That's the goal of most reporters. I want to do serious news, important issues of the day."

Senator Morse looked at the two aides and nodded. They pulled files out from a briefcase as the senator continued. "Good. *Good.* We need somebody we can trust to report the truth. But I cannot be your quoted news source. You may know, I'm not particularly well liked among some of the more hawkish senators. But the truth must get out. The people must know."

Rita looked puzzled. "What are you talking about? *What* must the people know? *What truth?*"

Senator Morse drew a deep breath and let it out slowly. "I'm prepared to give you some information regarding the attack on the Maddox in the Gulf of Tonkin a couple of days ago. Information the people need to know."

Rita leaned forward in her seat and repeated herself. *"What are you talking about?* The North Vietnamese attacked our Navy ships in international waters."

Senator Morse nodded with a half-smile on his lips. "Understand, young lady, the news media relies almost solely on the government to give them the story, specifically when it comes to battles and such. More importantly, I have it on very good information that it was not an unprovoked attack on August 2. *But* the attack the next night on both the Maddox and Turner Joy *was not quite as reported.*"

Rita reached in her purse for her steno pad and pencil. "*Okay,* you have my attention."

Senator Morse leaned forward and rubbed his mouth and chin with his left hand. "If you can be that reporter, I can get you information to write about what is going on. I can put you in touch with others who have information as well. We need a voice, a fresh voice, and we think you could be it."

Rita felt herself blush. She nodded, realizing she might be on the edge of the career break she'd been seeking. "Senator, I am very interested, but the executive editor of the newspaper may not like these types of articles. He is very pro-Johnson Administration, very pro-Vietnam."

Senator Morse sat back in the plush limo seat and pulled out a handkerchief to wipe his face. "You report. If it causes issues with your employer... well, we can handle that when the time comes."

Rita continued to nod her head. "Okay, I'm game, but I need my job desperately."

Senator Morse pointed his two aides. "Let her look at those files."

The first aide offered her a file. Rita grabbed one, reached in her purse for her glasses and began reading. After a minute, she looked at the senator and shrugged. "This was almost exactly what was reported. The USS Maddox was in international waters, came under attack by three small boats. They fired on the Maddox. The Maddox returned fire and hit all three boats, sinking one. Everybody knows that story."

The senator nodded. "The official report omitted a very important fact. The Maddox was going into North Vietnamese water. It was not routine mission. They were gathering intelligence. The plan was to coordinate an attack on North Vietnam by the Laotian Air Force, which is really our CIA, and the South Vietnamese Army, which is really our Navy Seals and another

Special Forces mission team. Just two days before, the North Vietnamese lodged a formal complaint about these activities."

The senator nodded at the other aide, who handed her another file. She read it closely:

> On the night of 4 August, the Maddox and the C. Turner Joy entered the Gulf of Tonkin, sailing within eight (8) miles of the North Vietnamese coast. The intelligence data was used to allow South Vietnamese swift boats to attack defenses on their coast. However, as night set in, a thunderstorm formed over the bay. This threw off the electronic instruments, specifically their sonar. Initially, what was reported as an attack by Captain Herrick. Both US vessels opened fire, but Herrick quickly speculated there was a problem and called for a re-assessment of the data and a review. The captain's review uncovered several discrepancies. It seemed sonar man who was overly excited actually heard the Maddox's propellers. Captain Herrick issued a second report of these findings that night that there was no North Vietnamese attack.

Rita pushed her glasses back up her forehead as she made eye contact with Senator Morse.

Senator Morse pointed at the file. "As soon as Captain Herrick completed his finding, he issued another report. There were no small North

Vietnamese boats present, attacking or anything else. President Johnson ignored that report. You draw your own conclusions."

Rita took her left hand and patted the back of her head and stroked her hair. "According to everything I've read, the North Vietnamese and the Viet Cong have been pouring over the border into South Vietnam and intimidating the South Vietnamese."

Senator Morse frowned at Rita. "I am not exonerating the communists. I'm only saying I don't want this conflict to escalate on a lie—*this* lie."

Rita gazed out the window as the limousine traversed its way along the streets of Washington DC. The lighted streets she had walked earlier had just gotten darker. Now, she was about to do something that she always wanted to do, but to write this report could cost her dearly. No one spoke for several minutes. Finally, the senator cleared his throat.

"So, are you *really* game, Miss Sullivan?"

Rita looked down at the two files sitting on her lap but didn't say anything. She had to think.

The senator tapped on the glass between them and his driver. When the glass slid down, the senator looked at Rita.

"Where can we drop you off?"

Rita was still staring out the window. "At my apartment." She gave out the address.

The remainder of the drive was quiet, and Rita refused to make eye contact with either the senator or his two aides. She chose instead to look out the window as the busy night streets paraded by rhythmically. When they arrived at her apartment, the limousine pulled to the curb. Rita did not utter a single word despite their encouragements. Realizing she still had the files on her lap, she handed them back to the two aides and climbed out.

Before the large car pulled away, the senator rolled down his window. "Miss Sullivan, we need someone with your talent and drive for the truth."

Rita looked up toward the sky, seeking divine intervention, and drew a deep breath. She turned back toward the limo and nodded. A tear came in her eye as she turned her head away and walked off quickly as if trying to out-walk the tremendously heavy responsibility that had just been placed on her.

Can I handle this?

Don Kesterson

CHAPTER TWENTY-FIVE

EARLY MORNING

AUGUST 7, 1964

WASHINGTON DC

Rita hung up the phone and sat staring at it. She had just made the most expensive phone call of her life, one she could hardly pay for on her salary. Rita picked her prized possession off the coffee table, a picture of her mother holding her just after birth with her father looking over her shoulder. Her mother had moved recently and found the picture and sent it to her. She tried to find some solace in holding it.

Rita was always a risk taker, but this phone call had turned out to be a total bust. Her best friend, Meredith Brown, knew nothing except for the official story. Rita could not believe she'd made such a crazy move. By the time she hung up the phone, she had accomplished only two things: one, burning money and, two, tipping her friend to a question she should never have asked. Rita glanced up and the wall clock told her she'd have to get coffee on the run to make it to work on time.

On the bus ride, Rita thought more about old times with her best friend. Meredith's family was very wealthy and part of the political elite of the United States and the world. Meredith was destined for great things. As the bus approached her stop, out came her compact to check her hair and lipstick. The thirty-minute ride to the stop for the short walk to the *Washington Star News* was spent imagining she was breaking news on a very big story. The sunny morning had taken the sting off her failed phone call. Rita could not get upset with Meredith; in her college days Meredith's family had virtually adopted her. They knew her divorced mother could not afford to give her many things, and they found ways to fill that gap while allowing her to maintain her dignity.

After Rita put her purse on her desk, she headed straight for Chief Petit's office. She tapped lightly on his door, and once she heard the grunt from the other side, she stepped in to deliver the column she was hoping would run the next evening. Rita cleared her voice, but again, without looking up, the Chief just pointed to the edge of his desk as he continued to read. He waved her out of the office. She stood for a minute, but when she realized he would not give her his attention, she dropped it on the top of the stack.

Rita went back to her small desk in the middle of the news center area. She had hoped her column would be quickly approved. She looked at the board at the front door, which had chalk marks that indicated Miriam Ottenberg and John Sherwood were already out on assignments.

After about thirty minutes of sitting at her desk, doing nothing, she heard the Chief bellow from his office. "Sullivan, get in here immediately!"

She jumped up and gracefully moved toward his office. In the last year, she had gotten used to his gruff style. He had made her a better newspaper reporter. When she got there, he exclaimed, "Close the door, young lady."

Rita closed the door and slid into the chair in front of his desk. With Rita looking on, the Chief picked up her column and casually dropped it in the waste basket. He stared at her. Rita didn't know what to think or say. Finally, he spoke but in an uncharacteristically low voice: *"Who the hell* was your source for *that* crock?"

Rita bit her lip to keep calm. "Senator Wayne Morse of Oregon."

The Chief snapped, "Well, I certainly know who *he* is." The Chief sat up straight and glared. Rita twisted around in the chair, then slid to the edge, ready for the confrontation.

"Calm down, young lady. Let me tell you a little story. During World War II, I worked for naval intelligence. We were aware that there was a worldwide communist movement. Now, I was never involved in any investigations of the communists, but you can be assured, I read everything I got my hands on. Classified reports. And I can tell you one thing, young lady, I think Morse is *at least* a subversive. You can throw that damn Ernest Gruening in with him, as well."

Rita was now more startled than upset. She was unaware of the depth of the Chief's experience. She knew not to question what he might know. But she was still going to defend her research. "Chief, Morse said he got his information from someone in the Pentagon. I worked on several other sources to verify. I think this story is accurate."

Continuing to stare at her, the Chief leaned up and placed both hands firmly on the desk. "Our country supports this President. Our ships were attacked. We don't need to get on the wrong side of the White House. If Johnson turns against us, we will have real problems getting stories in the future. Do. You. *Hear*. Me?"

Rita nodded, but she struggled to control her growing anger.

The Chief pointed toward the door. "Go find something else to report on. *Do your damn job*. You are a Sunday Community and Art Section columnist. Stop stirring up trouble."

249

Rita struggled to control her emotions as best she could and rose from the chair. She grabbed her column out of the waste basket and headed for the door with both fists clinched. It was all she could do to resist slamming the door when she left.

Rita went over and sat at her desk. She wished Miriam Ottenberg or John Sherwood were in the office. They might be able to help her. What was her next move? Rita looked at her typewriter—a new column or rewrite the old one, make it acceptable. The more she thought, the more it came clear. She had another move: to pursue the truth. Rita picked up her purse and walked out of the office.

NEXT MORNING

SAIGON

Tao sat up straight in bed. He had awakened from a deep sleep, his body wet with sweat. A nasty dream. The Buddhist monk sitting in the street on fire…

that look on his face… so peaceful, while he was consumed by fire… . Then the monk turned into his deceased wife. The pain, the haunting!

Tao looked at his watch—a little after 3 AM. Tao had only slept for four hours; he was still tired but now wide awake. The dream had been intense, pure adrenaline flowing through his veins. The smell of burning flesh seemed so real. How could that possibly have been a dream?

Tao decided the best thing to do was pack and head up to the runway, see if he could get to Saigon early. All the way, Tao could not shake his dream. The reoccurring dream had haunted him for more than a year. Every time he had it he was filled with a raging hunger for finding the Viet Cong who had killed his family. He decided that as soon as possible he would place a call to his son Luc, his last living family member. Tao and his son had exchanged several letters, but Tao thought a letter would not satisfy his need this time. Luc was doing well at Duke University and would graduate at the end of this semester.

As the plane was coming in for a landing at Tan Son Nhut Air Base, Tao thought that after calling his son, he would try to catch up with Hebert. Also, it might be a good idea to catch up with Pham Xuan An. Tao believed staying in Saigon would give him an opportunity to get the most recent update regarding the Gulf of Tonkin incident.

Tao walked into his Scooter Shop, went up front and turned on the store lights and the open sign. He walked to the back of his shop and picked up a broom to begin cleaning. *Yes, I think I would be happier being back in Saigon.* If he was going to re-open the shop as a front business, it desperately needed tidied up. Tao finished sweeping and was about to pick up a dust rag to go over the scooters when he heard a rapping at the back door. Tao scurried to the door, opened it and let Steven in. Tao just blurted out. "This Gulf of Tonkin incident has changed everything."

Steven was taken aback by Tao's harsh attitude. "What do you mean?"

Tao shook his head. "Watch what Johnson does next."

Steven opened his arms, palms up. "What do you mean?"

Tao straddled a wooden stool. "There was no attack the night of August 4 on either of our destroyers. Johnson ignored the second message from the captain because it didn't suit his needs."

Steven nodded. "I heard the same thing from both de Silva and Allen. De Silva also said Captain Herrick corrected his first message fairly quick, but it was the first one that President Johnson chose to focus on."

Tao waved his arm in the air. "Yeah, that's what I mean, it met his need." Tao rubbed his chin. "He was told by Ambassador Taylor the only way to win was to send a bunch of troops."

Steven sat down on a dusty wooden stool. "How do you know that? I work around the Ambassador and I haven't heard that."

Tao kept glancing away then back at Steven, ignoring his remark. "Look, Johnson is going to start bombing the North. Maybe that will work but look at the facts." Tao held his hand up in front of Steven and with the index finger on his opposite hand, poked his fingers as he held them up. "Taylor, army man, Wheeler, army man, and Westmoreland, army man. What does that tell you?"

Steven sat quietly for a minute. The reality grabbed him. While Tao was speculating, it was clear—if the bombing did not work, ground troops were inevitable. Steven lowered his head. "We have failed our mission. Troops are inevitable."

Tao shook his head. "Not inevitable but we are losing precious time."

Steven paced the Embassy building. He could not get the conversation with Tao out of his head. As he walked past the Ambassador's office, he thought he would poke his head in and talk with Meredith for a moment. As his luck would have it, she was in the office. He pointed at the Ambassador's office.

Meredith looked surprised but mouthed the word no. Steven started the idle conversation to take his mind off his own dilemma. "Meredith, you're working even though the Ambassador isn't in?"

Meredith shook her head. "The Ambassador is a workaholic. He's in and out at all hours and leaves work, filing, letters, even notes asking about how prior Ambassadors handled political issues."

Steven nodded. "I've always heard General Taylor was like that." Steven didn't mention that he was prejudiced about Taylor because of information he had heard from Lansdale.

Meredith smiled. "What do you hear from your Marine buddy, Ethan?"

Steven drew a deep breath. "Not much. Since he was sent to Da… his assignment here in the country, I have only heard from him once. He said he was bored."

Meredith nodded. "I imagine he will be in Saigon when he gets leave. Will you all be getting together?"

Steven smiled. "I sure hope so. He is one of my oldest and most trusted friends." He wondered why she brought up Ethan. *Strange.*

Meredith looked serious. "Can I confide in you with something? I mean, can I trust you?"

Steven nodded. "Why, of course, unless you tell me you are an ax murderer or something." Steven laughed. "You're not Lizzie Borden's granddaughter, are you?"

"No." Meredith looked down, obviously not enjoying his joke. Something else was on her mind. "I have a friend, a newspaper reporter in the United States. Her name is Rita. She wrote to me right after Ambassador Lodge won the New Hampshire primary. She wanted to talk to me or get information from me about Ambassador Lodge and his potential run for President."

Steven drew another deep breath. "I don't see any big deal about that."

"Well, I ignored her request, didn't even reply to her. She was my best friend in college. But I just didn't know what to say. You know, being new on the job and everything."

Steven shrugged. He started to speak she interrupted him. "She called me last night, wanted to know what I knew about the Gulf of Tonkin incident."

Steven started to speak, but Meredith kept talking, clearly agitated. She ran her hand repeatedly through her brunette hair. "I told her all I knew about was there were two attacks on our destroyers on consecutive days. Major, she would not have called me if she didn't know something. That's just how she is. I know *her*."

Steven worked to keep his face expressionless as he shrugged. "You know the official story."

Meredith looked at Steven. "Major, just before she hung up the phone she said it was probably good I didn't know what was going on. It would be safer for me. I don't get that. We're here—don't we know the actual story?"

Steven leaned forward. "You and I have seen the official reports. That is all we know, isn't it?" Steven wondered where Meredith's friend had sourced the story. He had come in here to have a light conversation with Meredith, only to find out that the truth might be circulating back home already.

Tao decided to walk over to the Lafayette Restaurant, hoping to kill enough time that he could nonchalantly run into Pham Xuan An sitting, enjoying lunch. Tao slowly entered the restaurant. He took a seat where he could watch the door and waited. An never awakened early in the day. Tao ordered a light breakfast and some strong Vietnamese coffee. As he was finishing up his sticky rice, seafood, and papaya, he saw Pham Xuan An walk in smoking a cigarette. Tao waved his hand, and An strolled over to join him at his small corner table.

An plopped down in the chair. "You sure seem to be in Saigon a lot for a man who says he is selling his business to live out in the countryside."

Tao was prepared for that question this time. "Well… I have not been able to find a suitable buyer for my business, so I may be moving back into Saigon to re-open until I can facilitate a sale." Tao thought he would see if he could An to give up more information. "Anyway, what has been going on with the Buddhists since I saw you last?"

An nodded as he took a drag off his cigarette. "Thich Tri Quang continues to lead the Buddhist movement against the South Vietnamese government. However, it seems he has fewer followers at the moment. The monk has been on one of his rants against the Catholics in the country. I don't think this gets his fellow Buddhists as excited with Diem, Nhu, and Can all dead. However, Khanh continues to play up to the Buddhists in hope of growing his power as he fights with the Catholics in the upper echelon of the military."

Tao was surprised at that comment. "How is Tri Quang getting along with the new Ambassador?"

An shook his head and smiled. "It appears Ambassador Taylor is not the politician that Ambassador Lodge was, and he doesn't seem to have the time of day for him."

Tao nodded. "From what I have heard, it seems to me he has been focused on Khanh's presidency." Tao waited for a response. When none came, he changed the subject. "So what else is going on around Saigon?"

Right then, a waiter came to the table and set it down a cup of coffee. As he snuffed out his cigarette, An did not say a word while the waiter was at the table. Once he'd left, An took his first sip of coffee. "Nothing in Saigon to speak of, but let's talk about the Gulf of Tonkin events."

Tao nodded, not knowing what to expect. "The attacks on the Maddox and the Turner Joy took place because they were in North Vietnamese waters. The US Navy is lying."

Tao thought he would test An. "The official report was that both ships were in international waters. Where do you get your information?"

An stared hard at Tao as he sipped. "My sources are good, as you know." An fumbled around for another cigarette. "You know, I cannot give up my sources. But we both know that President Johnson is using this."

Tao faked a frown and rubbed his chin as if he were contemplating, but he was surprised at how fast the real story had gotten out.

An continued. "The Maddox had been providing data for raids on the Viet Cong and into North Vietnam for at least a week."

Tao knew An had access to United States military information, but this was highly classified.

Just then a waitress carried over a plate of breakfast and set it in front of An. Tao thought the man had not even ordered, but assumed the staff knew exactly what An was to have.

Tao thought he would play the card he had just been dealt. "What's the American military's next move?"

An laughed then he leaned forward and whispered. "Come on now, Tao, you know the US better than me. They will start bombing the North any day. What comes after that, who knows, but I'm guessing there will be US troops in South Vietnam soon."

Tao thought he would press Pham Xuan An. "How deep do you think the NLF have penetrated into South Vietnam? Are they at the edge of Saigon?"

Tao was puzzled that An did not seem to like the question. An took another sip of his coffee and his first bite of breakfast. "We both know that the National Liberation Front is moving into South Vietnam, but I have no idea how far they have penetrated. I spend all my time here in Saigon. I'll say neither the US nor the South Vietnamese army seem to be too excited about it."

"I am buying breakfast." *Since you have been a wealth of information.*

This brought a smile to come to An's face. "I will take you up on that, my old friend."

Tao raised his hand to call over the waiter.

CHAPTER TWENTY-SIX

AUGUST 7, 1964

WASHINGTON DC

President Johnson was reading over a draft of the Gulf of Tonkin Resolution, He slowly placed it back down on his desk, took off his glasses, and leaned back in his chair. He rubbed his eyes and blinked several times. Secretary of Defense Robert McNamara and Secretary of State Dean Rusk exchanged glances then looked at the President, waiting for his comments. The President got up from his desk. The pain in his right shoulder just didn't let up. He walked over to the couch and sat down next to McNamara. Johnson leaned back casually as he broke into a confident smile. "I can't imagine anyone voting against this, can you?"

Secretary McNamara nodded. "I think your meeting went well with the congressional leaders. We had to pressure several of the senators, make deals with a few others. I think they're all on board. They're going to go along with whatever you and the Pentagon wish."

Secretary Rusk frowned. "Assuming the vote goes as expected, what is your next step, Mr. President?"

The President rubbed his chin. "My next move... will be to get with General Wheeler and select some sites from our original list of ninety-four targets in North Vietnam. Damn it, I wish Seaborn had been able to get us something to work with from the North Vietnamese. We'll see if they are willing to wait us out when we start bombing the hell out of 'em."

Rusk sniffed. "I think you need to see what the media and the public think before you get too aggressive."

President Johnson nodded as he raised his right hand. "No question. But I think with this Resolution in hand and with the press reporting the story the way we want it, there should be no problems. But my moves will be calculated and guarded because of the coming election."

McNamara continued to frown. "How do you think Goldwater will respond to this resolution and your actions?"

Johnson pursed his lips. "He has no choice but to support it. We could only hope he says we aren't going far enough." Johnson chuckled after he thought about his own remark.

Rusk bit his lower lip. "This could be a risky move at this stage in the election."

McNamara started to speak, but was interrupted by President Johnson, red-faced, pounding his fist on the coffee table. "I keep playing Ambassador Taylor's latest message over and over in my head. He raised the estimated strength of the Viet Cong in the South up to 34,000, He said the increase of 6,000 VC was due to better intelligence data. We've been feed bad intelligence for some time."

Rusk raised his eyebrows. "Did the bad intel come from the CIA or military Intelligence?"

Johnson ignored the question. "Damn it, the GOP blamed Truman for losing China and Korea. I will not let them blame me for losing Vietnam."

The room sat silent for a brief period as Johnson cooled off. "General Taylor, I mean, *Ambassador* Taylor, says we need to get troops in there now and start fighting. We've run out of time waiting on the South Vietnamese. Taylor thinks that Khanh is incapable of leading either the military or the country. General Wheeler has expressed a desire for aggressively bombing the North. He thinks that could get the job done." Johnson leaned his head back. "I think he is following General LeMay's playbook."

Rusk shook his head. "I'm still not sure that promoting Wheeler to Chairman of the Joint Chiefs was the right move. He lacks the experience of some of the other generals and the admiral."

Johnson could feel his face flush again. "I wanted an army man in that role. We need continuity! It will be best to have Taylor, Wheeler, and Westmoreland, all working together, all army."

Once again, the room fell silent.

After a while. President Johnson then spoke up. "Can we get Seaborn to carry another message to the Premier Dong?"

Rusk nodded. "I believe so, Mr. President."

President Johnson placed his hand over his mouth to cover up a yawn and closed his eyes. "Do we know when his ICC team is going back to Hanoi?"

Rusk said, "Should be soon. I'll get a date."

Johnson got back up from the couch. "Hopefully, we can get this resolution in our back pocket and get a couple of bombing runs in to help persuade them before he gets over there. Dean, get working on a draft of another message for Seaborn to deliver to the Premier Dong."

McNamara ran his hand over his slicked back hair. "What is your best-case scenario? The bombing causes the North Vietnamese to come to the table? Get them to agree to stop sending communists into the South or do you think we can get them to agree to mutual autonomy?"

Rusk spoke up as he shook his head. "We are putting a lot of trust in Seaborn. Maybe too much? Premier Dong told him that the North Vietnamese were willing to take whatever steps to overcome our efforts."

Johnson placed both hands on the couch as he leaned over. "Damn it, we don't have many options. I'm trying to keep South Vietnam from falling. If Vietnam and Laos falls to the communists, Red China will become the power broker for that region. The next thing you know we will be fighting the communists in Hawaii." Johnson went back to pacing behind the couch.

Rusk glanced over to McNamara, who discreetly shook his head. "There are several members of the CIA who no longer subscribe to the Domino Theory."

The President stopped again. "And exactly which faction of the CIA is that?"

AUGUST 8, 1964

SAIGON

Major Steven Hebert had been ordered to Ambassador Maxwell Taylor's office. Secretary Meredith Brown was sitting there with a bewildered look on her face. Meredith asked him what his opinion was of the developments of the last twenty-four hours. Steven stammered an answer that only caused her to roll her eyes. One thing was clear, the situation in Vietnam was getting more intense. The more they talked, the more frustrated Meredith got. Steven thought if she knew the whole story, she might lose it, and he did not want any part of that. Steven wondered if these situations were causing her to rethink her desire to stay in Foreign Service.

The Ambassador buzzed Meredith to send the major in. Before Steven could even take a seat, the Ambassador began to fill him on the latest developments in the United States. General Taylor advised Steven of the congressional vote; the House voted unanimously for the Gulf of Tonkin Resolution, while the Senate voted eighty-eight to two. Steven sat erect, waiting for the reason the Ambassador had called him down. It couldn't be just to describe the political situation in Washington DC. Finally, the Ambassador got to the point.

"Major, President Johnson is going to commence bombing certain targets in North Vietnam within the next forty-eight hours. Therefore, I think you need to start beefing up security around the Embassy within the next twenty-four hours. I want to be out ahead of any potential problems."

Steven remained motionless. "Yes, Sir, Ambassador. I'll get right on it."

Ambassador Taylor leaned forward, both hands on his desk as he stood up. "I have reviewed your security plan in the event of an emergency. It seems sound. However, the situation here is about to change. Do we need to bring in more military personnel to accomplish my objective?"

Steven considered that a strategic question that required a well thought out answer and wondered why it was necessary for Taylor to attempt to intimidate him with body language. Steven continued to sit straight in his chair without changing his expression. "No, Sir, Mr. Ambassador, I believe we have all of our bases covered, complete with contingency plans."

The Ambassador sat back down. "Well, I intend to review all the files over the next few weeks to make some changes to staff and assignments, particularly, if we are going into an enhanced conflict status in theater. Our time is short as this situation really cranks up."

Steven was not really surprised by the Ambassador's statements. The man had been a general used to running things. Steven felt confident that the review would result in few, if any changes.

Ambassador Taylor took his glasses off and laid them on the desk. "I want you to go back to see Tri Quang, and this time, I want you to take George Allen with you."

Steven did not change his expression, but he had little hope of getting Allen in to see the monk. It was unlikely the monk trusted the CIA. Ambassador Taylor was pushing, and Steven did not expect Tri Quang to give in.

"When do you want me to go?"

"President Johnson wants this silent endorsement as soon as possible. He feels it's critical to the bombing mission on the North."

Steven got up from the chair and saluted. "I'll get ready, Mr. Ambassador."

Steven and CIA Analyst George Allen arrived at the Buddhist Temple where Thich Tri Quang had been residing. Several monks met them as they entered the Hall of Heavenly Kings. Steven informed them of their desire to speak with Tri Quang again. The monks told them he was not here. Steven asked when he would return. One of the monks spun around: "He won't be back. After his last visit, he felt he should go to another location to protect his safety.

Steven frowned. "He knew he was safe with me."

The monk nodded. "Yes, with you, but we were concerned the Special Police may have followed you and discovered his location."

Steven looked over at Allen, then back at the remaining monk. "Will you take us to where he is?"

The monk walked back toward the two men then pointed at Steven. "We will take you." He pointed at Allen. "But not you."

Steven shook his head. "No deal."

The monk turned and started to walk toward the back of the middle alter.

Steven turned to George Allen. "What do we do, Mr. Allen?"

Allen bit his lower lip. "Damn it." Then whispered so that only Steven could hear: "We must get these questions answered for the President. You have to go." Allen reached in his hip pocket, pulled out a piece of paper and handed it to Steven. "Get these answered. Tri Quang cannot know that the President wants these answers. From Lodge's notes, he believes Tri Quang is power hungry. Taylor concurs. If he knows this is for Johnson. He may use it against us."

Steven nodded at Allen then turned and shouted at the monk. "Okay, I will go alone."

The monk stopped in his tracks, turned and slowly walked back to where both men were standing. "We must put a hood on you to keep his location a secret."

Steven's insides twisted. *A Negro man allowing another man to put a hood over his head.* Not to mention he was in a country surrounded by Viet Cong. Moreover, he still was not sure that he trusted Tri Quang that much. Steven walked back over to George Allen. "I don't know?"

Allen looked at the ground. "If they kidnap you, we'll send a team to find you. You are on a mission for the President."

With those words, Steven knew that to regain his honor, he had no choice but to follow through with the mission. "Well that's reassuring." Steven laughed. He turned and walked straight up to the orange clad monk. "Let's go."

The monk turned to Allen. "Go back to the Embassy. We will make sure the he is returned."

Steven nodded toward Allen, then followed the monk.

They continued to walk down the hallway then outside to a small, waiting Renault. As Steven was ready to get in the car, two other monks appeared; one was carrying a black cloth hood. Steven stood up straight and defiantly looked at the monks. He tried to be cool on the outside, but his heart pounded in his chest. They motioned for him to stoop down; as soon as he did they slipped the bag over his head.

Steven assumed they would travel on back roads. In a small car with a black hood over his head he would stick out more than the other passengers. They drove for what Steven estimated was a good forty-five minutes, making many turns. When they finally stopped, they did not remove the black hood. Steven drew a deep breath to see if there were any unique smells that would tip him where he was. It was quiet, no traffic or inner city sounds. The monks walked him several steps before telling him to be careful on the three steps to enter.

Steven was walked through several different areas before they stopped. He heard the monk's voice. "Close your eyes, so that we might remove your hood." Steven closed his eyes just in time as the hood was pulled off. Steven blinked several times then quickly looked around.

The monk nodded. "Are you all right, Mr. Hebert?"

Steven nodded without speaking. His training allowed him to regain his wits about him faster than most humans but having the hood on for that long was disorienting.

The monk waved his arm. Steven walked down the windowless hallway. He still had no idea where he was. After a few steps, the monk stopped and waved his arm toward a closed door. Steven stepped up to the door and knocked on it. A muffled voice on the other side said, "Enter."

Steven opened the door and once again found Thich Tri Quang seated on a mat in a lotus position. Steven once again sat down on the floor and leaned against the wall. He stretched his legs across the floor toward the Tri Quang. "Why did you think after meeting with me that you had to move?"

Tri Quang nodded. "I am not in a position to trust many people. I don't know who is following who and who is watching who. I am sorry for how we had to put a hood over your head. For a colored man it must have been *very*... difficult. We do understand."

270

Steven thought he would be clear about his position. "The Embassy wanted some answers and had some requests of you. Ambassador Taylor wanted George Allen to come and talk with you. But he was not permitted."

Tri Quang pursed his lips. "I do not know George Allen. I have been told he is CIA. Since I do not know the man, I could not take any chances."

Steven drew a deep breath. "You do not trust the CIA?"

Tri Quang frowned. "Again, I don't trust many people. I cannot afford to do so."

Tri Quang looked at Steven, seemingly waiting for him to speak.

Steven finally reached in his pocket and pulled out the slip of paper George Allen had given him. Steven read over the paper then began. "Has your opinion of President Khanh changed recently?"

"Khanh is weak. At any point he could decide that I'm causing the Buddhist and student protests, which is not true."

Steven knew the monk was behind the protests but was there a special meaning to his remark. "So you are not the organizer of these protests?"

The monk stared straight at Steven. "Perception is not always reality."

Steven decided not to pursue the subject further and glanced at the piece of paper. Steven read out loud the next question.

Steven looked straight at the monk. "How would you react if the United States started bombing the North?"

Tri Quang looked down at the ground for a long time then put his hands together in a prayer position. "The Buddhist leadership and the people would approve. I told you before, Khanh is weak and I don't trust him. Such a decision by the US would show strength in these military measures. I can tell from your expression this surprised you. While we are peaceful religion, there is wisdom in this decision, as it could shorten the conflict and result in fewer deaths, certainly of many innocent in the South."

Steven nodded. "So why don't you trust Khanh? Since Diem's removal there has been several leaders of South Vietnam. Are there any that you believed in?"

Tri Quang squinted and pursed his lips. "Let me say, there are still too many Diemists in government and military."

Steven knew not to push too hard if he wanted to come back. Or better still, bring back someone from the State Department. *This diplomatic stuff was not pleasant and I'm certainly not suited for it.*

Tri Quang closed his eyes and tilted his head back. "Major Hebert, do you have any more questions?"

Steven stood up. "As a matter of good faith, would you be willing to meet with someone from the Embassy? You can imagine this is not my forte and it isn't…"

Tri Quang paused for a moment licked his lips then nodded. "You are ready to return to the Embassy?"

"I was not of the impression we were finished."

Tri Quang stood up and moved toward the door.

Steven dreaded having that black hood go back over his head, but this time he was somewhat more confident they would take him back to the Embassy. He resisted the urge to repeat his question and moved toward the door.

As Steven grabbed the doorknob, Tri Quang spoke, "I'll agree to meet someone from the Embassy, as long as it is not Ambassador Taylor. It must be at a place of mutual convenience for my safety."

Steven turned back toward the monk, cracked half a smile, then exited the room. As soon as he was outside Tri Quang's room, he was met by the three monks, who had escorted him to wherever he was. One of the monks was holding the hood that was about to go over his head.

Steven drew a deep breath, stared at all three monks, then bent over to have the hood placed over his head. They gently grabbed him by each arm and started walking him through the structure. Steven lost track of how many steps he took before exiting the building. He guessed he was at a different door. This time he smelled incense when he walked, and there were no steps down to the parking lot to enter the car. When the car took off, the motor sounded different. Steven squirmed around in his seat; he felt like he had more room. It was definitely a different car. The drive was much longer than before. There were more turns on this trip. Steven began to wonder if he was in fact being taken back to the US Embassy. He tried to listen to the sounds of his surroundings as they drove. They still seemed to be in Saigon. Finally, the car stopped. The three monks were speaking Vietnamese, Steven heard one of the monks in the front seat say, "Tiếng cho rời bỏ đây." Steven understood every word. The monk on his left was advocating leaving Steven here. After a few more minutes of discussion, they pulled his hood off. Steven looked around. He did not recognize exactly where he was.

They pulled back into traffic and drove several more blocks. When they drove up to the Cambodian Embassy, Steven knew where they were and that is where they stopped. Where Steven had stood and helplessly watched the Thich Quang Duc burn himself to death. The one monk who had spoken to him throughout this process said, "We are leaving you here. You probably don't remember, but I was one of the monks who grabbed you last year when you tried to stop Thich Quang Duc from his self-immolation. We wished to remind you of how serious we are of our cause. Much like the negroes have a cause in the United States, we, the Buddhist monks, have a cause in Vietnam. You must tell your government to ponder these things. You have witnessed firsthand how serious we are. Deliver that message."

Steven got out of the car and turned to watch the monks drive off. His focus shifted to the intersection in the street where the self-immolation had occurred. *The monks wield considerable power in this country. Plus they*

have rallied the students to their side. Could US officials comprehend how
badly this might play out?

SAME DAY
WASHINGTON DC

Rita Sullivan sat in her small apartment, periodically trying to reach Senator Morse on the phone in his office. In an effort to calm herself, she had a radio on the jazz music station in the background. Even tapping her foot to her favorite Count Basie songs, her frustrations increased as time passed. She even danced herself around the room when "One O'Clock Jump" came on.

Senator Morse had told her to call at any time if something went wrong with her newspaper job. It had. She had gone to the library earlier in the day to research the senator; he first came to Congress as a Republican, then had switched to Independent, and now he was a Democrat. Had he changed for his constituents or his philosophy? Rita was in college during his brief unsuccessful run for the Democratic Nominee for President in 1960.

Finally, at 10:15 PM someone answered the phone. Rita asked to speak to the senator. The female voice on the other end of the phone advised her that the senator and all of his aides were out. Rita bit her lower lip, then asked to have the senator call her as soon as possible. For some reason her irritation grew when she was asked for her phone number.

Within a few minutes, Rita's phone rang. She quickly picked up: "Hello."

"Miss Sullivan, this is Senator Morse. I am sending a driver to pick you up. It's imperative I meet with you this evening."

Rita ran her fingers through her blonde hair. "Finally returned my call. And don't bother sending a car for me. Nothing I have done—"

"There is some information that I must show you.

Rita interrupted the senator. "Excuse me, why did it take you so long to return my call? Meeting with you hasn't worked out so well for me. I have lost my job because of my reporting. You said you would help me."

Senator Morse paused for a moment. "Miss Sullivan, I have some major developments. I want you to break this story."

Rita laughed. "So you are not aware I have been trying to call you over the last couple of days?"

The senator cleared his throat. "I was aware of one of your phone calls, but I have been out of my office since the Senate vote. As you can imagine, I'm pretty much 'persona non grata' around the Capital Building."

Frustrated, Rita shook her head. "Look, Senator Morse, I'm not really worried about your problems at the moment. Did you hear me? I am out of a job and it's your fault. And I distinctly remember you promising me another job."

There was silence on the other end. "It is essential we meet tonight. Please, come down and meet my car."

"Okay, but you better be able to find me a job on a newspaper." Rita slammed the phone down.

Rita picked up her purse and charged out of her apartment. She stomped up the street looking for limousine. About halfway up the block, Rita noticed a black Cadillac on the opposite side of the street with a man reading a newspaper, in the dark. *That's very weird.* Rita put her head down and picked up her pace. After just a few more steps, she saw the senator's car approaching.

When it stopped, before the driver could get out to open the door, Rita grabbed the handle and slipped in. She glanced back at the black Cadillac. As they drove by it, she pulled out her steno pad with the intention of getting the number off the license plate but it was not illuminated. The limo driver continued to maneuver the back streets until they were beside a restaurant on the far west side of Washington DC. The driver opened the petition to inform her that the senator was waiting for her inside.

Rita calmly pulled out her compact, checked her hair and lipstick before exiting the limousine. The senator was the only one in the quiet restaurant surrounded on both sides by his aides. Rita rapidly walked over to the table and sat down without being invited, then stared at the senator.

The senator looked at Rita. "There are a few things we need to discuss. As you can imagine, Senator Gruening and I are not very popular at the moment. This is the last time we can meet, but I need to tell you some things first."

Rita frowned. "What do you mean? As I said earlier, you could have told me this on the phone."

A cute waitress showed up to the table and flirted with one of the aides before asking Rita for her order. Rita asked for a glass of sweet tea.

Senator Morse paused while the waitress remained at the table, then he glanced at both aides, shushing them. The waitress turned and walked away. Rita thought the girl was playing up to the senator and his two aides.

Senator Morse continued. "I assume by now you know I have always been on a list around here. You know since Senator McCarthy went after me. I thought time had kind of swept that under the rug, but in the last twenty-four hours has proven that I may still be on that list."

Rita wondered if this was at least part of why the man was sitting in the black Cadillac, reading the newspaper in the dark. Maybe the senator had been watched longer than the last twenty-four hours. Now, she may have been added to the watch list.

"Well, again," Rita said, "you could have told me that over the phone. What was so important that we meet?"

Senator Morse lowered his head. "If we continue to meet, it could become too dangerous for both of us. I can put you—"

Rita interrupted him. "*What the hell do you mean* too dangerous?

The senator shook his head and stared hard. "I am afraid President Johnson will, shall we say, keep an eye on me. You know Bobby Baker's boys and others. I can't let you get drawn into this web."

Just then the waitress returned to the table with Rita's sweet tea and topped off the other's coffee cups. She asked if they were ready to order. Everybody shook their heads no.

While the waitress was at the table, Rita thought again of the man in the black Cadillac. It might be too late; she may already be on the list. "What if I am already on it? I'm afraid."

Senator Morse shook his head. "I will check, but I'm sure I still have enough power to keep you off it. I think."

Rita interrupted again. "*You think.* What good is that doing me?"

Senator Morse stuck his tongue in the side of his check. "They are after me, you are in the press. The government *expects* the press to be liberal. They want it that way. Besides the people that are after me won't go after women. They don't operate that way. If you distance yourself from me, you should be okay. What I was about to say is, I can get you a job with a phone call to the *Register–Guard* out in Eugene, Oregon. Also, I can put people with stories and events in touch with you. If you can write, you will be a national reporter before too long."

Rita sat up straight with that comment. This was risky but it might just catapult her into the spotlight she longed for. "So, you are trying to tell me that these creeps have morals. They won't go after women?"

The senator nodded. "They have never taken it that far in the past. So yes, this shadowing will likely stop with me... and Senator Gruening."

Rita did not get a lot of comfort from that, but she also thought it might be too late. Rita reached in her purse and pulled out some tightly folded papers. She unfolded them and placed them on the table. With the heel of her hand, she attempted to press out the folds. She got them as flat as she thought she could and handed them to the closest aid.

The table sat quietly while he passed the papers to the senator. He quickly ran his finger over the pages, reading. He passed each page to an aide who quickly read and passed them it back to the senator. Once they had completed their review, Rita spoke.

"*The Register–Guard* will need a sample of my unprinted writing to see what my capabilities are."

Senator Morse shook his head. "They won't need it. They'll do what I ask."

Rita saw both aides nod in affirmation.

As the senator slipped the papers in his pocket and looked at Rita. "You will get a phone call from the executive editor within the next couple of days."

This brought a half smile to Rita's face. She finally took her first sip of her iced tea. "I am ready to get back to work. This is…"

Senator Morse held his hand up to stop her. "As I originally said, this is the last time I am going to meet with you. However, if you are okay with all this, I want to also get you connected into the network of people who will help you get the truth out."

Rita didn't understand exactly what he was trying to tell her. "What do you mean, network of people who want the truth out?"

Senator Morse rubbed his mouth with his right hand. "Young lady, I'm afraid we are about to enter into an unauthorized war in Vietnam. The whole reason I voted against the Tonkin Resolution was Congress was giving the President a lot of power, and we only have the authority to authorize war under the War Powers Act. This is a real concern to me. He was going to get the votes, but he still strong-armed some of the senators. I want the press to keep the people advised of what is really going on."

Rita could see how serious Morse was about the authority this resolution had granted. She still felt there was more to the story. She had nothing to lose.

"Congressional War Powers Act. That's what this is about? Sorry, not buying it. What is your position on Vietnam, really?"

The senator frowned. "Young lady, you have no right to ask me that."

Rita got up from the table. "Yes, I do. I'm done here." Rita turned toward the door.

"Where are you going?"

Rita turned back to him. "I'm getting on a bus and getting out of here. I've put myself in a very bad position."

Morse continued. "What do you mean *a bad position*?"

Rita turned and pointed at him. "You have no principals. This is just to keep yourself in a position of power. I'm out of here."

Morse stayed very calm. "You can't take a bus home from here. You'll be on buses all night getting home. We can't give you a ride home, but the same limousine is sitting outside to take you home."

Rita turned and walked out the door.

A half-hour limousine ride back across town, and when the cab turned down her street, she peered around intently for the black Cadillac. It was not there. *Rita did not know whether to feel relieved or not. Perhaps a man had been there shadowing the senator, but how would he know the senator was going to meet with her. Was the senator's phone tapped or was hers? Was this the same man who had watched her two meeting with Mary Meyer? His presence could not logically be explained.*

Rita got out of the cab and slowly walked the steps to her apartment. She set her purse down on the kitchen table and went over to the refrigerator. She looked in causally, then closed it again. Time for bed. She picked up the picture of her mother holding her with her father looking on and stared at it for a minute. It relieved a little bit of her tension. Despite the fact she was unemployed, she wanted to stay in her routine. She slowly proceeded to her bedroom.

Rita had been asleep for less than an hour when her phone rang. She started to cover her head with the pillow as she looked at the clock. Senator Morse said the name of the newspaper; it was in Oregon. They were three hours behind her time. She focused and picked up the phone.

The voice on the other end of the phone said, "Miss Sullivan, we have some advice for you: Stay away from Senator Morse and his false stories."

Before Rita could reply, the voice continued. "You better listen to me, young lady. We don't want you to have a bad accident and end up injured or dead in a ravine. You are too pretty of a girl to have something like that happen to you."

The line went dead.

Chapter Twenty-Seven

August 15, 1964
Saigon

Tao paced around his back office contemplating his next move. Lansdale had ordered him back to Saigon to keep his eye on developments. He wondered how much of him wanting to stay in Saigon had to do with the drug operation of the French Corsicans, the CIA, and Vang Pao. *Must get this out of my head if my country is to survive. Must I learn to look the other way?* One thing was certain, the loss of Plaines des Jarres made watching the Ho Chi Minh Trail a much greater risk.

Tao dreaded his next decision. Time to call Lansdale. He had not spoken with Lansdale in some time and events were stacking up fast. Tao went to the phone, dialed Lansdale.

"I wanted to check in," Tao said when Lansdale picked up. "We haven't talked in a while."

"Good. I need some good intel."

Tao paused and breathed deeply. "A couple of months ago, I escorted Shackley into Vang Pao's camp."

Lansdale mumbled something inaudible, then said, "If the Blonde Ghost has been there, something must be up."

Tao sniffed a couple of time. "Vang Pao had me escort him from Saigon to his camp. Came in and out of Saigon dark. Still met with Conein."

Lansdale almost screamed through the phone. "He came to get Conein's blessing!"

Quiet for a second, Tao could sense Lansdale thinking.

"You were ordered back to Saigon," Lansdale said. "When do you plan to follow my orders?"

Tao decided to sidestep his question. "I'll keep my eye on some developments. Like the Buddhist situation, and I'll watch around Saigon for Viet Cong activity."

Lansdale added to his list. "I like your plan to scout the Viet Cong's position around Saigon."

Tao took a deep breath. *Should I bring up the press inside knowledge? I'd Better.* "The Press already knows the truth about the Gulf of Tonkin situation, including Pham Xuan An." Tao held the phone away from his head.

Lansdale screamed, "That is unbelievable! How the *hell* did that happen?"

Tao put the phone back to his head. "I don't know that's what I want to find out."

Lansdale paused for a minute. "Johnson really snowed Congress on the Tonkin Resolution. What is going on with Hebert?"

Tao wiped his mouth. "Hebert has had little contact with Taylor or de Silva, but some with Allen. We have little from the Embassy."

"That figures."

Tao frowned. "What do you mean?"

"Since Dallas, he has been totally worthless. I have received zero information from the Embassy."

Tao nodded. "What happened in Dallas, anyway? He wouldn't tell me anything."

There was a long pause on the other end. So much so, Tao thought he had been disconnected. Finally, Lansdale replied, "We flew to Dallas together on November 21. I was recruiting for my team, wanted him involved. Anyway, I came back to Washington, he went with Howard Hunt. According to all I've been able to learn, the next morning, the driver came to get him to take him to the Trade Mart for the Kennedy speech and he wasn't there."

Tao let out a low whistle.

Lansdale continued, "I wrote him a letter covering his ass since I needed him back in the Embassy. I finally caught up with Hunt to get his version of the story. He said when he dropped Hebert off at the hotel that night, he was fine."

Tao sat down in the chair. "That doesn't add up."

"Hunt's story just didn't feel right, but I can't tell you why."

Tao rubbed his chin. "So, there are ten, twelve hours unaccounted for before the driver showed up."

"The only thing he has done of any significance since then was his mission with Nixon."

Tao pondered what he had just been told. It made sense: Hebert had never opened up about the events of November 22. "I figured you were involved in the Nixon thing. How is everything going in Washington? Much going on there?"

Lansdale growled, "I think I've been played like a fiddle. President Johnson is getting ready to bomb North Vietnam. I was promised I would return to Vietnam with my team several months ago and now Johnson has sent General Taylor."

"I would think bombing was a good thing?"

"Yes, of course. It was part of my proposal. But if you believe that that is all they will do... but I believe that as soon as the election is over, either Johnson or Goldwater will send in troops. Think about it—everybody Johnson has sent are army men."

Tao squinted as he absorbed what Lansdale had told him. "I told Hebert the same thing about the Army appointments. What do your other contacts say?"

Lansdale huffed over the phone. "Nothing. Get me some information until I can get over there."

The line went dead before Tao could say anything else. It had been years since he had had heard Lansdale that angry.

CHAPTER TWENTY-EIGHT

AUGUST 30, 1964

SAIGON

TAN SON NHUT AIRPORT

Tao was on an Air America flight destined for Saigon. Tao about had his scooter shop back open full time with a couple of men running the business. It was imperative he start watching the Viet Cong around Saigon. Also, he wished to get a better understanding of the Buddhist and student protests and their impact on the South Vietnamese government. Before leaving, Tao found several highly qualified, highly motivated men who could replace him trail watching. If they worked out, he could really limit his time in Laos.

Tao looked out the window as the plane made its final approach to Tan Son Nhut Airbase. The lights around Saigon looked peaceful from 5,000 feet. Tao knew it was anything but peaceful. Conflicts within the South

Vietnamese military brass were causing more battles within their military than with the Viet Cong. It occurred to him that it was a metaphor for his own life. He remained conflicted about not patrolling the Ho Chi Minh Trail, in the now long-shot hopes of ever finding the men who had killed his family. However, he needed to distance himself from the branch of the CIA that seemed interested in financing illicit drugs.

The plane glided to the runway with a gentle touch-down. As the plane taxied up to the Air America hanger operated by the CIA, Tao exited to the tarmac. He watched another Air America plane landing as he walked toward the CIA hanger. The flight deck commander had advised him it was arriving from Bangkok. Tao noticed several South Vietnamese officers standing in the shadows of a nearby hanger. They seemed to be trying to blend into the background as they watched the arriving plane.

Tao continued to the CIA hanger, grabbing one last glance of those South Vietnamese officers before checking in. All three of the duty clerks were standing at the one window looking out at the arriving Air America plane. The men were startled to see Tao walk in. *Had they not noticed him walking across the tarmac? These men were trained by the CIA. Why were they looking past?* Tao checked in and left.

Tao paced toward his old Peugeot, watching the Air America plane pull up on the tarmac. As soon as he felt he was hidden, he repositioned himself to watch. *Something must be up.* An Air Force officer deplaned. Tao strained to get a good look at the man. *I think I've seen this man before. Perhaps at Vang Pao's Long Tieng Camp. Yes, that's him. What is his name?*

Tao moved to get a better view. The Air Force officer was carrying two large suitcases as he walked toward the South Vietnamese officers. When they were all face to face, the Air Force Officer set down the two suitcases and made several gestures toward the officers. These gestures were exaggerated and not very friendly. *He must not know these officers. I wish I could hear their conversations.*

After a brief conversation, the Air Force officer motioned down at the suitcases and indicated they should be taken to the hanger. The men walked toward that hanger. Out of the corner of his eye, Tao noticed a black car driving up. Tao changed his focus from the officers to the black car then back to the group of officers. They did not notice or pay attention to the black car. Suddenly, the car stopped about one hundred feet from the three officers. Those officers still did not notice as they continued toward the dark hanger. *Was the driver of the black car supposed to join those officers?* The man who had emerged from the black car was wearing black slacks and a black windbreaker, started moving quickly toward the officers.

Tao scanned around the tarmac. Two of the three clerks from the CIA hanger came out and started walking toward the South Vietnamese officers and the air force officer. The South Vietnamese officers and air force officer entered the abandoned hanger. No lights came on. No one else on the tarmac seemed to be paying any attention. The CIA clerks started moving faster toward the abandoned hanger. Tao continued to observe all of the action from across the tarmac. The man dressed in black reached the abandoned hanger door, pulled a gun and entered. Tao started in the direction of the hanger, but before he could get within a hundred feet of the door the two CIA clerks saw him and pulled their guns. One motioned for Tao to stop. *I have no weapons, I don't have to be told twice to stop.*

Within a minute, the door to the abandoned hanger opened slowly. The air force officer slowly stepped out with his hands behind his back. Behind him the man in black struggled to carry the two suitcases in one hand. Tao couldn't see the other hand but assumed it still held the gun. *Was this a robbery?* As soon as they were outside, the man in black ordered the air force officer to stop. He set down the two suitcases and pointed his gun at the two CIA clerks. They stopped in their tracks. The man pulled a badge and held it with his other hand

He identified himself as Bowman Taylor, an agent with the Federal Bureau of Narcotics, an agency Tao had never heard of. Agent Taylor positioned himself between his car and air force officer. He struggled to pick up the two suitcases with one hand, shuffling backwards toward his car. He noticed Tao, apparently for the first time, and pointed the gun at him. He ordered Tao to show his hands. Tao wasn't going to eat a bullet over a situation he knew nothing about and held his open hands high.

Agent Taylor resumed carrying the two suitcases toward his car. Taylor nervously scanned the tarmac. Finally, he put down the suitcases and started to drag them backwards toward his car. When he had finally made it to the car, he pushed the air force officer into the back seat, then opened the trunk and tossed the suitcases in, all the while shifting his eyes and gun back and forth between Tao and the two CIA clerks.

What the hell happened to the South Vietnamese officers? Tao wondered. *I didn't hear any shots.*

Agent Taylor slipped into the front seat and pointed his gun out the window as he backed the car rapidly across the tarmac. He threw the car into drive and spun around, accelerating as he drove away.

Tao looked at the two CIA clerks, who ignored him as they ran back toward the CIA hanger. Tao followed them and leaned beside the door. He paused, took a deep breath, and passed through the open door.

Tao couldn't see anyone in the dark. He fumbled around until he found a light switch. No one in the large structure. No bodies either. *What the hell had just happened?* As Tao investigated, he found a door in the back of the hanger. The South Vietnamese officers must have exited there. *Did the FBN agent let them go or could he not control all those men and grabbed the contraband? Likely, he let them go. He had no authority over South Vietnamese.*

Not much of a mystery to be solved in the hanger. The real mystery had left. Tao needed answers, but they were not here.

Tao had gotten a message to Steven Hebert asking they meet that evening. The incident the night before still weighed on his mind. It was the drug bust. Was one government organization starting a war with another government agency? Not as uncommon as one would think, but this was different. Some agency was taking on the CIA, one of the most powerful agencies in the world. *They may be signing their own death warrant.*

Tao had never heard of the Federal Bureau of Narcotics until the previous night. If they were real, they were likely not very large, certainly not big enough to take on the CIA. Tao had seen first-hand how even the FBI had fared against the CIA: They lost. However, that battle was ongoing, Hoover against whoever was running the CIA. *But the Federal Bureau of*

Narcotics? Tao knew at some point Agent Bowman Taylor would lose, but Tao wanted to find out what was really going on…

Tao's thoughts were interrupted by a pounding on the back door. Major Hebert was on time. Tao opened the door to let him in. Before Hebert could speak, Tao proceeded to lay out the events of the night before. Before Major Hebert could respond, Tao said, "I know just what we are going to do. We're going to go talk to *Lieutenant Colonel Lucien Conein.*"

Steven cracked a smile. "Count me in. When do you want to do this?"

Tao pounded his fist on the table. "Now."

Steven started laughing. "Where to?"

Tao looked frustrated, then sheepish. "Let's go to his favorite bar?"

"The Caravelle Hotel."

Tao nodded. "That's always a good place to start."

Once in Steven's vehicle, Tao said, "Can't wait to see Conein's face when we walk in together."

Steven sat silently for a few blocks, then started singing.

"Stars shining bright above you,

Night breeze seem to whisper,

I love you.

Birds singin' in the sycamore trees,

Dream a little dream of me."

Tao started laughing while he was singing. "You *must* love that song."

"Yea, was my Father's favorite song. Pops into my head often."

They pulled up in front of the Caravelle Hotel. Tao pointed to his left.

"There's his jeep. What do you think?"

Steven squinted. "We walk in together, just like you said. You know he'l have some of his boys around him."

Tao nodded. "Head on."

"Head on."

Steven pulled into the parking place and drew a deep breath. Tao reached over and gently punched him in the arm. "Ready?"

"Ready."

Tao and Steven entered the bar, and it was obvious where Lucien Conein was. Tao looked around—no one seemed to notice. He waved his hand low to Steven. Each moved in opposite directions from one another, circling around toward Conein. When Tao got within ten feet of Conein, three of Conein's men pulled guns and pointed them at Tao and Steven. Tao and Steven stopped in their tracks. Conein leaned on the bar as he looked at both men.

"Well, if it isn't *my favorite tizzun and the gook*. You guys couldn't sneak up on a corpse in a coffin." Conein let out a big belly laugh as he waved at his men to put down their guns.

The gesture did not relieve either Tao or Steven. Conein pointed toward a nearby booth and walked over to where four Vietnamese sat. Conein kicked the table, sending the drinks in the air. He sharply snapped his thumb over his shoulder, and the Vietnamese men scurried away. Conein shouted at the bartender.

"This table is a mess! Send someone to clean it up, *immediately*!"

Conein pointed at the table and held up three fingers. The three men sat down just as the waiter arrived to clean up the spilled alcohol and the six glasses. Another waiter quickly showed up at the table with three shots of tequila. Conein shouted so that everyone in the bar would hear: "The worm belongs to my little gook friend!"

Tao leaned forward. "Colonel Conein, we need to talk. I saw something at the airport last night, and I need to know what I saw."

Conein grabbed the shot of tequila, threw it down, and growled at Tao. "Agent Taylor is barking up the wrong tree. He has no idea who he is messing with."

Tao pressed. "Who was the air force officer who flew in on the Air America flight?"

Conein looked at both men. "You boys don't like my hospitality. You haven't enjoyed the beverages I had brought to the table."

Tao picked up the drink and swirled it around then downed it.

Conein looked at Steven, who shook his head. "Not interested, Colonel."

Conein let out a loud laugh, grabbed Steven's shot glass, and chugged it down. He slammed the empty glass down on the table. He leaned forward.

"The man who came in on the plane is none of your business. Now do you have more dumb questions?"

Tao leaned forward and whispered, "This opium movement is driving me crazy, Colonel. I want to help Vang Pao, I want to fight the Viet Cong. Is the CIA more concerned with drugs than fighting the enemy?"

Conein knocked all the shot glasses off the table with a quick backhand. "Outside. *Now.*"

Steven looked at Tao and nodded. Conein's men got up from the table and walked toward the door. Conein held his hand down, pushing toward the floor, indicating they should stop. Conein, Tao, and Steven exited the bar. When they got to Steven's vehicle, Conein pulled a toothpick out of his pocket and leaned against Steven's vehicle.

Tao folded his arm on his chest. "Now, answer my question about the opium business going on right under the nose of the US."

Steven was nodding while staring at Conein.

Conein rubbed his jaw. "You both are getting a little pushy, but I'm going to give you children a lesson. Tao, where is Vang Pao operating?"

"Laos, why?"

Conein huffed. "Who is working with Vang Pao? And, where do they get their funding?"

Steven jumped in. "Colonel, we all know the CIA gets their funding from Congress. What's your point?"

Conein shook his head. "You boys must have missed that day in civics class. The US government officially doesn't know we…" Conein pointed at all three of them. "Operate in Laos, so it is not officially funded. Tao, I know you know this because you have sat in on meetings in Vang Pao's office with the French Corsican Brotherhood."

Both Tao and Steven nodded.

"Our entire operation is funded off the books, so we had to come up with a way. We picked a *very select few* Air America pilots we could trust. The others don't *even* know about this operation. Vang Pao knows when they are scheduled to fly in. Surely, I don't have to explain more."

Tao drew a deep breath. "What is going to happen to the air force officer?"

Conein pushed off the vehicle and started walking back inside. Before he re-entered the building, he shouted back, "Watch and learn."

Tao stared blankly at Steven. Steven reached over and despondently grabbed his shoulder. "Let's go."

Tao pushed his hand away and walked around the other side of the vehicle without saying a word.

LATE NIGHT

AUGUST 31, 1964

NEW ORLEANS

Carlos Marcello was sitting in his limousine along the waterfront with the lights off. Workers at the commercial loading dock moved about paying little attention to the limousine. His two bodyguards sat silently in the front seat. Marcellos looked down at his watch. *Those two new bozos are late again. I'm going to have to shape them up or get rid of them if they don't get their act together.* After a few more minutes, a black Lincoln drove through a gate about four hundred yards ahead. They drove past the several dock workers performing various tasks. The Lincoln pulled alongside Marcello's limo and stopped.

Marcello leaned up toward the front seat. "Get their money and see what they want? Then get it out of the trunk."

His bodyguards both exited the limo, the one on the passenger's side pulled his gun and pointed at the two men in the Lincoln. Then he gestured to the two men to get out of their car. They got out, and the driver moved around to confront them. Marcello carefully watched the two men pass a bank bag to his driver then watched as the three men talked and made various hand gestures. The two men continued to glance back and forth from the backseat window where Marcello was sitting to the man holding a gun on them. They walked around to the trunk of the limousine and the driver opened it. Marcello could hear some shuffling in the trunk then watched them walk around to their Lincoln, open their trunk, and place the packages inside. As the two men walked back to their car, Marcello rolled down his window.

"You two, listen to me. I want the names of all the dealers in your group and what colleges and cities they are covering. I want more dealers in more colleges, so I want to see what areas are covered. If you guys can't do it, I'll get someone who can. Do you hear me? You guys are loafing too much."

The two men made eye contact with him and together replied. "Yes, Sir, Mr. Marcello. Anything you need, Sir. We haven't been…"

Marcello cut them off with a wave of his hand out the window. "I want that list in two weeks. Push your dealers harder. If you have to rough them up a little, do it. I need more sales or I'm cutting you all off. Find some people who can produce, do you hear me?"

"Yes, Sir, Mr. Marcello."

As Marcello rolled up the window, he shouted, "Don't be late again or I'm cutting you off. My time is too important to waste on people like you."

He watched the two men get in the Lincoln and drive off slowly. His bodyguards slipped back into the limo. The driver turned around and handed him the bank bag with the money. Marcello leaned forward and pointed ahead. "Pull up to that man standing at the end of the dock."

The driver pulled up to the man with the blonde hair standing on the very edge of the dock and stopped. He told his men to stay put and turn up the radio. Marcello got out of the car and walked over to the man with the horn-rimmed glasses. "Ted, I'll have that list for you in two weeks. Did you get the pictures of those two goons working for me?"

Shackley didn't respond to the question, but pulled the camera partway out of his pocket for Marcello to see. "I let that list slip into the right hands of the FBI, so they have some people to watch. That will keep their focus right where we want it. Anybody but you and Trafficante. You can afford to lose that small network, right? Those guys don't know they are being set up?"

Marcello nodded, as he took two more steps up beside Shackley and both men starred out on the New Orleans Harbor. He pulled his fedora down.

"No, they have no clue. Too new to know the difference. They did me a favor. One of my bookies was carrying markers too long. They wanted into my operation, so I let them run some product for me, so I've been setting this up."

The two men looked out of the harbor. Marcello reached in his breast pocket and pulled out a cigar.

"Are you making progress with Vang Pao? Trafficante says you are. What do you say?"

Shackley pushed his glasses back up on his nose. "Real progress. Everything is almost in place. Conein knows what's going on but I'm not sure he wants in the middle of this. He'll still get a cut, but he's still tight with the Corsicans. We have to be careful."

Marcello started chewing on the cigar as he drew a deep breath. "You make sure when the FBI gets that list, they just go after those kids and those two bozos."

Shackley turned his head and made eye contact. "I got this handled. With the heat getting turned up we're prepared. The FBI will need to bring down some drug networks. Just be sure this won't impact your operation?"

Marcello finally lit the cigar as he spoke. "They'll disappear before they get caught, I'll see to it. They just are small-time marijuana dealers with some occasional opium or hashish. They don't know anything about my herion operation and I intend to keep it that way. As to the college kids, the FBI will bust them then scare them. I need to let this happen. There are three FBI agents here in the city that have been watching me for about a year. This will give them something. Hell, Shackley, I'm just a real estate investor you know." Marcello blew out some smoke as he raised both arms and laughed.

Shackley looked back out on the harbor. "We don't need any screw ups in this operation."

Marcello took a big draw off his cigar. "By the time you're ready to move H and O, I'll have my network in place from Alabama through Texas."

His hair ruffled by the sea breeze, Shackley tried to push it back in place. "Good. I'll be here in two weeks."

Marcello waved his cigar in a circular motion. "I'll wire you some money in your Cayman account, as agreed."

He went back to his car and signaled for his driver to drive on. He turned around and looked back for Shackley. The Blonde Ghost had disappeared.

Chapter Twenty-Nine

September 1, 1964
Saigon

Lieutenant Colonel Lucien Conein reached in the drawer for his favorite pearl-handled .357 Magnum revolver then placed his Aussie bush hat on his head. He looked in the large mirror next to his front door. It was time to leave for a meeting he dreaded. His appointment was with both Ambassador Maxwell D. Taylor and CIA Station Chief Peer de Silva.

Conein had just returned the night before from a meeting with South Vietnamese President Khanh at his residence in Da Lat. Conein was tired of dealing with the South Vietnamese generals; they were always whining about something. Worse yet, now he had to meet with Ambassador Taylor, who was treating the generals as though they should be taking orders from him. President Johnson could not have selected a less political individual to fill a very political role. Conein had grown weary of all the politics that seemed now to dominate his life. As he walked to his jeep he longed for the days of fighting with the French Underground or help Lansdale sabotage the North Vietnamese. He looked at himself in the jeep's rearview mirror. *I miss drinking all night then going out to kill a few enemy and blow stuff up.*

Conein walked into the front door of the US Embassy in Saigon, where he was met by Major Steven Hebert. Conein decided to play it stoic. He informed Steven he was early for his scheduled meeting with Peer de Silva. They walked silently up the hallway to de Silva's office where Major Hebert knocked on the door. After Steven informed de Silva from the other side of the door that Conein had arrived, de Silva opened the door to let Conein in. He dismissed Steven, and Conein took off his Aussie bush hat and sat opposite the Station Chief.

De Silva initiated the conversation. "What did you learn from General Khanh?"

Conein scratched his chin. "What the hell do you think I learned? He is tired of Ambassador Taylor belittling him, treating him like... Anyway, Khanh requested I deliver the message directly to the Ambassador."

De Silva shook his head. "You know this is not a good idea?"

Conein looked at him and smacked the table. "You think I really care? You think General Taylor is going intimidate me? He can save his attitude for Khanh or you or anybody else. What's he going to do, fire me? I'm the only one over here these generals trust."

De Silva squinted at Conein, then raised his eyebrows as he got up from his desk. "Come on. Let's go."

The two men walked toward the exit then to the grounds where the tennis courts were located. When the two men arrived, Ambassador Taylor had just walked off the court with a towel around his head. Taylor saw them and pointed to a shady spot near one of the embassy compound buildings.

Conein nonchalantly walked to the shady spot, took off his Aussie bush hat and began fanning himself. "I was asked to deliver a message directly to you from President Khanh."

Ambassador Taylor look went from distain to total disgust. "What *does* the President of South Vietnam have to say that I haven't already heard?"

Conein began listing all the grievances of the Khanh Administration—Taylor, in particular—including being treated with a total lack of respect. Conein could tell Ambassador Taylor was barely listening as he fidgeted with the strings on his racquet.

After Conein finished relaying his message, Ambassador Taylor made eye contact with Conein for the first time. "Are you sure you understood the French that President Khanh was speaking in your meeting?"

Conein was beyond his own limits with Ambassador Taylor, tilted his head back. "Who knows, I've only been speaking their language since 1946.

You be the judge, Mr. Ambassador." Conein maintained eye contact while deciding he'd said enough. It was best to hold his tongue at this point, something he had always struggled with.

Ambassador Taylor looked at de Silva, then at Conein. "That will be all, Lieutenant Colonel."

Conein put his hat back on, turned and walked away as fast as he could. He was trying to show respect for the office of the US Ambassador. It was an extreme test. As he walked he heard Ambassador Taylor tell de Silva to meet him in the office first thing in the morning to discuss Conein and his revelations from "our good South Vietnamese." Conein knew the Ambassador's remarks had been made so he heard them. He also knew he did not need Taylor as much as Taylor needed him. Nobody on the Indochinese peninsula had a better relationship with the South Vietnamese generals: He knew it and they knew it.

As Conein walked around the corner where his jeep was parked, he saw Steven leaning on it. The last thing he wanted was to have another unwanted conversation. "Shouldn't you be protecting the Ambassador or some secretary?"

Steven replied, "Maybe I am."

Conein tilted his head back and jacked his jaw. "What the hell do you want? I have very little patience for you or anyone else."

Steven nodded. "I just want to know what the hell is going on."

Conein squinted, "You aren't entitled to know anything, but since you are here working for Lansdale, I'll tell you this: Tell your boss he better get his ass over here soon or this whole situation in Vietnam is going very bad. I've just about had it with this entire shit storm."

Steven straightened up. "What do you mean?"

Conein decided to give Steven something to really think about. "Johnson has screwed this up royal. Westmoreland wants US troops only doing the fighting. Johnson doesn't want the South Vietnamese involved, then he sends Taylor over here as an ambassador. The man has no diplomatic experience and is ordering all the South Vietnamese around like they are subordinates. As I told you and your little gook friend, Vang Pao is the only one fighting the commies and our own government is trying to kill my financing with that goof ball narcotics agent over here arresting people. I have that handled for now, but I'm getting tired of all this incompetence. I need some help and I think Lansdale is the only one who can help me. Now get out of my way before I lose my patience with you. Be a good boy, tell Lansdale."

SEPTEMBER 1, 1964

WASHINGTON DC

WHITE HOUSE

President Johnson finished his meeting with his campaign adviser. The man was nothing more than a figurehead. Johnson was running this campaign and everybody knew it, including the adviser. They just needed to sit back and let Republican candidate Barry Goldwater continue to make far-right statements and mistakes on the campaign trail and the election should be in the bag. *No surprises.*

Both men believed that Goldwater's slogan, "In your heart, you know he's right" was not inspired or inspiring. Johnson wanted his campaign manager to find some individuals who would make commercials saying that Goldwater was a member of the John Birch Society. Johnson continued to read over the official Republican campaign brochures, plus all the notes that surrogates had brought him. *The man has come right out and all but said he would use tactical nuclear weapons in Vietnam. Most Americans won't support that position.*

President Johnson was snapped back to his surroundings by the buzz of the intercom. Gerri advised him that his attorney and adviser Abe Fortas had arrived. Fortas was shown into the Oval Office by a Secret Service Agent and proceeded to the couch. President Johnson remained at his desk, reading. Fortas sat quietly until Johnson asked him about the legal issues surrounding Johnson's association with Bobby Baker. Fortas, who also represented Baker, handled the questions with legal jargon. Johnson reiterated his concern as the election approached that the corruption related to Baker was going to come back to the Senate floor and that Goldwater would use the information against him. Johnson knew Goldwater was smart enough not to let it come directly from his campaign but from some of his larger supporters.

President Johnson had concerns about Director J. Edgar Hoover, who up until now had killed information regarding kickbacks and Baker's association with the Mafia. Johnson got up from his desk, walked over to the window and peered out. Johnson and Hoover were tight, but Johnson knew that Hoover served Hoover first. If it came down to protecting one or the other, Johnson knew he would finish in second place. The fight would be very ugly, as both men had so much on each other. Fortas reassured him that nothing new regarding his relationship with Baker would come up before the election. The legal process was too complicated.

President Johnson relaxed with that bit of news. He walked over to the couch and stood towering over Fortes for a moment. His demeanor changed as he sat down on the couch.

"I'm going to win this election." Johnson sat quietly for a minute. "Abe, you and Dulles have the Warren Commission under control. Goldwater signed off on the Gulf of Tonkin Resolution and that took the Vietnam issue off the table. No more problems in Vietnam then my only problem is Baker."

Fortas pinched his nose with thumb and fore finger. "You said the Vietnam issue is off the table? Are you sure?"

Johnson leaned forward. "Yes, on the US involvement side, but I'm still concerned about the political side and how the press covers it."

Fortas shook his head. "The press has been on your side so far. Why would they turn on you now? Goldwater is so far to the right and that's not where the American public is on these issues."

Johnson got up from the couch and walked around the office. Concern flushed back over him about his old friend. "Bobby Baker has been very loyal to me… Getting me information when I needed it, but if people knew the lengths he has gone to protect me, this could hurt me."

Fortas nodded.

Johnson leaned over the couch. "Abe, you got to keep us clean. We got to keep the Senate from digging any further into these issues. I worked hard all year to put up blocks to stop the Senate on their investigations. If the press were to get wind of this… well, I just got to keep the press on my side. You got it?" Johnson walked back around the couch and sat down. *I have concerns there may be one defection in the press. I've got to think Baker has*

this handled, but I won't contact him. Too risky, damn it.

Fortas raised an eyebrow. "Most of that will be up to you."

Johnson stared hard at Fortas. "Of course. But if Baker's association with Giancana and Lansky were to ever come out, my God, that could be devastating to me."

Fortas leaned toward the coffee table. "Mr. President, if you're so worried about him, don't you think you should start distancing yourself?"

Johnson started pacing again. "Abe, in my judgment, Bobby has some bad marks on him, but he has done some things for me..." Johnson leaned over the couch, "anyway, I don't have any direct contact with him now."

CHAPTER THIRTY

SEPTEMBER 7, 1964

SAIGON

US EMBASSY

Steven heard that today was the day the final report of the Warren Commission was to be released. He contemplated asking Lansdale for a copy of the official report, knowing full well he would get it. But it would only raise Lansdale's suspicions of him, so he passed on that idea. His desperation became so great, he even thought about breaking into the Ambassador's office. But he didn't know where to look or even if the Ambassador would have an official copy. He realized he'd have to rethink his very bad idea. He did have an appointment with the Ambassador that afternoon; he could look around the office while he was in there.

At the time of his appointment, Steven entered Meredith's office. He quickly scanned her desk to see if there was a copy of the report there. For her part, Meredith was almost bubbling out of her chair. She was looking forward to going out on the town as soon as everyone was off duty. Steven asked if the Ambassador was ready as he sat down. Meredith ignored the question as she looked at him. "So where are you taking me and Tim later?" Meredith giggled.

Steven smiled. "There are a couple of nice restaurants in Saigon that I believe are still safe, good, and quiet. I thought once we were out of here, we could just drive by and all come to an agreement. They are all in the same area."

Meredith giggled. "This is going to be so much fun. I've been afraid to go out in the evenings since I've been here."

Steven looked at Meredith. *I can't imagine being cooped up in this compound that long. I'd be stir crazy, too.* "Well, I'm glad I can show you and Tim around. Get the two of you out of here for a short time."

Just then Tim came out of the Ambassador's office carrying a stack of papers. The top page header read, "Warren Commission Report-State Department Summary."

Steven couldn't take his eyes off the stack of reports, as Tim exited the Ambassador's office. The Ambassador buzzed Meredith. "Major, the Ambassador said for you to come in."

Steven got up and slid past Tim into the office. The Ambassador asked him to close the door. Steven sat as the Ambassador dropped his copy of the report on his desk. "I've been reviewing soldier's efficiencies at the gun range. I'd like to get updated scores."

Steven sat up straight. "Yes, Ambassador Taylor. We test everyone on a weekly basis for rifle and handgun efficiency. I'll bring in the results immediately."

Taylor came right back. "Your evacuation plan of getting everyone to Tan Son Nhut is okay, but you need to add a route to ships sitting offshore. As there is the buildup in troops, there will be a buildup in naval involvement. This may be a better option and maybe our only route of escape."

Steven maintained eye contact. "As to the evacuation plan, I'll get right on it and make the appropriate contingency plans for an escape route to off-shore vessels, Mr. Ambassador."

Ambassador Taylor nodded. "Please make those alterations for my review to the evac plan ASAP, Major. Things are getting ready to pick up around here, and we need to be out in front of this. You're dismissed."

Steven stood and saluted. He made a beeline for Communication to catch up with Tim. In Communications, he saw several copies of the Warren Commission Report on the side of Tim's desk. Steven initiated the conversation.

"Are you ready to hit the town?"

Tim blushed as he replied. "I'm so excited to go out, you can't imagine. I get to go hang out with Meredith."

Steven started laughing, which caused Tim to blush even more. "So… you are more interested in hanging out with Meredith than me?"

Tim looked worried. "You know what I mean."

Steven smiled and nodded. Tim pushed a summary that the State Department had wanted distributed to all Embassy Staff around the world. Steven tried to act as nonchalant as possible while leaning in to read it.

Tim looked up at Steven as he was reading. "Yes, you were supposed to meet the President at the Trade Mart that afternoon."

Steven nodded. *He couldn't possibly know I never made it. Hopefully, he only knows that Lodge had made that arrangement.* "Yes, anyway. I was wondering what was their final conclusion?"

Tim shook his head. "You know, I still believe some crazy guy assassinated President Kennedy."

Steven anxiously read the report about the conclusions of the Warren Commission. He desperately wanted to find the complete report. According to the official memo, they concluded Lee Harvey Oswald, once a Marine marksman, fired three shots from a 6.5mm Carcano rile. One missed entirely, but two hit President Kennedy and one of those two also hit Governor Connelly. The trajectory of the bullet seemed impossible. Steven did not know whether to be relieved or apprehensive. How can they have missed all the facts? Steven knew his own capabilities. He consistently scored 240 to 250 on his range scores. He was one of the best snipers in the US Marine Corp and was little bit familiar with the Soviet rifle used. He knew there was no way he could pull off those shots.

Steven said, "As soon as I am relieved by Captain Jefferson, I get cleaned up and come get you and Meredith."

Steven wanted to contemplate what he had read. Let it sink in. He went outside to walk around the compound. The question that kept popping into his mind was, Did this clear him of any possible association with assassination plot? How could the French Corsicans still blackmail him? The irony in all of this was it had become exactly what Lucien Sarti predicted. They concluded a lone gunman in a sniper's nest pulled off the assassination. If Steven said anything now, would anybody even believe him? Or would somebody try to keep him quiet, possibly by sending one of their hit men? Steven actually came away with more questions than answers.

When Steven was off duty he went by and picked up his mail on the way to his quarters. There was his monthly letter from his mother. He sat down on the edge of his bed to read it. As he glanced over it, the words of Julian Romano played out in his head. Her letters had gotten shorter and her script had become harder to read. It was obvious her arthritis was now in her hand. Clearly, his mother was struggling. But as he read what the letter had to say, his attention shifted.

Mother could not get in touch with Jeremiah at Southern Miss. She had called twice. Whoever was answering the phone said they would leave a message, but so far no return call. *Very strange.* Jeremiah's grades had been terrible in the spring semester and had put his track scholarship in jeopardy. Steven had wanted to talk to Jeremiah when he was home the previous summer, but Jeremiah had stayed in Hattiesburg for summer school to bring up his grades. Supposedly. The one time Steven had gotten him on the phone, his brother had been gruff, non-communicative. Steven had ended up screaming into the phone, and Jeremiah had simply refused to speak and dropped the phone. Steven had come to believe he could not trust anything Jeremiah told him. And now, Jeremiah had disappeared—or at least severed all contact with their mother. *What was he up to?*

Tip-toeing around this situation was over. Steven looked at the clock, quickly calculated the time in Louisiana and picked up the phone to call his mother.

When she answered the phone, her voice was weak. "Hello?"

"Momma, hi. What is the latest on my dumb-shit brother?"

Even over the static of the long distance connection, Steven could hear her starting to cry. "I am so glad you called. Within the last couple of hours, I called Jeremiah's dorm floor. Whoever answered the phone just stammered around without providing any sound answers. He had no idea where he was. He may have moved out or even dropped out of Southern Miss. I have no idea where he is either."

Steven dropped his head down. "Momma, you don't need this. I'll take over from here."

The phone was silent. Steven could hear his mother blow her nose before speaking. "Steven, exactly how are you going to do that? You are in Vietnam. I'm going to hang up and figure this out. This call is costing you a lot of money. I'll find him. I love you, Steven. Pray for me. Goodbye."

Steven choked back tears himself and swallowed hard. "No, Momma." But the line was already dead. He pounded his fist on the bed stand several times.

His mother did not need this, nor did he. Where in the hell was his brother? Again, the words of Romano played in his head. Smoking pot now, plus Steven believed his brother had stolen from their mother. Now it sounded like the situation had gotten critical. And Steven was more than six thousand miles away.

Steven was beginning to question his decision to re-up. Last year, he was headed home to take care of his family, then Lansdale and MacArthur requested he take on this mission. Now, he was just over one year into his four-year enlistment, he was regretting that decision. He was stuck with Embassy duty and felt irrelevant. Kennedy was dead, MacArthur was dead, and Lansdale didn't trust him. His family needed him and he was stuck with three more years of service. Up until now, he had wanted to get back in combat; now he just wanted out. Worse yet, he was stuck in the middle of a bunch of politicians. If Lodge was still here, he might be able to get leave, but not from General Taylor.

Steven walked over and looked at the evacuation plan for the Embassy that he needed to update. With a swipe of his hand, he knocked those papers off his small desk, and they scattered all over the floor.

He looked at the mess on the floor, his jaw tightening. He had to compose himself. He could not let anyone know what was going on in his personal life. He had promised to take Tim and Meredith out to a restaurant for a dinner away from the Embassy compound. It was the last thing he wanted to do, but he had promised his friends and perhaps it would help him get his head right.

Steven finally got to lie down for the night in his quarters he just stared at the ceiling, it was going to be another restless night. Lately, he had slept but only sporadically, and he expected his mother did as well. His frustration stemmed from his own circumstances. He had been in Indochina so long he'd lost touch with any friends he once had who might be able to help him find Jeremiah. Until he could return to the States, his prospects of being able to hunt down his brother seemed bleak. Moreover, Steven was afraid to even approach Ambassador Taylor, just expected to hear a resounding no. He guessed Taylor would give him some statement like his brother was of age, and the major had a duty to serve at the Embassy. Steven felt great despair with his family dilemma.

SEPTEMBER 11, 1964
HATTIESBURG, MS

Jeremiah hung up the phone. He believed his conversation with his mother had gone well and he had straightened everything out. It definitely took some talking to calm her down. He believed he had convinced her he was still enrolled at Southern Miss, still living in the dorm, all of which was true. She seemed to buy his explanation that he'd been working with tutors every time she called and that he had not taken the time to call her back. Jeremiah claimed the floor-mates she'd spoken to had just not known he was still living there because he spent little time in his room. He acted pissed off about them telling her he had dropped out of school and moved out of the dorm. She now believed his grades were Bs and Cs; he hadn't mentioned the two incompletes in his toughest classes.

Jeremiah thought he'd convinced her he was not involved in drugs. He was, but it wasn't a big deal. He liked to smoke reefer and opium when he could get it, which wasn't that often. He was still trying to work off his debt to Marcello by selling drugs around the campus. His tab was going down but not as fast as he'd hoped because Marcello's men kept charging him high interest. Jeremiah was legitimately scared. Since the day after those two shady characters had stopped him in the street, Nick's Pool Hall had been closed. He kept thinking about how no one had seen Nick since that night. The word on the street was that he'd left town over a family emergency, but Jeremiah didn't buy that. Still, he wasn't talking about it either.

Jeremiah could tell even over the phone how upset his mother was. He figured by convincing her of his story, he had talked her out of doing something drastic. Lord knew what she would have done. His mother could be fierce when she wanted to be. She'd probably been thinking about sending some of his father's old cop friends to track him down. That would have put both him and his mother in jeopardy with Marcello's men. They'd told him if he worked with them—like he had any choice—they would all be safe. The men had given him choices, and all Jeremiah knew was that his choice was not to disappear like Nick.

Jeremiah hoped his mother would also pass his story on to his big lug of a brother. The only thing worse than his mother sending the cops after him was, if Steven thought there was a problem. As fierce as his mother could be, his big brother could actually be dangerous. Not dangerous to Jeremiah, but just the opposite: If Steven thought Jeremiah was being threatened—or worse yet, really harmed—he'd be back here in a heartbeat, and he'd do anything to protect Jeremiah and their mother. His brother would go crazy! He could even start a killing spree from Louisiana to Mississippi. Jeremiah couldn't let that happen.

No, Jeremiah had to work this problem out for himself.

CHAPTER THIRTY-ONE

OCTOBER 10, 1964

WASHINGTON DC

Rita Sullivan was sitting at her tiny roll top desk in her apartment researching her current story. She yawned and looked up at the clock. Just a little before 2 AM. She stood and walked over to her "trusted friend", the coffee pot. Working on the East Coast and reporting to the West Coast, sleep came at a premium. Rita was preparing her report on the speech President Lyndon B. Johnson gave at the Jung Hotel, New Orleans. The typical campaign speech: The Great Society, Vietnam, and how far to the right Barry Goldwater was. Rita's challenge was to find a way to report on the same story and add something new. With the election just a month away, everything was becoming very routine. Johnson was polished, and it was boring.

Her telephone rang. Rita could not believe someone from the *Register–Guard* was calling her for her report already. Her plane had not been on the ground more than three hours, and she hadn't been in her apartment more than two. She collected herself, picked up the receiver, and plopped down in the chair.

"I promise I have you my report in the next hour."

Rita heard a giggle on the other end of the phone. "Excuse me. Is this Rita Sullivan?"

Rita did not recognize the female voice. "Why, yes, to whom am I speaking?"

"This is Mary Meyer. I'm sorry to call you so late. Yesterday, I tried to get in touch with you at the desk phone. Whoever answered informed me you had a new job. I took the risk of calling you at home."

Rita sat up straight. "I am so glad you did. Yes, I have a new job. I'm the Washington DC correspondent for the *Register–Guard* in Eugene, Oregon."

"I guess you're no longer interested in art and music events in the area?"

Rita smiled, she knew how important it was to have an elite acquaintance like Mrs. Meyer. "Not at all. I'm certainly still interested, and I'm sure my editor will give me the latitude of reporting anything. I've been covering the election and find it quite boring. I just got back from a speech President Johnson made in New Orleans."

Mary's voice changed. "Ugggh. You have to hang around with Johnson. Doesn't sound like fun. Umh. Perhaps we should meet. I have many things I'd like to discuss but won't do it over the phone."

Rita thought it was strange that she would not talk about art and music events over the phone. "Mrs. Meyer, just let me know when you want to meet."

"Why don't you come over to my house this Monday, the twelfth. We can go for a walk. I have many things we can talk about, including politics. *Many things*." Mary began breathing hard in the phone. "Please call me Mary." Mrs. Meyer sounded apprehensive. "My home is easy to find. Come by about 10. In the morning. We can take a walk on the canal. That way we can talk privately. It's a beautiful walk, so bring your best walking shoes."

Rita reached over and grabbed her steno pad and pencil. "Give me your address, please."

"Fifteen twenty-three 34th street northwest."

"I'll call you Monday morning, Mrs. Meyer." Rita thought it strange that she wanted to talk privately. *What did she want to tell me?* "Okay, I have the address. Will be there. Goodbye."

MONDAY, OCTOBER 12, 1964

Rita was sipping her morning coffee, waiting on an official from a call from State Department to confirm the rumor that Nikita Khrushchev may be ousted as the leader of the Soviet Union for his handling of the Cuban Missile Crisis. This was very big news. Most Americans hated Khrushchev and would relish the news of him being removed. Rita had been tipped to this potential development by an anonymous phone call, likely set up by Senator Morse. She called the official at the State Department in the Vietnam area who had been help her research the Buddhist protests. He promised to have someone from the Soviet area call, but so far nothing. Very disappointing. She had tried to get a comment from the communication director at the White House but was rebuffed. She was also scheduled to meet Mary Meyer. Rita looked at her watch—time was running short.

She went over to the phone, sat down and dialed Mary Meyer to tell her she couldn't meet her to walk but would be freed up in time for lunch.

"Hello?"

"Miss Meyer, this is Rita Sullivan. I'm sitting here waiting on someone from the State Department to call me regarding a major development. Unless I get the call in the next few minutes, I'm not going to be able to meet at the scheduled time to walk."

Mary Meyer's voice was stern. "You *must* come. It's very important that we meet face to face. We have many private things to discuss."

Rita shifted uncomfortably in her chair. Mary had always been very proper and polite, but now she sounded downright pushy. "Miss Meyer, I shouldn't tell you this, but I'm waiting on word that Khrushchev might be ousted. Potentially huge breaking news. My staff wants me in place to take this call."

"I have something for you that might be just as revolutionary. Maybe more so. I'm scared, and I have to give someone a copy of my journal for my own protection. You're my someone."

Rita scooted to the edge of her chair. *What could be* more *revolutionary?*

"Can you give me a clue?"

Mary snapped, "Not on the phone. It's too dangerous. They might be listening."

Rita leaned back. *Why is she so paranoid?* "I'll be over as soon as possible. I can't afford to lose my job if I miss this call. Is there some place I can meet you after you walk? In case I don't get there when you are ready to go." Rita could hear Mary breathing hard.

Mary spoke in a low voice. "If something should happen to me, I just want to make sure my… this gets out."

Rita put her hand up to her mouth. Something or someone must really have her spooked. She has never been like this before. "I will do *anything* I can. I'll get there as soon as I can. *Please* understand."

Mary was barely audible. "Yes, yes, of course. Just wait for me at my house. If I go for a walk before you arrive. It will be brief. I just need to get out and get some fresh air. Think. I'm sorry to have been so rude to you. *Please* hurry though. It's important, *very important*."

"Yes, Ma'am."

Mary whispered, "Goodbye."

Rita slowly hung up the receiver. After sitting for a minute she got up and paced around her studio apartment. What could Mary Meyer possibly have that was as important as Khrushchev getting removed? Surely, she was exaggerating. Could anything a DC socialite have be that important? If there was, Rita couldn't think of what it might be.

Rita hung up the receiver; Khrushchev was in fact being ousted. She quickly looked over her notes and placed a call to the *Register–Guard* for her news flash.

Time to hustle over to Mary Meyer's residence. As soon as she pulled out of the small office that served as the Washington Bureau, she noticed the black Cadillac right behind her. Rita was more concerned with getting to Meyer's residence than worrying about being tailed. So far the man in the black Cadillac had only followed or watched her, *spied* on her.

Rita drove like a maniac across the city, running her car through the gears and the yellow traffic lights. Her speed didn't matter. The man in the black Cadillac stayed right behind her. She made a sharp turn onto 34th Street NW and looked in the rearview mirror. All she could see was the grille of the black Cadillac. Just as she crossed over 30th Street, the Cadillac tried to pull up beside her at the traffic light. Just in time, the light turned green.

Rita slammed the shifter into first for a jack rabbit start. She tried to time the next traffic light so she could get through on yellow, leave the Cadillac behind. But another car pulled out in front of her, throwing off her timing. At that next traffic light, the Cadillac slammed into the back of Rita's car. Her head snapped forward and hit the steering wheel; she shook her head to try to focus then jumped out of the car. The man in the black Cadillac threw his car in reverse. Despite the steam coming out of the front in his car, he peeled out and hid his face as he drove around Rita. She ran after the car for a couple of steps. But it was hopeless.

Feeling faint, she wobbled back to her car so as not to collapse in the street. She caught a glimpse of herself in the side window. Blood was all over her face and the pain was beginning to register. She crawled behind the steering wheel and grabbed some Kleenex from her purse and pressed it to her bleeding forehead. By then several cars had stopped and passersby came up to her car to check on her. Anxiety clutched her stomach as she realized she needed to get to Mary Meyer's house—now! Awkwardly, she pushed the shifter into first, let off the clutch, and lurched off toward the Meyer residence.

As Rita approached the address, she saw two police cars in front of Mary's house. Rita stopped in the middle of 34th Street and jumped out of her car. She ran as hard as she could up to the two police cars. *No officers.* Rita frantically looked around for them. *No one.* She ran up to the house. The front door was slightly open. She rang the doorbell. A young police officer opened the door, Rita flashed her press credentials.

The police officer looked at her credentials and pointed her through the door. The police sergeant looked at her.

"How did you hear so fast?" The sergeant frowned. "What happened to you anyway? Do we need to get you to the hospital?"

Rita's heart pounded in her chest as a trickle of new blood ran down her forehead and dripped off her nose. "I'm fine. Hear what? I have a meeting with Mary Meyer."

The sergeant looked at the other three policemen in the room. "Get her out of her. You all may need to take her to the hospital. That head wound looks bad. Then immediately take her down to a detective at the station. We want to know what she knows." The sergeant stepped toward Rita and looked closely at her. "Ma'am, you're going to need stitches. There's blood all over you. What happened to you?"

Two officers walked toward her and grabbed her arms. "Come on, go with us."

Rita jerked both of her arms away. She ignored the question about the blood. "Why am I being taken to the station?"

The sergeant faked a smile. "You may have some clues as to why Mary Meyer was murdered."

Rita's legs threatened to collapse for a second. As she was getting control over her limbs, the two police officers grabbed her again. Rita recovered quickly, now with total rage. "Mary Meyer was murdered. Where?"

The sergeant pointed toward the door. "The detective downtown will fill you in on everything. Please cooperate with our investigation. Being a reporter, you above all should understand the importance of gathering evidence. Certainly, you would want to help us find her killer."

Rita's mind raced. Mary's words exploded in her brain: "Something revolutionary," she'd said. "I'm scared, and I have to give someone a copy of my journal for my own protection. You're my someone… not on the phone. It's too dangerous. They might be listening."

Rita knew she had to be coy with her information or she would be drawn deep into this investigation. Was the black Cadillac part of the plot to murder Mary? *Am I being drawn into this?* Rita focused on the room, glancing around to see if there was a package or book or something that Meyer had wanted to give her. *Nothing.* Then she focused on the policemen in the room. "My car is literally parked in the middle of the street. I need to move it. I'll meet your officers and the detective at the station."

The sergeant grabbed his chin with his right hand. "Since you're the press, I'll let you do that, but see to it that you follow the black-and-white down to the precinct. We don't want to come looking for you."

Rita sensed the sergeant's eyes checking out the blood on her dress. *Better get out to the car before they start asking questions about the accident.*

Rita thought about going home and changing her dress, but she was afraid to do that because she'd said she would follow the police car back to the station. At the moment, her best bet was to stay on the side of law enforcement. She thought if she was going to hold back on some of the comments made to her on the phone, it would be best to show cooperation.

When she arrived at the police station and got out of her car, her neck and back were hurting as bad as her head. She walked toward the junior police officer she had followed. She looked behind her and saw another police officer walking around her car. *Better come up with a story for smashed rear end.* The young officer must have seen her looking, because he grabbed her arm. "Come on, the lead detective is waiting on us up in the lieutenant's office."

Rita gently pulled her arm away from the aggressive police officer. They walked through the precinct and toward a small office. The blinds were drawn to keep her from seeing inside, but the plate on the door read, Lieutenant Brodie. The junior officer rapped once and opened the door for Rita.

Inside, two men were sitting behind a wooden desk that had three wooden chairs on the other side. One man stood and pointed Rita to one of the wooden chairs. She sat down and looked at the man She assumed he was the lieutenant and the other man, still sitting, must be the lead detective.

"Thank you for coming down to the station," the lieutenant said. "We wanted to talk to you about your relationship with Mary Meyer. I understand you spoke with her this morning. You may have been the last person to talk to her."

Rita looked up at the detective then over to the lieutenant, as she ran her fingers through her blonde hair. "I didn't have any relationship with her. We were just starting to build one. Earlier in the year, I met her regarding Cherry Blossom Festival events, and she liked the article I wrote. We met on one other occasion, in August, I believe it was. Then today we were going to meet. She called me about the meeting but never told me what it was about. I assumed it was regarding upcoming art and music events. Will you tell me what happened to Mrs. Meyer?"

The detective pulled out his small notepad. "Miss Sullivan, I have some questions for you. What was her mood like when you talked to her?"

Rita bit her lower lip, frustrated that the detective was ignoring her question. "Her mood was fine. She was rushed and wanted me to get over there. I just assumed she had other plans for the day."

The detective scribbled something on his notepad, then looked at the junior police officer. "What did you observe?"

The police officer looked at the three people in the room. "The sergeant on site wanted me to determine why Miss Sullivan had a bleeding forehead and blood all over her dress when she showed up at the Meyer residence. Miss Sullivan's car has quite a lot of damage to its rear end, black paint. There is a lot of blood on her front seat."

The detective looked at Rita. "What exactly happened to your forehead, your dress, and your car?"

Rita had anticipated these questions. "On my drive over, I was the subject of a hit and run. I didn't get a good look at the driver or the car, so I continued on to my appointment."

As the detective was writing, he did not look up but asked, "Why didn't you call the police? Your insurance company is certainly going to ask for a police report, don't you think?"

Rita nodded. "By the time I got to the Meyer's residence I realized that. I was dazed from my head hitting the steering wheel. Perhaps your officer would be willing to write me up a report now."

The detective looked over at the lieutenant, who waved the police officer out of the room, then looked back at Rita. "It is not a good police practice to write a police report when both cars have left the scene of the accident."

Rita thought she had put the accident out of her mind so she pushed for answers regarding Meyer. "Will you tell me what happened to Mary Meyer?"

The lieutenant leaned forward, nodded at the detective, who flipped over a couple of pages in his notepad. "The deceased was found down from the 4300 block along the C & O Canal towpath. She'd been shot twice at close range, one on the left side of her head by her ear and the other over her right shoulder blade straight down. She likely would have died from the first shot. We have notified her ex-husband and her sister. We do have a suspect in custody at this time but everything is preliminary."

Oh, my God, Rita thought. *The night the phone rang and the man said, "end up in some deep ravine." Sounds like a professional hit.*

The detective looked over at the lieutenant, who nodded. "We may want to ask you more questions in the future. Once your head clears up. Can we have someone take you over to the hospital to get checked out? You could have a concussion."

The last thing Rita wanted was to go to the hospital and have more questions. The detective's words burned into her brain: "The deceased was found… shot twice, close range."

I just need to think. Clear my head. It is on overload, too much going on to process. Then there is the man in the black Cadillac… It's time to figure this out.

CHAPTER THIRTY-TWO

THURSDAY OCTOBER 29, 1964
WASHINGTON DC

President Johnson leaned back in his chair. He'd just finished reviewing his campaign manager's latest internal poles. Johnson smiled then got up and walked over to the couch and sat down opposite Robert McNamara. Johnson handed McNamara the poling, who looked at it and smiled. Both men believed that come next Tuesday, Johnson was going to win big. Goldwater was barely going to win his own home state. According to the last polls, Goldwater was leading in the five southern states—Louisiana, Mississippi, Alabama, Georgia, and South Carolina--that Johnson had campaigned very little in. He knew full well that many in the South viewed his War on Poverty as focused solely on the minorities, which didn't play well in those states. But Goldwater's campaign had affectively turned off most of the American public with some of his rhetoric.

Goldwater had campaigned to abolish many of the social welfare programs, including Social Security, while Johnson had promised to expand them with his "Great Society," which included his War on Poverty. Johnson had also pushed Goldwater to the far right on Vietnam, saying he might even be willing to use tactical nuclear weapons. Johnson had stated on numerous occasions on the campaign trail that he was not willing "to send American boys nine or ten thousand miles away from home to do what Asian boys ought to be doing for themselves." The voting public had stark contrasts to choose from, and the polls said they were going to choose Johnson in a big way.

Johnson had been able to keep his plans for Vietnam quiet, as well as the Bobby Baker and Billy Sol Estes scandals out of the press. Johnson had portrayed himself as a man who would continue the same programs and vision for the American people that had been held by the assassinated John F. Kennedy. Johnson believed he would get a large number of sympathy votes because the American public still mourned the death of President Kennedy.

McNamara handed Johnson back his poling data. "I don't know that any candidate has had polling data like this."

Johnson continued to grin. "If these hold up until Tuesday night, we'll have an ole fashion Texas barbeque. We'll continue to hope the Viet Cong do something or those South Vietnamese lunatics don't pull another coup between now and then."

"The Press has kept all of the foreign issues off the front pages."

Johnson picked up the polling data, stared at it. "Bob, as soon as this election is over, I want you to get with the Joint Chiefs and start working up our plans for Vietnam. Also, I am going to start 'promoting' some of our appointed officials, who won't support our war effort." Johnson smiled. "I'll teach them to get on board or get out. I must have a unified front."

McNamara nodded. "I agree, Mr. President. Dissenters in the Administration would look bad."

"Our domestic side issues will take care of themselves. If I do win all of these states, this election will have some coattails. The Congress we'll have to work with will handle getting the bills entered and passed quickly. But we have a real quagmire developing in Vietnam. I think that's where we'll need to focus our attention."

McNamara took off his glasses and cleaned them with his tie. "What do you think the Soviets or the Chinese will do when we start bombing the North?"

Johnson was still staring at the polling data when he mumbled under his breath, "As long as we stay out of the North, I doubt they'll do anything.

341

Hell, they are already supplying the North and the VC." Johnson got up and stood there with both hands on his hips. "Let's go win us an election."

NOVEMBER 4, 1964
TAN SON NHUT AIR BASE
SAIGON

Steven boarded the helicopter with his gear to provide security for CIA Station Chief Peer de Silva, who was on a mission to the Quang Ngai Province of South Vietnam. Once in the helicopter, Steven was introduced to Major Haskill, Sector Advisor, and his deputy, Major Osborne. Immediately, de Silva began to debrief Steven. He advised Steven that his absence from the Embassy over the past few months was because he had conceived this program, with blessings from the very top of the CIA. Major Haskill advised everyone they would be meeting South Vietnamese Major Ly, the other operative in this program in Quang Ngai Province.

On the flight up, the men discussed the program, "Police Forces." It had been implemented in as many areas possible once they proved they could assemble and train the necessary team. It had gone into effect in most of the northern provinces. Today, they were going to visit several of the most successful. However, de Silva stated that he wanted to determine what was successful and what did not work. De Silva wanted to take two days to review the program in order to then send a written report back to William Colby, Chief of the CIA's Far East Division and Richard Helms, CIA Deputy Director for Plans.

When they landed just outside of Quang Ngai, they were met by Major Ly, who took them to the makeshift headquarters. Ly began to describe their operation; forty South Vietnamese men with their primary objectives to protect and earn the trust of the families in each village. The teams moved from village to village, which kept the Viet Cong from having a base to attack. Also, this prevented the VC from gaining an influence over the villagers through fear tactics. Once the basic briefing was over, de Silva asked if they could be taken around the village.

As they walked, Ly continued brief the contingency. Ly stopped in front of a small residence and described the equipment provided to the Police Force Concept. Steven believed de Silva's program was very similar to what Lansdale wished to implement, and even had the same name: Concept for Victory. These men were well equipped with three Browning automatic rifles, nine M-1 rifles, twenty-five submachine guns, and seventeen pistols. Plus, they had a number of grenades and grenade launchers. Ly told de Silva that they had been in operation since April, and they had 3 forty-man teams in the middle of Vietnam. When they started walking again, Steven overheard de Silva ask under his breath, "Did Ambassador Taylor tell Westmoreland to fight like we did in France?" Haskill just nodded affirmatively.

Upon completing their review, as they walked back to Ly's headquarters. It was too late to move on to the next village. They decided to stay overnight at this camp. Shortly after dark, one of the perimeter scouts returned to the command to inform they had spotted Viet Cong activity outside the village. Steven asked de Silva, "Peer, can I go out with the team? Let me take some shots at the VC."

De Silva cracked a smile and nodded. "You know you're here to protect me, right?"

Steven held out both hands palms up. "I am."

Steven disappeared immediately only to emerge in two minutes in full black pajamas with his M14MN and 1911 ready. *I feel alive again in these black pajamas. Perhaps I am more like Ethan than I thought.* De Silva looked startled by Steven's appearance in the black pajamas. Steven went out the door to scout the perimeter.

When they arrived at the perimeter, the leader gave several hand signals, motioning where they had seen the VC activity. Steven moved silently behind the perimeter line to the eastern edge when two men motioned him down then pointed off at ten o'clock, then held up three fingers. Steven laid down on his stomach and pulled his rifle into position. Through his scope he failed to see any activity. He refocused his sniper's mentality, waiting for the targets to show themselves.

Thirty minutes passed. Everyone remained at their stations, barely breathing, waiting for something to happen, for someone to move. When the night jungle creatures got very quiet, everyone heightened their readiness. Steven did not remove his eyes from his scope, remaining focused on the area that was initially identified. Finally, there was a rustle in the tall grass just on the edge of his scope. Steven locked in on that position. He held up two fingers on his left hand but did not remove his fixed gaze from his scope, hoping the men in this position saw his signal and knew what it meant. Steven moved his finger from the side of the rifle down to the trigger, fired three shots as fast as possible. There was no more movement in the area, but to the west of their position, a firefight broke out instantaneously.

Steven and several South Vietnamese men moved toward the gunfire, in hopes of supporting their position. Two men remained in their position so no one could approach their flank. As they approached the battle, they all sat where they could return fire. Steven again positioned himself on the ground and focused on the area where the VC were firing. He started firing, then quickly swapped out the magazine and continued. This time, as Steven was firing, the South Vietnamese started firing with greater intensity. Within five minutes, the jungle fell silent. Everyone sat quietly for more than an hour. The assumption among the Police Force team was the VC had been forced to retreat into the jungle. Steven told the team leader he was going back to the compound.

Early the next day, de Silva and Major Haskill were ready to move on to the next location, at Tu Nghia, where there was another forty-man team operating. Major Ly informed Haskill and de Silva that at this smaller village, during the daytime, this team assisted with construction projects, even did household chores. At night, they were guarding the perimeter against the VC.

After about an hour of observation of this team's operations and the general activities in Tu Nghia, de Silva advised Major Ly that he had seen enough of this operation. He wished to return to Saigon to send his report to Washington DC.

Before boarding their respective helicopters, de Silva asked Major Ly why he thought the Police Force had been successful. Ly was quick to advise that the province chiefs were providing intelligence to the teams as soon as they arrived. The primary objective of these teams was to be welcomed into the villages as they moved through. They never spent more than a couple of days before moving on to the next village. The villagers had come to trust these teams, as each team had some men from their village and all were from the same general region. These were men who were not going anywhere; they were protecting their homeland with a sense of personal pride. Additionally, the teams were equipped like LARPs, which allowed them to move easily through the territory without being bogged down.

On the drive back to the Embassy at the end of his mission, de Silva was writing as they moved through Saigon. Finally, he looked over at Steven.

"What did you think of what you saw over the last few days?"

Steven gave him a quick glance to ascertain if he was really interested in his opinion. "These men were effective. Very impressive. I would like to know more about the teams up north that are failing. Why are they failing while these teams are doing so well?"

"Major, I concur," de Silva said as he went back to writing. "This program is in its infancy and needs considerable study both on the positive and the negative. The one thing I really like is there are no military installations for the VC to strike. I'm curious how my report will be received by our government and military once it reaches the highest levels. So far, the MACV has kept it under the radar, but with Westmoreland and Taylor, in time it will likely get out."

Steven didn't respond to that observation. He knew the answer, but as a junior officer it was best to keep it to himself.

De Silva chuckled. "What is the old saying... your silence speaks volumes. Look, Major, your background was why you were selected to go with me. I can't prove it, but I assume you are getting messages to Lansdale somehow. You were a part of Lansdale's old team, which is why I wanted you to see these teams. I know all about Lansdale's "Concepts for Victory" and I'm guessing if he ever were allowed to implement it you would be a part of the team. I'd also guess that if he were to listen to you, you could add depth to his plan. I believe this country is about to see our military move in here. That is, if Westmoreland and Taylor have their way—and they will. I believe in what we saw. I'm sending over a very positive report. I just hope someone listens, hopefully really *studies*, and maybe helps expand on this. This is why I don't want it going to our high government officials or the military brass."

Steven really liked what he was hearing, de Silva's vision for Vietnam was similar to his. No ground troops. Keep our boys out of this country, yet with a vision for winning the conflict with the Viet Cong and the North Vietnamese army.

Wish I could ask him what he thinks about Conein—the answer would be telling.

Steven carefully folded up his most recent letter from his mother. She had only heard from Jeremiah once in the last month. His mother said she had called the dorm several times and Jeremiah never seemed to be there. When confronted the only time he had actually called home, he did not have a good explanation for his absence. He could not even offer up a bad excuse for his actions. She had called a couple of her late husband's old friends in New Orleans about some advice, they said they would check on it for her but she had not heard anything back yet. This behavior really concerned Steven; Jeremiah had always respected and been truthful with their mother. Over the last year, he had really let them down.

Steven sensed this was something more than just a kid in college who thinks he knows everything. The words of Romano played out in Steven's head, *discovered marijuana*. His brother claimed he was getting his grades up and was looking forward to the Spring track season. He said he would be home as soon as finals were over, which should in a little more than a month, as he had an important final on the last day. Steven could not wait to get home and get his hands on his brother's neck. He was going to knock some sense into him one way or another. Steven's mother was very concerned that Steven was not came home until after Christmas. She thought Steven was delusional to believe that when he got back home that they could get everything turned around in a positive direction. Steven was determined to deliver the message: His brother was going to live at the foot of the Cross by the time Steven got done with him.

Equally disturbing was Steven's mother wrote that on a couple of different nights she had seen automobile lights late at night on the road leading to her house. She had not gone out and checked on it but was considering buying a shotgun. Steven wondered if this was some of the doings of Lucien Sarti's bunch. The last thing Steven wanted to contemplate was his mother having to purchase a shotgun for her personal safety. The situation at home was deteriorating rapidly, he was helpless to do anything about it.

NOVEMBER 5, 1964

Lyndon Johnson sat impatiently at his desk, experiencing both the agony and the ecstasy of being the President of the United States. The ecstasy: He had just won the Presidency of the United States in one of the biggest victory in the history, 43 million votes to Goldwater's 27 million, or 61% of the popular vote. The Electoral College would give him 486 votes from the 44 states he had won. Johnson had a mandate to carry out his domestic agenda.

Then there was the agony: a final report from General Westmoreland. The Viet Cong had carried out a mortar attack on the United States Air Base at Bien Hoa. Just after midnight on November 1, mortars rained down on the base, damaging twenty B-57s, four helicopters, and three A-1H Skyriders. Johnson believed this attack was a direct retaliation to the US bombing North Vietnam. What pissed Johnson off the most was the Viet Cong had escaped back into the jungle without suffering a single casualty, while four US and two Vietnamese soldiers had died. Nineteen were wounded.

Johnson pushed away from his desk and walked over to where McNamara was seated. "Where did those sons a bitches get these mortars?"

McNamara shifted on the couch trying to move away from the President. "Well, we must assume the North Vietnamese are getting these 81 millimeter mortars from either the Soviets or the Chinese. Hell, maybe both."

Johnson tapped his fist several times gently on the couch. "We had to know that the Soviets would be getting in there sometime, but I thought they'd wait until we started winning. How much longer must we wait for the

Joint Chief's plan to build up forces in South Vietnam? This is getting ridiculous."

McNamara looked down. "They say they're debating two distinct philosophies for our execution of the future battle plans: one side the rapid buildup, while the other side wanted to move slow."

Johnson got up and walked around the Oval Office. *I can't make up my mind, either.* "Get those generals moving. I need a plan."

McNamara pulled out a notepad, made a note. "I'll get with General Wheeler."

Johnson walked over to his desk and sat down. "Everyone around here *has to be* on the same page regarding sending troops to Vietnam. I am not sure about Roger Hilsman and Averell Harriman—they may be against that move. It's funny, they were the driving forces to remove Diem and now... They may be the first ones to get ambassadorships, somewhere out of the way."

CHAPTER THIRTY-THREE

DECEMBER 16, 1964

SAIGON

US EMBASSY

Ambassador Taylor had summoned Steve Hebert to his office to discuss the latest developments around the city. The Ambassador told Steven he was aware he was about to go off duty for the evening, but he wanted to review a communication he was about to send to President Johnson. He began by reading over the draft.

First, his letter ran on where he complained about the deteriorating situation between the South Vietnamese young generals and the old generals including High National Council.

Steven wondered as Taylor read why he wanted him to hear this. It was all diplomatic gobbledygook. Steven already knew Taylor had little respect for the South Vietnamese government and less for their military. Steven sat straight and waited.

As Taylor continued to read, his complaints focused on his concerns regarding the Buddhist protests. He expressed reservations about Tri Quang's leadership affecting the general Buddhist population. Yet, he continued to worry about the impact of three Buddhist leaders carrying out a hunger strike.

In conclusion, he believed there would soon be a confrontation between the government and the Buddhists. Was this a conclusion he had drawn from his Embassy staffers meeting with Tri Quang, since he refused to talk with the monk?

When Taylor finished reading his draft, he looked at Steven. "Do you think that Tri Quang will ever come around to cooperate with the government? Specifically, do you believe it could cause a security risk here at the Embassy?"

Steven maintained direct eye contact with the Ambassador. "I believe his resentment for Khanh and his government has grown very strong, and I doubt if it changes. I don't believe the situation represents a security risk."

Ambassador Taylor pursed his lips as he looked down at his memo. Remaining silent, he appeared to reread it. He looked back up. "The Buddhists are going to be the undoing of the Khanh government before this is all over."

Steven wondered what Taylor's role in this was going to be. Clearly, he appeared to be looking for a side to take in the brewing confrontation. It was unlikely the South Vietnamese government would win.

Meredith buzzed Ambassador Taylor to tell him he had an incoming call from the State Department. Taylor quickly dismissed Steven.

Steven walked back into Meredith's office. *Did Taylor had a reason to call him into the office? Security threat seemed low. Was there something else he was going to ask.*

Meredith smiled. "What are your plans for Christmas? This is my first away from my family, I'm open for ideas. Tim wants us all to do something, but I don't know."

Steven had too much on his mind to give it much thought. He had gone out of his way to grant leave to as many of the nonessential staff as possible, plus Captain Jefferson, but this decision was haunting him because it delayed his getting back to the States and fixing his own personal problems. More particularly, his brother's situation. *Was someone really watching my mother?* He tried to clear his mind. He was on his way to meet with Tao, who was supposed to be back in Saigon after spending a couple of weeks in Vang Pao's headquarters. Steven rubbed his chin with his right hand. "I don't know offhand, let me think about it."

Meredith put on a pouty face. "You better hurry up Major, Christmas is coming fast."

"Will do," he said, with a thumbs-up over his shoulder as he headed for the motor pool. Still he fought to repress events of the past year. It had been more than a year since he'd gone through his dreadful experience with the French Corsicans and the hit on the President Kennedy. He still couldn't decide whether the Warren Commission report would keep them from implicating him in their hit. It was only natural to have these thoughts around Christmas time: The top of the list was the serious trouble his brother was in. Whatever it was? He was supposed to go home from Southern Miss to take care of their frail mother, but Steven could not count on him to do anything right. Steven had not planned to go home this year.

Steven was off to Tao's Scooter Shop. As he drove through the city, he realized Saigon didn't reflect the Christmas spirit. With the Buddhists in control this December, it might have well been June. When he was a child, his mother and father would take him and his brother into New Orleans to shop. He loved to look at the Christmas lights and decorations. The memory just made him wish he was at home, with his mother and brother. Part of him still believed that whatever was wrong with Jeremiah, he could make it right, if only he was there.

Once at Tao's shop, Steven watched Tao talking with two customers. Watching their body language as Steven passed through the shop made him chuckle; Tao was a *terrible* salesman. The man couldn't sell bait to a fisherman. When the two men left, without buying, Tao joined Steven in the back room. Steven was shaking his head. "You are the worst salesman of all time."

Tao laughed and faked a punch at Steven, who started bouncing around like Muhammad Ali, feigning lightning jabs at Tao. After about ten seconds of that Tao stopped and walked to his small desk. "My salesman would have closed that deal. He has actually turned this place around over the last couple of weeks."

Steven turned the wooden chair around backwards and sat down as Tao did the same. He briefed Tao on the growing problems between Ambassador Taylor and President Khanh. Then Tao proceeded to tell him about the Buddhist problem that was also applying considerable pressure on Khanh. Steven remained steadfast keeping his two meetings with Tri Quang from Tao.

"So, Tao, what's going on with Vang Pao?"

Tao glanced away for a moment the made eye contact with Steven. "You know Operation Barrel Roll was implemented just two days ago? The US air force is really striking hard at the Pathot Lao and along the northern portion of the Ho Chi Minh Trail. I was part of the team that picked the strike points. Anyway, I met with An last night. He already knew about the program and where we were going to bomb."

Steven drew a deep breath. "I believe I can shed some light on that. Ambassador Taylor sent me over to one of Westmoreland's press briefings. To show Meredith Brown and Tim Mitchell how the military conducts press conferences. When Westmoreland finished his briefing, after he and bureau chief left the room, we stood there talking to some reporters. I watched An walk over and review the clipboard for limited distribution, not the clipboard for the news publications."

Tao just stared at Steven for a minute, then looked at his watch. He got up and walked to the front of his Scooter Shop with Steven following. Tao turned the "Closed" sign over. Tao looked back at Steven. "No one questioned An looking at that information?"

Steven shook his head. "No. No one paid any attention. Ambassador Taylor has told me that Westmoreland wants to establish a good working relationship with the press, *but I just don't know* if that is part of his plan. As you know, An is the go-to guy for all of the other reports when it comes to the military."

Tao continued to think for a minute. "Hebert, that's important, but this is different. This was a top secret operation. I think he is getting information from somewhere else? That information should not have been on any clipboard."

Steven scratched his head. Something did not make sense with respect to An. Both he and Tao knew he worked for the CIA when they were working with Lansdale in the late 1950s. Was he getting information from someone in the CIA? Who in the CIA could be giving him information?

DECEMBER 18, 1964
SAIGON

Lieutenant Colonel Lucien Conein was impatiently sitting at a table in the Caravelle Hotel bar, continually looking at the clock behind the bar. *Where the hell are they? I'm not waiting around much longer.*

Conein held his hand up to order another whiskey on the rocks. He saw CIA Bureau Chief Peer de Silva and his guard Major Steven Hebert finally enter. The two men glanced around the bar until they made eye contact with him. They sat down at his table. Immediately, Conein waved to the waiter to come take their orders. Conein appreciated that de Silva was sharp enough to know that his connections with the South Vietnamese generals were still important despite Ambassador Taylor putting him on the sideline.

As soon as de Silva settled in, he nodded to Conein to start his briefing. Conein stated that over the last several weeks, he'd met with the old generals, whose advice was being ignored by the Khanh government. The most important thing he learned was little attention was being paid to the voices on the High National Council; Khanh is losing the trust of a large segment of the population. As Conein continued to deliver the laments of the generals, de Silva finally raised his hand to stop him. Just as de Silva was about to speak, the waiter arrived at the table to get their orders. After both men ordered green tea, de Silva advised Conein he was more concerned about the Viet Cong camps on three sides of Saigon.

Conein looked at both men as he leaned forward. "What exactly do you want to know that you don't already know?"

De Silva frowned as he whispered. "I've got too many men in the field at risk. We need to know something, anything about their strength in each camp. You have been here long enough to have sources. Me, I can't get my people close enough to get figures. I need another set of eyes, *experienced* eyes. Villagers already there that won't appear suspicious."

Conein slugged down the last of his whiskey on the rocks and smiled. "Well, tell you what I'm gonna do. I grab a machine gun and a couple of men, and we'll drive through all the camps shooting and counting. I'll report back next week."

De Silva lowered his head. "Okay, I really don't need the sarcasm. It's all about the men at risk. If this were a game of chess I'd say we got two kings in check, neither of them wants to move. Me, I'm trying to do something to change the game. I need to know where to place them. You are

Pawns: Kings in Check

familiar with the operations I'm running. I'd like to start moving them into position to be effective, but I need intel."

Conein rubbed his chin with his left hand. "I'll try to find some individuals near those camps who will talk to me. It won't be easy, it won't happen quick, but I'll get you *that* intel."

De Silva looked at Steven Hebert and pointed toward the door. "We're done here. Let's go."

Conein folded his hands on top of the table. "De Silva, I need you to give me about five minutes with Hebert, privately?"

De Silva looked back and forth at both men. "You're taking my bodyguard, who has my back in here?"

Steven leaned up on the table as he looked at Conein. "No, Lieutenant Colonel, *Sir*. Mr. de Silva is my responsibility. I cannot leave his side. You can say it here, in front of both of us."

Conein leaned toward both men. "No. I've got four men in here who have been watching us the whole time. They know I'm going to talk to Hebert privately." Conein pointed at de Silva. "You'll be fine. They'll take a bullet for me; they'll take a bullet for you."

De Silva looked at his watch. "Go. Your five minutes just started."

Conein got up from the table, motioning to Steven to follow him out the door. Steven looked back at de Silva, who nodded, so Steven followed

361

Conein out the door. Conein led him to his jeep and both men got in. Conein reached in his breast pocket and pulled out a piece of paper. "This is a list of names and addresses that my boss, William Colby, sent to me."

Steven started to speak, but Conein shook his head no as he held a finger up to his lips. "Why, you ask, did I bring you out here to tell you this. You remember when I told you and your gook friend that that dick head Agent Bowman Taylor was going to be a problem. Well, he has created a big problem for you."

Steven twisted around on the bench set to look directly at Conein. "What are you trying to feed me?"

Conein smiled. "Well, I told you that I would handle Taylor and I will. When someone started cracking down on our drug operations, the FBI found out that many of the FBN agents were on the take, except for that dick head Agent Taylor. The FBI opened up an investigation on the drug operations. This led them to focus on Carlos Marcello in New Orleans and Santos Trafficante in Miami. According to Colby, Hoover shut down these investigations two summers ago, but the local offices have quietly picked them up again because some agent in Washington DC tipped them off about Corsican drug runners and assassins in the United States. Both offices have restarted an undercover, low-key investigation."

Steven shook his head. "Colonel, so now you and the Corsicans are going to implicate me as part of this network? That's what is on that paper. What about your drug speech and funding the war effort in Laos?"

Conein frowned. "You're not being implicated in anything. Stop your damn whining and pay attention to what I'm telling you. I'm about to get in the middle of a drug war between my old friends, the Corsican Brotherhood and the US mafia families. There is even going to be conflict within the CIA, and agents will be falling out on both sides. I don't know how this is going to play out, but it's going to get messy. This FBN and FBI investigation is going to play a role in this, both here and in the US. We'll continue our financing effort, but things are going to change."

Steven just stared at him, blankly.

Conein handed him the paper. "On this paper…"

Steven took the paper.

"On this paper is the list of people the FBI are following in New Orleans."

Steven opened the paper and scanned the list. His jaw dropped. "My brother? What's my brother's name doing on this list? Why are you doing this?"

Conein nodded. "Shit, boy, *I like you*. I've been trying to tell you that, but you just wouldn't believe me. I told you I'm a boy scout." Conein's laughter, loud and hard, sounded to Steven like a shotgun burst. "You and me are on the same team. You saved my life a couple of times with your sniper bullet back when we were working for Lansdale, so I owed you. Now, I've paid my tab. We are even. What you do with that information is up to you. Now give me the paper back. No one was to see this, just me."

Staring at the paper, Steven slowly handed it back. "There is no address in New Orleans, I thought he was still in Hattiesburg? Why is he in New Orleans? How good is Colby's source?"

Conein took the paper and continued. "Don't you get it? Your brother is selling drugs for Marcello. Colby got this from a source of his in New Orleans, who knew what we were up to and he wanted us, the CIA, to protect ourselves. The FBI has been watching him for a few months. They watched him get in the car with two of Marcello's guerillas and go to New Orleans. Those thugs are with him always. They move their dealers around to different houses. They must think that keeps them from being watched."

Steven lowered his head as he looked out the jeep window.

Conein continued. "Look, eventually, the FBI will ask us to help them pick up some people outside the US, so we'll have to take sides, too." Conein paused. "And now it is likely that Hoover will not let them lay a glove on either Marcello or Trafficante, but he will let them work on the network once he gets wind of their investigation. But if your name is on this list, let me tell you how it is going to work. You will be arrested then either go to jail or become an informant. Colby said all of those on this list were selling drugs at schools. I wouldn't want anyone in my family going to jail. Or work as an informant."

Steven slowly opened the door to the jeep and walked away.

Conein started his jeep and drove off. He knew he had done the right thing, but it had to be a bomb shell to Hebert.

Steven returned to the bar to get Peer de Silva. The two men silently walked back to vehicle. Steven could hardly process what Conein had told him. If his information was right, his brother may have dropped out of Southern Miss right before finals. Then he moved to New Orleans. Why? Steven knew his mother had not heard from Jeremiah since the month before his finals. His brother was taken to New Orleans by two thugs who worked for Marcello. Steven knew he was more than a week out before he was scheduled for leave to the United States. He had made a huge mistake, thinking everything was okay with his brother and letting most of the other soldiers serving at the Embassy have leave for Christmas before him. Now he had to wait on Captain Jefferson to return before he could leave. Would Jeremiah be brought in for questioning by the FBI before he got there to do something about it? Would those thugs do something to harm him in the mean time? Steven had never felt so helpless in his life.

WASHINGTON DC

Rita Sullivan was writing in her journal, detailing her morning. Her newsroom was very small, barely room for her desk, a chair on the other side, and the teleprinter. This afternoon she was scheduled for her last treatment for whiplash at the chiropractor. She couldn't afford to go to a real doctor but as it worked out the chiropractor was better. She wrote about no longer suffering from headaches or neck or back pain.

She had not seen the black Cadillac since the day he smashed into her, but that had not provided her any mental relief. Was it her gut feeling or fear that made her believe she had not seen the last of him? *Mary Meyer's murder.* She still believed the murder and her "accident" were connected, somehow. Since the murder, she had started writing in her journal in George shorthand, so if anyone stole it, it would be harder to read. She flipped back to her notes on the murder. Mary Meyer's friends were some of the most influential people in this city and all of them had very high contacts into the US government. Rita wondered why she had not been protected. After all her ex-husband was a high ranking CIA official. Her sister was married to a current or former CIA operative, who was now the Washington Bureau chief for *Newsweek*. Rita's research on Meyer's background still pointed to her being a typical socialite. Nothing unusual stuck out. *Am I missing something?*

The lead detective had told her that they had taken someone into custody the day of the murder that they believed was the likely perpetrator. The suspect's name was Raymond Crump, Jr. Rita had done research on the suspect. The statement from the only witness said he heard a woman's voice shout, "Someone help me! Help me!" right before he heard two gunshots. He ran to the towpath and saw a black man in a light jacket, dark slacks, and a dark cap standing over the body of a white woman. He estimated the man was five-eight and 185 pounds. This did not match Crump, who was five foot five and a half inches and weighed 145 pounds.

Maybe at a distance, the witness was not able to accurately determine his size, Rita thought. But no gun was mentioned. Further, there was no physical evidence that could link Crump to the murder: no blood, no hairs, and no fibers. *The dark halo of gunpowder around the bullet hole says she was shot at almost point-blank range.* Rita sat back in her chair. *Wouldn't close range shots splatter gun powder residue on him? None was found.* Initially, she'd been told the head shot would have killed Meyer. Now the second shot was directly into the heart. No eyewitnesses, no gun had been found, so all the evidence was circumstantial. *I'm convinced it was a professional hit.*

Plus, there was still the unanswered question: Was the information Mary wanted to give her the reason she was killed? What had changed between the call on October 10 and the day of her murder—two days? *Was my hit-and-run to keep me from getting the information? What did she have that she was so desperate to give to me? Did it really cost her her life! Or am I making too much of it?*

Rita sat back and closed her eyes. She flinched as she had a flash of the black Cadillac smashing into her car. She worked her neck and shoulders around. She had been trying to figure out who she'd caught a glimpse of driving the black Cadillac, and so far, she'd struck out. *No recall of what he looked like.* She had even gone back by the Quorum Club but had not seen the black Cadillac there since the day she met Meyer there.

The phone on her desk rang. She jerked again, her heart racing as she grabbed the receiver. "*Register–Guard*, Washington Bureau, Rita Sullivan speaking."

The voice replied, "I am one of the organizers of a nationwide protest around the country tomorrow. I'm a member of the Student Peace Union.

One of the protests will take place in Washington DC tomorrow. We would like you to come and cover it."

Rita slid her steno pad into position with her right hand and picked up the pen in her left hand. "First, I have several questions for you."

The person on the phone said, "Well, yes, I suppose. Can we meet and discuss these questions?"

Rita replied, "Come by my office after lunch. Let's talk here."

After lunch, Rita was sitting in her office when a slender man with long blonde hair wearing a sweater that was too big and scruffy bell bottom jeans walked in. He looked around suspiciously then sat down opposite her.

"Hello, Ms. Sullivan, I'm Billy. As I said on the phone, I'm here for the Student Peace Union. I was given your name by Mario Savio of the War Resisters League in San Francisco. He said you would give us a fair write-up on our planned protest. Maybe you could attend and help our cause. We've heard you're not a fan of President Johnson."

Rita opened her steno pad and picked up her pen. "Okay, first of all, I'm a reporter, so I won't be going to help your cause. But if your protest makes a good story, I'll write it up. What is your cause?"

Billy frowned. "We are protesting what is going on in Vietnam. Johnson campaigned over and over that he would not, quote-unquote 'send American boys nine or ten thousand miles away from home to do what Asian boys ought to be doing for themselves.' Yet even before the election is over, we were bombing North Vietnam. I have it on good information we already have troops fighting in Vietnam and are about to send more. This is not what he campaigned on. We want our voices heard."

Rita wrote in shorthand on her steno pad. She believed Senator Wayne Morse or someone at that level had provided them this information. "How many demonstrators are you expecting to show up tomorrow?"

Billy looked around, nervously. "We are hoping for more than a thousand."

Rita continued writing without looking up. "Where are you planning to start your demonstration?" Rita looked up to make eye contact with Billy. Out of the corner of her vision she saw a black Cadillac slowly drive by the entrance to her office. *Was that the one—or am I just paranoid?* Rita jumped up and ran out the door. She held it open as she looked up and down the street. *Nothing. I'm just being paranoid. There must be hundreds of black Cadillacs in this city.*

Billy turned around and looked out toward the front. "What's wrong?"

Rita ignored the question as she came back and sat down. She pulled her blonde hair back, straightened her glasses, and drew a deep breath. "I'm sorry. Go ahead."

Billy shifted in the chair. "If you are willing to cover this protest, I'll call you in the morning and give you a starting point. We want you on board. We've heard that you believe the same way we do."

Rita nodded. "Again, I am here to cover the news. My thoughts and opinions are irrelevant."

Billy ran his hand through his hair and pushed it back off his forehead. "Will you give me your home phone?"

Rita shook her head no. "Call me here. I'll be in early." She had become very cautious, as a single girl, of giving out her number. She walked to the door with Billy then discreetly looked up and down the street again. *Nothing.*

WASHINGTON, DC

NEXT MORNING

Rita was in the office early reading the news tape. The South Vietnamese government had had another coup of sorts. The President, General Khanh, remained in power, but he had removed some of the elder statesmen. *Vietnam is becoming a quagmire. It's hard to understand why we're involved in what appears to be a civil war.* Rita knew the answer to her own question; it was just a continuation of the Cold War, the communists versus free world. Rita was not so sure that the participants of the protest she was waiting to hear about had their facts straight. She had seen no indication that President Johnson was about to commit ground troops and more military to the cause. While she was not a fan of Johnson, there had not been any information made public that would tip her to that pending development. *Where did Billy get his information?*

About that time, the phone rang. It was Billy giving her the time and location for the protest march. Billy told her that as many as five organizations were participating: The War Resisters League, the Fellowship of Reconciliation, the Committee for Nonviolent Action, the Socialist Party, and the Student Peace Union. This excited Rita, it seemed the protest would be bigger than she had initially expected. This could be a real stepping stone in her career, as there had not been many organized protests around the country and this could really make the news. Rita made notes as Billy spoke and was glad she had comfortable walking shoes. She'd have to get herself settled into the crowd and interview several of the more informed participants. When she hung up the phone, she put her steno pad and a couple of pencils in her purse. Rita put on her heavy jacket and left.

Rita parked her car several blocks away from the designated starting point of the protest. At that distance, if she wanted to get away, she wouldn't be trapped. When she was a block away she noticed several buses and cars had filled all available spaces. She began to hear some faint chants, but she could not make out what they were saying. Despite how cold it was that day, the walk warmed her up and she felt the loud chanting charge her adrenaline.

When she finally could see the gathering, she was shocked by the size of the crowd. They had filled a large courtyard and could easily number than five thousand participants. It appeared that many of them had signs. She looked around to see if there was someone making the signs or if they had been made in advance. That would tell her if the protest was well organized. While there were some hand-made signs, most premade, so she concluded it was well organized.

After the crowd did several more random chants, Billy climbed up on a scaffolding and waved his hands to quiet everyone. Once accomplished, another young man stepped out of the crowd onto the scaffolding carrying a megaphone. He started a series of chants he wanted the protestors to quickly learn, which they performed as he held up the appropriate hand signals as they marched. Rita looked at her watch. She wondered who was this individual. Clearly, where Billy was new to protesting, this young man was organized. He knew how to get the crowd going and how to keep them involved. He even told some individuals with signs where to march to be seen. Rita thought she was the only one from any news organization covering the protest, and that brought a half smile to her lips. After about fifteen minutes, the young man pronounced them ready and jumped off the scaffolding to get them moving.

Rita tried to work her way up to the leader. She tried to catch up with Billy to see if he could get her to the young man. Rita moved through the crowd talking to individuals, first trying to determine where most of them lived and what they were upset about. For the most part, all the people she interviewed understood and believed in protesting the insertion ground troops into South Vietnam.

After walking a little more than three blocks, Rita had finally caught up with Billy. Just as she was about to ask him the name of the leader, the crowd broke into a series of chants. She could not even hear herself think. She tried to stay by him but got bumped around and ended up about twenty feet behind him. As Rita scanned around the moving protest, she noticed the leader had separated himself from the crowd out in front to orchestrate the protest chants. Rita was mesmerized by the rhythm the man was able to get out of the crowd in just a quick, fifteen-minute training session. Rita began to believe that some of the other participants were experienced protesters.

Just before reaching their destination, the protesters slowed as they walked slowly down the street. Rita thought this was her chance to catch up with the leader. She pushed her way through the throng and double-timed her pace to catch up with him. She flashed her credentials, simultaneously requesting an interview. He agreed, all the while continuing to lead the chants. The man appeared to be about her age; she asked him to identify himself, but he refused. She agreed to continue the interview without his name, understanding his desire to keep his anonymity. She was able to get five questions answered, but as the protestors continued moving past them, he quickly ended the interview to run in front of the protestors to invigorate the chanting to their final destination. Rita was satisfied she had a good feature and decided then to head back to her car.

It took Rita several minutes to walk back through the chanting protestors. Then there was the thirty-minute walk back to her car. The day had not warmed up, and her feet got cold. She could see her breaths as she walked. She focused on the article she was going to write. As she stepped off the curb at the intersection she heard a rumble behind her and turned just in time to see the black Cadillac barreling into the intersection. Rita jumped back just in time to avoid being run down. She tried to get a look at the driver, but he turned his head away and accelerated past her. *Someone is really trying to hurt me? Send me a message. What am I doing to cause this? Who is behind this? This is more complex than just the Mary Meyer murder but what?*

Rita hustled to her car and back to her office. She locked the door and started writing her column on the protest. After her second read over it, she sat at the teleprinter and typed it out for the home office.

Rita was ready to go home for the evening, satisfied with her column. Just then her desk phone rang. She contemplated not answering but it could be the *Register-Guard* with a question. She picked up the receiver.

"Don't write a negative column about President Johnson or a positive column on the protest, if you know what is good for you." The line went dead.

Rita raised her eyebrows as she looked at the receiver and slowly put it down. With a deep breath she walked outside to her car. She continued to check the rearview mirror all the way home. *Is the man in the black Cadillac and the man on the phone one and the same? Mary Meyer was murdered, and someone is trying to hurt or intimidate me. Why? What am I doing?*

DECEMBER 20
SAIGON

Major Steven Hebert had not had a typical day. It started with a briefing from Ambassador Taylor regarding the overnight coup that had not been a typical coup. General Khanh was scheduled to come by the US Embassy the next morning for a meeting with the Ambassador. Steven was not looking forward this meeting. Khanh and Taylor's relationship had continued to deteriorate. The meeting could be disastrous.

As soon as he got off duty, Steven headed to Tao's Vespa Scooter Shop. It was good having Tao back in town, easier for him to communicate with Lansdale, plus it kept him from feeling he had failed Lansdale every time they spoke. Over the past year this feeling had become oppressive. When he arrived, Tao was sitting at the back of his shop going over the inventory list.

"You won't believe what I'm working on," Tao said. "Inventory. This place is turning into a business. The boy I hired is selling scooters so fast, I have to order more inventory."

Steven told him what had gone on at the Embassy that morning after the latest South Vietnamese coup and that Khanh was coming over tomorrow.

Tao let out a low whistle. "Not good. That meeting could get downright ugly. I understand why he'd want security in his office for *that* meeting. I need to catch up with An to get his input."

Steven shrugged. "Do you know what really happened? Taylor was too busy putting down the Khanh regime to really give me much detail. However, Taylor believes Tri Quang is behind the uprising and the Khanh moved to short-circuit it."

Tao shook his head as he moved to the edge of his desk. "Taylor has it all wrong. I'm not sure you can call it a coup. Khanh dissolved the High National Council. He even arrested some of them. This is a battle between the younger generals and the South Vietnamese elders on the council. Khanh and his young generals are still focused on their own power. They are Nero fiddling while Rome burns around them."

Steven frowned at Tao.

"Ancient Roman history." Tao smacked his hand on the desk. "The Viet Cong and the North Vietnamese are gaining control of more and more of the countryside. Khanh is paying it no attention."

Steven nodded. "Wasn't much into the study of ancient history, except the battles of the Spartans and the Roman Army. The rest is boring and inessential."

Tao was swinging his legs back and forth. "The other thing I learned at Vang Pao's camp, the OPLAN 34A and Seal Team missions have been very effective. They are using many of the techniques Lansdale talked about. You know, the things we used to do." Tao nodded morosely as he spoke.

Steven looked around room, contemplating what Tao had just told him.

Tao persisted. "You know the only actual military action has been at An Lao up in the Binh Dinh Province."

Steven jumped in, interrupting. "Taylor thinks the pacification program is progressing slowly around Saigon, they're behind schedule. One of my contacts at MACV said they had stopped the program, but that turned out to be not true." Steven pursed his lips.

Tao raised both arms. "An called it a total failure several months ago. But between the typhoons last month and the heavy rains it's no wonder they're behind, is it? I'll say this, I don't think it will work as many of the people feel displaced."

Steven leaned back in his chair and changed the subject. "What are you doing for Christmas?"

"I have a drop then I'm going back to the States to see my son. Haven't seen him in a couple of years. I missed his graduation from Duke. He and his best friend Frank Young are fighting in a Tae Kwon Do tournament to qualify for the nationals. I told him I would come and watch. Why?"

"When do you fly out?"

Don Kesterson

"I'm leaving Christmas night."

"A bunch of us from the Embassy are going to the Brinks Hotel on Christmas Eve. Care to join us?"

Tao shrugged. "I'm not sure that is such a good idea, since no one knows we're working together. Besides, the drop is supposed to take place sometime on Christmas Eve. It is to an old friend, Colonel Fabian Ver. He's coming back from Thailand, he went through military police training there in the past. He is going back to the Philippines to protect a high political official, and the CIA wanted him to get some dossiers on several known individuals in that country to keep an eye on."

Steven nodded. "Did you know him back when you were assigned there?"

"Let's just say we crossed paths. I'm to hand-deliver these dossiers at Tan Son Nhut when he notifies me he is on the ground. Then I'm going to Mass."

Steven looked at his watch. "Better get back to the Embassy. When you supposed to speak with Lansdale again?" Steven got up and started toward the back door.

Tao got up to walk out with Steven. "After making this drop."

"May have more to update you on before that phone call." Steven continued talking on his way out the back door.

380

DECEMBER 21, 1964

SAIGON

US EMBASSY

Steven stepped through the front door of the Embassy as the South Vietnamese motorcade arrived. He was expecting General Khanh; instead General Thi, Premier Ky, Admiral Chung Tan Cang, and IV Corp Commander General Nguyen Van Thieu exited the vehicles to meet with Ambassador Maxwell Taylor. Steven asked if they were the advance team. They advised Steven they were the only ones coming to the meeting. Steven turned and escorted the four men into the building, knowing this change of plans was bound to upset the Ambassador.

Steven showed them to the conference room and urged them to take their seats around the conference table. Steven excused himself and went to get the Ambassador. On their way back to the conference room, he let the Ambassador know that Khanh was not part of the entourage. Ambassador

Taylor didn't say anything, but Steven saw his jaw muscle bulge as he clenched his teeth. No, not happy. Not happy at all.

In the conference room, Ambassador Taylor calmly took his seat opposite the four Vietnamese dignitaries. He asked them to do their best to explain what had transpired over the previous two days. After each offered their opinions, Taylor looked at each of the men.

"Do all of you understand English?" For the next twenty minutes he exceeded diplomatic protocol, putting the four men down in a variety of ways. He made several threats to cut off financial aid to their government. He demanded they reinstate the High Council, talked about Khanh's Constitution not being followed, and claimed that the Buddhists had turned against his government. Lastly, with extreme vigor Taylor told them he was tired of the coups and the refusal to engage with the Viet Cong.

Steven was shocked at Ambassador Taylor's tone, and he was equally shocked that the government officials sat there and took it.

As soon as Steven was off duty, he headed off to Tao's Vespa Scooter Shop. He needed to unwind, and he wanted to come clean with Tao. When he arrived, Tao was on the phone talking to Lansdale. Tao put his index finger to his lips. Steven twisted his back and neck, trying to relax the tension built up in his body.

Steven wondered why Tao did not want Lansdale to know he was there. Tao was informing Lansdale about the latest Viet Cong activity just outside Saigon. Steven listened as their conversation grew tense, Tao's responses becoming brief and terse. Tao finally hung up, a little too hard, Steven thought. "Glad you are talking to him, Tao."

Tao sat with his head lowered. "Lansdale is on the warpath. He has read more of Colonel Vann's reports about the South Vietnamese army's lack of readiness. And he thinks Johnson used him."

Steven knitted his brows. "Good thing he didn't talk to me. Ambassador Taylor just completely humiliated several South Vietnamese government officials."

Tao raised both hands palms up, as he pursed his lips. "So far I have to say Taylor hasn't proven to be very diplomatic. I don't like him disrespecting my people. It's not good for our relations."

Steven rubbed his forehead with two fingers. "I have to tell you about a mission Taylor sent me on last month." He stuck his chin out. "I was sent to open conversations with Thich Tri Quang."

Tao frowned. "You. Why?"

"Taylor thought he would talk to me since he knew me from the Lodge days. Anyway, he is on the side of the US. He confirmed he believed Khanh was a weak leader. Since then, he has sent one of the junior diplomats from the Embassy to talk with him periodically."

Tao looked at Steven. "Why didn't you tell me this before?"

Steven just shrugged. For a moment he was at a loss for words. "I... um... I was under strict orders from Taylor, but after today, I realized my mistake."

Tao just stared at Steven.

Steven knew he had violated trust with both Tao and Lansdale, all for the purposes of getting in the good graces of the Embassy "higher ups." He was beginning to think he had made a foolish error in judgement.

SAME DAY
WASHINGTON DC

Rita went straight to the office teleprinter for the morning news. Her report on the big protest in Washington DC had been picked up by the Associated Press and United Press International. Finally, she had achieved her first step towards being a national reporter. She was really proud of herself. Threatening phone call be damned! If she could play this up one more level and get it in a bigger newspaper, the story could provide her the high level profile she needed to keep the man in the black Cadillac from trying to intimidate or injure her. *One more big story, and I should be able to develop that next big break.*

None of this was stopping her from trying to learn the identity of Cadillac Man. Rita pulled her compact out of her purse and looked herself in the eyes. *You're a newspaper reporter, for goodness sakes. You can't find this man or who he is? That's inexcusable. Really time to get to the bottom of this. Whoever he was he was protecting the President, but how did Mary Meyer fit into it? There were no ties between Johnson and Meyer. That was what didn't seem to fit. Maybe I need to try to get into the Quorum Club, see if Mr. Cadillac Man frequents the bar.* Then she remembered a conversation with Miriam and John. *The Meyer family and the Kennedy family were once friends. Plus, Mary's brother-in-law was married to Ben Bradlee. Need to see if these relationships can provide some leads before going back to the Quorum Club for Cadillac Man.* Lecture over, she put the compact back in her purse.

Within a few minutes, her mother called. She was so excited to see Rita's name in the national section of her hometown paper. Mother and daughter chatted for a bit before Rita had to cut the conversation short. It had been difficult for her not to mention Cadillac Man to her mother. *Mom doesn't need the worry.*

Later in the morning, the executive editor of the *Register–Guard* called her to congratulate her on her news report being picked up. He said he had already received several calls about it. He even went on to say he did not want to lose her, and that felt good.

As she was getting ready to go home for the evening, her desk phone rang. It was Meredith calling to tell her she had seen her article and how thrilled she was for her. This was the icing on the cake of a great day. Meredith did say the Ambassador had some not-so-nice things to say about the protest. Meredith said she just sat there quietly so as not to tip him off that she knew the author.

CHAPTER THIRTY-FOUR

CHRISTMAS EVE

SAIGON

Ambassador Taylor was far from being in the Christmas Spirit. The last three days had been brutal. General Khanh, the South Vietnamese government, himself, and to a lesser extent, the US government had participated in a vicious game of diplomatic hardball. Khanh had come over and met with Taylor, face to face.

The only outcome of that had been a very undiplomatic confrontation, which included Khanh telling Taylor the US just wanted his government to be a puppet to their wishes and desires. In one conversation, Ambassador Taylor told Khanh that he had lost confidence in his leadership, as had others in the US government. Taylor demanded the High National Council be restored and given even more power. He told Khanh he was going to cut the financial aid to the country; while Taylor did not have that much power, he did have President Johnson's ear so Khanh perceived the threat as credible.

But it was Khanh who played Taylor like a fiddle on the phone: he told the Ambassador he would leave the country, along with his young generals, if Taylor told him which ones he wanted gone. Khanh had taped the conversation then spliced it together in such a way as to make it look like Taylor was threatening to expel some of the young generals from their own country. It was an impossible threat but it got the desired effect of keeping the young generals on Khanh's side. Next, Khanh leaked the tape to the Saigon Press, which spilled the diplomatic squabbling into the public. Khanh had even gone on radio and said, "We make sacrifices for the country's independence and the Vietnamese people's liberty, but not to carry out the policy of any foreign country." These remarks only created more chaos in South Vietnam, just what the effort to defeat the communists didn't need. The public diplomatic battle put the Embassy's security staff on a high alert.

In the ensuing meetings, Ambassador Taylor believed that despite his desire that this not go public, it might bring the Buddhists and students onto his side. Might not work that way, though. Taylor might be the disappointed one. His position had been destroyed by Washington's decision to back down on demands for the restoration of the High National Council. The elders were being pushed aside just like General "Big" Minh had been and there was nothing Taylor could do. This only made the Embassy a more unpleasant place to be. Taylor was not accustomed to politics and diplomacy; he was used to ruling with an iron fist, which rarely worked in the diplomatic world.

Nguyen Tao was on the phone ordering inventory in the back of his shop when the bell on the front door rang. As Tao stepped through the curtain, he saw Pham Xuan An milling around looking at one of the Vespa scooters on the showroom floor. An said he had just stopped by to see Tao, see how his business was going since he was in Saigon more. *Is An checking up on me?*

Tao chuckled as he described how busy he was and what a good job the boy he had hired was doing. An advised him the real reason he stopped by was to tell him that the South Vietnamese government was considering expelling Ambassador Taylor. He claimed that most of the leadership in South Vietnam had grown tired of Taylor trying to run their government. They were also sick of being talked down to. An then laid a bomb shell.

"You know Khanh is trying to secretly negotiate a peace deal with the North Vietnamese so they can tell the Americans to get out of our country."

Tao could not believe his ears.

An was not done with bomb shells. "I heard a rumor he is planning to execute Captain Nguyen Van Nhung soon. Naturally, that is a secret."

"That's Big Minh's bodyguard! The man who killed Diem and Nhu, right?"

An nodded then waved his hand. "Yes, but somehow, word of this got out to Thich Tri Quang. He has cancelled a planned pilgrimage to India so that he can organize more street protests. This is significant, the Buddhists have lost faith in Khanh."

Tao looked away as he ran his hand through his dark hair. He could not find the words to reply. *Every time something negative was brought up, An seemed to blame it on the Buddhists. This was a clear pattern.*

As An was getting ready to leave, he asked, "If you aren't doing anything later, Tao, stop by the hotel for dinner. I'm going to try to get some more information on the Buddhist and student protests."

Tao folded his arms on his chest. "I have a meeting in several hours. I'm getting ready to go back to the States to see my son Luc. I even turned down a party invitation at the Brinks Hotel. Somehow this evening I'll make it to a Christmas Eve Mass."

An smiled first. "I just want my old friend Lansdale to know what is really going on here. Tell Luc I asked about him." Then he looked worried. "Perhaps you are the lucky one that you have to work."

Silently, An walked out of the scooter shop, leaving Tao wondering what he had meant. Tao flipped the closed sign, looked the door, and headed to the back of his shop.

Steven Hebert walked into Meredith Brown's office. She had called him down under the pretext of a meeting with Ambassador Taylor. When he walked in, Steven saw his old friend, Ethan Graham. After some brief conversation, Ethan told Steven he was on his way home for leave. He wanted to stop by and see Steven on his way.

When Steven found out Ethan was not flying out until the next morning, he suggested they get together at the Brinks Hotel later in the afternoon for their own little Christmas Eve celebration. Plus, there would be a lot of military brass there, too. Ethan suggested they go right then, but Steven was the duty-first kind and could not leave until he was off duty at 16:00. The

Embassy staff was already low and security concerns were high. Ethan agreed to meet them at the hotel as soon as he could get there.

After Ethan left, Steven wanted to know what the Ambassador wanted. Meredith laughed.

"That was just my excuse to get you down here."

Steven pointed at the door. "Is he in there?"

Meredith shook her head.

Steven drew a deep breath. "Good. This political hot potato has become almost too much to handle."

Meredith whispered, "I really don't want to say anything, but I came here to work with Henry Cabot Lodge. Working with General Taylor has been, well... very different."

Steven pursed his lips. "It really makes me miss combat duty, to be honest."

Meredith frowned. "You can't be serious! Bullets flying around your head is better than this? As crazy this place is, I don't believe that."

All Steven could do was raise his eyebrows.

Meredith changed the subject. "I think I've talked Tim into going to Christmas Eve Mass. Are you interested in going with us?"

Steven had not felt the least bit religious in years. His mother used to make him go with his little brother, Jeremiah, but since then he had not been inside a church. He looked down at the ground.

"Perhaps, but I probably will be hanging out at the Brinks with Ethan." He thought that would close the subject.

With a big smile on her face, Meredith asked, "Isn't that the hotel where all the single majors and colonels live?"

Steven just smiled.

Meredith almost wiggled out of her chair. "What time should we leave?"

Steven put his hand over his mouth to hide his sly grin. He knew exactly what Meredith was thinking.

"As soon as I can get relieved," he said. "Likely a little after 16:00. I'll be ready."

By now Meredith's smile looked like it would become a permeant feature of her pretty face.

"I'm so excited!" she said, "A Christmas Eve party may alleviate some of my homesickness."

Steven escaped to the hallway and started walking his security routine, checking on all the guards and securing the premises. He expected things to be very quiet since most of the staff had returned to the States or gone to Australia or Singapore for a few days.

Steven stepped outside for some fresh air. The humidity was oppressive from the rain over the last month. The last few days had been a whirlwind, and it only amplified the deteriorating situation in South Vietnam. Lansdale still believed he'd be able to make a difference with his team, but Steven was beginning to doubt that as too much time may have passed.

At 4:45 PM Steven pulled up to the front door of the Embassy in his assigned motor pool car. He sat there for a couple of minutes waiting for Meredith and Tim to come out. Once in the car, they drove off toward the Brinks Hotel. Tim and Meredith were so excited that Steven felt like a chaperon escorting two teenagers on their first date. Tim probably thought something similar, but Steven figured Meredith did not.

The traffic across the city was very heavy. Steven couldn't wait to get out of the car and away from his two giddy friends. Their small talk was more than he could handle. He ignored all the questions he could as they drove. What he could answer with a nod or a grunt seemed to be sufficient. They asked about restaurants, about bars, about Christmas in Saigon, and what Buddhists did during Christmas. They were giggling so much, he believed they hardly paid any attention to his answers. Steven knew the Tim was in love and Meredith was just having fun. Finally, it dawned on him this was a part of life that he had missed. His father had been killed in the line of duty when he was very young, and he had never had an older adult male to look up to. Steven tried to feed off Tim and Meredith's giddy energy for the rest of the trip, hoping to lighten up his attitude.

Meredith reached up from the backseat and tapped Steven on the shoulder. "It's after five. We're running late. How much longer before we get to the hotel?"

Steven laughed. "As soon as the traffic gets out of my way. *Actually*, we are almost there."

Meredith sat back and continued to look out the car windows as Tim tried to keep her attention turned on him. Steven could tell she was starting to tire of Tim's chatter. Finally, Steven pulled into the hotel parking lot. Meredith sprang from the car with Tim in hot pursuit. Steven slowly got out of the car, closed the door and leaned against it for just a minute to catch his breath. He stretched his back and twisted his neck to relieve his tension. *Try to relax, after all it was Christmas Eve.*

He looked around the parking lot—a lot of brass at this hotel. *Time to go find Ethan. Hopefully, he is not fully inebriated yet.*

Steven started walking toward the entrance. He looked at his watch: 17:30. Happy hour was still going. *This crowd is going to be too drunk for me. Don't know that I'm in the mood for this.*

As Steven walked toward the hotel, he noticed two South Vietnamese military cars driving up to the security guard at the entrance to the underground garage. He watched the South Vietnamese major flash his credentials to the guard, then start to argue with him. Finally, the guard let the two cars through. Since Steven was now nothing more than a glorified security guard himself, he walked over and flashed his credentials to the same guard. "What was that all about?"

The frustrated guard just shook his head. "I told that major that the colonel he was looking for had left the country for Christmas, but he kept saying the colonel had gone to Da Lat to meet some other South Vietnamese dignitaries. He was supposed to meet the colonel here. I finally just gave up. He thinks he is sending his chauffeur to pick him up. I'd say they're wasting their time."

Steven laughed, then he put both hand on his hips, as he tilted his head at the guard. It seemed strange to him that a South Vietnamese major would send a chauffeur to pick up a US colonel.

"Well, Merry Christmas. Hope the rest of your evening goes better." Steven walked on toward the front door.

Steven decided to head for the bar first, where he expected to find Ethan. He would catch up with Tim and Meredith later in the larger conference room that was being used as a ballroom, with tables surrounding an area for dancing. As he walked toward the bar, he passed the dance floor and saw Tim and Meredith already doing the twist to a Chubby Checker song. He shook his head and snickered as he continued toward the bar.

Steven stopped in the restroom where he washed his hands and checked himself in the mirror. He headed toward the bar. Undoubtedly by now, since they were late, Ethan had had several stiff drinks.

He'd barely taken two steps before entire hotel exploded into a fiery inferno from an explosion that came up through the floor. Steven fought to keep from passing out. Part of his uniform had been ripped from his body, and he felt pelts of something imbedded in his skin everywhere he touched. *Don't pass out. Don't pass out.*

His eyes stung from dust, but he was able to blink them clear enough to see. He stumbled to his feet but immediately fell against what was left of the hallway. Again, he stumbled to his feet then moved as rapidly as possible into the ballroom, staggering and bouncing against what was left of the wall. *Where were Tim and Meredith? There were people on the floor everywhere he could see though the thick smoke and dust hanging in the air.*

Steven went from person to person, shouting their names: "Tim! Meredith!" More and more officers climbed to their feet and joined him, each searching for individuals. Names were being called, but the cries for help could still be heard among the injured. It was a haunting sound. A couple of officers shouted out they were doctors. "Who needs help?" The doctors moved from injured to injured, determining who needed immediate assistance and who could wait.

After about a minute, Steven heard Tim's and Meredith's voices behind him. They came running in, not a scratch on them. They told Steven they had gone outside just as the hotel exploded. Steven drew a deep breath, then coughed from inhaling the smoke and dust, relieved nonetheless. Both of them were in shock from what they were seeing around them. As they got closer to Steven, Meredith shouted, "You're hurt bad! We need to get you to the hospital."

Steven shook his head no. He pointed at them. "Go help the doctors. I'm going to look for Ethan."

Tim said, "I want to come with you?"

Again, Steven shook his head no and pointed to his left. "Help these people. I'll come back for you if I need help." The scream of sirens filled the streets outside. On his way to the bar, Steven passed emergency personnel already moving through the ballroom. The mirror behind the bar and all the bottles where completely shattered, and glass was strewn about the place. As he moved carefully through the bar, very few of the patrons could be seen sitting up, let alone rising to their feet. Steven could hear glass crushing under his feet. There must be twenty people in this tiny bar. After checking a few people Steven started shouting, "E! Ethan!" No answer.

Steven continued to go through the injured, trying to find Ethan. Steven stopped for a second to wipe the sweat from his brow only to find it was his own blood. Finally, Steven got to Ethan. He was still unconscious and very badly cut up from flying glass. Steven yelled, "I need a medic over here!"

An individual across the room shouted, "How bad? Everyone in here needs a doctor."

Steven's frustrations grew. He got up from Ethan and walked toward the medical people working the room. He noticed one of them covering up one of the patrons who was already dead. Just as he was about to physically grab the man, Tim and Meredith caught up with him to try to calm him down. Steven aggressively pulled his arms free from the two of them, but they just grasped him again. Meredith stepped between him and the doctor.

"You need to sit down, Steven," she said. "You are badly injured."

Steven stopped resisting. "Not until a doctor tends to Ethan."

Meredith pointed for Steven to turn around to see that someone with a medical bag had made it to Ethan.

For the first time since the explosion, Steven could feel himself relax. As soon as he did, he collapsed. A Vietnamese nurse who had just entered the bar area immediately started toward him. Steven started to crawl over to Ethan. The nurse tried to hold him down, but Steven was too strong for the tiny nurse. Finally, when Steven made it over to Ethan, he asked the doctor, "Is he going to be okay?"

The doctor nodded without looking up as he continued to dress wounds and pick glass out of his patient.

Steven rolled over on his back next to his friend and let the nurse dress his wounds. Then Tim and Meredith appeared over him. Steven tried to smile, but it was impossible to hold.

Ethan opened his eyes, tried to look around. He called out, "Where am I?

Steven tried to reach out and grab his arm. "E, you were in an explosion of some kind."

Ethan rolled his head around the best he could. "Hebert! Where are you?"

Steven grimaced as the nurse pulled a piece of concrete from his leg. "Right here, buddy. Right beside you. Semper Fi."

CHAPTER THIRTY-FIVE

DECEMBER 26, 1964

SAIGON

Two days later, Steven was hobbling down the hallway of the Embassy when he ran into Tim coming in the opposite direction. This was the day that Captain Jefferson was to return, and Steven was determined to head to New Orleans.

Tim's eyes widened. "Thought you were supposed to be in the hospital?"

Steven grimaced. "Was. Discharged myself." *Got to go take care of my brother.*

Tim frowned. "Is that such a good idea?"

"Of course it is, if you hate hospitals."

"How's Ethan?"

Steven swallowed hard. "That boy's too tough to kill him with just some shrapnel."

"Do you know what the hell happened?"

Steven leaned against the wall. "I saw individuals going into the garage. I think they were behind the bombing. Must be VC."

Tim leaned close to Steven and whispered, "I shouldn't tell you this but Ambassador Taylor has been trying to get the President to retaliate, but so far he hasn't convinced him."

Steven squinted at Tim then pushed off from the wall. "Doesn't that just figure? Another strike at the heart of our troops and nothing. I've got to go talk to de Silva about what I saw. We must get these men."

DECEMBER 28, 1964

BELL CHASSE, LA, OUTSIDE NEW ORLEANS

Steven picked up his duffle bag and headed to the cab line to get a ride to Bell Chasse Naval Base. He'd wanted to stay in downtown New Orleans but changed his mind at the last minute. He decided to go to the Base because of his race—might be the safest way, the most discreet way to search for his brother.

Steven figured it would be best to look for his brother between now and New Year's Eve afternoon. If Jeremiah was selling drugs, he would be out and active, working bars in New Orleans; users would want to make a score before partying all night on New Year's Eve. This was his best window of time to find his brother, but it was short. Most importantly, Steven wanted to avoid a direct confrontation with Carlos Marcello. It was known around New Orleans, Marcello was a big investor in real estate. He likely cleaned up some of his illegal money that way.

As he drove to the Base, Steven wondered if the drugs his brother was selling were coming from Laos, but his biggest problem was that he didn't know what the two thugs who had grabbed his brother looked like.

Steven would blend in better hanging out in the Negro bars, but he rarely drank. The best thing to do was start hanging around some of the bars and watch the clientele that patronized each establishment. There would be risk takers coming to town not knowing anybody but looking to score. Lastly, if Marcello's goons were in charge of Jeremiah, they would be close by but not too close to get busted. If they were a couple of white mobsters, they should be easy to spot. Steven believed his days as a sniper helped him work at a distance.

Steven sat out mid-day in a vehicle from the car pool to scout several bars in the Negro section. He hung around until almost one o'clock in the morning. No sign of Jeremiah. He was exhausted and his wounds from the explosion were starting to bleed again. He was still very sore. By the end of the day, the only thing he was able to accomplish was eliminate about six bars.

DECEMBER 29, 1964

Steven was nursing his wounds with some balm. He pulled out a city map of New Orleans and marked off all the bars he had covered the previous day. He pulled out a phonebook and made a new list, marking them on the map. He decided to start out just a little later today so that he could stay out longer. *Druggies probably aren't earlier starters.* Lastly, Steven grabbed a piece of paper and scribbled: *It is over. Debt paid in full.* Then stuck it in his pocket

Steven drove off the base toward the rougher part of town. According to the people he saw, this was a part of town where drugs were already rampant. It was unlikely many New Year's Eve revelers would come to this part of town, even to score some marijuana. As Steven drove, it hit him that hardcore users already had whatever drugs they were going to celebrate with on New Year's Eve. *What had Conein said? Colby told him all of those on this list were selling drugs at schools. I wasted a day yesterday. Shit. I need to go over by Tulane. College kids that went to school would likely come back to New Orleans to party for New Year's Eve.* Jeremiah was a college kid and would fit in much better in that area. He looked at his watch: five o'clock in the afternoon. He turned the car around in the middle of the street and headed toward Tulane. *I wasted a day because I didn't remember what Conein told me. That explosion really rattled my brain more than I thought.* He pounded the steering wheel several times.

The bars near the campus gave Steven the feeling this was where he would find his brother. He drove past the last bar on the block and parked. He put on his Chicago Cub's baseball cap, pulled it down low, and started walking by all of the bars on the street. He started moving about the various bars surrounding the campus, watching people going in and out. For a while, he struck out-until he noticed a nice Lincoln Continental with two white guys watching a bar halfway down the block. They did not look like college kids or the parents of college kids— not the type. Those guys weren't people anyone would want as a neighbor.

Steven decided to watch the two men. They just seemed out of place. *I hope this is my lead.* As Steven walked, he continued to watch the Lincoln, making sure it remained right where it was. Steven assumed if these were the men watching his brother, as long as they were here, Jeremiah *could be* around here, too. Steven entered each bar, looked around briefly then moved on to the next one. No Jeremiah. Each time making sure the Lincoln was still setting on the street. He entered the last bar, looked around. Still no sign of his brother, and he was very disappointed. Could it be he was wrong about the two men? *Maybe they were here for some other reason. Should I stay and watch or move on to other bars away from Tulane?*

The night was getting cold, a sensation Steven had not experienced in a long time. He decided to go back to his vehicle, where he could watch the two men in the Lincoln. Steven walked right by the Lincoln and quickly peered inside. He kept walking to his car, which was some two blocks away. Steven saw two young men, probably his brother's age, walk up to the Lincoln and crawl into the backseat. As Steven stopped in front of college clothing store pretended to look in, so that he could continue to keep his eye on activity in the Lincoln. The young men were in the Lincoln for a couple of minutes, doing a lot of moving around but too low to determine what they were passing back and forth. Then they got out and headed on. Steven started toward his vehicle, he noticed another car with two men sitting in it looking up the street toward the Lincoln. They seemed out of place, too. Steven continued up the street past the newly discovered car, he glanced at the two men then the license plate. *Uh oh. They might be FBI. Time is getting very short.*

Just before Steven made it to his vehicle, he looked back up and down the street. He caught a glimpse of his brother several blocks away walking down the opposite side of the street. Steven started walking back toward his brother. Jeremiah crossed in the middle of the street and headed toward the same Lincoln. Steven picked up his pace toward Jeremiah and the Lincoln. Before he could get there, the man in the passenger seat got out of the car and opened his suit coat. Steven assumed he was showing his brother a gun. Jeremiah walked up to the man with his head down looking at the concrete. The man slapped Jeremiah hard across the face. Steven glanced back at the FBI car to get their reaction; they were sitting up, intently watching.

For a second, Jeremiah and the man froze, but then the man opened the back door and pushed Jeremiah in. Enraged, Steven started walking as fast as he could. He couldn't draw attention to himself. He was not sure what he would do when he got there since he was unarmed, but he was determined to grab his brother. *Gun or FBI be damned.* Before he got there, the Lincoln pulled into traffic.

Steven made a mental note of the license plate then hustled to his vehicle. *Why did the two thugs let the first two boys walk away but force Jeremiah into the car?* He spun his vehicle around in the middle of the street and took off after the Lincoln. Steven scanned the streets, looking for the Lincoln as he drove behind the slowing moving traffic. *These people couldn't drive any slower!* He pounded the steering wheel.

Steven spotted the Lincoln turning right at the next intersection. Steven followed them, trying to stay back, particularly since there were not as many cars on the side street. They continued to drive into what looked like a dormitory and apartment section near Tulane.

It was dark when they stopped in front of a house that looked like a flop house. Steven parked. Both men got out of the car, then Jeremiah got out. The two men stood on both sides of Jeremiah and walked him to the house. They were met at the front door by a giant of a man who pushed Jeremiah in the door. The men went back to their car and drove off.

Steven needed to do a little recon before he decided how to handle this. He walked around the neighborhood, finally stopping with a full view of the back of the dilapidated house. As he suspected would be the case, he could see another large man pacing around on a shabby, broken-down back porch. He was either smoking a cigarette or a joint.

Steven went back around to his vehicle and observed other boys—well, *young men*, Jeremiah's age—go into the house. *It didn't make sense that*

Marcello was getting his pushers from a group of young kids. These were clearly amateurs, who could get busted at any moment. They were disposable, but still might be getting their supplies from Marcello.

Steve figured the two thugs were just a couple of flunkies who moved drugs and handled gambling establishments—for Marcello, but at arms-length. Marcello would be untouchable. Very cunning.

This boosted Steven's confidence about handling the situation. If he moved at the right time, all he had to worry about were the two big guys in the house and the two thugs who had slapped Jeremiah around. Steven figured he had time to go pick up a few items he might need; his brother was obviously being held captive in the house. Just as his confidence was peaking, he looked in his rearview mirror and saw the FBI vehicle park several blocks back but in full view of the front of the house.

His task of getting his brother to safety became more complicated. No matter, he was determined. Over the next couple of hours, Steven bought 1911 handgun, an extra magazine, his USMC Marine tactical knife, some WD-40, a small mirror, and a role of duct tape. He returned to the same neighborhood, drove by the FBI agents still in place. This time he parked in a different spot, but still close to the house where they were holding Jeremiah. Steven tried to channel his inner Lucien Conein: *How would he handle this?* Steven had watched him from afar: Conein had brass ones, for sure. Time to focus his sniper mentality, wait for just the right time to execute his plan—go in the back door and kidnap his brother. His opportunity would come with patience. He assumed the FBI would stay watching the two thugs or the front of the house.

Just past 03:00, Steven moved up to the back of the house. He held the small mirror up to each window, looking for the man guarding the back door. The man appeared to be asleep in a chair. Steven continued to watch. Within a half hour he checked again. The man was still asleep; time to move. First, Steven cut a piece of duct tape from the length of his thumb to his little finger and stuck it lightly on his shirt. He wondered if there was an alarm on the door but remembered a lesson he had learned in combat—doubt was an enemy, preparation was a friend. Steven crept to the back door.

Steven grabbed the door handle, turned it. Unlocked. Definitely amateurs. He sprayed WD-40 on the hinges and quietly opened the back door. Steven easily crept past the sleeping guard. He needed to find his brother without waking any of the other residents. Steven moved like a lion stalking his prey.

As he ascended the stairway to the upper floor of the two-story house, he stayed close to the wall, stepping as close to the corners, so they would not creak. Hard to believe, none creaked in the old house. Steven started at the farthest room down the hallway. He sprayed hinges and cracked a door. The three bedrooms on the top floor all checked out. Everyone was asleep, no sign of his brother. Just as Steven stepped on the first step to the ground floor he heard someone walking around on the first floor. Steven pulled his knife, stepped backward up the step, then pressed his body against the wall. Someone was walking down the hallway. A door opened.

Steven stayed in place and listened. There was a flushing sound downstairs. The door opened again and footsteps returned to the back of the house. Good news and bad news: The guard returned to the back of the house, but he was awake. Steven returned to his one objective: find Jeremiah.

Steven moved silently down the stairs to the ground floor. He crept to the front door and looked out. The man guarding the front door was standing out at the curb smoking a cigarette, talking to the men in the Lincoln. *Timing is everything, but I'm lucky.* Steven moved back down the hallway to the remaining two bedrooms. He sprayed the hinges, tried to open the door but it was locked. He reached over top of the door on the sill hoping to find the skeleton key. *Found it.* He slipped in the keyhole and peeked inside the door. *Jeremiah.* Steven looked around the room to make sure Jeremiah was the only one in the room. *Yes.* Steven stepped in and closed the door behind him.

Steven moved to his bedside. He pulled the piece of duct tape off his shirt and with a single, smooth motion, he slapped it over Jeremiah's mouth. Jeremiah woke up immediately with terror in his eyes. Steven made eye contact and held his finger to his lips. He wrested Jeremiah onto his back and pinned his hands behind his back. Steven whispered in his brother's ear: "I'm getting you out of here. Cooperate, do you understand? Or I'll tape you up and carry you out of here."

Under Steven's weight, Jeremiah squirmed, trying to speak through the tape, "Ummph Mmphh!" All he could do was nod, and a tear ran down his cheek that Steven thought was regret, or maybe despair.

"Don't fight me," Steven hissed, "and we'll get out of this alive. Fight me, and we could both die."

Steven tightened his grip to get his brother's attention, even at the risk of hurting him. They started toward the door. Steven maintained his grip on Jeremiah. As soon as they were in the hallway, Steven raised his knife and started down the hallway toward the back door. He moved slowly, while maintaining his grip on Jeremiah. He twisted his brother's arm every few seconds to keep his attention.

They reached the room where the man was guarding the back door. Steven put the knife in his mouth and pulled out the mirror. The man had his back toward them, pacing back and forth. Steven waited as he timed the cadence of his pacing. He placed the knife in his boot, on his second pivot the man turned his back to Steven. Steven drew a deep breath and pulled his gun.

Steven closed the distance on the guard silently and struck the man on the back of the head, knocking him out. Placed the gun back in his belt. Quickly, Steven dragged the guard over and duct taped him to the chair. Steven reached in his pocket and pulled out a piece of paper and showed it to Jeremiah, who squirmed as he read it. *It is over. Debt paid in full.*

After Jeremiah calmed down, Steven placed the note on the man's chest. Just then he heard the front door close. Steven looked up the hallway. No one. Steven and Jeremiah hurried to the back door. Just as he started to open the door, he heard heavy pounding footsteps running down the hallway. Steven pushed Jeremiah behind him as he spun to face the charging giant guard. The giant man was easily six foot six and over three hundred pounds. He swung at Steven when Steven ducked the punch, the guard brought his knee up into Steven's face, knocking him up and backwards into Jeremiah.

The big man continued his attack. Thrusting his full body weight at Steven, the man knocked Steven's wind out and crushed him up against Jeremiah with a massive thud. He had eliminated Steven's leverage, and the pressure on his wounds from the explosion brought searing pain. Still, Steven managed to headbutt the giant man's nose. Blood sprayed everywhere and the man staggered backwards with a roar. Steven brought his knee up into the man's groin, but the giant landed a punch to the side of Steven's head, causing his ears to ring and disorienting him for a second. Steven attempted to block the second round house punch from the big man with his right hand. The punch smacked against the left side of Steven's face, but Steven was able to follow the big man's arm recoil with a hard open palm strike to the giant's busted nose. More blood sprayed as the big man staggered backwards.

Again. Steven jumped straight up, landing his size thirteen army boot in a front snap kick to the giant's chin, the finishing blow. The big man toppled with a huge thud. Steven pounced on top of the downed man, delivering left-right combination to the downed man's face. The second punch sounded as though it broke the big man's jaw. He pulled back to deliver another palm strike to the nose but stopped out of fear of killing the man. *I can't afford to kill anyone.* Steven gritted his teeth and focused his breathing, trying to control his inner rage. He got up and grabbed his duct tape and taped the man's beefy arms and fat legs together, as well as piece over his mouth.

As Steven got up, he realized how lucky he was the giant was an inexperienced fighter and just a big brawler. Had he delivered any of blows to Steven's body wounds with those beefy punches, he would have been in big trouble. He turned to Jeremiah who was still frozen wide eyed in the corner by the back door.

Steven moved as fast as he could while he dragging his unwilling brother to his car, then pushed him in. When Steven got in, he yanked the duct tape off Jeremiah's face. Jeremiah jabbed a right, connecting with

Steven's jaw. Before he could pull back his right hand to punch again, Steven grabbed it and put a wrist lock on him.

"Calm down. We're going to Labadieville. We're going home to get Momma and get the two of you in hiding until this mess all blows over." He released his grip on his brother and started the car. *Got to avoid the FBI, I assume they are still in the same parking space, watching. Hope they haven't made me or my vehicle.* "Now, do you care to tell me what happened so I know what you got yourself into?"

Jeremiah just looked out the side window.

Steven did not wait for the answer. He had to get out of New Orleans and get to their mother's. He threw the vehicle into drive and sped west across the city. He wanted to be home by daylight. Steven took the backroads that he had grown up riding to New Orleans with his father, now mostly tar or hard gravel.

As he drove in the silent car, compassion for his brother began to creep in. What he must have gone through!

After about forty-five minutes of driving, Steven stopped at a gas station just after daylight. He looked over at his brother. "Are you hungry?"

Jeremiah nodded but did not speak.

Steven did not want to take the time to stop at a restaurant but wanted to see what the gas station might have in a couple of vending machines. He still did not trust Jeremiah enough to leave him in the car, so he made

Jeremiah go inside with him. They found two vending machines, one with Coca-cola, the other with a selection of candy bars. They each got a Coke and two Three Musketeers bars. Once back outside, they found the attendant had just finished checking the oil. Steven handed him three dollars to pay for the gas. Within the next thirty minutes, mud and loose gravel were flying as they traveled the long parish road that led toward their home.

No sooner did Steven turn up the long road leading to his mother's home, Jeremiah looked over. "I gotta use the bathroom?" He sounded surly.

Enough! Steven slammed on the brakes, throwing Jeremiah forward to crack against the dash as the car stopped. While Jeremiah got out Steven laid his 1911, extra magazine on the seat. *Don't know what I'll find outside Momma's house.* He looked around and saw Jeremiah was gone. Both knew this country like the back of their hands. *Rotten little bastard.*

Steven got out of the vehicle, gun in hand and extra magazine in the other and called out his name. No answer. This time Steven shouted out. "You're going to make this pretty rough on yourself if I have to come and find you."

Steven stuck the gun in his belt, the magazine in his pants pocket, and walked around looking at the ground in the back of the vehicle where Jeremiah had gone to the bathroom. He picked up the tracks in the direction his brother escaped. Steven moved silently through the woods. Broken twigs and partial shoe prints led him about a quarter mile into the woods where he came on his brother just sitting on a stump. Steven paused; he recognized where he was.

It was a place he and his brother had come to talk growing up, when they wanted to get away from their mother to be alone. Steven went over and sat down beside him. "Are you ready to talk?"

Jeremiah jutted his jaw in defiance. "*I thought* you were going to kill the big man in the fight."

Steven gritted his teeth as he looked away. "It was hard not to, but my objective was to get my brother that I love out of harm's way."

Jeremiahs paused for a long time, biting his lower lip. "It all started out with a gambling debt at the pool hall near campus. First, I lost some games shooting pool. I won some, too. The owner, Nick, started letting me bet on pro football games, and I won for a while. I had a knack. I was doing pretty good picking games. One night while we were playing eight ball, one of my friends borrowed some money from me to go outside and buy some marijuana. He came back in just giggling like crazy. He was having so much fun and was so funny. Anyway, I beat him several more games, and we decided to get back to the dorm."

Steven held both palms up. "Then what?"

Jeremiah shrugged. "To make a long story short, I ended up trying the marijuana because Bobby, that's my friend, was always laughing after he smoked. So, I thought I'd try it, too. Looked fun. I bought a joint or two off from him. Next thing you know I was buying smoke regularly. I hit a losing streak at Nick's and I was down a couple of hundred bucks on a weekend. Anyway, Nick liked me and let me slide a week. The next weekend I tried to double down on my bets and lost. Now, I'm down twelve hundred dollars. Nick's pissed off at me and cuts me off. Kicks me out of the pool hall in fact."

Steven looked down at the ground. *Twelve hundred dollars. Where was his brain? He was talking gambler's mentality.*

Jeremiah continued. "I was scared. By Christmas, I was trying to figure out a way to make some money to pay Nick back. But there was nothing I could do to make that kinda money. Not here. Anyway, when I went back to school, I thought everything had kinda blown over until one night I was at the pool hall and these two guys were giving Nick a rough time. I figured it was over me, so I left only they were outside waiting on me. They hit me a couple of times, they stopped when a car approached. They left because I told them I would pay them some money in a couple of weeks. I was scared, but they seemed satisfied and left. I didn't think it was any big deal. Anyway, Nick disappeared. No one has heard from him since."

"Then I got really scared. The next time I saw them, they threatened me so I went home that next weekend and took Momma's money from the coffee can. The following weekend I met those guys and gave them the money—two hundred-fifty dollars. They told me they'd let me work off the debt and gave me an ultimatum. If I didn't work it off, they'd hurt me bad—and Momma. So, I started selling marijuana and opium for them."

Steven stopped Jeremiah. "Do you know where they were getting the drugs?"

Jeremiah nodded. "They said it came from Carlos Marcello. At first, my debt started coming down fast. I was selling a lot on campus. But then they started charging me interest on what I owed them. Or Nick, really. But Nick wasn't around anymore."

"After the semester was over they came and got me, made me move to New Orleans. They said I could finish working off the debt there. They said I had to have them paid off by the time school started back up at Southern Miss. That's why I was in New Orleans. They kept telling me they were afraid I'd run, so they kept telling they would kill me and Momma."

Steven ignored that comment, keeping his cool, and acting like his big brother. "So do you still smoke marijuana?"

Jeremiah nodded. "Opium too, when I can get it."

Steven said, "You probably should be more scared of me and Momma than those guys."

Jeremiah pushed him away. *"I'm not being funny.* We're all in big trouble. They're watching Momma."

Steven nodded. "I know, at least that is what they say. Did you know you were being watched by the FBI?"

Jeremiah's eyes got great big, then he dropped his head into his hands.

Steven did not wish to scare him, but he felt it was necessary to show him the gravity of his troubles. "Now, let's go talk to Momma. I'll handle them, if need be."

The two of them got up from the stump and walked back to the vehicle. They drove up to an old sign: LaBelle Hebert's Home. The address under it was barely legible. Steven was relieved to see his old home. He got out of the vehicle and looked around. No sign of anyone. Time to go in and fell his mother Jeremiah's story. When they walked into the house, LaBelle started to cry.

Steven punched his brother lightly in the shoulder. "Go hug your mother." He pointed to the couch for both to sit down.

"Tell your mother the whole story. Don't leave anything out. I want her to understand what we're facing."

Steven went into the bathroom and sat down on the edge of the bathtub. He pulled out his medicine to treat his wounds. They were all bleeding again. He put new bandages on the worst cuts. Once everything was secure, he went back out to the living room. His mother and brother were talking softly. *Time to take a walk around the property. ee if there was anyone from Marcello or the French Corsican Brotherhood watching.* Steven did not expect to find anyone, but it was time to take all the precautions.

Steven went out the back door to the deepest point of his mother's property. As he moved forward he did not see any evidence of anyone being in the back of the property. He walked along the perimeter up to the front of

420

the tract along the dirt road leading to the house. Then he walked back along the other perimeter of the property back toward the house. As he worked his way along the western side of the property, he discovered some tracks in the woods made with street shoes. *Very unusual.*

Steven carefully examined the shoe prints; they were not fresh. He had no way of knowing when someone had been here last. He followed them. They did not veer very far off from the road, but where they stopped one clearly had an unobstructed view of the house. Steven also saw cigarette butts on the ground. Someone had stood here and watched, for a long time. He searched around some more. These cigarettes were left here on purpose. Professionals didn't make this mistake. *Someone wanted me to find them and know his mother's home was being watched.*

Steven followed the shoe prints back to the dirt road to look for tire tracks, but there had been too much traffic on this road to learn anything. Steven walked back to the house. His mother was sitting on the couch trying to sew, but her arthritic hands slowed her down. Steven looked at his mother.

"What do you think?"

LaBelle raised her eyebrows. "I'm just glad Jeremiah is home. Other than that this is just too much. Ask me later."

Steven sat down next to his mother and hugged her. "I want to get you and Jeremiah out of here. Let things die down. Cool off."

LaBelle shook her head. "I will not be intimidated out of my own home."

Steven grasped her hand. "Momma, I agree with you, but I can't protect you once I'm back in Vietnam. I must leave on the second of January. We both know that Jeremiah can't go back to Southern Miss, at least not now. I want to protect both of you."

LaBelle picked up the sewing. "Steven, I'll be okay and so will Jeremiah."

Steven drew a deep breath; he did not want to tell her his story. She did not need to know, particularly if this was all behind them.

LaBelle put the sewing back down on her lap. "If I must leave, then take me to my brother's place out in the Bayou. No one will find us there. I'll be close to home, and we'll be safe there."

Jeremiah walked back into the living room and sat down on the old chair opposite them. "Momma has the right idea. No one will find us there. Uncle Jake's place doesn't even have a mailbox or a road in."

Steven looked at his brother. "You agree to go there, too? I'm sorry you can't return to college, at least right now. I think you have two choices. Figure out where to transfer, a long way away, or enlist in the service, maybe the navy or the air force."

Jeremiah shook his head. "Steven, I am scared. I can't make any decisions right now."

Steven stretched his back as he folded his arms across his chest. "You need to keep Momma safe and you need to get your act together. Get off those guys' radar. Everybody's radar. That is the smart thing. Let's get ready to go to Uncle Jake's home for a while."

THE END